P9-AGQ-925

RISE OF THE GOVERNOR

Center Point
Large Print

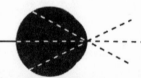

**This Large Print Book carries the
Seal of Approval of N.A.V.H.**

the walking dead:
RISE OF THE GOVERNOR

ROBERT KIRKMAN
and JAY BONANSINGA

CENTER POINT LARGE PRINT
THORNDIKE, MAINE

This Center Point Large Print edition
is published in the year 2015 by arrangement with
St. Martin's Press.

The text of this Large Print edition is unabridged.
In other aspects, this book may vary
from the original edition.
Printed in the United States of America
on permanent paper.
Set in 16-point Times New Roman type.

ISBN: 978-1-62899-459-9

Library of Congress Cataloging-in-Publication Data

Kirkman, Robert.
 The walking dead : rise of the Governor / Robert Kirkman and Jay
Bonansinga. — Center Point Large Print edition.
 pages cm
 Summary: "In The Walking Dead universe, there is no greater villain
than The Governor. The despot who runs the walled-off town of
Woodbury has his own sick sense of justice. Now, fans of The Walking
Dead will discover how The Governor became the man he is, and what
drove him to such extremes"—Provided by publisher.
 ISBN 978-1-62899-459-9 (library binding : alk. paper)
 1. Large type books. I. Bonansinga, Jay R. II. Title.
PS3611.I7555W35 2015
813´.6—dc23
                                                        2014044045

acknowledgments

Special thanks to Robert Kirkman, Brendan Deneen, Andy Cohen, David Alpert, Stephen Emery, and all the good people at Circle of Confusion.

—Jay

Big ups to Jay Bonansinga, Alpert and the rest at Circle of Confusion, the fine folks at Image Comics, and Charlie Adlard for steering the ship. Much respect for Rosenman, Rosenbaum, Simonian, and Lerner. And, of course . . . Brendan Deneen.

—Robert

RISE OF THE GOVERNOR

PART 1

The Hollow Men

There's nothing glorious in dying.
Anyone can do it.
—Johnny Rotten

one

It occurs to Brian Blake as he huddles in the musty darkness, the terror constricting his chest, the pain throbbing in his knees: If only he possessed a *second* pair of hands, he could cover his *own* ears, and maybe block out the noise of human heads being demolished. Sadly, the only hands Brian currently owns are busy right now, covering the tiny ears of a little girl in the closet next to him.

The seven-year-old keeps shuddering in his arms, jerking at the intermittent *THWACK-GAHHHH-THUMP* outside the closet. Then comes the silence, broken only by the sticky sound of boot steps on bloody tile, and a flurry of angry whispers out in the vestibule.

Brian starts coughing again. He can't help it. For days he has been fighting this goddamn cold, a stubborn blight on his joints and sinuses that he cannot shake. It happens to him every fall, when the Georgia days start getting dank and gloomy. The dampness gets into his bones, saps his energy, and steals his breath. And now he feels the pounding stab of a fever with each cough.

Doubling over in another hacking, wheezing fit, he keeps his hands pressed down on little Penny's ears as he coughs. He knows the sound of his rasping is attracting all kinds of attention outside

13

the closet door, out in the convolutions of the house, but there's nothing he can do about it. He sees tracings of light with each cough—like tiny filigrees of fireworks across his blind pupils.

The closet—barely four feet wide, and maybe three feet deep—is as dark as an inkwell, and it reeks of mothballs, mouse droppings, and old cedar. Plastic coat bags hang down in the darkness, brushing the sides of Brian's face. Brian's younger brother Philip told him it was okay to cough in the closet. In fact, Brian was free to cough his fucking head off—it would draw out the monsters—but Brian better not give his goddamn cold to Philip's little girl. If he did, Philip would crack *Brian's* head open.

The coughing fit passes.

Moments later, another pair of lumbering footsteps disturbs the silence outside the closet—another dead thing entering the kill zone. Brian squeezes his hands tighter against Penny's ears, and the child flinches at another rendition of Skull Splitting in D minor.

If asked to describe the racket outside the closet, Brian Blake would probably revert to his days as a failed music store entrepreneur and tell you that the head-cracking sounds are like a percussive symphony they might play in hell—like some trippy outtake from Edgard Varèse or a druggy drum solo from John Bonham—with repeating verses and choruses: the heavy breathing of humans . . . the shambling footsteps of another moving corpse . . . the whistle of an axe . . . the *thunk* of steel sinking into flesh . . .

. . . and finally, the big finale, the splat of moist, dead weight on the slimy parquet.

Another break in the action sends fever chills down Brian's spine. The silence closes in again. Eyes now adjusted to the darkness, Brian sees the first shimmer of thick arterial blood seeping under the bottom of the door. It looks like motor oil. He gently yanks his niece away from the spreading puddle, pulling her back against the boots and umbrellas along the back wall.

The hem of Penny Blake's little denim dress touches the blood. She quickly pulls the fabric away, and frantically rubs at the stain, as if the very absorption of the blood will infect her somehow.

Another convulsive coughing fit doubles Brian over. He fights it. He swallows the broken glass of a sore throat and pulls the little girl into a full-on embrace. He doesn't know what to do or say. He wants to help his niece. He wants to whisper something reassuring to her but cannot think of a single reassuring thing to whisper.

The girl's father would know what to say. Philip would know. He always knows what to say. Philip Blake is the guy who says the things that everybody else *wishes* they had said. He says what needs to be said, and he does what needs to be done. Like right now. He's out there with Bobby and Nick, doing what needs to be done . . . while Brian hunkers here in the dark like a scared rabbit, wishing he knew what to say to his niece.

Considering the fact that Brian Blake is the oldest of the two siblings, it's odd how Brian has always been the runt. Barely five feet seven in his boot heels, Brian Blake is a raw-boned scarecrow of a man scarcely able to fill out his black peg-leg jeans and torn Weezer T-shirt. A mousey goatee, macramé bracelets, and a thatch of dark Ichabod Crane hair complete the picture of a thirty-five-year-old Bohemian waif stuck in Peter Pan limbo, now kneeling in the mothball-scented gloom.

Brian sucks in a hoarse breath and looks down at the doe-eyed Penny, her mute, horrified face ghostly in the darkness of the closet. The child has always been a quiet little girl, with an almost porcelain complexion, like that of a china doll, which has given her face a rather ethereal cast. But since her mother's death she has turned even further inward, becoming more wan and stoic, to the point of appearing almost translucent, with tendrils of raven-black hair obscuring her huge eyes.

For the last three days, she has hardly said a word. Of course, they have been three *extraordinary* days—and trauma works differently on children than it does on adults—but Brian is worried that Penny is perhaps slipping into some kind of shock.

"It's gonna be okay, kiddo," Brian whispers to her with a lame little cough as punctuation.

She says something without looking up at him. She mumbles it, staring down at the floor, a tear pearling on her dirty cheek.

"What was that, Pen?" Brian cradles her against him and wipes her tear.

She says something again, and again, and again, but not exactly to Brian. She says it more like a mantra, or a prayer, or an incantation: *"It's never-ever going to be okay, never-ever-ever-ever-ever."*

"Sshhhhh." He holds her head, pressing it gently against the folds of his T-shirt. He feels the damp heat of her face against his ribs. He covers her ears again as he hears the *THWACK* of another axe blade outside the closet, smashing through the membrane of a scalp, into the hard shell of a skull, through the layers of dura, and into the pulpy gray gelatin of an occipital lobe.

It makes a smacking noise like a baseball bat hitting a wet softball—the ejaculate of blood like a mop head slapping the floor—followed by a ghastly, wet thud. Oddly, that's the worst part for Brian: that hollow, moist thump of a body landing on expensive ceramic tile. The tile is custom made for the house, with elaborate inlay and Aztec designs. It's a lovely house . . . or at least, it once was.

Again the noises cease.

Again the horrible dripping silence follows.

17

Brian stifles a cough, holding it in like a firecracker that's about to pop, so he can better hear the minute changes in breathing outside the closet, the greasy footsteps shuffling through gore. But the place is dead silent now.

Brian feels the child seize up next to him—little Penny girding herself for another salvo of axe blows—but the silence stretches.

Inches away, the sound of a bolt clicking, and the closet doorknob turning, rashes Brian's body with gooseflesh. The door swings open.

"Okay, we're good." The baritone voice, whiskey-cured and smoky, comes from a man peering down into the recesses of the closet. Eyes blinking at the darkness, face shimmering with sweat, flush with the exertion of zombie disposal, Philip Blake holds a grue-slick axe in his workman's hand.

"You sure?" Brian utters.

Ignoring his brother, Philip gazes down at his daughter. "Everything's okay, punkin, Daddy's okay."

"Are you *sure?*" Brian says with a cough.

Philip looks at his brother. "You mind covering your mouth, sport?"

Brian wheezes, "You sure it's clear?"

"Punkin?" Philip Blake addresses his daughter tenderly, his faint Southern drawl belying the bright, feral embers of violence just now fading in his eyes. "I'm gonna need y'all to stay right there for a minute. Awright? You stay right there until

Daddy says it's okay to come out. You understand?"

With a slight nod, the pale little girl gives him a feeble gesture of understanding.

"C'mon, sport," Philip urges his older brother out of the shadows. "Gonna need your help with the cleanup."

Brian struggles to his feet, pushing his way through the hanging overcoats.

He emerges from the closet and blinks at the harsh light of the vestibule. He stares and coughs and stares some more. For a brief moment, it looks as though the lavish entryway of the two-story Colonial, brightly lit by fancy copper chandeliers, is in the throes of being redecorated by a work crew afflicted by palsy. Great swaths of eggplant-purple spatters stain the teal green plaster walls. Rorschach patterns of black and crimson adorn the baseboards and moldings. Then the shapes on the floor register.

Six bodies lie akimbo in bloody heaps. Ages and genders are obscured by the wet carnage, the mottled, livid skin tones, and the misshapen skulls. The largest lies in a spreading pool of bile at the foot of the great circular staircase. Another one, perhaps the lady of the house, perhaps once a convivial hostess offering peach cobbler and Southern hospitality, is now splayed across the lovely white parquet floor in a contorted mess, a stringer of wormy gray matter flagging from her breached cranium.

Brian Blake feels his gorge rising, his throat involuntarily dilating.

"Okay, gentlemen, we got our work cut out for us," Philip is saying, addressing his two cronies, Nick and Bobby, as well as his brother, but Brian can barely hear over the sick thump of his own heartbeat.

He sees the other remains—over the last two days, Philip has started calling the ones they destroy "twice-cooked pork"—strewn along the dark, burnished baseboards at the threshold of the living room. Maybe the teenage children who once lived here, maybe visitors who suffered the Southern *in*hospitality of an infected bite, these bodies lie in sunbursts of arterial spray. One of them, his or her dented head lying facedown like a spilled soup pan, still pumps its scarlet fluids across the floor with the profusion of a breached fire hydrant. A couple of others still have small hatchet blades embedded in their crania, sunk down to the hilt, like the flags of explorers triumphantly stuck into once unattainable summits.

Brian's hand flies up to his mouth, as if he might stem the tide rising up his esophagus. He feels a tapping sensation on the top of his skull, as though a moth is ticking against his scalp. He looks up.

Blood drips from the overhead chandelier, a droplet landing on Brian's nose.

"Nick, why don't you go grab some of them tarps we saw earlier in the—"

Brian falls to his knees, hunches forward, and roars vomit across the parquet. The steaming flood of khaki-colored bile sluices across the tiles, mingling with the spoor of the fallen dead.

Tears burn Brian's eyes as he heaves four days of soul-sickness onto the floor.

Philip Blake lets out a tense sigh, the buzz of adrenaline still coursing through him. For a moment he makes no effort to go to his brother's side, but simply stands there, setting down his bloody axe, rolling his eyes. It's a miracle Philip doesn't have a groove worn into the tops of his eye sockets from all the eye rolling he's done over the years on his brother's account. But what else is Philip supposed to do? The poor son of bitch is family, and family is family . . . especially in off-the-scale times such as these.

The resemblance is sure there—nothing Philip can do about *that*. A tall, rangy, sinewy man with the ropy muscles of a tradesman, Philip Blake shares the same dark features as his brother, the same dark almond eyes and coal-black hair of their Mexican-American mother. Mama Rose's maiden name was Garcia, and her features had dominated the lineage over those of the boys' father, a big, coarse alcoholic of Scots-Irish descent named Ed Blake. But Philip, three years younger than Brian, had gotten all the muscle.

He now stands over six feet tall in his faded

jeans, work boots, and chambray shirt, with the Fu Manchu mustache and jailhouse tats of a biker; and he is about to move his imposing figure over to his retching brother, and maybe say something harsh, when he stops himself. He hears something he doesn't like coming from across the vestibule.

Bobby Marsh, an old high school pal of Philip's, stands near the base of the staircase, wiping an axe blade on his size XXL jeans. A portly thirty-two-year-old junior college dropout, his long greasy brown hair pulled back in a rattail, Bobby Marsh is not exactly obese, but definitely overweight, definitely the type of guy his Burke County High classmates would call a butterball. He now giggles with nervous, edgy, belly-shivering laughter as he watches Brian Blake vomit. The giggling is colorless and hollow—a sort of tic that Bobby cannot seem to control.

The anxious giggling had started three days ago when one of the first of the undead had lumbered out of a service bay at a gas station near the Augusta airport. Clad in blood-soaked overalls, the grease monkey shuffled out of hiding with a trail of toilet paper on his heel, and the thing had tried to make a meal out of Bobby's fat neck before Philip had stepped in and clobbered the thing with a crowbar.

The discovery that day—that a major blow to the head does the job quite nicely—had led to more nervous chortling on Bobby's part—

definitely a defense mechanism—with a lot of anxious chatter about it being "something in the water, man, like the black-fucking-plague." But Philip didn't want to hear about reasons for this shit storm then, and he sure doesn't want to hear about them now.

"Hey!" Philip addresses the heavyset man. "You still think this is *funny?*"

Bobby's laughter dies.

On the other side of the room, near a window overlooking the dark expanse of a backyard, which is currently shrouded in night, a fourth figure watches uneasily. Nick Parsons, another friend from Philip's wayward childhood, is a compact, lean thirty-something with the kind of prep-school grooming and marine-cut hair of an eternal jock. The religious one of the bunch, Nick has taken the longest to get used to the idea of destroying things that were once human. Now his khakis and sneakers are stippled with blood, and his eyes burn with trauma, as he watches Philip approach Bobby.

"Sorry, man," Bobby mutters.

"My daughter's in there," Philip says, coming nose to nose with Marsh. The volatile chemicals of rage and panic and pain can instantly ignite in Philip Blake.

Bobby looks at the blood-slicked floor. "Sorry, sorry."

"Go get the tarps, Bobby."

Six feet away, Brian Blake, still on his hands and

knees, expels the last of his stomach contents, and continues to dry-heave.

Philip goes over to his older brother, kneels by him. "Let it out."

"I'm—uh—" Brian croaks, sniffing, trying to form a complete thought.

Philip gently lays a big, grimy, callused hand on his brother's hunched shoulders. "It's okay, bro . . . just let it all out."

"I'm—s-sorry."

"It's all right."

Brian gets himself under control, wipes his mouth with the back of his hand. "Y-you think you got all of them?"

"I do."

"You sure?"

"Yep."

"You searched . . . everywhere? In the basement and stuff?"

"Yes, sir, we did. All the bedrooms . . . even the attic. Last one came out of hiding at the sound of that fucking cough, loud enough to wake the fucking dead. Teenage girl, tried to have one of Bobby's chins for lunch."

Brian gulps down a raw, painful swallow. "These people . . . they . . . *lived* here."

Philip sighs. "Not anymore."

Brian manages to look around the room, then gazes up at his brother. Brian's face is wet with tears. "But they were like . . . a family."

Philip nods, and he doesn't say anything. He feels like giving his brother a shrug—*so fucking what*—but all he does is keep nodding. He's not thinking about the zombified family he just dispatched, or the implications of all the mind-numbing butchery he's already wreaked over the last three days—slaughtering individuals who were recently soccer moms and mailmen and gas station attendants. Yesterday, Brian had gone off on some bullshit intellectual tangent about the difference between morals and ethics in this situation: Morally, one should never kill, *ever,* but ethically, which is subtly different, one should maintain the policy of killing only if it's in self-defense. But Philip doesn't see what they're doing as killing. You can't kill a thing that's already been killed. What you do is squash it like a bug, and move on, and stop *thinking* so much.

The fact is, right now, Philip isn't even thinking about the next move his little ragtag group will make—which is probably going to be entirely up to him (he has become the de facto leader of this bunch, and he might as well face it). Right now, Philip Blake is focused on a single objective: Since the nightmare started less than seventy-two hours ago, and folks started turning—for reasons nobody has yet been able to figure out—all that Philip Blake has been able to think about is protecting Penny. It is why he got the hell out of his home-town, Waynesboro, two days ago.

A small farming community on the eastern edge of central Georgia, the place had gone to hell quickly when folks had started dying and coming back. But it was Penny's safety that had ultimately convinced Philip to fly the coop. It was because of Penny he had enlisted the help of his old high school buddies; and it was because of Penny he had set out for Atlanta, where, according to the news, refugee centers were being set up. It was all because of Penny. Penny is all that Philip Blake has left. She is the only thing keeping him going—the only salve on his wounded soul.

Long before this inexplicable epidemic had broken out, the void in Philip's heart would pang at 3 A.M. on sleepless nights. That's the exact hour he had lost his wife—hard to believe it's been nearly four years now—on a rain-slick highway south of Athens. Sarah had been visiting a friend at the University of Georgia, and she'd been drinking, and she lost control of her car on a winding road in Wilkes County.

From the moment he had identified the body, Philip knew he would never be the same. He had no qualms about doing the right thing—taking on two jobs to keep Penny fed and clothed and cared for—but he would never be the same. Maybe that's why all this was happening. God's little gag. When the locusts come, and the river runs red with blood, the guy with the most to lose gets to lead the pack.

"Doesn't matter who they were," Philip finally says to his brother. "Or *what* they were."

"Yeah . . . I guess you're right." By this point, Brian has managed to sit up, cross-legged now, taking deep wheezing breaths. He watches Bobby and Nick across the room, unrolling large canvas tarps and shaking open garbage bags. They begin rolling corpses, still dripping, into the tarps.

"Only thing that matters is we got this place cleaned out now," Philip says. "We can stay here tonight, and if we can score some gas in the morning, we can make it to Atlanta tomorrow."

"Doesn't make any sense, though," Brian mutters now, glancing from corpse to corpse.

"What are you talking about?"

"Look at them."

"What?" Philip glances over his shoulder at the gruesome remains of the matriarch being rolled up in a tarp. "What about 'em?"

"It's just the family."

"So?"

Brian coughs into his sleeve, then wipes his mouth. "What I'm saying is . . . you got the mother, the father, four teenage kids . . . and that's like *it*."

"Yeah, so what?"

Brian looks up at Philip. "So, how the hell does something like this happen? They all . . . *turned together?* Did one of them get bitten and bring it back inside?"

Philip thinks about it for a moment—after all, he's still trying to figure out just exactly what is going on, too, how this madness works—but finally Philip gets tired of thinking about it and says, "C'mon, get off your lazy ass and help us."

It takes them about an hour to get the place cleaned up. Penny stays in the closet for the duration of the process. Philip brings her a stuffed animal from one of the kid's rooms, and tells her it won't be long before she can come out. Brian mops the blood, coughing fitfully, while the other three men drag the canvas-covered corpses—two large and four smaller ones—out the back sliding doors and across the large cedar deck.

The late-September night sky above them is as clear and cold as a black ocean, a riot of stars shining down, taunting them with their impassive, cheerful twinkling. The breaths of the three men show in the darkness as they drag the bundles across dew-frosted planks. They carry pickaxes on their belts. Philip has a gun stuffed down the back of his belt. It's an old .22 Ruger that he bought at a flea market years ago, but nobody wants to rouse the dead with the bark of gunfire right now. They can hear the telltale drone of walking dead on the wind—garbled moaning sounds, shuffling footsteps—coming from somewhere in the darkness of the neighboring yards.

It's been an unusually nippy early autumn in

Georgia, and tonight the mercury is supposed to dip into the lower forties, perhaps even the upper thirties. Or at least that's what the local AM radio station claimed before it petered out in a gust of static. Up to this point in their journey, Philip and his crew have been monitoring TV, radio, and the Internet on Brian's BlackBerry.

Amid the general chaos, the news reports have been assuring people that everything is just peachy-keen—your trusty government is in control of the situation—and this little bump in the road will be smoothed out in a matter of hours. Regular warnings chime in on civil defense frequencies, admonishing folks to stay indoors, and keep out of sparsely populated areas, and wash their hands frequently, and drink bottled water, and blah, blah, blah.

Of course, nobody has any answers. And maybe the most ominous sign of all is the increasing number of station failures. Thankfully, gas stations still have gas, grocery stores are still stocked, and electrical grids and stoplights and police stations and all the infrastructural paraphernalia of civilization seem to be hanging on.

But Philip worries that a loss of power will raise the stakes in unimaginable ways.

"Let's put 'em in the Dumpsters behind the garage," Philip says so softly he's almost whispering, dragging two canvas bundles up to the wooden fence adjacent to the three-car garage. He wants to do this swiftly and silently. He doesn't want to attract any zombies. No fires, no sharp noises, no gunshots if he can help it.

There's a narrow gravel alley behind the seven-foot cedar fence, serving the rank and file of spacious garages lining the backyards. Nick drags his load over to the fence gate, a solid slab of cedar planks with a wrought-iron handle. He drops the bundle and opens the gate.

An upright corpse is waiting for him on the other side of the gate.

"LOOK OUT, Y'ALL!" Bobby Marsh cries out.

"Shut the fuck up!" Philip hisses, reaching for the pickaxe on his belt, already halfway to the gate.

Nick recoils.

The zombie lurches at him, chomping, missing his left pectoral by millimeters, the sound of yellow dentures snapping impotently like the clicking of castanets—and in the moonlight, Nick can see that it's an elderly adult male in a tattered Izod sweater, golf slacks, and expensive cleats, the lunar gleam shining in its milky, cataract-filmed eyes: *somebody's grandfather.*

Nick gets one good glimpse at the thing before stumbling backward over his own feet and falling onto his ass on the lush carpet of Kentucky bluegrass. The dead golfer lumbers through the gap and onto the lawn just as a flash of rusty steel arcs through the air.

The business end of Philip's pickaxe lands

squarely in the monster's head, cracking the coconutlike shell of the old man's skull, piercing the dense, fibrous membrane of the dura mater and sinking into the gelatinous parietal lobe. It makes a sound like celery snapping and sends a clot of dark brackish fluid into the air. The insectile verve on the grandfather's face instantly dims, like a cartoon whose projection system has just jammed.

The zombie folds to the ground with the inelegant deflation of an empty laundry sack.

The pickaxe, still deeply embedded, pulls Philip forward and down. He yanks at it. The point is stuck. "Shut the motherfucking gate now, shut the gate, and do it quietly, goddamnit," Philip says, still affecting a frenzied stage whisper, slamming his left Chippewa steel-toed logger boot down on the breached skull of the cadaver.

The other two men move as if in some synchronized dance, Bobby quickly dropping his load and rushing over to the gate. Nick struggles to his feet and backs away in a horrified stupor. Bobby quickly latches the wrought-iron lever. It makes a hollow metallic rattle that is so noisy it echoes across the dark lawns.

At last, Philip wrenches the pick from the stubborn crag of the zombie's skull—it comes out with a soft smooch sound—and he turning toward the remains of the family, his mind swimming with panic, when he hears something odd, something unexpected, coming from the house.

He looks up and sees the rear of the Colonial, the window glass lit brilliantly from within.

Brian is silhouetted behind the sliding glass door, tapping on the pane, motioning for Philip and the others to hurry back, right now. Urgency burns in Brian's expression. It has nothing to do with the dead golfer—Philip can tell—something is wrong.

Oh God, please let it not *have to do with Penny.*

Philip drops the pickaxe and crosses the lawn in seconds flat.

"What about the stiffs?" Bobby Marsh is calling after Philip.

"Leave 'em!" Philip yells, vaulting up the deck steps and rushing to the sliding doors.

Brian is waiting with the slider ajar. "I gotta show you something, man," he says.

"What is it? Is it Penny? Is she okay?" Philip is out of breath as he slips back into the house. Bobby and Nick are coming across the deck, and they too slip into the warmth of the Colonial.

"Penny's fine," Brian says. He's holding a framed photograph. "She's fine. Says she doesn't mind staying in the closet a little while longer."

"Judas Priest, Brian, what the fuck!" Philip catches his breath, his hands balled into fists.

"I gotta show you something. You want to stay here tonight?" Brian turns toward the sliding glass door. "Look. The family died together in here, right? All six of them? Six?"

Philip wipes his face. "Spit it out, man."

"Look. Somehow they all turned *together.* As a family, right?" Brian coughs, then points at the six pale bundles lying near the garage. "There's six of them out there on the grass. Look. Mom and dad and four kids."

"So fucking *what?*"

Brian holds up a portrait in a frame, the family from a happier time, all smiling awkwardly, dressed in their starchy Sunday best. "I found this on the piano," he says.

"And . . . ?"

Brian points at the youngest child in the photo, a boy of eleven or twelve years old, little navy blue suit, blond bangs, stiff smile.

Brian looks at his brother and says very gravely, "There's seven of them in the picture."

two

The graceful two-story Colonial that Philip selected for their extended pit stop sits on a manicured side street deep in the tree-lined labyrinth of a gated enclave known as Wiltshire Estates.

Situated off Highway 278, about twenty miles east of Atlanta, the six-thousand-acre community is carved out of a forest preserve of dense longleaf pine and massive, old live oaks. The southern boundary fronts the vast, rolling hills of a thirty-six-hole golf course designed by Fuzzy Zoeller.

In the free brochure, which Brian Blake found on the floor of an abandoned guard shack earlier that evening, a flowery sales pitch makes the place sound like a Martha Stewart wet dream: *Wiltshire Estates provides an award-winning lifestyle with world-class amenities . . . named the "Best of the Best" by* GOLF Magazine Living *. . . also home to the Triple-A Five Diamond Shady Oaks Plantation Resort and Spa . . . full-time security patrols . . . homes from $475,000 to 1 million-plus.*

The Blake party happened upon the fancy outer gates at sunset that day—on their way to the refugee centers in Atlanta—all of them crammed into Philip's rust-pocked Chevy Suburban. In the spill of the headlights, they saw the fancy cast-iron finials and great arched legend with the Wiltshire name hammered in metal across the spires, and they stopped to investigate.

At first, Philip thought the place might serve as a quick pit stop, a place to rest and maybe forage for supplies before completing the last leg of the journey into the city. Perhaps they would find others like them, other living souls, maybe a few good Samaritans who would help them out. But as the five tired, hungry, wired, and dazed travelers made an initial circle of the winding roads of Wiltshire, with the darkness quickly closing in, they realized that the place was, for the most part, *dead.*

No lights burned in any of the windows. Very few cars remained in the driveways or at the curbs. A fire hydrant gushed at one corner, unattended, sending a foamy spray across a lawn. At another corner, an abandoned BMW sat with its shattered front end wrapped around a telephone pole, its twisted passenger door gaping open. People had apparently left in a hurry.

The reason they left, for the most part, could be seen in the distant shadows of the golf course, in the gullies behind the resort, and even here and there on the well-lighted streets. Zombies shambled aimlessly like ghostly remnants of their original selves, their slack, yawning mouths letting out a rusty groan that Philip could hear well enough, even through the sealed windows of the Suburban, as he circumnavigated the maze of wide, newly paved roads.

The pandemic or the act of God—or whatever the hell started it all up—must have hit Wiltshire Estates hard and fast. Most of the undead seemed to be off in the berms and pathways of the golf course. Something must have happened there to speed the process. Maybe golfers are mostly old and slow. Maybe they taste good to the undead. Who the hell knows? But it is apparent, even from hundreds of yards away—glimpsed through trees or over the tops of privacy fences—that scores, maybe hundreds, of undead are congregated in the vast complex of clubhouses, fairways, footbridges, and sand traps.

In the dark of night, they resemble insects lazily swarming a hive.

It's disconcerting to look at, but somehow the phenomenon has left the adjacent community, with its endless circuit of cul-de-sacs and curving lanes, relatively deserted. And the more Philip and his wide-eyed passengers circled the neighborhood, the more they began to long for a small chunk of that award-winning lifestyle, just a taste, for just long enough to replenish themselves and recharge.

They thought that they could maybe spend the night here, get a fresh start in the morning.

They chose the big Colonial at the bottom of Green Briar Lane because it seemed far enough away from the golf course to avoid the attentions of the swarm. It had a big yard with good sight lines, and a high, sturdy privacy fence. It also seemed empty. But when they carefully backed the Suburban across the lawn and up to a side door—leaving the vehicle unlocked, the keys in the ignition—and they sneaked in a window, one by one, the house almost immediately started working on them. The first creaking noises came from the second floor, and that's when Philip had sent Nick back to the Suburban for the assortment of axes stored in the back well.

• • •

"I'm telling you, we got 'em all," Philip is saying now, trying to calm his brother down, who sits across the kitchen in the breakfast nook.

Brian doesn't say anything, just stares at his bowl of soggy cereal. A bottle of cough medicine sits nearby, a quarter of which Brian has already chugged down.

Penny sits next to him, also with a bowl of Cap'n Crunch in front her. A little stuffed penguin the size of a pear sits next to her bowl, and every now and then Penny moves her spoon to the toy's mouth, pretending to share her cereal with the thing.

"We checked every inch of this place," Philip goes on as he throws open cabinet after cabinet. The kitchen is a cornucopia, brimming with upper-class provisions and luxuries: gourmet coffees, immersion blenders, crystal goblets, wine racks, handmade pastas, fancy jams and jellies, condiments of every variety, expensive liqueurs, and cooking gadgets of every description. The giant Viking range is spotless, and the massive Sub-Zero refrigerator is packed with expensive meats and fruits and spreads and dairy products and little white Chinese carryout boxes full of still-fresh leftovers. "He might have been visiting a relative or something," Philip adds, making note of a nice single-malt Scotch sitting on a shelf. "Might've been with his grandparents, staying over at a friend's house, whatever."

"Holy freaking Jesus, look at this!" Bobby Marsh exclaims across the room. He stands in front of the pantry, and he's lustily inspecting the goodies inside it. "Looks like Willy-damn-Wonka and the Chocolate Factory in here . . . cookies, lady fingers, and the bread's still fresh."

"The place is safe, Brian," Philip says, pulling the bottle of Scotch down.

"Safe?" Brian Blake stares at the tabletop. He lets out a cough and cringes.

"That's what I said. Matter of fact, I'm thinking—"

"Just lost another one!" a voice pipes in from the other side of the kitchen.

It's Nick. For the past ten minutes, he's been nervously surfing through the TV channels on a little plasma screen mounted under a cabinet to the left of the sink, checking the local stations for updates, and now, at a quarter to twelve Central Standard Time, Fox 5 News out of Atlanta has just crumbled into snow. All that leaves on the cable box—other than national networks showing reruns of nature programs and old movies—is Atlanta's stalwart, CNN, and all *they're* showing at the moment are emergency robo-announcements, the same warning screens with the same bullet points that have been airing for days. Even Brian's BlackBerry is giving up the ghost, the signal very spotty in this area. When it *does* work, the device is full of blind e-mails and Facebook tags and anonymous tweets with cryptic messages such as:

. . . AND THE KINGDOM WILL BE IN DARKNESS . . .

. . . IT'S THE BIRDS FALLING FROM THE SKY, THAT'S WHAT STARTED IT . . .

. . . BURN IT ALL DOWN BURN IT ALL . . .

. . . BLASPHEMIES AGAINST GOD . . .

. . . U SUCK U DIE . . .

. . . THE HOUSE OF THE LORD HAS BECOME A DWELLING PLACE OF DEMONS . . .

. . . DON'T BLAME ME FOR THIS I'M A LIBERTARIAN . . .

. . . EAT ME . . .

"Turn it off, Nick," Philip says gloomily, plopping down on a chair in the breakfast nook with his bottle. He frowns and reaches around to the back of his belt, where his pistol is digging into the small of his back. He lays the Ruger on the table and thumbs the cap off the Scotch, then takes a healthy swig.

Brian and Penny both stare at the gun.

Philip puts the cap back on the bottle, then tosses the Scotch across the kitchen to Nick, who catches it with the aplomb of an all-state second basemen (which he once was). "Tune in to the all-booze channel for a while . . . you need to get some sleep, stop watching screens."

Nick takes a taste. He takes another one, then caps the bottle and tosses it to Bobby.

Bobby nearly drops it. Still standing at the

pantry, he is busily wolfing down an entire package of Oreos, the black crust already forming in the corners of his mouth. He washes the cookies down with a big pull of single-malt, and lets out a grateful belch.

Drinking is something Philip and his two friends are accustomed to doing together, and they need to do it tonight more than ever. It started in their freshman year at Burke County, with crème de menthe and watermelon wine in pup tents in each others' backyards. Later, they graduated to boiler-makers after football games. Nobody can hold his liquor like Philip Blake, but the other two men are close rivals in the juicer sweepstakes.

Early in his married life, Philip would go out carousing with his two high school buddies on a regular basis, mostly to remind himself what it was like to be young and single and irresponsible. But after Sarah's death, the three men drifted apart. The stress of being a single parent, and working days at the muffler shop, and nights driving the freightliner with Penny in the sleeper compartment, had consumed him. The boys' nights out became less and less frequent. Once in a while, though—in fact, as recently as last month—Philip still finds time to meet Bobby and Nick down at the Tally Ho or the Wagon Wheel Inn or some other Waynesboro dive for an evening of good-natured debauchery (while Mama Rose watches Penny).

In recent years, Philip had started wondering if he was just going through the motions with Bobby and Nick to remind himself that he was alive. Maybe that was why, this past Sunday—when the feces hit the fan in Waynesboro, and he decided to take Penny and shuffle off to a safer place—he rounded up Nick and Bobby for the journey. They felt like a piece of his past, and that helped somehow.

He had never intended to take Brian along, though. Bumping into Brian had been an accident. That first day on the road, about forty miles west of Waynesboro, Philip had taken a quick detour into Deering, to check on his mom and dad. The elderly couple lived in a retirement community near the Fort Gordon military base. When Philip arrived at his folks' little town house, he found that the entire population of Deering had been moved to the base for safekeeping.

That was the good news. The bad news was that Brian was there. He was holed up in the deserted town house, huddling in the basement crawl space, petrified by the growing number of walking dead in the backcountry. Philip had almost forgotten about his brother's current status: Brian had moved back home after his marriage to that crazy Jamaican girl from Gainesville had gone south—*literally*. The girl had pulled up stakes and had gone back to Jamaica. This, coupled with the fact that every single one of Brian's harebrained business schemes had all crashed and burned—most of them financed with their parents' money (like his latest brilliant idea of opening a music store in Athens, when there was already one on every corner)—made Philip cringe at the thought of having to watch over his brother for any length of time. But what was done was done.

"Hey, Philly," Bobby says from across the room, polishing off the last of the cookies, "you think those refugee centers in the city are still up and running?"

"Who the hell knows?" Philip looks at his daughter. "How you doing, punkin?"

The little girl shrugs. "Okay." Her voice is barely audible, like a broken wind chime in the breeze. She stares at the stuffed penguin. "I guess."

"What do you think of this house? You like it?"

Penny shrugs again. "I don't know."

"What would you say if we stayed here a while?"

This gets everyone's attention. Brian looks up at his brother. All eyes are on Philip now. Nick finally speaks up: "Whattya mean 'a while'?"

"Gimme that hooch," Philip says, motioning at Bobby for the bottle. The bottle comes over and Philip takes a long pull, letting it burn nicely. "Look at this place," he says after wiping his mouth.

Brian is confused. "You said just for the night, right?"

Philip takes a deep breath. "Yeah, but I'm sorta getting over that idea right now."

Bobby starts to say, "Yeah, but—"

"Look. I'm just saying. Might be best for us to lay low for a spell."

"Yeah, but Philly, what about—"

"We could just stay put, Bobby, see what happens."

Nick has been listening intently to this. "Philip, come on, man, they've been saying on the news that the big cities are the safest—"

"The news? Jesus Christ, Nick, blow the wax outta your head. The news is going down the tubes with the rest of the population. Look at this place. You think some government halfway house is gonna have *these* kinds of goodies, beds for everyone, enough food for weeks, twenty-year-old Scotch? Showers, hot water, washing machines?"

"We're so close, though," Bobby says after a moment's thought.

Philip sighs. "Yeah, well . . . close is a relative term."

"It's twenty miles, tops."

"Might as well be twenty *thousand* miles, all them wrecks on the interstate, 278 crawling with those things."

"That ain't gonna stop us," Bobby says. His eyes light up. He snaps his fingers. "We'll build a— whattya call it?—on the front end of the Chevy— a scoop—like in fucking *Road Warrior*—"

"Watch your language, Bobby," Philip says, nodding at the little girl.

Nick speaks up. "Dude, we stay here, and it's only a matter of time until those things out at the—" He stops himself, glancing at the child. Everybody knows what he's talking about.

Penny studies her soggy cereal as though she's not listening.

"These places are solid, Nicky," Philip counters, setting down the bottle, crossing his muscular arms across his chest. Philip has been giving a lot of thought to the problem of those wandering hoards out on the golf course. The key would be keeping quiet, masking out the light at night, not sending up any signals, or smells, or undo commotion. "As long as we got power, and we keep our wits about us, we're golden."

"With one gun?" Nick says. "I mean, we can't even use it without drawing their attention."

"We'll check out the other houses, look for weapons. These rich bastards are big on deer huntin', maybe we can even find a silencer for the Ruger . . . hell, we can make one. You see that workshop downstairs?"

"C'mon, Philip. What are we, gunsmiths now? I mean . . . all we got to defend ourselves right now is a few—"

"Philip's right."

Brian's voice startles everybody—the way it comes out on a hoarse, wheezing tone of certainty.

44

He pushes his cereal away and looks up at his brother. "You're right."

Philip is probably the one who is the most taken aback by the conviction in Brian's nasally voice.

Brian stands up, comes around the table, and stands in the doorway leading into the spacious, well-furnished living room. The lights are off in there, and all the shades are drawn. Brian points toward the front wall. "Basically, the front of the house is the problem. The sides and the back are pretty well protected by that tall fence. The dead don't seem to be able to, like, penetrate barriers and stuff . . . and every house on this block has a fenced-in backyard." For a moment, it looks as if Brian's going to cough but he holds it in, puts his hand to his mouth for a moment. His hand is shaking. He goes on: "If we can, like, borrow materials from the other yards, other houses, maybe we can secure a wall across the front of the house, maybe across the neighbors' houses, too."

Bobby and Nick are looking at each other now, nobody reacting, until Philip finally says with a faint smile, "Leave it to the college boy."

It's been a while since the Blake boys have smiled at each other, but now Philip sees that at least his ne'er-do-well brother wants to be useful, wants to do something for the cause, wants to man up. And Brian seems to be absorbing confidence from Philip's approval.

Nick is unconvinced. "For how long, though? I feel like a sitting duck in this place."

"We don't know what's gonna happen," Brian says, his voice raw and yet somehow manic. "We don't know what caused this thing, how long it's gonna last . . . they could, like, figure this thing out, come up with an antidote or something . . . they could drop chemicals from crop dusters, the CDC could contain it . . . you never know. I think Philip's totally right. We should cool our jets here for a while."

"Damn straight," Philip Blake says with a grin, still sitting with his ropy arms crossed. He gives his brother a wink.

Brian returns the wink with a satisfied little nod, wiping a strand of hair as thick as straw from his eyes. He takes a shallow breath into wheezing lungs and then triumphantly walks over to the bottle of Scotch, which sits on the table next to Philip. Grabbing the bottle with a gusto that he hasn't shown in years, Brian lifts it to his lips and takes a massive gulp with the victorious swagger of a Viking celebrating a successful hunt.

Instantly, he flinches, doubles over, and lets out a fusillade of coughs. Half the liquor in his mouth goes spraying across the kitchen, and he coughs and coughs and coughs and wheezes furiously, and for a moment, the others just stare. Little Penny is thunderstruck, gawking with her huge eyes, wiping droplets of liquor from her cheek.

Philip looks at his pathetic excuse for a brother and then looks at his buddies. Across the room, Bobby Marsh struggles to stifle a laugh. Nick tries to repress his own twitching grin. Philip tries to say something but can't help but start laughing, and the laughter is contagious. The others start chortling.

Soon, everybody is laughing hysterically—even Brian—and for the first time since this whole nightmare kicked in, the laughter is genuine: a release of something dark and brittle lurking in all of them.

That night, they try to sleep in shifts. Each one of them gets their own room on the second floor—the remnants of former inhabitants like eerie artifacts in a museum: a bedside table with a half-full glass of water, a John Grisham novel open to a page that will never be finished, a pair of pompoms hanging off a teenage girl's four-poster bed.

For most of the night, Philip sits watch downstairs, out in the living room, with his gun on a coffee table next to him and Penny tucked under blankets on a sectional sofa beside his chair. The child tries unsuccessfully to fall asleep, and around three in the morning, as Philip finds his mind casting back to those tormented thoughts of Sarah's accident, he notices out of the corner of his eye that Penny is tossing and turning restlessly.

Philip leans over to her and strokes her dark hair and whispers, "Can't sleep?"

The little girl has the covers pulled up to her chin, and she looks up at him. She shakes her head. Her ashen face is almost angelic in the orange light of a space heater, which Philip has rigged next to the couch. Outside, in the distant wind, barely audible over the soft drone of the heater, the dissonant chorus of groaning is relentless, like an infernal series of waves lapping a shore.

"Daddy's here, punkin, don't worry," Philip says softly, touching her cheek. "I'll always be here."

She nods.

Philip gives her a tender smile. He leans down and plants a kiss on her left eyebrow. "Ain't gonna let nothin' happen to you."

She nods again. She has the little penguin lodged snugly in the crook of her neck. She looks at the stuffed animal and frowns. She moves the penguin to her ear, and she acts as though she's listening to the animal whisper a secret. She looks up at her father. "Daddy?"

"Yeah, punkin?"

"Penguin wants to know somethin'."

"What's that?"

"Penguin wants to know if them people are sick."

Philip takes a deep breath. "You tell Penguin . . . yeah, they're sick all right. They're more than sick. That's why we've been . . . puttin' them outta their misery."

"Daddy?"

"Yeah?"

"Penguin wants to know if we're gonna get sick, too."

Philip strokes the girl's cheek. "No, ma'am. You tell Penguin we're gonna stay healthy as mules."

This seems to satisfy the girl enough for her to look away and stare into the void some more.

By four o'clock that morning, another sleepless soul in another part of the house is asking imponderable questions of his own. Lying in a tangle of blankets, his skinny form clad only in T-shirt and briefs, his fever breaking in a film of sweat, Brian Blake stares at the stucco plaster of a dead teenage girl's ceiling and wonders if this is how the world ends. Was it Rudyard Kipling who said it ends "not with a bang but a whimper." No, wait a minute . . . it was *Eliot*. T. S. Eliot. Brian remembers studying the poem—was it 'The Hollow Men'?—in his twentieth century comparative literature class at the U of G. A lot of good *that* degree had done him.

He lies there and broods about his failures—as he does every night—but tonight the ruminations are intercut with carnage, like frames of a snuff film inserted into his stream of consciousness.

The old demons stir, mingling with the fresh fears, wearing a groove into his thoughts: Was there something he could have done or said to keep his ex-wife, Jocelyn, from drifting away, from lawyering up like she did, from saying all those hurtful things before she went back to Montego Bay? And can you kill the monsters with a simple blow to the skull or do you have to destroy the brain tissue? Was there something Brian could have done or begged for or borrowed to keep his music shop open in Athens—the only one of its kind in the South, his brilliant fucking idea of a store that catered to hip-hop artists with refurbished turntables and used bass cabinets and gaudy microphones festooned with Snoop Dogg bling? How fast are the unlucky victims out there multiplying? Is it like an airborne plague, or is it passed in the water like Ebola?

The circular ruminations of his mind keep going back to more immediate matters: the nagging feeling that the seventh member of the family that once lived here is still somewhere in the house.

Now that Brian has closed the deal among his compatriots that they should indeed stay here indefinitely, he can't stop worrying about it. He hears every creak, every faint ticking of the foundation settling, every hushed whirr of the furnace coming on. For some reason that he cannot explain, he is absolutely certain that the blond-haired kid is still here, in the house, waiting, biding his time for . . . what? Maybe the kid is the only one in the family who didn't turn. Maybe he's terrified and hiding.

Before turning in that night, Brian had insisted

they check the nooks and crannies of the house one last time. Philip had accompanied him with a pickaxe and a flashlight, and they had checked every corner of the basement, every cabinet, every closet and storage locker. They looked inside the meat freezer in the cellar, and even checked the washer and dryer for unlikely stowaways. Nick and Bobby looked up in the attic, behind trunks, in boxes, in wardrobes. Philip looked under all the beds and behind all the dressers. Coming up empty, they still made some interesting discoveries along the way.

They found a dog's food bowl in the basement, but no sign of the animal. They also found an array of very useful power tools in the workshop: jigsaws, drills, routers, and even a nail gun. The nail gun would be especially handy for building barricades since it is somewhat quieter than a pounding hammer.

In fact, Brian is thinking about other uses for that nail gun when, all at once, he hears a noise that instantly frosts his scantily clothed body in goose bumps.

The sound is coming from above him, on the other side of the ceiling.

It's coming from the attic.

three

Upon hearing the noise—almost subconsciously identifying it as something other than the house settling, or the wind in the dormers, or the furnace rattling—Brian sits up on the edge of the bed.

He cocks his head and listens more carefully. It sounds like somebody scratching at something, or the faint sound of fabric tearing in fits and jerks. At first, Brian feels compelled to go get his brother. Philip would be the best one to deal with this. It could be the kid, for God's sake . . . or something worse.

But then, almost as an afterthought, Brian stops himself. Is he going to puss out again . . . as usual? Is he going to run, like always, to his brother— his *younger* brother, for God's sake—the same individual whose hand Brian had once held at the crosswalk every morning when the two of them were grade school kids at Burke County Elementary? No, goddamnit. Not this time. This time, Brian is going to grow a pair.

He takes a deep breath, turns, and searches for the flashlight he had left on the bedside table. He finds it and switches it on.

The narrow beam shoots across the dark bedroom, spreading a silver pool of light on the opposite wall. *Just you and me, Justin,* Brian thinks as he rises to his feet. His head is clear. His senses are crackling.

The truth is, Brian had felt incredibly good earlier that night when he had concurred with his brother's plans, when he had seen the look in Philip's eyes, like maybe Brian is not a hopeless loser after all. Now it's time to show Philip that the moment in the kitchen was not a fluke. Brian can get the job done just as well as Philip.

He moves quietly toward the door.

Before leaving the room, he grabs the metal baseball bat that he found in one of the boys' bedrooms.

The papery rustling noises can be heard more clearly in the hallway, as Brian pauses under the attic hatchway, which is a glorified trapdoor embedded in the ceiling above the second-floor landing. The other bedrooms along the hallway—filled with the deep snores of Bobby Marsh and Nick Parsons—are situated on the other side of the landing, on the east side of the house, out of earshot. That's why Brian is the only one hearing this right now.

A leather strap hangs down, low enough for Brian to jump up and grasp. He pulls the spring-levered hatch open, and the accordionlike stairs unfold with a pinging noise. Brian shines the flashlight up into the dark passage. Dust motes drift in the beam. The darkness is impenetrable, opaque. Brian's heart chugs.

You fucking pussy, he thinks to himself. *Get your pussy ass up there.*

He climbs the steps with the baseball bat under one arm, the flashlight in his free hand, and he pauses when he reaches the top of the ladder. He shines the light on a huge steamer trunk with Magnolia Springs State Park stickers on it.

Now Brian smells the cold putrid odors of must and mothballs. The autumn chill has already seeped into the attic through the seams of the roof. The air is cool on his face. And after a moment, he hears the rustling again.

It's coming from a deeper place in the shadows of the attic. Brian's throat is as dry as bone meal as he climbs to his feet on the threshold. The ceiling is low enough to force him to hunch. Shivering in his underwear, Brian wants to cough but doesn't dare.

The scratching noises stop, and then start again, vigorous and angry sounding.

Brian raises the bat. He gets very still. He's learning the mechanics of fear all over again: When you're really, really scared, you don't shake like in the movies. You grow still, like an animal bristling.

It's only afterward you start shaking.

The beam of the flashlight slowly scans across the dark niches of the attic, the detritus of the well-to-do: an exercise bike laced with cobwebs, a rowing machine, more trunks, barbells, tricycles, wardrobe boxes, water skis, a pinball machine furry with dust. The scratching noises cease again.

The light reveals a coffin.

Brian practically turns to stone.

A *coffin?*

Philip is already halfway up the staircase when he notices, up on the second-floor landing, the attic stepladder hanging down, unfolded.

He pads up to the landing in his stocking feet. He carries an axe in one hand and a flashlight in the other. The .22 pistol is shoved down the back of his jeans. He is shirtless, his ropy musculature shimmering in moonbeams filtering down through a skylight.

It takes him mere seconds to cross the landing and scale the accordion steps, and when he emerges into the darkness of the attic, he sees the silhouette of a figure across the narrow space.

Before Philip even has a chance to shine his flashlight on his brother, the situation becomes clear.

"It's a tanning bed," the voice says, making Brian jump. For the past few seconds, Brian Blake has been paralyzed with terror, standing ten feet away from the dusty, oblong enclosure shoved up against one wall of the attic. The top of the thing is latched shut like a giant clamshell, and something scratches to get out of it.

Brian jerks around and finds in the beam of his flashlight his brother's gaunt, sullen face. Philip stands on the threshold of the attic with the axe in his right hand. "Move away from it, Brian."

"You think it's—"

"The missing kid?" Philip whispers, cautiously moving toward the object. "Let's find out."

The scratching noise, as if stimulated by the sound of voices, surges and rises.

Brian turns toward the tanning bed, braces himself, and raises the baseball bat. "He might have been hiding up here when he turned."

Philip approaches with the axe. "Get outta the way, sport."

"I'll take care of it," Brian says bitterly, moving toward the latch, his baseball bat poised.

Philip gently steps in between his brother and the tanning bed. "You don't have to prove nothing to me, man. Just move outta the way."

"No, goddamnit, I got this," Brian hisses, reaching for the dusty latch.

Philip studies his brother. "Okay, whatever. Go for it, but do it quick. Whatever it is—don't think about it too much."

"I know," Brian says, grasping the latch with his free hand.

Philip stands inches behind his brother.

Brian unlatches the enclosure.

The scuttling noises cease.

Philip raises the axe as Brian throws open the lid.

Two quick movements—a pair of blurs in the darkness—shoot across Philip's sight line: a rustling of fur and the arc of Brian's bat.

It takes a second or two for the animal to register in Philip's heightened senses—the mouse darting out of the glare of the flashlight and scurrying across the fiberglass trough toward a hole gnawed in one corner.

The baseball bat comes down hard, missing the fat, oily-gray rodent by a mile.

Pieces of the bed's switch panel and old toys shatter at the impact. Brian lets out a gasp and recoils at the sight of the mouse vanishing down the hole, slithering back into the inner workings of the bed's base.

Philip lets out a sigh of relief and lowers the axe. He starts to say something when he hears a little metallic tune playing in the shadows next to him. Brian looks down, breathing hard.

A little jack-in-the-box, thrown by the impact of the bat, lies on the floor.

Triggered by the fall, the tinny music plays a few more notes of a circus lullaby.

Then the toy clown pops out—sideways—from the fallen metal container.

"Boo," Philip says wearily, with very little humor in his voice.

● ● ●

Their moods improve slightly the next morning after a huge breakfast of scrambled eggs and slab bacon and grits and ham and griddlecakes and fresh peaches and sweet tea. The fragrant mélange fills with entire house with the welcoming odors of coffee and cinnamon and smoked meats sizzling. Nick even makes his special redeye gravy for the group, which sends Bobby into ecstasy.

Brian finds cold remedies in the master bedroom medicine cabinet and starts feeling a little better after he downs a few DayQuil capsules.

After breakfast, they explore the immediate vicinity—the single square block known as Green Briar Lane—and they get more good news. They find a treasure trove of supplies and building materials: woodpiles for fireplaces, extra planking under decks, more food in the neighbors' refrigerators, cans of gas in the garages, winter coats and boots, boxes of nails, liquor, blowtorches, bottled water, a shortwave radio, a laptop, a generator, stacks of DVDs, and a gun rack in one of the basements with several hunting rifles and boxes of shells.

No silencer; but beggars can't be choosers.

They also get lucky in the undead department. The houses on either side of the Colonial are empty; their residents evidently got the hell out of Dodge before the shit had gone too far down. Two houses away from the Colonial, on the west side,

Philip and Nick encounter an elderly couple who have turned, but the oldsters are easily, quickly, and most importantly, *quietly* dispatched with some well-placed hatchet blows.

That afternoon, Philip and company cautiously begin work on the barricade across the front parkway of the Colonial and its two neighbors—a total span of a hundred and fifty feet for the three lots, and sixty down either side—which sounds to Nick and Bobby like a daunting amount of territory to cover, but with the ten-foot-long prefab sections they find under a neighbor's deck, combined with fencing cannibalized off the place across the street, the work goes surprisingly fast.

By dusk that evening, Philip and Nick are connecting the last sections on the northern edge of the property line.

"I've been keeping an eye on 'em all day," Philip is saying, pressing the forked tip of the nail gun against the bracing of a corner section. He's referring to the swarms out near the golf club. Nick nods as he butts the two support beams against each other.

Philip pulls the trigger, and the nail gun makes a muffled snapping noise—like the crack of a metal whip—sending a six-inch galvanized nail into the boards. The nail gun is baffled with a small piece of packing blanket, secured with duct tape, to dampen the noise.

"I ain't seen a single one of them wander closer,"

Philip says, wiping the sweat from his brow, moving to the next section of support beams. Nick holds the boards steady, and the tip presses down.

FFFFFUMP!

"I don't know," Nick says skeptically, moving to the next section, the sweat making his satin roadie jacket cling to his back. "I still say it's not *if*... but *when*."

FFFFFFFUMP!

"You worry too much, son," Philip says, moving to the next section of planking, tugging on the gun's cord. The extension cable snakes off toward an outlet on the corner of the neighbor's house. Philip had to connect a grand total of six twenty-eight-foot cords to get the thing to reach. He pauses and glances over his shoulder.

About fifty yards away, in the backyard of the Colonial, Brian pushes Penny in a swing. It's taken a little getting used to for Philip, putting his hapless brother in charge of his precious little girl, but right now Brian is the best nanny he's got.

The play set—of course—is deluxe. Rich folks love to spoil their kids with shit like this. This one—more than likely a haunt of the missing kid—has got all the bells and whistles: slide, clubhouse, four swings, climbing wall, jungle gym, and sandbox.

"We got it made here," Philip goes on, turning back to his work. "Long as we keep our heads screwed on straight, we're gonna be fine."

As they position the next section, the rustling sounds of their movements and the creak of the planks mask the telltale noise of shuffling foot-steps.

The footsteps are coming from across the street. Philip doesn't hear them until the errant zombie is close enough for its odor to register.

Nick is the first one to smell it: that black, oily, mildewy combination of rotting protein and decay—like human waste cooking in bacon grease. It immediately puts Nick's guard up. "Wait a minute," he says, holding a section of planking. "You smell—"

"Yeah, smells like—"

A fish-belly arm bursts through a gap in the fencing, grabbing a hank of Philip's denim shirt.

The assailant was once a middle-aged woman in a designer running suit, now an emaciated wraith with torn sleeves, blackened, exposed teeth, and the button eyes of a prehistoric fish, her hooked hand clutching Philip's shirttail with the vise grip of frozen dead fingers. She lets out a low groan like a broken pipe organ as Philip spins toward his axe, which lies canted against a wheelbarrow twenty feet away.

Too damn far.

The dead lady goes for Philip's neck with the autonomic hunger of a giant snapping turtle, and across the yard, Nick fumbles for a weapon, but it's all happening too fast. Philip rears backward with a grunt, just now realizing that he still holds the nail gun. He dodges the snapping teeth, and then instinctively raises the muzzle of the nail gun.

In one quick movement, he touches the tip to the thing's brow.

FFFFFFFFFFFUMP!

The lady zombie stiffens.

Icy fingers release their grip on Philip.

He pulls himself free, huffing and puffing, gaping at the thing.

The vertical cadaver teeters for a moment, wobbling as if drunk, shuddering in its soiled velveteen Pierre Cardin warm-up, but it will not go down. The head of the six-inch galvanized nail is visible above the ridge of the lady's nose like a tiny coin stuck there.

The thing remains upright for endless moments, its sharklike eyes turned upward, until it begins to slowly stagger backward across the parkway, its ruined face taking on a strange, almost dreamy expression.

For a moment, it looks as though the thing is remembering something, or hearing some high-pitched whistle. Then it collapses in the grass.

"I think the nail does just enough damage to take 'em out," Philip is saying after dinner, pacing back and forth across the shuttered windows of the lavish dining room, the nail gun in his hand like a visual aid.

The others are sitting at the long burnished oak table, the remnants of dinner lying strewn in front of them. Brian cooked for the group that night, defrosting a roast in the microwave and making gravy with a vintage cabernet and a splash of cream. Penny is in the adjacent family room watching a DVD of *Dora the Explorer*.

"Yeah, but did you see the way that thing went down?" Nick points out, pushing an uneaten gob of meat across his plate. "After you zapped it . . . looked like the damn thing was stoned for a second."

Philip keeps pacing, clicking the trigger of the nail gun and thinking. "Yeah but it *did* go down."

"It's quieter than a gun, I'll give you that."

"And it's a hell of a lot easier than splitting their skulls open with an axe."

Bobby has just started in on his second helping of pot roast and gravy. "Too bad you don't have a six-mile extension cord," he says with his mouth full.

Philip clicks the trigger a few more times. "Maybe we could hook this puppy up to a battery."

Nick looks up. "Like a car battery?"

"No, like something you could carry more easily, something like one of them big lantern batteries or something outta one of them electric mowers."

Nick shrugs.

Bobby eats.

Philip paces and thinks.

Brian stares at the wall, mumbling, "Something to do with their brains."

"Say what?" Philip looks at his brother. "What was that, Bri?"

Brian looks at him. "Those things . . . the sickness. It's basically in the brain, right? It's gotta be." He pauses. He looks at his plate. "I still say we don't even know they're dead."

Nick looks at Brian. "You mean after we take 'em out? After we . . . destroy 'em?"

"No, I mean *before,*" Brian says. "I mean, like, the condition they're in."

Philip stops pacing. "Shit, man . . . on Monday, I saw one of 'em get squashed by an eighteen-wheeler and ten minutes later, it's dragging itself along the street with its guts hanging out. They've been saying it on all the news reports. They're dead, sport. They're *way* dead."

"I'm just saying, the central nervous system, man, it's complicated. All the shit in the environ-ment right now, new strains of shit."

"Hey, you want to take one of them things to a doctor for a checkup, be my guest."

Brian sighs. "All I'm saying is, we don't *know* enough yet. We don't know shit."

"We know all we need to know," Philip says, giving his brother a look. "We know there's more of them fucking things every day, and all they seem to want to do is have us for lunch. Which is why we're gonna hang here for a while, let things play out a little."

Brian breathes out a painful, weary sigh. The others are silent.

In the lull, they can hear the faint noises that they've been hearing all night, coming from the darkness outside: the muffled, intermittent thudding of insensate figures bumping up against the makeshift barricade.

Despite Philip's efforts to erect the rampart quickly and quietly, the commotion of the day's construction project has drawn more of the walking corpses.

"How long do you think we're gonna be able to stay here?" Brian asks softly.

Philip sits down, lays the nail gun on the table and takes another sip of his bourbon. He nods toward the family room, where the whimsical voices of children's programming drift incongruously. "She needs a break," Philip says. "She's exhausted."

"She loves that play set out back," Brian says with a weak smile.

Philip nods. "She can live a normal life here for a while."

Everybody looks at him. Everybody silently chews on the concept.

"Here's to all the rich motherfuckers of the world," Philip says, raising his glass.

The others toast without really knowing just exactly what they're toasting . . . or how long it will last.

four

The next day, in the clean autumn sun, Penny plays in the backyard under the watchful gaze of Brian. She plays throughout the morning while the others take inventory and sort through their supplies. In the afternoon, Philip and Nick secure the window wells in the basement with extra planking, and try unsuccessfully to rig the nail gun to DC power, while Bobby, Brian, and Penny play cards in the family room.

The proximity of the undead is a constant factor, swimming sharklike under the surface of every decision, every activity. But for the moment, there's just an occasional stray, an errant wanderer bumping up against the privacy fence, then shambling away. For the most part, the activity behind the seven-foot cedar bulwark on Green Briar Lane has, so far, gone unnoticed by the swarm.

That night, after dinner, with the shades drawn, they all watch a Jim Carrey movie in the family room, and they almost feel normal again. They're all starting to get used to this place. The occasional muffled thump out in the darkness barely registers now. Brian has practically forgotten the missing twelve-year-old, and after Penny goes to bed, the men make long-term plans.

They discuss the implications of staying in the

Colonial as long as supplies hold out. They've got enough provisions for weeks. Nick wonders if they should send out a scout, maybe gauge the situation on the roads into Atlanta, but Philip is adamant about staying put. "Let whoever's out there duke it out among themselves," Philip advises.

Nick is still keeping tabs on the radio, TV, and Internet . . . and like the failing bodily functions of a terminal patient, the media seem to be sparking out one organ at a time. By this point, most radio stations are playing either recorded programming or useless emergency information. TV networks— the ones on basic cable that are still up and running—are now resorting to either twenty-four-hour automated civil defense announcements or inexplicable, incongruous reruns of banal late-night infomercials.

By the third day, Nick realizes that most of the radio dial is static, most of basic cable is snow, and the Wi-Fi in the house is gone. No dial-up connections are working, and the regular phone calls Nick has been making to emergency numbers —which, up to this point, have all played back recordings—are now sending back the classic "fuck you" from the phone company: *The number you have dialed is not available at this time, please try again later.*

By late morning that day, the sky clouds over.

In the afternoon, a dismal, chill mist falls on the community, and everybody huddles indoors, trying to ignore the fact that there's a fine line between being safe and being a prisoner. Other than Nick, most of them are tired of talking about Atlanta. Atlanta seems *farther away* now—as if the more they ponder the twenty-some miles between Wiltshire and the city, the more impassable they seem.

That night, after everybody drifts off to sleep, Philip sits his lonely vigil in the living room next to a slumbering Penny.

The mist has deteriorated into full-blown thunder and lightning.

Philip pokes a finger between two shutter slats, and he peers out into the darkness. Through the gap, he can see—over the top of the barricade— the winding side streets and massive shadows of live oaks, their branches bending in the wind.

Lightning flickers.

Two hundred yards away, a dozen or so humanoid shapes materialize in the strobe light, moving aimlessly through the rain.

It's hard to tell for sure from Philip's vantage point, but it looks as though the things might be moving—in their leaden, retarded fashion, like stroke victims—*this way*. Do they smell fresh meat? Did the noises of human activity draw them out? Or are they simply lumbering around randomly like ghastly goldfish in a bowl?

Right then, for the first time since they arrived at Wiltshire Estates, Philip Blake begins to wonder if their days in this womb of wall-to-wall carpet and overstuffed sofas are numbered.

The fourth day dawns cold and overcast. The pewter-colored sky hangs low over the wet lawns and abandoned homes. Although the occasion goes unspoken, the new day marks a milestone of sorts: the beginning of the plague's second week.

Now Philip stands with his coffee in the living room, peering out through the shutters at the jury-rigged barricade. In the pale morning light, he can see the northeast corner of the fence shuddering and trembling. "Son of a *buck*," he mutters under his breath.

"What's the matter?" Brian's voice snaps Philip out of his stupor.

"There's more of 'em."

"Shit. How many?"

"Can't tell."

"What do you want to do?"

"Bobby!"

The big man trundles into the living room in his sweatpants and bare feet, eating a banana. Philip turns to his portly pal and says, "Get dressed."

Bobby swallows a mouthful of banana. "What's going on?"

Philip ignores the question, looks at Brian. "Keep Penny in the family room."

"Will do," Brian says, and hurries off.

Philip starts toward the stairs, calling out as he

goes: "Get the nail gun and as many extension cords as you can carry . . . hatchets, too!"

FFFFFFFOOOMP! Number five goes down like a giant rag doll in tattered suit pants, the dead, milky eyes rolling back in its head as it slides down the other side of the fence, its putrid body collapsing to the parkway. Philip steps back, breathing hard from the exertion, damp with sweat in his denim jacket and jeans.

Numbers one through four had been as easy as shooting fish in a barrel—one female and three males—all of whom Philip had sneaked up on with the nail gun as they bumped and clawed against the weak spot at the fence's corner. At that point, all Philip had to do was stand on the bottom strut with a good angle on the tops of their heads. He put them down quickly, one after another: *FFFFOOOMP! FFFFOOOMP! FFFFOOOMP! FFFFOOOMP!*

Number five had been slippery. Inadvertently jerking out of the line of fire at the last moment, it did a little intoxicated shuffle, then craned its neck upward at Philip, jaws snapping. Philip had to waste two nails—both of which ricocheted off the sidewalk—before he finally sent one home into the suit-wearing asshole's cerebral cortex.

Now Philip catches his breath, doubled over with exhaustion, the nail gun still in his right hand, still plugged into the house with four twenty-five-foot cords. He straightens up and listens. The front parkway is silent now. The fence is still.

Glancing over his shoulder, Philip sees Bobby Marsh in the backyard, about a hundred feet away. The big man is sitting on his fat ass, trying to catch his breath, leaning against a small abandoned doghouse. The doghouse has a little shingle roof and the word LADDIE BOY mounted above the opening at one end.

These rich people and their fucking dogs, Philip thinks ruefully, still a little manic and wired. *Probably fed that thing better than most kids.*

Over the back fence, about twenty feet away from Bobby, the limp remains of a dead woman are draped over the crest, a hatchet still buried in her skull where Bobby Marsh put out her lights.

Philip gives Bobby a wave and a hard, questioning look: *Everything cool?*

Bobby returns the gesture with a thumbs-up.

Then . . . almost without warning . . . things begin happening very quickly.

The first indication that something is decidedly *not* cool occurs within a split second of Bobby signaling the thumbs-up sign to his friend and leader and mentor. Drenched in sweat, his heart still pumping with the burden of his huge girth as he sits leaning against the doghouse, Bobby manages to accompany the thumbs-up signal with a smile . . . completely oblivious to the muffled noise coming from inside the doghouse.

For years now, Bobby Marsh has secretly yearned to please Philip Blake, and the prospects of giving Philip the thumbs-up after a messy job well done fills Bobby with a weird kind of satisfaction.

An only child, barely able to make it out of high school, Bobby clung to Philip in the years before Sarah Blake had died, and after that—after Philip had drifted away from his drinking buddies—Bobby had desperately tried to reconnect. Bobby called Philip too many times; Bobby talked too much when they were together; and Bobby often made a fool of himself trying to keep up with the wiry, alpha dog of a ringleader. But now, in a strange way, Bobby feels as though this bizarre epidemic has—among other things—given Bobby a way to bond again with Philip.

All of which is probably why, at first, Bobby doesn't hear the noise inside the doghouse.

When the thump comes—as if a giant heart were beating inside the little miniature shack—Bobby's smile freezes on his face, and his upturned thumb falls to his side. And by the time the realization that there's something inside the doghouse—something moving—manages to travel the synapses of Bobby's brain and register plainly enough for him to move, it's already too late.

Something small and low to the ground bursts out of the doghouse's arched opening.

• • •

Philip is already halfway across the yard, running at a full sprint, when it becomes clear that the thing that has just thrust its way out of the doghouse is a tiny human being—or at least a rotting, bluish, contorted *facsimile* of a tiny human being—with leaves and dog shit in its filthy, matted blond bangs, and chains tangled around its waist and legs.

"F-FUH-FFUHHHHK!" Bobby yelps and jerks back away from the twelve-year-old corpse as the thing that was once a boy now pounces on Bobby's ham-hock-sized leg.

Bobby tumbles sideways, ripping his leg free in the nick of time, just as the little contorted face— like a sunken gourd with hollow cavities for eyes—gobbles the grass where Bobby's leg had been one millisecond earlier.

Philip is now fifty feet away, charging toward the doghouse at top speed, raising the nail gun like a divining rod aimed at the miniature monster. Bobby crawls crablike through the damp grass, his ass crack showing pathetically, his gasps high and shrill like those of a little girl.

The pint-sized fiend moves with the graceless energy of a tarantula, scuttling across the grass toward Bobby. The fat man tries to struggle to his feet and run, but his legs get tangled and he tumbles again, backward this time.

Philip is twenty feet away when Bobby starts

shrieking in a higher register. The zombie child has hooked a clawlike hand around Bobby's ankle, and before Bobby can wrest his leg away from the thing, it sinks a mouthful of putrefying teeth into Bobby's leg.

"GODDAMNIT!" Philip booms as he approaches with the nail gun.

A hundred feet behind him, the extension cord pulls free of the outlet.

Philip slams the tip of the nail gun down on the back of the thing's skull as the monster latches on to Bobby's quivering, fat body.

The nail gun trigger clicks. Nothing happens. The zombie burrows down into Bobby's flaccid thigh, piranhalike, breaching his femoral artery and taking half his scrotum with it. Bobby's scream deteriorates into a ululating howl as Philip instinctively tosses the gun aside, then lurches at the beast. He tears the thing off his friend as though removing a giant leech and heaves it— head over heels—across the lawn before it has a chance to take another bite.

The dead child flops and rolls twenty feet across the muddy grass.

Nick and Brian burst out of the house, Brian grabbing for the extension cord, Nick roaring across the lawn with a pickaxe. Philip grabs Bobby and tries to stop him from squirming and screaming, because the extra exertion is making the big man hemorrhage faster, the ragged wound already sending up geysers of blood in rhythm with Bobby's quickening pulse. Philip slams his hand down on Bobby's leg, stanching the flow slightly, the blood oozing between Philip's greasy fingers, as other figures move across Philip's peripheral vision. The dead thing is crawling back across the moist ground toward Philip and Bobby, and Nick does not hesitate, approaching at a sprint, raising the axe, eyes wide with panic and rage. The axe sings through the air, the rusty point coming down on the back of the zombie-child's skull, sinking three inches into the cranial cavity. The monster deflates. Philip screams up at Nick something about a *belt,* a *BELT,* and now Nick is hovering, fumbling for his belt. Philip has no formal training in first aid but he knows enough to try and stop the bleeding with some kind of tourniquet. He wraps Nick's belt around the shivering fat man's leg, and Bobby is trying to talk again but he looks like a man experiencing extreme cold, his lips moving, quivering silently. Meantime—as all this is going on—Brian is a hundred feet away, plugging the extension cord back in the outlet, probably because it's all he can think of doing. The nail gun lies in the grass fifteen feet behind Philip. At this point, Philip is shouting at Nick to *GO GET SOME FUCKING BANDAGES AND ALCOHOL AND WHATEVER!!!* Nick hurries off, still carrying the pickaxe, while Brian approaches, staring at the

75

dead thing lying facedown in the grass, its skull stoved in. Brian gives it a wide berth. He picks up the nail gun—just in case—and he scans the hill behind the back fence as Philip now holds Bobby in his arms like a giant baby. Bobby is crying, breathing quick, shallow, rattling breaths. Philip comforts his friend, murmuring encouragement and assuring him that it's all going to be okay . . . but it's clear, as Brian cautiously approaches, that things are definitely not going to be okay.

Moments later, Nick returns with an armful of large sterile cotton bandages from inside, as well as a plastic bottle of alcohol in one back pocket and a roll of cotton tape in the other. But something has changed. The emergency has transformed into something darker—a deathwatch.

"We gotta get him inside," Philip announces, now soaked in his friend's blood. But Philip makes no effort to lift the fat man. Bobby Marsh is going to die. That much is clear to all of them.

It's especially clear to Bobby Marsh, who now lies in a state of shock, staring up at the gunmetal sky, struggling to speak.

Brian stands nearby, holding the nail gun at his side, staring down at Bobby. Nick drops the bandages. He lets out an anguished breath. He looks as though he might start to cry, but instead he simply drops to his knees on the other side of Bobby and hangs his head.

"I—I—n-n-nn—" Bobby Marsh tries desperately to get Philip to understand something.

"Sssshhhhh . . ." Philip strokes the man's shoulder. Philip cannot think straight. He turns, grabs a roll of bandages, and starts dressing the wound.

"Nnn-n-NO!" Bobby pushes the bandage away.

"Bobby, goddamnit."

"NN-NO!"

Philip stops, swallows hard, looks into the watery eyes of the dying man. "It's gonna be okay," Philip says, his voice changing.

"N-no—it ain't," Bobby manages. Somewhere way up in the sky, a crow yammers. Bobby knows what's going to happen. They saw a man in a ditch back in Covington come back in less than ten minutes. "S-ss-stop saying that, Philly."

"Bobby—"

"It's over," Bobby manages in a feeble whisper, and his eyes roll back for a moment. Then he sees the nail gun in Brian's hand. With his big bloody sausage fingers, Bobby reaches for the muzzle.

Brian drops the gun with a start.

"Goddamnit, we gotta get him inside!" Philip's voice is laced with hopelessness as Bobby Marsh blindly reaches for the nail gun. He gets his fat hand around the pointed barrel and tries to lift it to his temple.

"Jesus Christ," Nick utters.

"Get that thing away from him!" Philip waves Brian away from the victim.

Bobby's tears track down the sides of his huge head, cleansing the blood in streaks. "P-please, Philly," Bobby murmurs. "J-just . . . *do* it."

Philip stands up. "Nick!—C'mere!" Philip turns and walks a few paces toward the house.

Nick rises to his feet and joins Philip. The two men stand fifteen feet away from Bobby, out of earshot, their backs turned, their voices low and strained.

"We gotta cut him," Philip says quickly.

"We gotta what?"

"Amputate his leg."

"What!"

"Before the sickness spreads."

"But how do you—"

"We don't know how fast it spreads, we gotta try, we owe the man at least *that*."

"But—"

"I'm gonna need ya to go get the hacksaw from the shed and also bring—"

A voice rings out behind them, interrupting Philip's tense litany: "Guys?"

It's Brian, and from the grim sound of his nasally call, the news is most likely bad.

Philip and Nick turn.

Bobby Marsh is stone-still.

Brian's eyes well up as he kneels next to the fat man. "It's too late."

Philip and Nick come over to where Bobby lies in the grass, his eyes closed. His big, flabby chest does not move. His mouth is slack.

"Oh no . . . Sweet Jesus Christ no," Nick says, staring at his dead pal.

Philip doesn't say anything for quite a long time. No one does.

The immense corpse lies still, there on the wet ground, for endless minutes . . . until something stirs in the man's extremities, in the tendons of his massive legs, and in the tips of his plump fingers.

At first, the phenomenon looks like the typical residual nerve twitches that morticians might see now and again, the dieseling engine of a cadaver's central nervous system. But as Nick and Brian gape, their eyes widening—both of them slowly rising, then slowly beginning to back away—Philip comes closer still, kneeling down, a sullen businesslike expression on his face.

Bobby Marsh's eyes open.

The pupils have turned as white as pus.

Philip grabs the nail gun and presses it to the big man's forehead just above the left eyebrow.

FFFFFFFFFUMP!

Hours later. Inside the house. After dark. Penny asleep. Nick in the kitchen, drowning his grief in whiskey . . . Brian nowhere to be found . . . Bobby's cooling corpse in the backyard, covered in a tarp next to the other bodies . . . and Philip now standing at the living room window, gazing out through the slatted shutters at the growing number of dark figures on the street. They shuffle like sleepwalkers, moving back and forth behind the barricade. There are more of them now. Thirty, maybe. Forty even.

Streetlights shine through the cracks in the fence, the moving shadows breaking the beams at irregular intervals, making the light strobe, making Philip crazy. He hears the silent voice in his head—the same voice that first made itself known after Sarah had died: *Burn the place down, burn the whole fucking world down.*

For a moment earlier that day, after Bobby had died, the voice had wanted to mutilate the twelve-year-old's body. The voice had wanted to take that dead thing apart. But Philip tamped it down, and now he's fighting it again: *The fuse is lit, brother, the clock is ticking . . .*

Philip looks away from the window, and he rubs his tired eyes.

"It's okay to let it out," a different voice says now, coming from across the darkness.

Philip whirls and sees the silhouette of his brother across the living room, standing in the archway of the kitchen.

Turning back to the window, Philip offers no response. Brian comes over. He's holding a bottle of cough syrup in his trembling hands. In the

80

darkness his feverish eyes shimmer with tears. He stands there for a moment.

Then he says in low, soft voice, careful not to awaken Penny on the couch next to them, "There's no shame in letting it out."

"Letting *what* out?"

"Look," Brian says, "I know you're hurting." He sniffs, wipes his mouth on his sleeve, his voice hoarse and congested. "All I wanted to say is, I'm really sorry about Bobby, I know you guys were—"

"It's done."

"Philip, c'mon—"

"This *place* is done, it's cooked."

Brian looks at him. "What do you mean?"

"We're getting out of here."

"But I thought—"

"Take a look." Philip indicates the growing number of shadows out on Green Briar Lane. "We're drawing 'em like flies on shit."

"Yeah, but the barricade is still—"

"The longer we stay here, Brian, the more it's gonna get like a prison." Philip stares out the window. "Gotta keep moving forward."

"When?"

"Soon."

"Like tomorrow?"

"We'll start packin' in the morning, get as many supplies in the Suburban as we can."

Silence.

Brian looks at his brother. "You okay?"

"Yeah." Philip keeps staring. "Go to sleep."

At breakfast, Philip decides to tell his daughter that Bobby had to up and go home—"to go take care of his folks"—and the explanation seems to satisfy the little girl.

Later that morning, Nick and Philip dig the grave out back, choosing a soft spot at the end of the garden, while Brian keeps Penny occupied in the house. Brian thinks they should tell Penny some version of what happened, but Philip tells Brian to stay the hell out of it and keep his mouth shut.

Now, in front of the rose trellis in the backyard, Philip and Nick lift the massive tarp-wrapped body and lower it into the hollowed-out earth.

It takes them quite a while to get the hole filled back up, each man tossing spade after spade of rich, black Georgia topsoil on their friend. While they work, the atonal moaning of the undead drifts on the wind.

It's another blustery, overcast day, and the sounds of the zombie horde carry up across the sky and over the tops of houses. It drives Philip nuts as he sweats in his denims, heaving dirt on the grave. The oily, black, rotten-meat odor is as strong as ever. It makes Philip's stomach clench as he puts the last few shovelfuls of earth on the grave.

Now Philip and Nick pause on opposite sides of the huge mound, leaning on their shovels, the sweat cooling on their necks. Neither says a word for a long moment, each man lost in his thoughts. Finally, Nick looks up, and very softly, very wearily, and with great deference, says, "You want to say something?"

Philip looks across the grave at his buddy. The moaning noises are coming from all directions like the roar of locusts, so loud Philip can barely think straight.

Right then, for some strange reason, Philip Blake remembers the night that the three friends got drunk and sneaked into the Starliter Drive-In Theater out on Waverly Road and broke into the projection booth. Waving his fat little fingers in front of the projector, Bobby had made shadow puppets appear on the distant screen. Philip had laughed so hard that night he thought he was going to puke, watching the silhouettes of rabbits and ducks cavorting across the flickering images of Chuck Norris spin-kicking Nazis.

"Some folks thought Bobby Marsh was a simpleton," Philip says with his head lowered, his gaze down-turned, "but they didn't know the man. He was loyal and he was funny, and he was a goddamn good friend . . . and he died like a man."

Nick is looking down, his shoulders trembling slightly, his voice breaking, his words barely audible over the rising clamor around them: "Almighty God, in your mercy turn the darkness of death into the dawn of new life, and the sorrow of parting into the joy of heaven."

Philip feels tears welling up and he grits his teeth so hard his jaw throbs.

"Through our Savior, Jesus Christ," Nick says in a shaky voice, "who died, rose again, and lives for evermore. Amen."

"Amen," Philip manages in a faint croak that sounds almost alien to his own ears.

The relentless din of the undead swells and surges louder and louder.

"SHUT THE FUCK UP!" Philip Blake bellows at the zombies, the noises coming from all directions now. "YOU DEAD MOTHER*FUCKERS!*" Philip turns away from the grave, slowly pivoting: "I WILL SKULL-FUCK EVERY ONE OF YOU CANNIBAL-COCKSUCKERS!!! I WILL RIP EVERY STINKING HEAD OFF EVERY FUCKING ONE OF YOU AND SHIT DOWN YOUR ROTTEN FUCKING NECKS!!!"

Hearing this, Nick starts sobbing as Philip runs out of gas and falls to his knees.

While Nick cries, Philip just stares down at the fresh dirt as though some answer lies there.

If there was ever any doubt about who was in charge—not that there ever was—it is now made abundantly clear that Philip is the alpha and omega.

They spend the rest of that day packing, Philip

issuing orders in monosyllables, his voice low and gravelly with stress. "Take the toolbox," he grunts. "Batteries for the flashlights," he mumbles. "And that box of shells," he mutters. "Extra blankets, too."

Nick thinks that maybe they should consider taking two cars.

Although most of the abandoned vehicles in the community are ripe for the picking—many of them late-model luxury jobs, many with the keys still in them—Brian worries about splitting the ragged little group into two. Or maybe he's just clinging to his brother now. Maybe Brian just needs to stay close to the center of gravity.

They decide to stick with the Chevy Suburban. The thing is a tank.

Which is exactly what they'll need to get into Atlanta.

His stubborn cold now settling into his lungs, causing a perpetual wheeze that may or may not be early-stage pneumonia, Brian Blake focuses on the task at hand. He packs three large coolers with food stamped with the furthest expiration dates: smoked lunch meats, hard cheeses, sealed containers of juice and yogurt and soda and mayonnaise. He fills a cardboard box with bread and beef jerky and instant coffee and bottled water and protein bars and vitamins and paper plates and plastic utensils. He decides to throw in an array of chef's knives: cleavers, serrated knives, and boning knives—for whatever close encounters they might stumble into.

Brian fills another box with toilet paper and soap and towels and rags. He rifles through the medicine cabinets and takes cold remedies and sleeping pills and pain relievers, and while he's doing this, he gets an idea: something he should do before they depart.

In the basement, Brian finds a small can half full of Benjamin Moore Apple Peel Red and a two-inch horsehair paintbrush. He finds an old three-by-three-foot-square piece of plywood, and quickly but carefully, he writes a message: five simple words in big capital letters, large enough to be seen from a passing vehicle. He nails a couple of short legs on the bottom edge of the sign.

Then he takes the sign upstairs and shows it to his brother. "I think we should leave this outside the gate," Brian says to Philip.

Philip just shrugs and tells Brian it's up to him, whatever he wants to do.

They wait until after dark to make their exit. At the stroke of 7 P.M.—with the cold, metallic sun drooping behind the rooftops—they hurriedly pack the Suburban. Working quickly in the lengthening shadows, while monsters swarm against the barricade, they form a sort of bucket brigade, quickly passing suitcases and containers from the side door of the house to the open hatch of the SUV.

They take their original axes with an assortment of additional picks and shovels and hatchets and saws and cutting blades from the toolshed out back. They bring rope and wire and road flares and extra coats and snow boots and fire-starter blocks. They also pack a siphoning tube and as many extra plastic tanks of gasoline as they can fit into the rear storage well.

The Suburban's tank is currently full—Philip managed to siphon fifteen gallons' worth earlier in the day from an abandoned sedan in a neighbor's garage—as they have no clue about the status of local gas stations.

Over the last four days, Philip had discovered a variety of sporting guns in neighboring homes. Rich folks love their duck season in these parts. They love picking off green heads from the luxury of their heated blinds with their high-powered rifles and purebred hounds.

Philip's old man used to do it the hard way, with nothing but waders, moonshine, and a mean disposition.

Now Philip chooses three guns to stow in vinyl zip-up bags in the rear compartment—one is a .22-caliber Winchester rimfire, and the other two are Marlin Model 55 shotguns. The Marlins are especially useful. They're known as "goose guns." Fast and accurate and powerful, the 55s are designed for killing migratory fowl at high altitudes . . . or, in this case, the bull's-eye of a skull at a hundred-plus yards.

It's almost eight o'clock by the time they get the Suburban packed, and get Penny situated in the middle seat. Bundled in a down coat with her stuffed penguin at her side, she seems oddly sanguine, her pale face drawn and languid, as though she were about to visit the pediatrician.

Doors click open and shut. Philip climbs behind the wheel. Nick takes the front passenger seat, and Brian settles in next to Penny in the middle. The sign sits on the floor, pressed against Brian's knees.

The ignition fires. The growl of the engine carries across the still darkness, making the undead stir on the other side of the barricade.

"Let's do this quick, y'all," Philip says under his breath, slamming it into reverse. "Hold on."

Philip puts the pedal to the floor, and the four-wheel drive digs in.

The gravitational force throws everyone forward as the Suburban roars backward.

In the rearview mirror, the weak spot in the makeshift barricade looms closer and closer until . . . BANG! The vehicle bursts through the cedar planking and into the dim streetlight of Green Briar Lane.

Immediately, the left rear quarter panel collides

with a walking corpse as Philip stands on the brakes and jacks it into drive. The zombie launches twenty feet into the air behind them, doing a limp pirouette in a mist of blood, a piece of its moldering arm detaching and pinwheeling in the opposite direction.

The Suburban blasts off toward the main conduit, smashing through three more zombies, sending them flinging off into oblivion. With each impact, the dull thumping sensations traveling through the chassis—as well as the yellowish buglike smears left on the windshield—make Penny cringe and close her eyes.

At the end of the street, Philip yanks the wheel and screeches around the corner, then pushes north toward the entrance.

A few minutes later Philip barks another order: "Okay, do it quick—and I mean QUICK!"

He slams down on the brakes, making everybody lurch forward in their seats again. They've just reached the great entrance gate, visible in a cone of streetlight across a short expanse of shrub-lined gravel.

"This'll just take a second," Brian says, grabbing the sign, clicking his door handle. "Leave it running."

"Just get it done."

Brian slips out of the car, carrying the big three-by-three sign.

In the cold night air, he hastens across the gravel

threshold, his ears hyperalert and sensitive to the distant thrum of groaning noises: They're coming this way.

Brian chooses a spot just to the right of the entrance gate, a section of brick wall unobstructed by shrubbery, and he positions the sign against the wall.

He sinks the wooden legs into the soft earth to stabilize the board, and then hurries back to the car, satisfied he's done his part for humanity, or whatever is left of it.

As they drive off, each and every one of them—even Penny—glances back through the rear window at the little square sign receding into the distance behind them:

ALL DEAD
DO NOT
ENTER

five

They head west, slowly, through the rural darkness, keeping their speed down around thirty miles per hour. The four lanes of Interstate 20 are littered with abandoned cars, as the macadam snakes toward the sickly pink glow of the western horizon, where the city awaits like a bruise of light on the night sky. They are forced to weave through the obstacle course of wrecks with agonizing slowness, but they manage to put nearly five miles behind them before things start going wrong.

For most of these five miles, Philip keeps thinking of Bobby and all the things they could have done to save him. The pain and regret are burrowing deep down in the pit of Philip's gut, a cancer metastasizing into something darker and more poisonous than grief. In order to fight the emotions he keeps thinking of that old trucker's adage: *Scan don't stare.* Gripping the wheel with the practiced clench of a longtime hauler, he sits forward in his seat, his gaze alert and fixed on the margins of the highway.

For five miles only a handful of dead brush the ghostly edges of their headlights.

Just outside of Conyers they pass a couple stragglers shuffling along the shoulder of the road like blood-spattered AWOL soldiers. Passing the Stonecrest Mall they see a cluster of dark figures hunkered down in a ditch, apparently feasting on some sort of roadkill, either animal or human, impossible to tell in the flickering darkness. But that has been the extent of it—for five miles, at least—and Philip keeps his speed at a steady (but safe) thirty miles per hour. Any slower and they risk hooking a stray monster; any faster and they risk sideswiping the growing number of wrecks and abandoned vehicles cluttering the lanes.

The radio is dead, and the others ride in silence, their gazes glued to the passing landscape.

The outer rings of metro Atlanta roll past them in slow motion, a series of pine forests broken by an occasional bedroom community or strip mall. They pass car dealerships as dark as morgues, the endless ocean of new models like coffins reflecting the milky moonlight. They pass deserted Waffle Houses, their windows busted out like open sores, and office parks as barren as war zones. They pass Shoney's, and trailer parks, and Kmarts, and RV Centers, each one more desolate and ruined than the last. Small fires burn here and there. Parking lots look like the dark playrooms of mad children, the abandoned cars strewn across the pavement like toys thrown in anger. Broken glass glitters everywhere.

In less than a week and a half, the plague has apparently savaged the outer exurbs of Atlanta. Here, in the rural nature preserves and office campuses, where middle-class families have emigrated over the years to escape the arduous commutes, backbreaking mortgages, and high-stress urban life, the epidemic has laid waste to the social order in a matter of days. And for some reason, it's the sight of all the devastated churches that bothers Philip the most.

Each sanctuary they pass is in a progressively worse state: The New Birth Missionary Baptist Center outside of Harmon is still smoldering from a recent fire, its charred ruin of a cross rising against the heavens. A mile and a half down the road the Luther Rice Seminary features hastily hand-scrawled signs over its portals warning passers-by that the end is nigh and the rapture is here and all you sinners can kiss your asses good-bye. The Unity Faith Christian Cathedral looks as though it's been ransacked and scoured clean and then pissed upon. The parking lot at the St. John the Revelator Pentecostal Palace resembles a battlefield littered with bodies, many of the corpses still moving with the telltale, somnam-bulant hunger of the undead. *What kind of God would let this happen? And while we're on the subject: What kind of God would let a simple, innocent good old boy like Bobby Marsh die in such a way? What kind of—*

"Oh shit!"

The voice comes from the backseat, and it shakes Philip out of his dark musings. "What?"

"Look," Brian says, his voice weak from either his cold or the fear, or maybe a little of both. Philip glances at the rearview mirror, and he sees his brother's anxious expression in the green glow of the dash. Brian is pointing toward the western horizon.

Philip gazes back through the windshield, instinctively pumping the brakes. "What? I don't see anything."

"Holy crap," Nick says from the passenger seat.

He is staring through a break in the piney woods off to the right, where light shines through the trees.

About five hundred yards ahead of them, the highway banks off in a northwesterly direction, cutting through a stand of pines. Beyond the trees, through clearings in the foliage, flames are visible.

The interstate is on fire.

"God*damnit*," Philip says on a tense sigh. He slows the vehicle to a crawl as they make the turn.

Within moments the overturned tanker truck comes into view, lying jackknifed in a cocoon of flames, like an upended dinosaur. The truck's carcass blocks the two westbound lanes, its cab detached and lying in pieces, tangled with three other cars across the median and both of the eastbound lanes. The scorched shells of other cars lie overturned behind the burning wreckage.

Beyond the wreck the lanes look like a parking lot, with scores of cars, some burning, most of them tangled in the chain reaction.

Philip pulls the Suburban over and brings it to a stop on the shoulder fifty yards from the dwindling flames. "That's just fantastic," he says to no one in particular, wanting to launch a barrage of profanity, but barely containing himself (on account of Penny's ears being inches away).

From this distance—even in the flickering darkness—several things are clear. First, and foremost, it is obvious they are either going to have to find a team of firefighters and heavy-duty towing equipment in order to continue on course or they're going to have to figure out a fucking detour. Second, it looks as though whatever happened here took place in the very recent past, perhaps earlier today, perhaps only hours ago. The pavement around the wreck is blackened and scarred, as though a meteor had punched a hole in it, and even the trees lining the highway are charred from the shock waves. Even through the closed windows of the Suburban, Philip can smell the acrid stench of burning diesel and melted rubber.

"What now?" Brian finally says.

"Gotta turn around," Nick says, looking over his shoulder.

"Just lemme think for a second," Philip says, staring at the overturned truck cab, the roof sheared off it like the lid of a tin can. In the darkness, charred bodies lie sprawled across the muddy median. Some of them are twitching with the lazy undulations of snakes waking up.

"C'mon, Philip, we can't get around it," Nick says.

Brian speaks up. "Maybe we can cut across to 278."

"GODDAMNIT, SHUT UP AND LET ME THINK!"

The sudden flare of rage makes Philip's skull throb with the force of a splitting migraine, and he grits his teeth, clenching his fists and stuffing the voice back down inside himself: *Crack it open, do it, tear it open now, tear the heart out . . .*

"Sorry," Philip says, wiping his mouth, glancing over his shoulder at the frightened little girl huddling in the darkness of the backseat. "I'm real sorry, punkin, Daddy lost it there for a second."

The little girl stares at the floor.

"What do you want to do?" Brian asks softly, and from the forlorn tone of his voice it sounds as though he would follow his brother into the flames of hell if Philip thought that was the best option right now.

"Last exit was—what?—maybe a mile or so back there?" Philip glances over his shoulder. "I'm thinking that maybe we should—"

The slapping noise comes out of nowhere, cutting Philip off mid-thought.

Penny shrieks.

"SHIT!"

Nick jerks away from the passenger window, where a charred corpse has materialized out of the darkness.

"Get down, Nick. Now." Philip's voice is flat and unaffected, like a radio dispatcher, as he quickly leans over to the glove box, pops the tiny door, and fishes for something. The thing outside the window presses up against the glass, barely recognizable as human, its flesh blistered to a crisp. "Brian, cover Penny's eyes."

"SHIT! SHIT!" Nick ducks down and covers his head, as though in an air raid. "SHIT! SHIT! SHIT!"

Philip finds the Ruger .22 pistol where he left it, already with a round in the chamber.

In one fluid motion Philip raises the weapon with his right hand, while simultaneously jacking down the power window with his left. The burned zombie reaches through the opening with its scorched, emaciated arm, letting out a guttural moan, but before it can grab hold of Nick's shirt, Philip squeezes off a single shot—point-blank, into the thing's skull.

The bark of the Ruger is enormously loud inside the Subrban's interior, and it makes everybody jump, as the charred corpse whiplashes—a direct hit above its left temple sending brain matter spitting across the inside of the windshield.

The thing slides down the outside of the passenger door, the muffled sound of its body hitting the pavement barely audible over the ringing in Philip's ears.

Twenty-two-caliber semiautos like the Ruger have a unique bark. The blast sounds like a hard flat slap—a two-by-four smacking concrete—and the gun invariably jumps in the shooter's hand.

That night, despite the muffling effect of the interior of the Suburban, that single boom echoed out across the dark landscape, reverberating over treetops and office parks, carrying on the wind.

The slapback could be heard a mile away, piercing the silence of the deep woods, penetrating the mortified auditory canals of shadowy creatures, awakening dead central nervous systems.

"Everybody awright?" Philip looks around the dark interior, setting the hot gun down on the carpeted hump next to him. "Everybody cool?"

Nick is just now rising back up, his eyes wide and hot, taking in all the residue on the inside of the glass. Penny, curled up in Brian's arms, keeps her eyes shut, as Brian frantically looks around, peering through all the windows, looking for any other intruders.

Philip slams the Suburban into reverse, kicking the accelerator as he quickly rolls the window back up. Everybody jerks forward as the vehicle screeches backward—a hundred feet, a hundred and fifty feet, two hundred feet—away from the smoking tanker truck.

Then the Suburban skids to a stop, and they sit there in stunned silence for a moment.

Nothing moves outside in the flickering shadows. Nobody says anything for the longest time, but Philip is convinced he's not the only one, at this moment, wondering if this twenty-mile trek into the city is going to be a lot harder than they originally thought.

• • •

They sit there in the idling Suburban for quite some time, debating their best course of action, and this makes Philip very antsy. He doesn't like sitting in one place for very long, especially with the engine running, burning gas and time, with those moving shadows behind the burning trees, but the group cannot seem to come to a consensus, and Philip is trying his hardest to be a benevolent dictator in this little banana republic.

"Look, I still say we try to drive around it." Philip gives a nod toward the darkness to the south.

The far shoulder of the oncoming lanes is littered with smoldering vehicles, but there's a narrow gap—maybe the width of the Suburban, with a few inches to spare—between the gravel shoulder and the thicket of pines along the highway. The recent rains combined with the oil spill from the over-turned tanker have turned the land to slop. But the Suburban is a big, heavy vehicle with wide tires, and Philip has driven the thing through far worse conditions.

"It's too steep, Philly," Nick says, wiping the gray matter from the inside of the windshield with a grimy towel.

"Yeah, man, I have to agree," Brian says from the shadows of the backseat, his arm around Penny, the anguished features of his face visible in the flicker of firelight. "I vote for heading back to the last exit."

"We don't know *what* we'll find on 278, though, it could be worse."

"We don't know that," Nick says.

"We gotta keep moving forward."

"But what if it's worse in the city? Seems like it's getting worse the closer we get."

"We're still fifteen, twenty miles away—we don't know shit about what it's like in Atlanta."

"I don't know, Philly."

"Tell you what," Philip says. "Let me take a look."

"What do you mean?"

He reaches for the gun. "I'll just take a quick look."

"Wait!" Brian speaks up. "Philip, come on. We gotta stick together."

"I'm just gonna see what the ground is like, see if we can make it through."

"Daddy—" Penny starts to say something, and then thinks better of it.

"It's okay, punkin, I'll be right back."

Brian looks out the window, unconvinced. "We agreed we'd stick together. No matter what. C'mon, man."

"It'll take two minutes." Philip opens his door, shoving the Ruger into his belt.

The cool air and the sound of crackling flames and the smell of ozone and burning rubber waft into the Suburban like uninvited guests. "You guys sit tight, I'll be right back."

Philip climbs out of the car.
The door slams.

Brian sits in the silent Suburban for a moment, listening to his heart thudding in his chest. Nick is looking through each and every window, scanning the immediate vicinity, which is alive with flickering shadows. Penny gets very still. Brian looks at the little girl. The child looks like she's shrinking into herself, like a little night bloom, contracting into itself, pulling its petals shut.

"He'll be right back, kiddo," Brian says to the kid. He aches for her. This is not right, a child going through this, but on some level Brian knows how she feels. "He's a tough old boy, Philip. He can beat the crap outta any monster comes along, believe me."

From the front seat Nick turns and says, "Listen to your uncle, sweetie. He's right. Your daddy can take care of himself and then some."

"I saw your daddy catch a rabid dog once," Brian says. "He was maybe nineteen, and there was this German shepherd terrorizing the neighbor kids."

"I remember that," Nick says.

"Your daddy chased that thing—foaming mouth and all—down to the dry creek bed, and he wrestled the damn thing into a trash barrel."

"I totally remember that," Nick says. "Grabbed it with his bare hands, threw it halfway across the

101

gully before slamming the trash can down on it like he was catching a fly."

Brian reaches down and tenderly brushes a strand of hair from the little girl's face. "He'll be okay, honey . . . trust me. He's a mean *muchacho*."

Outside the vehicle, a piece of burning wreckage falls to the ground. The clatter makes everybody jump. Nick looks at Brian. "Hey, man . . . you mind reaching back into that zipper bag by the wheel well?"

Brian looks at Nick. "What do you need?"

"One of them goose guns."

Brian stares at him a moment, then turns and leans over the back headrest. He roots out the long, canvas hunting bag wedged between a cooler and a backpack. He unzips it and finds one of the Marlin 55s.

Handing the shotgun across the backseat to Nick in the front, Brian says, "You need the shells, too?"

"I think it's already loaded," Nick says, hinging open the barrel and peering down into the breech.

Brian can tell Nick is handy with the thing, has probably hunted before, although Brian never witnessed it. Brian had never been the type to participate in the manly pursuits of his younger brother and his cronies, although he secretly yearned to do just that. "Two shells in the breech," Nick says, snapping the barrel shut.

"Just be careful with that thing," Brian says.

"Used to hunt feral hogs with one of these babies," Nick says, cocking and locking it.

"Hogs?"

"Yep . . . wild hogs . . . up to Chattahoochee reservation. Used to go on night hunts with my dad and my uncle Verne."

"Pigs you're talking about," Brian says incredulously.

"Yeah, basically. A hog is just a big ol' pig. Maybe they're older, too, I'm not—"

Another loud metallic crash comes from outside Nick's window.

Nick jerks the barrel toward the noise, finger on the trigger, his teeth gnashing with nervous tension. Nothing moves outside the passenger window. Muscles uncoil inside the Suburban, a long sigh of relief from Nick. Brian starts to say, "We gotta get our butts in gear before—"

Another noise.

This time it comes from the driver's side, a shuffling of feet—

—and before Nick can even register the identity of the shadowy figure approaching the Suburban's driver-side window, he swings the Marlin's muzzle up at the window, takes aim, and is about to squeeze off a couple of twenty-gauge greetings, when a familiar voice booms outside the car.

"JESUS CHRIST!"

Philip is visible outside the window just for an instant, before ducking out of the line of fire.

"Oh God, I'm sorry, I'm sorry," Nick says, instantly recognizing his mistake.

Philip's voice outside the window is lower now, more controlled, but still seething with anger. "You want to point that thing away from the goddamn window?"

Nick lowers the barrel. "I'm sorry, Philly, my bad, I'm sorry."

The door clicks and Philip slips back into the car, breathing hard, his face shiny with sweat. He shuts his door and lets out a long breath. "Nick—"

"Philly, I'm sorry . . . I'm a little jumpy."

For a moment Philip looks like he's going to take the other man's head off, then the anger fades. "We're all a little jumpy . . . I get that."

"I'm totally sorry."

"Just pay attention."

"I will, I will."

Brian speaks up. "What did you find out there?"

Philip reaches up to the stick shift. "A way around this damn mess." He flips it into four-wheel drive and slams the lever down. "Everybody hold on."

He turns the wheel, and they slowly roll across a spray of broken glass. The shards crunch under the Suburban's massive wheels, and nobody says anything, but Brian's thinking about the potential for flat tires.

Philip steers the vehicle down across the center

median—which is a shallow culvert overgrown with switchgrass, weeds, and cattails—and the rear wheels dig into the rutted earth. As they approach the other side, Philip gives it a little more juice, and the Suburban lurches upward and across the eastbound lanes.

Philip keeps his hands glued to the steering wheel as they approach the far shoulder. "Hold on!" he calls out, as they suddenly plunge down a slope of muddy weeds.

The Suburban pitches sideways like a sinking ship. Brian holds on to Penny, and Nick holds on to the center armrest. Yanking the wheel, Philip kicks the accelerator.

The vehicle fishtails toward a narrow gap in the wreckage. Tree branches scrape the side of the SUV. The rear wheels slide sideways, then chew into the mud. Philip wrestles the wheel. Everybody else holds their respective breaths, as the Suburban scrapes through the opening.

When the car emerges out the other side, a spontaneous cheer rings out. Nick slaps Philip on the back, and Brian whoops and hollers triumphantly. Even Penny seems to lighten up a little, the hint of a smile tugging at the corners of her tulip-shaped lips.

Through the windshield they can see the tangle of vehicles in the darkness ahead of them—at least twenty cars, SUVs, and light trucks in the westbound lanes—most of them damaged in the pileup. All of them abandoned, many of them burned-out shells. The empty vehicles stretch back at least a hundred yards.

Philip puts the pedal to the metal, muscling the SUV back toward the road. He jerks the wheel. The rear of the SUV wags and churns.

Something is wrong. Brian feels the loss of traction beneath them like a buzzing in his spine, the engine revving suddenly.

The cheering dies.

The car is stuck.

For a moment Philip keeps the pedal to the floor, urging the thing forward with his ass cheeks, as if his sheer force of will and white-hot rage—and the tightening of his sphincter muscles—can get the blasted thing to move. But the Suburban keeps drifting sideways. Soon the thing is simply spinning all four wheels, kicking up twin gushers of mud out the back into the moonlit darkness behind them.

"FUCK!—FUCK! FUCK! FUCK!" Philip slams a fist down on the steering wheel, hard enough to make the thing crack and send a splinter of pain up his arm. He practically shoves the foot feed through the floor, the engine screaming.

"Let up on it, man!" Nick hollers over the noise. "It's just digging us in deeper!"

"FUCK!"

Philip lets up on the gas.

The engine winds down, the Suburban leaning to one side, a foundering boat in brackish waters.

"We gotta push it out," Brian says after a moment of tense silence.

"Take the wheel," Philip says to Nick, opening his door and slipping outside. "Give it gas when I tell ya to. Come on, Brian."

Brian opens the rear door, slips outside, and joins his brother in the glow of the taillights.

The rear tires have sunk at least six inches into the greasy muck, each rear quarter panel spattered with mud. The front wheels are no better. Philip places his big, gnarled hands on the wood grain of the tailgate, and Brian moves to the other side, assuming a wide stance in order to get a better purchase in the mud.

Neither of them notices the dark figures lumbering out of the trees on the other side of the highway.

"Okay, Nick, now!" Philip calls out and shoves with all his might.

The engine growls.

The wheels churn, spewing fountains of mud, as the Blake brothers push and push. They push with everything they have, all to no avail, as the slow-moving figures behind them shamble closer.

"Again!" Philip shouts, putting all his weight behind the shoving.

The rear wheels spin, sinking deeper into the mire, as Brian gets sprayed with an aerosol of mud.

Behind him, moving through a fog bank of smoke and shadows, the uninvited close the distance to about fifty yards, crunching through broken glass with the slow, lazy, awkward movements of injured lizards.

"Get back in the car, Brian." Philip's voice has abruptly changed, becoming low and even. "Right now."

"What is it?"

"Just do it." Philip is opening the rear hatch. Hinges squeak as he reaches in and fishes for something. "Don't ask any questions."

"But what about—" Brian's words stick in his throat as he catches a glimpse in his peripheral vision of at least a dozen dark figures—maybe more—closing in on them from several directions.

six

The figures approach from across the median, and from behind the flaming debris of the wreck, and from the adjacent woods—all shapes and sizes, faces the color of spackling compound, eyes gleaming like marbles in the firelight. Some are burned. Some are in tatters. Some are so well dressed and groomed they look as though they just came from church. Most have that curled-lip, exposed-incisor look of insatiable hunger.

"Shit." Brian looks at his brother. "What are you gonna do? What are you thinking?"

"Get your ass in the car, Brian."

"Shit—shit!" Brian hurries around to the side door, throws it open, and climbs in next to Penny, who is looking around with a bewildered expression. Brian slams the door, and smashes down the lock. "Lock the doors, Nick."

"I'm gonna help him—" Nick goes for his goose gun and opens his door, but he stops abruptly when he hears the strange sound of Philip's flat, cold, metallic tone through the open rear hatch.

"I got this. Do what he says, Nick. Lock the doors and stay down."

"There's too many of them!" Nick is thumbing the hammers on the Marlin, already with his right leg out the door, his work boot on the pavement.

"Stay in the car, Nick." Philip is digging out a pair of matched log splitters. A few days ago he found the small axes in a garden shed of a mansion at Wiltshire Estates—two matched, balanced implements of razor-sharp carbon steel —and at the time he wondered what in the world some fat rich guy (who probably paid a yard service to split his firewood) would want a pair of small bad-axes for.

In the front seat, Nick pulls his leg back inside the SUV, slams his door, and bangs the lock down. He twists around with his eyes blazing and the gun cradled in his arms. "What the hell? What are you doing, Philly?"

The rear hatch slams.

The silence crashes down on the interior.

Brian looks down at the child. "I'm thinking maybe you ought to get down on the floor, kiddo."

Penny says nothing as she slides down the front of the seat, and then curls into a fetal position. Something in her expression, some glint of knowing in her big soft eyes, reaches out to Brian and puts the squeeze on his heart. He pats her shoulder. "We'll get through this."

Brian turns and peers over the backseat, over the cargo and out through the rear window.

Philip has a bad-axe in either hand, and is calmly walking toward the converging crowd of zombies. "Jesus," Brian utters under his breath.

"What's he doing, Brian?" Nick's voice is high and taut, his hands fingering the Marlin's bolt.

Brian cannot muster a response because he is now held rapt by the terrible sight through the window.

It's not pretty. It's not graceful or cool or heroic or manly or even well executed . . . but it feels good. "I got this," Philip says to himself, under his breath, as he lashes out at the closest one, a heavyset man in farmer's dungarees.

The bad-axe sheers off a grapefruit-sized lobe of

the fat one's skull, sending a geyser of pink matter into the night air. The zombie falls. But Philip doesn't stop. Before the next closest one can reach him, Philip goes to work on the big flaccid body on the ground, windmilling the cold steel in each hand down on the dead flesh. "Vengeance is mine; I will repay, saith the Lord." Blood and tissue fountain. Sparks kick off the pavement with each blow.

"I got this, I got this, I got this," Philip murmurs to no one in particular, letting all the pent-up rage and sorrow come out in a flurry of glancing blows. "I got this, I got this, I got this, I got this, I got this—"

By this point others have closed in—a skinny young man with black fluid dripping off his lips, a fat woman with a bloated, dead face, a guy in a bloody suit—and Philip spins away from the mangled corpse on the ground to go to work on the others. He grunts with each blow—*I GOT THIS!*—cleaving skulls—*I GOT THIS!*—severing carotid arteries—*I GOT THIS!*—letting his anger drive the cold steel through cartilage and bone and nasal cavities—*I GOT THIS!*—the blood and brain matter misting up across his face as he remembers the foaming mouth of rabid fangs coming for him when he was a kid, and God taking his wife Sarah, and the monsters taking his best friend Bobby Marsh—*I GOT THIS!*—*I GOT THIS!*—*I GOT THIS!!*

• • •

Inside the Suburban, Brian turns away from the scene outside the back window, coughs, and feels his gut rising at the nauseating sounds penetrating the sealed interior of the Suburban. He stifles the urge to vomit. He reaches down and gently puts his hands around Penny's ears, a gesture which, sadly, is becoming a routine.

In the front seat Nick cannot tear his eyes from the carnage behind them. On Nick's face Brian can see a weird mixture of repulsion and admiration—a kind of thank-God-he's-on-our-side type of awe—but it only serves to tighten Brian's gut. He will not throw up, goddamnit, he will be strong for Penny.

Brian slips down on the floor and holds the girl close to him. The child is limp and damp. Brian's brain swims with confusion.

His brother is everything to him. His brother is the key. But something is happening to Philip, something horrible, and it's beginning to gnaw at Brian. What are the rules? These walking abominations deserve every fucking thing Philip is dishing out . . . but what are the rules of engagement?

Brian is trying to put these thoughts out of his mind when he realizes the killing noises have ceased. Then he hears the heavy boot steps of a person outside the driver's side door. The door clicks.

Philip Blake slips back inside the Suburban,

dropping the bloody hand-axes on the floor in front of Nick. "There'll be more of 'em," he says, still winded, his face beaded with perspiration. "The gunshot woke 'em up."

Nick peers out the back window at the battlefield of bodies visible in the firelight on the slope, his voice coming out in a monotone, a combination of awe and disgust: "Home run, man . . . grand slam home run."

"We gotta get outta here," Philip says, wiping a pearl of sweat from his nose, catching his breath, and glancing up at the rearview mirror, searching for Penny in the shadows of the backseat as if he doesn't even hear Nick.

Brian speaks up. "What's the plan, Philip?"

"We gotta find a safe place to stay for the night."

Nick looks at Philip. "What do you mean exactly? You mean other than the Suburban?"

"It's too dangerous out here in the dark."

"Yeah, but—"

"We'll push it out of the mud in the morning."

"Yeah, but what about—"

"Grab whatever you need for the night," Philip says, reaching for the Ruger.

"Wait!" Nick grabs Philip's arm. "You're talking about leaving the car! Leaving all our shit out here?"

"Just for the night, come on," Philip says, opening his door and climbing out.

Brian lets out a sigh and looks up at Nick. "Shut up and help me with the backpacks."

· · ·

They camp that night about a quarter of a mile west of the overturned tanker, inside an abandoned yellow school bus, which sits on the shoulder, well illuminated by the cold glow of a sodium vapor light.

The bus is still fairly warm and dry, and it's high enough off the pavement to give them good sight lines on the woods on either side of the interstate. It has two doors—one in the front and one off the rear—for easy escape. Plus the bench seats are padded and long enough for each of them to stretch out for some semblance of rest. The keys are still in the ignition, and the battery still has juice.

Inside the bus it smells like the inside of a stale lunchbox, the ghosts of sweaty, rambunctious kids with their wet mittens and body odors lingering in the fusty air.

They eat some Spam and some sardines and some expensive pita crackers that were probably meant to adorn party trays at golf outings. They use flashlights, careful not to shine them off the windows, and eventually they spread their sleeping bags on the bench seats for some shut-eye, or at least some facsimile of sleep.

They each take turns sitting watch in the cab with one of the Marlins, using the huge side mirrors for unobstructed views of the bus's rear end. Nick takes the first shift and tries unsuccessfully for nearly an hour to raise a station on his portable weather radio. The world has shut down, but at least this section of Interstate 20 is equally still. The edges of the woods remain quiet.

When it's Brian's turn to sit watch—up to this point he has only managed a few minutes of fitful dozing on a squeaky bench seat in back—he gladly takes his place in the cab with all the levers and the dangling pine tree air fresheners and the laminated photograph of some long-lost driver's baby son. Not that Brian is very comfortable with the prospects of being the only one awake, or for that matter, having to fire the goose gun. Still, he needs some time to think.

At some point just before dawn, Brian hears Penny's breathing—just barely audible over the faint whistle of the wind through the ranks of sliding windows—becoming erratic and hyperventilated. The child has been dozing a few seats away from the cab, next to her father.

Now the little girl sits up with a silent gasp. "Oh . . . I got it . . . I mean . . ." Her voice is barely a whisper. "I got it, I think."

"Ssshhh," Brian says, rising from his seat, creeping back down the cabin to the little girl, whispering, "It's okay, kiddo . . . Uncle Brian's here."

"Um."

"It's okay . . . ssshhhh . . . let's not wake your dad." Brian glances over at Philip, who is tangled in a blanket, his face contorted with troubling dreams. He took half a pint of brandy before bed to knock himself out.

"I'm okay," Penny utters in her mousey little voice, looking down at the stuffed penguin in her small hands, squeezing it like a talisman. The thing is soiled and threadbare, and it breaks Brian's heart.

"Bad dreams?"

Penny nods.

Brian looks at her and thinks it over. "Got an idea," he whispers. "Why don't you come up and keep me company for a while."

The little girl nods.

He helps her up, and then, draping a blanket around her and taking her hand, he silently leads her back up to the cab. He flips down a little jump seat next to the driver's perch, and says, "There ya go." He pats the worn upholstery. "You can be my copilot."

Penny settles into the seat with her blanket pulled tightly around her and the penguin.

"See that?" Brian points to a filthy little video monitor above the dash, about the size of a paperback book, on which a grainy black-and-white image reveals the highway behind them. The wind rustles through the trees, the sodium lights gleaming off the roofs of wrecked cars. "That's a security camera, for backing up, see?"

The girl sees it.

"We're safe here, kiddo," Brian says as con-

116

vincingly as possible. Earlier in his shift he had figured out a way to turn the ignition key to the accessory position, lighting up the dash like an old pinball machine coming to life. "Everything's under control."

The girl nods.

"You want to tell me about it?" Brian says softly a moment later.

Penny looks confused. "Tell you about what?"

"The bad dream. Sometimes it helps to like . . . *tell* someone . . . you know? Makes it go away . . . *poof.*"

Penny gives him a feeble little shrug. "I dreamed I got sick."

"Sick like . . . those people out there?"

"Yes."

Brian takes a long, anguished, deep breath. "Listen to me, kiddo. Whatever these people have, you are not going to catch it. Do you understand? Your daddy will not let that happen, never in a million years. *I* will not let that happen."

She nods.

"You are very important to your daddy. You are very important to *me*." Brian feels an unexpected hitch in his chest, a catching of his words, a burning sensation in his eyes. For the first time since he departed his parents' place over a week and half ago, he realizes how deeply his feelings go for this little girl.

"I got an idea," he says after getting his emotions

in check. "Do you know what a code word is?"

Penny looks at him. "Like a secret code?"

"Exactly." Brian licks his finger, and then wipes a stain of dirt from her cheek. "You and I are going to have this secret code word."

"Okay."

"This is a very special code. Okay? From now on, whenever I say this secret word, I want you to do something for me. Can you do that? Can you, like, always remember to do something for me whenever I give you the secret code word?"

"Sure . . . I guess."

"Whenever I say the code word, I want you to hide your eyes."

"Hide my eyes?"

"Yeah. And cover your ears. Until I tell you it's okay to look. All right? And there's one more thing."

"Okay."

"Whenever I give you the secret code . . . I want you to remember something."

"What?"

"I want you to remember that there's gonna come a day when you won't have to hide your eyes anymore. There's gonna come a day when everything's all better, and there won't be any more sick people. Got that?"

She nods. "Got it."

"Now what's the word gonna be?"

"You want me to pick it?"

"You bet . . . it's your secret code . . . you should pick it."

The little girl wrinkles up her nose as she ponders a suitable word. The sight of her contemplating—so intently that she looks as though she's calculating the Pythagorean theorem—presses down on Brian's heart.

Finally the child looks up at Brian, and for the first time since the plague had begun, a glimmer of hope kindles in her enormous eyes. "I got it." She whispers the word to her stuffed animal, then looks up. "Penguin likes it."

"Great . . . don't keep me in suspense."

"*Away,*" she says. "The secret code word's gonna be *away.*"

The gray dawn comes in stages. First, an eerie calm settles around the interstate, the wind dying in the trees, and then a luminous pale glow around the edges of the forest wakes everybody up and gets them going.

The sense of urgency is almost immediate. They feel naked and exposed without their vehicle, so everybody concentrates on the task at hand: packing up, getting back to the Suburban, and getting the damn thing unstuck.

They make the quarter-mile hike back to the SUV in fifteen minutes, carrying their bedrolls and excess food in backpacks. They encounter a single zombie on the way, a wandering teenage girl, and

Philip easily puts out her lights by quickly and quietly chopping a furrow into her skull, while Brian whispers the secret word to Penny.

When they reach the Suburban, they work in silence, ever mindful of the shadows of adjacent woods. First they try to apply weight to the rear end by putting Nick and Philip on the tailgate, and having Brian give it gas from the driver's seat, pushing with one leg outside the door. It doesn't work. Then they search the immediate area for something to build traction under the wheels. It takes them an hour but they eventually unearth a couple of broken pallets scattered along a drainage ditch, and they bring them back, and wedge them under the wheels.

This also fails.

Somehow the mud beneath the SUV is so saturated with moisture and runoff and oil and God knows what else that it just keeps sucking the vehicle deeper, the leaning Suburban slipping progressively backward down the slope. But they refuse to give up. Driven by a relentless anxiety over unexplained noises in the adjacent pine forest—twigs snapping, low concussive booms in the distance—as well as the constant unspoken dread of having all their worldly possessions and supplies lost with the foundering Suburban, nobody is willing to face the encroaching hopelessness of the situation.

By mid-afternoon, after working for hours, and

breaking for lunch, and then going back at it for a couple more hours, all they have succeeded in doing is causing the SUV to drift nearly six feet farther down the muddy incline, while Penny sits inside the vehicle, alternately playing with Penguin and pressing her morose face to the window.

At that point, Philip steps back from the mud pit and gazes at the western horizon.

The overcast sky has begun its fade toward dusk, and the prospect of nightfall suddenly puts a pinch on Philip's gut. Covered with sludge, soaked in sweat, he pulls a bandana and wipes his neck.

He starts to say something, when another series of noises from the neighboring trees yank his attention to the south. For hours now the crackling, snapping noises—maybe footsteps, maybe not— have been getting closer.

Nick and Brian—both wiping their hands with rags—join Philip. None of them says anything for a moment. Each of their expressions reflects the hard reality, and when another snap from the trees crackles—as loud as a pistol shot—Nick speaks up: "Writing's on the wall, ain't it."

Philip shoves his handkerchief back in his pocket. "Night's gonna fall soon."

"Whattya think, Philly?"

"Time for plan B."

Brian swallows hard, looking at his brother. "I wasn't aware there *was* a plan B."

Philip gazes at his brother, and for a moment,

Philip feels a bizarre mixture of anger, pity, impatience, and affection. Then Philip looks at the old, rust-pocked Suburban, and feels a twinge of melancholy, as though he's about to say good-bye to another old friend. "There is now."

They siphon gas from the Suburban into plastic tanks they brought from Wiltshire. Then they get lucky enough to find a big, late-model Buick LeSabre, the keys still in it, left for dead on the side of the road, about an eighth of a mile west of there. They commandeer the Buick and roar back to the foundered SUV. They fill the Buick with gas and transfer as many supplies as they can squeeze into the car's huge trunk.

Then they take off toward the setting sun, each of them glancing back at the swamped SUV, receding into the distance like a shipwreck sinking into oblivion.

Indications of the looming apocalypse appear on either side of the interstate with alarming frequency now. As they draw nearer and nearer to the city, weaving with increasing difficulty through abandoned wreckage—the trees thinning and giving way to a growing number of residential enclaves, shopping plazas, and office parks—the telltale signs of doom are everywhere. They pass a dark, deserted Walmart, the windows broken, a sea of clothes and merchandise strewn across the parking lot. They notice more and more power outages, entire communities as dark and silent as tombs. They pass strip malls ravaged by looting, biblical warnings scrawled on exhaust chimneys. They even see a small single-engine plane, tangled in a giant electrical tower, still smoking.

Somewhere between Lithonia and Panthersville, the Buick's rear end starts vibrating like a son of bitch, and Philip realizes the thing has two blown tires. Maybe they were already flat when they acquired the car. Who knows? But there is no time to try and fix the infernal things, and no time to debate the matter.

Night is pressing in again, and the closer they get to the outskirts of metro Atlanta, the more the roads are knotted with the carcasses of mangled wrecks and abandoned cars. Nobody says it out loud, but they are all beginning to wonder whether they could get into the city faster on foot. Even the neighboring two-lanes like Hillandale and Fairington are blocked with empty cars, lined up like fallen dominoes in the middle of the road. At this rate, it will take them a week to get into town.

Which is why Philip makes the executive decision at that point to leave the Buick where it sits, pack up every last thing they can possibly carry, and set out on foot. Nobody's crazy about the idea, but they go along with it. The alternative of searching the frozen traffic jam in the pitch-darkness for spare tires or a suitable replacement vehicle doesn't seem viable right now.

They quickly dig their necessities out of the Buick's trunk, stuffing duffel bags and backpacks with supplies, blankets, food, weapons, and water. They are getting better at communicating with whispers, hand gestures, and nods—hyperaware now of the distant drone of dead people, the sounds waxing and waning in the darkness beyond the highway, percolating in the trees and behind buildings. Philip has the strongest back, so he takes the largest canvas duffel. Nick and Brian each strap on an overloaded backpack. Even Penny agrees to carry a knapsack filled with bedding.

Philip takes the Ruger pistol, the two bad-axes —one shoved down each side of his belt—and a long machetelike tool for cutting underbrush, which he shoves down the length of his spine between the duffel and his stained chambray shirt. Brian and Nick each cradle a Marlin 55 shotgun in their arms, as well as a pickaxe strapped to the sides of their respective backpacks.

They start walking west, and this time, not a single one of them looks back.

A quarter of a mile down the road, they encounter an overpass clogged with a battered Airstream mobile home. Its cab is wrapped around a tele-phone pole. All the streetlights have flickered out, and in the full dark, a muffled banging noise is heard inside the walls of the ruined trailer.

This makes everybody pause suddenly on the shoulder beneath the viaduct.

"Jesus, it could be somebody—" Brian stops himself when he sees his brother's hand shoot up.

"Sssshhhhh!"

"But what if it's—"

"Quiet!" Philip cocks his head and listens. His expression is that of a cold stone monument. "This way, come on!"

Philip leads the group down a rocky slope on the north edge of the interchange, each of them descending the hill gingerly, careful not to slip on the wet pea gravel. Brian brings up the rear, wondering again about the rules, wondering if they just deserted one of their fellow human beings.

His thoughts are quickly subsumed by the plunge into the darker territory of countryside.

They follow a narrow blacktop two-lane called Miller Road northward through the darkness. For about a mile, they encounter nothing more than a sparsely commercialized area of desolate industrial parks and foundries, their signs as dark as hieroglyphs on cave walls: Barloworld Handling, Atlas Tool and Die, Hughes Supply, Simcast Electronics, Peachtree Steel. The rhythmic shuffle of their footsteps on the cold asphalt mingles with the thrumming of their breaths. The silence starts working on their nerves. Penny is getting tired. They hear rustling noises in the woods off to their immediate right.

At last Philip raises his hand and points toward a sprawling, low-slung plant stretching back into the distance. "This place will do," he says in a low flat whisper.

"Do for *what?*" Nick says, pausing next to Philip, breathing hard.

"For the night," Philip says. There is no emotion in his voice.

He leads the group past a low, unlighted sign that says GEORGIA PACIFIC CORPORATION.

Philip gets in through the office window. He has everybody huddle in the shadows outside the entrance while he makes his way through empty, littered corridors toward the warehouse in the center of the building.

The place is as dark as a crypt. Philip's heart beats in his ears as he strides along with the bad-axes at his side. He tries one of the light switches to no avail. He barely notices the pungent aroma of wood pulp permeating the air—a gluey, sappy odor—and when he reaches the safety doors, he slowly shoves them open with the toe of his boot.

The warehouse is the size of an airplane hanger, with giant gantries hanging overhead, the rows of huge scoop lights dark, the odor of paper must as thick as talc. Thin moonlight shines down through gargantuan sky windows. The floor is sectioned off into rows of enormous paper rolls—as big around as redwood trunks—so white they seem to glow in the darkness.

Something moves in the middle distance.

Philip shoves the bad-axes down either side of his belt, then grasps the hilt of the Ruger. He draws out the gun, snaps back the slide, and raises the muzzle at a dark figure staggering out from behind a stack of pallets. The factory rat comes through the shadows toward Philip slowly, hungrily, the front of his dungarees dark with dried blood and bile, his long, slack face full of teeth gleaming in the moonbeams coming through the skylight.

One shot puts the dead thing down—the blast bouncing back like a kettledrum in the cavernous warehouse.

Philip makes a sweep of the remaining length of the warehouse. He finds a couple more of them— an older fat man, a former night watchman from the looks of his soiled uniform, and a younger one—each dragging his dead ass out from behind shelving units.

Philip feels nothing as he pops each one in the skull at point-black range.

On his way back toward the front entrance he discovers a fourth one in the shadows, caught between two massive paper rolls. The bottom half of the former forklift operator is wedged between the blinding white cylinders, crushed beyond recognition, all his fluids pooled and dried on the cement floor beneath him. The top half of the creature convulses and flails, its milk-stone eyes stupidly awake.

"What's up, bubba?" Philip says as he approaches with the gun at his hip. "Another day, another dollar . . . huh?"

The zombie chomps impotently at the air between its face and Philip.

"Lunch break overdue?"

Chomp.

"Eat this."

The .22-caliber blast echoes as the slug smashes through the forklift operator's orbital bone, turning the milky eye black, and sending a chunk of the parietal hemisphere flying. The spray—a mixture of blood, tissue, and cerebrospinal fluid—spatters the rows of pristine white paper, as the top half of the dead thing wilts like a noodle.

Philip admires his work of art—the scarlet tendrils on that field of heavenly white—for quite a long time before going to get the others.

seven

They spend the night in a glass-encased foreman's office, high above the main floor of the Georgia Pacific warehouse. They use their battery-powered lanterns and they move the desks and chairs aside, and they spread their bedrolls on the linoleum tiles.

The previous occupant must have practically

lived in the little two-hundred-square-foot crow's nest, because there are CDs, a stereo, a microwave, a small refrigerator (the food inside it mostly spoiled), drawers full of candy bars, work orders, half-full liquor bottles, office supplies, fresh shirts, cigarettes, check stubs, and porn.

Philip hardly says a word the whole night. He just sits near the window overlooking the warehouse floor, occasionally taking a swig of whiskey from the pint bottle he found in the desk, while Nick sits on the floor in the opposite corner, silently reading a small Concordance Bible by the light of a lantern. Nick claims he carries the little dog-eared leather-bound book wherever he goes; but the others have rarely seen him reading it . . . until now.

Brian forces down some tuna fish and saltine crackers, and he tries to get Penny to eat something but she won't. She seems to be drawing further into herself, her eyes now displaying a permanent glaze that looks vaguely catatonic to Brian. Later, Brian sleeps next to her, while Philip dozes in the swivel chair by the greasy wire-mesh window, through which past foremen have kept their eyes peeled for loafers. This is the first time Brian has seen his brother too consumed by his own thoughts to sleep next to his daughter, and it does not bode well.

The next morning, they awaken to the sounds of dogs barking somewhere outside.

The dull, pale light floods in through the high

windows, and they pack quickly. Nobody has any appetite for breakfast so they use the bathroom, tape their feet to ward against blisters, and put on extra socks. Brian's heels are already sore from the few miles they've trekked, and there's no telling how far they will go today. They each have one change of clothes, but nobody has the energy to put on anything clean.

On their way out, each one of them—except Philip—studiously avoids looking at the bodies lying in pools of gore in the warehouse.

Philip seems galvanized by the sight of corpses illuminated by daylight.

Outside, they discover the source of the barking. About a hundred yards west of the warehouse a pack of strays—mostly mutts—are fighting over something pink and ragged on the ground. As Philip and the others approach, the dogs scatter, leaving the object of their attentions in the mud. Brian identifies the object as they pass, and softly gives Penny the code word: *away*.

The thing is a severed human arm, chewed so badly it looks like it belongs to a wet rag doll.

"Don't look, punkin," Philip mutters to his daughter, and Brian pulls Penny next to him, covering the girl's eyes.

They trudge westward, moving silently, their footsteps furtive and careful like thieves creeping through the morning sun.

• • •

They follow a road called Snapfinger Drive, which runs parallel to the interstate. The blacktop ribbon winds through barren forest preserves, abandoned residential villages, and ransacked strip malls. As they move through increasingly populated areas, the side of the road holds horrors that no little girl should ever see.

A high school football field is strewn with headless torsos. A mortuary has been hastily boarded and nailed shut *from the outside*—the horrible muffled sounds of the recently risen scratching and clawing to get out. Philip fervidly searches for a suitable vehicle to highjack, but most of the cars along Snapfinger lie in ditches like burned husks or sit on the gravel shoulder with two or three tires blown. Traffic lights, most of them either blinking yellow or completely black, hang over clogged intersections.

The highway—visible up along a ridge a hundred yards to their left—crawls with the dead. Every so often the tattered remains of a person will cross through the distant pale rays of the rising sun, causing Philip to motion for everybody to get the hell down and stay quiet. But despite the arduous process of ducking behind trees or wreckage every time they sense another presence looming nearby, they cover quite a bit of ground that day.

They encounter no other survivors.

· · ·

Late that afternoon, the weather turns clear and sunny—ironically, a fine early autumn afternoon in any other context—the temperature in the low sixties. By five o'clock, the men are sweating, and Penny has tied her sweatshirt around her waist. Philip calculates their progress, subtracting a thirty-minute rest for lunch, and he figures that they've averaged about a mile an hour—crossing nearly eight miles of suburban wilderness.

Still, none of them realizes how close they are to the city until they come upon a muddy hillock rising out of the pines just west of Glenwood, where a Baptist church sits on a ridge, smoldering from a recent conflagration, its steeple a smoking ruin.

Exhausted, drained, and hungry, they follow the winding road up the grade to the top of the hill; and when they reach the church parking lot, they all stand there for a moment, gazing out at the western horizon, frozen with a sort of unexpected awe.

The skyline, only three miles away, looks almost radiant in the fading light.

For boys growing up within a couple hundred miles of the great capital of the New South, Philip and Brian Blake have spent precious little time in Atlanta. For the two and half years that he drove trucks for Harlo Electric, Philip occasionally made deliveries there. And Brian has seen his share of concerts at the Civic Center, the Earl, the Georgia Dome, and the Fox Theater. But neither man knows the town well.

As they stand on the edge of that church parking lot, with the acrid smell of the apocalypse in their sinuses, the skyline in the hazy distance reflects back at them a sort of unattainable grandeur. In the dreamy light they can see the capitol spire with its golden-clad dome, the mirrored monoliths of the Concourse Complex, the massive Peachtree Plaza towers, and the pinnacle of the Atlantic building, but it all seems to give off an air of *mirage*—a sort of Lost-City-of-Atlantis feeling.

Brian is about to say something about the place being so close and yet so far—or perhaps make a comment about the unknowable condition of the streets down below—when he sees a blur out of the corner of his eye.

"Look!"

Penny has darted away, unexpectedly and quickly, her voice shrill with excitement.

"PENNY!"

Brian starts after the little girl, who is scurrying across the western edge of the church parking lot.

"GRAB HER!" Philip calls out, chasing after Brian, who is charging after the girl.

"Lookit! Lookit!" Penny's little legs are churning frantically as she darts toward a side street, which winds along the far side of the hill. "It's a policeman!" She points as she runs. "He'll save us!"

"PENNY, STOP!"

The little girl scurries around an exit gate and down the side road. "He'll save us!"

Brian clears the end of the fence at a dead run, and he sees a squad car about fifty yards away, parked on the side of the road under a massive live oak. Penny is approaching the royal blue Crown Victoria—the Atlanta Police decal on the door, the trademark red swoosh, and the light bar mounted on the roof—a silhouette hunched behind the wheel.

"Stop, honey!"

Brian sees Penny pausing suddenly outside the driver's door, panting with exertion, staring in at the man behind the wheel.

By this point, Philip and Nick have caught up with Brian, and Philip zooms past his brother. He charges up to his little girl and scoops her off the ground as though pulling her out of a fire.

Brian reaches the squad car and looks in the half-open driver's side window.

The patrolman was once a heavyset white man with long sideburns.

Nobody says anything.

From her father's arms, Penny gapes through the car window at the dead man in uniform straining against his shoulder strap. From the looks of his badge and his garb, as well as the word TRAFFIC emblazoned on the front quarter panel of the vehicle, he was once a low-level officer, probably assigned to the outer regions of the city, feeding stray cars to the impound lots along Fayetteville Road.

Now the man twists in his seat, imprisoned by a seat belt he cannot fathom, openmouthed and drooling at the fresh meat outside his window. His facial features are deformed and bloated, the color of mildew, his eyes like tarnished coins. He snarls at the humans, snapping his blackened teeth with feral appetite.

"Now that's just plain pathetic," Philip says to no one in particular.

"I'll take her," Brian says, stepping closer and reaching for Penny.

The dead cop, catching the smell of food, snaps his jaws toward Brian, straining the belt, making the canvas harness creak.

Brian jerks back with a start.

"He can't hurt ya," Philip says in a low, alarmingly casual tone. "He can't even figure out the goddamn seat belt."

"You're kidding me," Nick says, looking over Philip's shoulder.

"Poor dumb son of a bitch."

The dead cop growls.

Penny climbs into Brian's arms, and Brian steps back, holding the child tightly. "C'mon, Philip, let's go."

"Wait a minute, hold your horses." Philip pulls the .22 from the back of his belt.

"C'mon, man," Nick pipes in, "the noise is gonna draw more of 'em . . . let's get outta here."

Philip points the gun at the cop, who grows still at the sight of the muzzle. But Philip doesn't pull the trigger. He simply smiles and makes a childlike shooting noise: *psssh-psssh-pssssh.*

"Philip, come on," Brian says, shifting Penny's weight in his arms. "That thing doesn't even—"

Brian stops and stares.

The dead cop is transfixed by the sight of that Ruger in his face. Brian wonders if his rudimentary central nervous system is somehow sending a signal to some far-off muscle memory buried deep in his dead brain cells. His expression changes. The monstrous abomination of a face falls like a rotten soufflé, and the thing almost looks sad. Or maybe even scared. It's hard to tell behind that beastly snarling mouth and mask of necrotic tissue, but something in those Buffalo-nickel eyes flickers then: a trace of dread?

An unexpected tide of emotion rises in Brian Blake, and it takes him by surprise. It's hard to put a name to it—it's partly repulsion, partly pity, partly disgust, partly sorrow, and partly rage. He suddenly puts Penny down, and he gently turns her around so that she's facing the church.

"This is an *away* moment, kiddo," Brian says softly, and then turns to face his brother.

Philip is taunting the zombie. "Just relax and

follow the bouncing ball," he says to the drooling creature, waving the barrel slowly back and forth.

"I'll do it," Brian says.

Philip freezes. He turns and gives his brother a look. "Say what?"

"Give me the gun, I'll finish it off."

Philip looks at Nick, and Nick looks at Brian. "Hey, man, you don't want to—"

"Give me the gun!"

The smile that twitches at the corners of Philip's lips is complex, and humorless. "Be my guest, sport."

Brian takes the gun and without hesitation steps forward, pokes it in the car, presses the muzzle against the dead cop's head, and starts to squeeze off a single shot . . . but his finger will not respond. His trigger finger will not obey the command his brain is giving it.

In the awkward pause the zombie drools as though waiting for something.

"Gimme the gun back, sport." Philip's voice sounds far away to Brian.

"No . . . I got this one." Brian grits his teeth and tries to pull the trigger. His finger is a block of ice. His eyes burn. His stomach clenches.

The dead cop snarls.

Brian begins to tremble as Philip steps forward.

"Gimme the gun back."

"No."

"Come on, sport, give it back."

"I got it!" Brian wipes his eyes with his sleeve. "Damnit, I got it!"

"Come on." Philip reaches for the gun. "Enough."

"God*damn*it," Brian says, lowering the gun, the tears welling in his eyes. He can't do it. He might as well face it. He gives the gun to his brother, and steps back with his head lowered.

Philip puts the policeman out of his misery with a single pop that sends a spray of blood mist across the inside of the prowler's windshield. The bark echoes up and out over the ruined landscape.

The dead cop slumps over the wheel.

A long moment passes as Brian fights his tears and tries to hide his trembling. He gazes through the car window at the cop's remains. He feels like saying he's sorry to the dead officer but decides against it. He just keeps staring at the limp body still held in place by the shoulder strap.

The faint sound of a child's voice, like the flutter of broken wings, comes from behind them. "Dad . . . Uncle Brian . . . Uncle Nick? Um . . . something bad is happening."

The three men whirl around almost simultaneously. Their gazes rise across the church parking lot, to the place toward which Penny is staring and pointing. "Son of a *bitch,*" Philip says, seeing the worst-case scenario unfolding before his very eyes.

"Oh my God," Nick says.

"Shit, shit—shit!" Brian feels his spine go cold as he sees the front of the church.

"Come on, punkin, this way." Philip goes over to the child and tugs her gently back toward the cruiser. "We're gonna borrow this nice policeman's car." He reaches inside the driver's door, unlatches it, kicks it open, unsnaps the seat belt, and yanks the limp body from the vehicle— the zombie sprawling to the pavement with the ceremonial splat of an overripe gourd.

"Everybody in—quick! Throw your shit in the back! And get in!"

Brian and Nick circle around to the other side, throw open the doors, toss in their backpacks, and get in.

Philip slides Penny over the center hump, setting her on the passenger seat and climbing behind the wheel. The keys are in the ignition.

Philip turns the key.

The engine ticks.

The dashboard barely lights, just a dull ember of power left.

"Damnit to hell! DAMNIT!" Philip glances out the window at the church. "Okay. Wait a minute. Wait . . . wait." He shoots a quick glance through the windshield, and he sees that the road ahead banks into a steep downgrade, which leads under a train trestle. He looks at Brian and Nick. "You two. Get out. Now!"

Brian and Nick look at each other, stunned. What

they see emerging from the church—most likely aroused by the commotion of voices and the pistol shot—would most likely burn itself into their memories for some time to come. Unfortunately it would also linger in Penny's imagination, probably more vividly: dead things materializing behind gaping holes in stained-glass portals and half-open doorways, some of them still clad in ragged, blood-soaked clerical vestments, some of them in Sunday-go-to-meeting suits and crepe dresses drenched with gore. Some of them are gnawing on severed human appendages, while others carry body parts at their sides, the organs still dripping from the gruesome orgy inside the chapel. There are at least fifty, maybe more, and they move side by side with a lurching purpose toward the police car.

For a single instant, before throwing open his door and joining Nick outside the car, Brian finds his mind flashing on a strange thought: *They are moving as one—even in death, still a tightly knit congregation—like puppets of some great overmind.* But the notion quickly flies from his thoughts as he hears the call of his brother from behind the wheel of the cop car.

"PUSH THE SON OF THE BITCH WITH EVERYTHING YOU GOT AND THEN HOP ON!"

Now Brian joins Nick behind the car and then, without really even thinking about it, begins to push. By this point Philip has jammed the thing into neutral, and has his door open, and his leg outside the car, and is shoving the thing with his boot with all his might.

It takes them a few moments to build up steam—the churchgoing hoard behind them approaching steadily, dropping their ghastly treasures amid the promise of fresh meat—but soon the cruiser is coasting rapidly down the hill, faster and faster, to the point where Brian and Nick have to hop on board. Nick grasps the whip antenna for purchase. Brian gets halfway inside the flapping rear door, but can't get himself the rest of the way inside without falling, so he holds tightly to the door's frame.

By this point the car is halfway down the hill, putting distance between them and the scores of undead shambling after them. The weight of the vehicle is building inertia. The Crown Victoria now feels as though it's a runaway train, bumping down the cracked pavement toward the inter-section at the bottom of the hill. The wind whips Brian's dark hair as he holds on for dear life.

Nick hollers something, but the noise of the wind and the thumping wheels drown out his voice. At the bottom of the hill lies a defunct Conrail switch-yard, its maze of ancient rails fossilized into the Georgia earth, its ramshackle sheds and office buildings as black and decayed as prehistoric ruins. Philip is yelling something that Brian cannot hear.

They reach the bottom of the hill and the steering wheel locks up.

The squad car bangs over the track and careens into the switchyard. Philip cannot turn the wheel. The car skids. The wheels cut into the cinders, the undercarriage sparking off the iron.

Brian and Nick hold on tight as the cruiser skids to a halt in a cloud of black dust.

"Grab your shit! Everybody! Now!" Philip already has his door open and he's already pulling Penny out. Brian and Nick hop off the rear end and join Philip, who hefts his duffel onto one shoulder and lifts his daughter onto the other. "This way!" He nods toward a narrow street to the west.

They hurry out of the switchyard.

A row of boarded storefronts and burned-out buildings stretches down a perpendicular cobblestone road.

They move quickly along, staying tight under a row of awnings on the south side of the street, their shoulders brushing graffiti-stained doors and Rust-Oleum-flecked windows. The dusk is closing in and shadows are lengthening, burying them in gloom.

The sense of being surrounded is overwhelming, although at the moment they don't see any creatures, just a long corridor of shitty, obsolete businesses once serving this corroded, forsaken part of Atlanta's outskirts: pawnshops, currency exchanges, bail bondsmen, auto parts places, taverns, and junk shops.

As they move along the scarred storefronts, huffing and puffing with the weight of their loads, not daring to speak or make any unnecessary noise, the urgency of getting inside somewhere begins to work on them. Night is falling again, and this place will be the dark side of the moon in less than an hour. They have no map, no GPS, no compass, no sense of where they are other than the misty landmark of the skyline miles to the west.

Brian feels the anxiety on the back of his neck like a cold finger.

They turn a corner.

Brian sees the mechanic's shop first, but Philip sees it a split second later and motions toward it with a nod. "Up there on the corner, see it?"

Nick sees it now. "Yeah, yeah . . . looks good."

It does *indeed* look good: On the southwest corner of a deserted intersection one block away, Donlevy's Autobody and Repair appears to be the only business in this godforsaken area that has any life still in it—although it currently appears closed for the season.

They hasten toward the building.

As they approach, they see that the half-acre lot is recently repaved. The two islands of gas pumps out front, clean and apparently operational, sit under a giant Chevron sign. The building itself— lined with columns of new tires, fronted on one

143

side by a pair of massive double garage doors—is a gleaming slab of silver metal siding and reinforced glass. There's even a second floor, housing either an office or more retail space.

Philip leads them around back. The rear of the place is tidy, with newly painted garbage Dumpsters shoved up against the cinder-block back wall. They search for a door or window but find neither.

"What about the front door?" Brian says in a breathless whisper as they pause next to the Dumpsters. They can hear the congregation coming down the street, the shuffling, groaning chorus of fifty-plus zombies.

"I'm sure it's locked," Philip says, his gaunt, hard face shiny from the labors of carrying his daughter and his duffel. Penny is compulsively, nervously sucking her thumb against his shoulder.

"How do you know?"

Philip shrugs. "Guess it's worth a try."

They creep around the far side of the building, and they stay in the shadows under the Chevron awning, as Philip sets Penny and duffel down and hurries up to the entrance door. He yanks the handle.

It's open.

eight

They huddle for some time inside the repair center's front office, under the cashier's counter, next to a spinner rack of candy bars and potato chips.

Philip locks the door and crouches next to the others in the shadows, watching the parade of undead out on the street, passing by the shop, oblivious to the whereabouts of their prey, stupidly scanning with their button eyes like dogs hearing high-pitched whistles.

From this vantage point, gazing through the meshed, reinforced windows, Brian gets a chance to scrutinize the dead clergy and ragged parishioners as they awkwardly promenade past the service station. How did this church full of true believers turn en masse? Did they gather as frightened Christians after the plague had broken out, cleaving to each other for succor and comfort? Did they hear fire-and-brimstone sermons from the preachers about the Revelation to John? Did the pastors furiously cant warning parables: " 'And the fifth angel blew his trumpet, and I saw a star fallen from heaven to earth, and he was given the key to the shaft of the bottomless pit!' "

And how did the first one turn? Was it somebody in a back pew having a heart attack? Was it a ritual suicide? Brian imagines one of those old black ladies—her system clogged with cholesterol, her plump, gloved hands waving with the spirit—suddenly clutching her massive bosom at the first twinge of a coronary. And minutes later—maybe in an hour or so—the woman rises, her porcine face full of a *new religion,* a singular, savage faith.

"Fucking Holy Rollers," Philip grumbles from across the cashier's counter. Then he turns to Penny and swallows contritely. "Sorry for the language, punkin."

They explore the repair center. The place is spotless and secure, cold but clean, the floors swept, the shelves well ordered, the cool air redolent with the odors of new rubber and the vaguely pleasant chemical fragrance of fuels and fluids. They realize they can stay here for the night, but it is not until they investigate the large repair garage that they make their most fortuitous discovery.

"Holy crap, it's a tank," Brian says, standing on the cold cement, shining a flashlight at the black beauty parked under canvas tarps in one corner.

The others gather around the sole vehicle standing in the darkness. Philip whips off the tarp. It's a late-model Cadillac Escalade in cherry condition, its onyx finish gleaming in the yellow light.

"Probably belonged to the owner," Nick ventures.

"Christmas comes early," Philip says, kicking one of the massive tires with his muddy work boot. The luxury SUV is enormous, with huge molded bumpers, giant vertical headlights, and big, shiny chrome wheels. It looks like the kind of vehicle a secret government agency would have in its fleet, the sinister tinted windows reflecting the bloom of the flashlight back at them.

"There's nobody inside it, right?" Brian shines the beam off the opaque glass.

Philip pulls the .22 from his belt, clicks a door open, and points the muzzle in at the empty, showroom-clean interior, with its wood trim, leather seats, and console that looks like a control center for an airliner.

Philip says, "Bet you a dollar to a doughnut there's keys in a drawer somewhere."

The whole incident with the cop and the church seems to have pushed Penny into a deeper stupor. She sleeps that night curled into a fetal ball on the floor of the repair area, covered in blankets, her thumb in her mouth.

"Haven't seen her do that in a coon's age," Philip remarks nearby, sitting on his bedroll with the last of the whiskey. He wears a sleeveless T-shirt and filthy jeans, his boots sitting next to him. He takes a sip and wipes his mouth.

"Do what?" Brian is sitting cross-legged, bundled

in his blood-spattered coat, on the other side of the little girl, careful not to speak too loudly. Nick dozes over by a workbench, zipped in a sleeping bag. The temperature has plunged into the forties.

"Suck her thumb like that," Philip says.

"She's dealing with a lot."

"We all are."

"Yeah." Brian stares into his lap. "We'll make it, though."

"Make it where?"

Brian looks up. "The refugee center. Wherever it is . . . we'll find it."

"Yeah, sure." Philip kills the rest of the bottle and sets it down. "We'll find the place and the sun'll come out tomorrow and all the orphans will find good homes and the Braves will win the fucking pennant."

"Something bothering you?"

Philip shakes his head. "Jesus Christ, Brian, open your eyes."

"Are you mad at me?"

Philip stands and stretches his sore neck. "Now why the fuck would I be mad at *you,* sport? It's business as usual. No big deal."

"What does that mean?"

"Nothing . . . just get some sleep." Philip walks over to the Escalade, kneels down, and looks under the chassis for something.

Brian climbs to his feet, his heart racing. He feels dizzy. His sore throat is better, and he stopped coughing after a few days of rest and rejuvenation in the Wiltshire house, but he still does not feel a hundred percent. Who does? He goes over and stands behind his brother. "What do you mean by 'business as usual'?"

"It is what it is," Philip mutters, checking the SUV's underbelly.

"You're mad about the cop," Brian says.

Philip stands up slowly, turns, and comes face-to-face with his brother. "I said go to sleep."

"Maybe I have a harder time shooting something that was once human—so sue me."

Philip grabs Brian by the nape of the T-shirt, spins him around, and slams him back against the side of the Escalade. The impact nearly knocks the breath out of Brian, and the noise wakes up Nick, and it even makes Penny stir. "You listen to me," Philip growls in a threatening, husky voice that's both sober and drunk at the same time. "Next time you take a gun from me, you make sure you're ready to put it to good use. That cop was harmless, but who knows about next time, and I ain't gonna be the one babysitting you with nothin' but my gonads in my hand, you understand? You read me?"

Brian is nodding, his throat dry with terror. "Yes."

Philip increases the pressure on Brian's shirt. "You better get past your namby-pamby bullshit sheltered life and start carrying your weight

149

around here and stoving some heads in because it sure as hell is gonna get worse before it gets better!"

"I understand," Brian says.

Philip doesn't let go, his eyes glinting with rage. "We're gonna survive this thing, and we're gonna do it by being bigger monsters than they are! You understand? There ain't no rules anymore! There ain't no philosophy, there ain't no grace, there ain't no mercy, there's only us and them, and all they wanna do is *eat* our ass! So we're gonna fucking eat *them!* We're gonna chew 'em up and spit 'em out, and we're gonna survive this thing or I will blow a hole through this whole fucked-up world! You follow me? You FOLLOW ME!"

Brian nods like crazy.

Philip lets him go and walks away.

By this point Nick is awake and sitting up, and staring agape.

Penny's eyes are wide and she furiously sucks her thumb, watching her father storm across the repair floor. He walks over to the massive reinforced garage doors, pauses, and stares out at the night though the slatted burglar bars, his big gnarly fists clenched.

Across the floor, still pinned against the side of the Escalade, Brian Blake wages a silent battle to keep from crying like a namby-pamby-bullshit-sheltered-baby.

• • •

The next morning, in the lambent daylight filtering into the shop, they hurry through a breakfast of cereal bars and bottled water, and then pour the contents of three five-gallon jugs of gas into the Escalade's tank. They find the keys in a drawer in the office, and they pack all their belongings in the SUV's cargo area. The tinted windows are fogged with condensation from the cold. Brian and Penny settle into the backseat while Nick stands at the garage door awaiting Philip's signal. Since the power is down—seemingly everywhere now—they are forced to spring the manual latch on the automated door opener.

Now Philip climbs behind the wheel of the Escalade and fires it up. The huge six-point-two-liter V-8 hums. The console lights up. Philip jacks it into gear and edges forward, giving Nick the signal.

Nick yanks the closest garage door, and the casters squeak, as the thing rises on its tracks. The light and air of the day explode through the windshield, as Nick hustles around to the passenger side door and climbs into the shotgun seat. The door slams.

Philip pauses for a moment, looking down at the dash.

"What's the matter?" Nick says in a shaky voice, still a little nervous about questioning anything Philip does. "Shouldn't we maybe get moving?"

"One second," Philip says, reaching down to a pull-out drawer.

Inside a spring-loaded map case he finds about two dozen CDs, neatly organized by the former owner—Calvin R. Donlevy of 601 Greencove Lane S.E. (according to the registration in the glove box). "Here we go," Philip says, rifling through the discs. Calvin R. Donlevy of Greencove Lane is apparently a lover of classic rock, judging by all the Zeppelin, Sabbath, and Hendrix in his collection. "A little somethin' to help with the concentration."

All at once a Cheap Trick disc goes in and Philip puts the hammer down.

The gravitational thrust of four hundred fifty horses pushes them against the seats, as the wide-body Escalade blasts off through the opening, barely making it through the gap without side-swiping the metal trusses. Daylight floods the interior. The buzz-saw guitar intro of the party anthem "Hello There" leaps out of the Bose 5.1 surround sound system, as they boom across the lot and into the street.

Cheap Trick's lead singer asks if all the ladies and gentlemen are ready to rock.

Philip roars around the corner and heads north on Maynard Terrace. The street widens. Lower-income homes blur by on either side of the vehicle. A wandering zombie in a torn raincoat looms off to the right, and Philip veers toward the thing.

The sickening thump is barely audible above the

roar of the engine (and the thunderous drum-beats of Cheap Trick). In back Brian sinks down lower in his seat, feeling sick to his stomach and worrying about Penny. She slumps in her seat next to him, staring straight ahead.

Brian reaches over and buckles her in and tries to give her a smile.

"Gotta be an entrance ramp north of here," Philip is saying over the noise, but the sound of his voice is almost completely drowned by the growl of the engine and the music. Two more walking dead loom off to their left, a man and woman in tatters, maybe homeless people, scuttling along the curb, and Philip happily swerves and takes them both down like soggy bowling pins.

A severed ear sticks to the windshield, and Philip puts the wipers on.

They reach the north end of Maynard Terrace, the entrance ramp straight ahead. Philip slams the brakes. The Escalade screams to a stop in front of a six-car pileup at the foot of the ramp, a cluster of upright corpses circling the wreckage like lazy buzzards.

Philip snaps the lever into reverse. The pedal goes down, the rock music thundering. The gravitational force sucks everybody forward. Brian braces Penny against her seat.

A yank of the wheel, and the Escalade does a one-eighty, then charges back down McPherson

Avenue—which runs parallel to the interstate.

They cross a mile of real estate in a couple of minutes, with kick drum and bass providing syncopated beats to the horrible thumping of errant dead, too slow to get out of the way, colliding with the massive quarter panels and launching into the air like giant flailing birds. More and more of them are emerging from the shadows and trees, awakened by the bellowing growl of the muscle car.

Philip's jaws tense with grim determination as they near another entrance ramp.

The brakes lock up at Faith Avenue, where a Burger Win burns out of control, the whole area fogbound with greasy smoke. This ramp is blocked worse than the last. Philip yells a garbled curse, and then slams the thing into reverse, rocketing backward.

The Escalade swerves over to an adjacent side street. Another yank of the steering wheel. Another kick of the pedal. Now they're burning rubber again, moving westward, weaving around roadblocks, heading toward the skyscrapers in the distance, which loom larger and larger like apparitions in the haze.

The increasing number of blocked streets, debris, ruined cars, and wandering dead seem insurmountable, but Philip Blake will not be denied. He sits hunched over the wheel, breathing thickly, eyes fixed on the horizon. He passes a Publix grocery store that looks as though it's been bombed in a blitzkrieg, its lot infested with dead.

Philip increases his speed in order to plow through a file of zombies in the street.

The tide of gore splashing up across the SUV's huge hood is spectacular—a lurid display of morbid tissue spraying up and blossoming across the windshield. Wipers swish and streak the gruesome remains.

In the backseat Brian turns to his niece. "Kiddo?" No answer. "Penny?"

The child's vacant stare is fixed on the Technicolor display across the windshield. She doesn't seem to hear Brian over the din of rock and roll and the rumble of the car, or perhaps she chooses *not* to hear him, or perhaps she's too far gone to hear anything.

Brian gently taps her shoulder, and she snaps her gaze at him.

Then Brian reaches across her, and carefully writes a single word on the inside of her fogged window:

AWAY

Brian remembers reading somewhere that the Atlanta metro area was up to almost six million people. He remembers being surprised at the number. Atlanta always seemed to Brian to be a sort of miniature metropolis, a mere token of

Southern Progress, isolated in a sea of sleepy little redneck burgs. The few visits he had taken to the city at ground level gave him the impression that the town was one giant suburb. Sure, it had its midtown canyon of tall buildings—it had Turner and Coke and Delta and the Falcons and all the rest—but mostly it seemed like a little sister to the great northern cities. Brian had been to New York once, visiting his ex-wife's family, and that vast, grimy, claustrophobic antfarm had seemed like a *real* city to Brian. Atlanta seemed like a *simulacrum* of a city. Maybe part of it was the town's history, which Brian remembers learning about in a college survey course: During Reconstruction, after Sherman had torched the place, the planners decided to let the old historic landmarks go the way of the dodo bird; and over the next century and a half Atlanta got tarted up in steel and glass. Unlike other Southern towns like Savannah and New Orleans—where the flavor of the Old South still proudly permeates—Atlanta turned to the bland surfaces of modern expressionism. *Look, Ma,* they seemed to say, *we're progressive, we're cosmopolitan, we're cool, not like those bumpkins in Birmingham.* But to Brian it always seemed like the Lady Atlanta "doth protested too much." To Brian, Atlanta had always been a pretend city.

Until now.

Over the course of those next horrible twenty-five minutes, as Philip relentlessly zigzags down desolate side streets and across leprous vacant lots running parallel to the interstate, carving their way closer and closer to the heart of town, Brian sees the real Atlanta like a flickering slide show of forensic crime scene photos outside the tinted windows of the hermetically sealed SUV. He sees blind alleys choked with wreckage, flaming trash heaps, housing projects plundered and abandoned, windows blown out everywhere, stained sheets hanging out of buildings scrawled with desperate pleas for help. This is *indeed* a city—a primeval necropolis—overcrowded and malodorous with death. And the worst part of it is, they are not yet to the border of the downtown area.

At approximately 10:22 A.M. Central Standard Time, Philip Blake manages to find Capital Avenue, a wide six-lane thoroughfare that wends past Turner Field and then downtown. He turns the stereo off. The silence booms in their ears as they turn onto Capital and then slowly proceed north.

The road is cluttered with abandoned cars, but they're spaced far enough apart for the Escalade to weave in between them. The spires of sky-scrapers—off to the left—are so close now they seem to glow in the haze like the mainsails of rescue ships.

Nobody says a thing as they roll past oceans of cement on either side of the street. The stadium parking lots are mostly empty. A few golf carts overturned here and there. Vending trucks sit in the corners, all closed up and defaced with graffiti. Scattered dead, way in the distance, wander the gray barrens in the cold autumn daylight.

They look like stray dogs about to fall over from malnutrition.

Philip rolls down his window and listens. The wind whistles. It has an odd smell to it—a mélange of burning rubber, melted circuits, and something oily and hard to identify like rotting tallow—and something chugs in the distance, vibrating the air like a vast engine.

A realization twists in Brian's gut. If the refugee centers are open somewhere to the west—somewhere in the ventricles of the city—wouldn't there be emergency vehicles out here? Signs? Checkpoints? Armed marshals somewhere? Police helicopters? Wouldn't there be some indication—this close to the downtown area—that relief is in sight? Up to this point, over the course of their journey into the city, they have seen only a few potential signs of life. Back on Glenwood Avenue they thought they saw someone on a motorcycle flash by but they couldn't be sure. Later, on Sydney Street, Nick said he saw someone darting across a doorway but he wouldn't swear to it.

Brian pushes the thoughts out of his mind when he sees the vast tangle of highways forming a cloverleaf about a quarter of a mile away.

This sprawling interchange of major arteries marks the eastern border of Atlanta's urban area—

the place where Interstate 20 meets up with 85, 75, and 403—and now it sits baking in the cold sun like a forgotten battlefield, clogged with wrecks and overturned semis. Brian feels the Escalade beginning to ascend a steep upgrade.

Capital Avenue rises on massive pilings over the interchange. Philip takes the incline slowly, snaking through an obstacle course of deserted wrecks at about fifteen miles an hour.

Brian feels a tapping on his left shoulder, and he realizes that Penny is trying to get his attention. He turns and looks at her.

She leans over and whispers something to him. It sounds like, "I can't see."

Brian looks at her. "You can't see?"

She shakes her head and whispers it again.

This time, Brian understands. "Can you hold it for a minute, kiddo?"

Philip hears this, and he glances in the rearview. "What's the matter?"

"She has to pee."

"Oh boy," Philip says. "Sorry, punkin, you're gonna have to cross your legs for a few minutes."

Penny whispers to Brian that she really, really, *really* has to go.

"She's gotta go, Philip," Brian informs his brother. "Really bad."

"Just hold it for a little bit, punkin."

They are approaching the zenith of the hill. At night, the view from this part of the city, as a motorist crosses Capital Avenue, must be gorgeous. There's a moment coming, about a hundred yards in the distance now, when the Escalade will clear the shadow of a tall building to the west. At night, the luminous constellations of city lights come into view at this point, providing a breathtaking panorama of the capitol dome in the foreground, and the sparkling cathedral of skyscrapers behind it.

They clear the shadow of the building, and they see the city spread out before them in all its glory. Philip slams on the brakes.

The Escalade lurches to a stop.

They sit there for an endless moment, all of them stricken speechless.

The street to the left runs along the front of the venerable old marble edifice of the capitol building. It is one-way going the wrong way, completely choked with abandoned cars. But that is not why everyone in the SUV is suddenly thunderstruck. The reason why nobody can muster a word—the silence lasting only a second, but seeming to go on for an eternity—is because of what they see coming at them down Capital Avenue from the north.

Penny wets herself.

The greeting party, as copious as a Roman army and as slapdash as a swarm of giant arachnids, comes from Martin Luther King Drive, a little over a block away. They come from the cool shadows where government buildings block out the sun, and there are so many of them that it takes a moment for the human eye to simply register what it is seeing. All shapes and sizes and stages of deterioration, they emerge from doorways and windows and alleys and wooded squares and nooks and crannies, and they fill the street with the profusion of a disordered marching band, drawn to the noise and smell and advent of a fresh automobile filled with fresh meat.

Old and young, black and white, men and women, former businessmen, housewives, civil servants, hustlers, children, thugs, teachers, lawyers, nurses, cops, garbage men, and prostitutes, each and every one of their faces uniformly pale and decomposed, like an endless orchard of shriveled fruit rotting in the sun—a thousand pairs of lifeless gunmetal-gray eyes locking in unison onto the Escalade, a thousand feral, primordial tracking devices fixing themselves hungrily on the newcomers in their midst.

Over the course of that single instant of horror-stricken silence, Philip makes a number of realizations with the speed of a synapse firing.

He realizes he can smell the telltale odor of the horde coming through the open window, and possibly even the air vents in the dash: that sickening, rancid bacon-and-shit stench. But more than that, he realizes that the strange drone he heard earlier, when he rolled down his window—that vibrating hum in the air like the twanging of a million high-tension wires—is the sound of a city full of the dead.

Their collective groaning, as they now labor as one giant multifaceted organism toward the Escalade, makes Philip's skin crawl.

All of which leads to one final realization that strikes Philip Blake between the eyes with the force of a ball-peen hammer. It occurs to him—considering the sight unfolding in almost dreamy slow motion in front of him—that the quest to find a refugee center in this town, not to mention anyone still alive, is fast becoming about as prudent as the boy looking for a pony in a pile of horseshit.

In that microsecond of dread—that minuscule soupçon of frozen stillness—Philip realizes that the sun will probably not be coming out tomorrow, and the orphans will stay orphans, and the Braves will never again win the fucking pennant.

Before jerking the shift lever he turns to the others and in a voice laced with bitterness says, "Show of hands, how many y'all still hot to find that refugee center?"

PART 2

Atlanta

He who fights too long against dragons
becomes a dragon himself; and if
you gaze too long into the abyss,
the abyss will gaze into you.
                    —Nietzsche

nine

Very few production cars on the road—in the U.S., at least—are capable of attaining any kind of speed in reverse. First of all, there's the gear problem. Most cars, vans, pickups, and sport-utility vehicles that come off the line have five or six forward gears but only one for reverse. Second of all, most vehicles have front suspensions designed to go forward not backward. This prevents drivers from getting up a head of steam in reverse. Third of all, in reverse you're usually steering by looking over your shoulder, and pushing cars to top speeds in this fashion usually terminates in spectacular spinouts.

On the other hand, the vehicle that Philip Blake is currently commandeering is a 2011 Platinum Cadillac Escalade with all-wheel drive and tricked-out torsion bars for any off-road applications that ace mechanic Calvin R. Donlevy of Greencove Lane might have endeavored to undertake in the backwaters of Central Georgia (in happier times). The vehicle weighs in at nearly four tons, and is close to seventeen feet long, with a StabiliTrak electronic stability control system (standard on all Platinum models). Best of all, it's equipped with a rearview camera that displays on a generous seven-inch navigation screen built into the dash.

Without hesitation, his nervous system wired to his right hand, Philip slams the lever into reverse, and keeps his gaze riveted to that flickering yellow image materializing on the navigation screen. The image shows the partly cloudy sky over the horizon line of pavement behind them: *the top of the overpass.*

Before the oncoming regiment of zombies have a chance to get within fifty yards, the Escalade rockets backward.

The g-forces suck everybody forward—Brian and Nick each twisting around to gaze out the tinted rear window at the overpass rushing toward them—as the tail end of the Escalade shimmies slightly, the vehicle building speed. Philip pushes it hard. The engine screams. Philip doesn't turn around. He keeps his gaze locked onto that screen, the little glowing yellow picture showing the top of the overpass growing larger and larger.

One slight miscalculation—a single foot-pound of pressure on the steering wheel in either direction—and the Escalade goes into a spin. But Philip keeps the wheel steady, and his foot on the gas, and his eyes on the screen, as the vehicle tears backward faster and faster—the engine now singing high opera, somewhere in the vicinity of C sharp. On the monitor Philip sees something change.

"Aw shit . . . look!"

Brian's voice pierces the noise of the engine but

Philip doesn't have to look. In the little yellow square of video he sees a series of dark figures appearing a couple hundred feet away, directly in their path, at the top of the overpass, like the pickets of a fence. They're moving slowly, in a haphazard formation, their arms opening to receive the vehicle now hurtling directly at them. Philip lets out an angry grunt.

He slams both work boots down on the brake pad, and the Escalade skids and smokes to a sudden stop on the sloping pavement.

At this point Philip realizes—along with everybody else—that they have one chance, and the window of that opportunity is going to close very quickly. The dead things coming at them from the front are still a hundred yards off, but the hordes behind them, shambling over the crest of the viaduct from the projects and vacant lots around Turner Field, are closing in with alarming speed, considering their ponderous, leaden movements. Philip can see in a side mirror that an adjoining street called Memorial Drive is accessible between two overturned trailers, but the army of zombies that are looming close and closer in his rearview will be reaching that cross street very soon themselves.

He makes an instantaneous decision, and bangs down on the accelerator.

The Escalade roars backward. Everybody holds on. Philip backs it straight toward the crowd of shuffling corpses. On the video monitor the image shows the columns of zombies excitedly reaching out, mouths gaping, as they grow larger and larger on the screen.

Memorial Drive comes into view on the camera, and Philip stomps on the brake.

The rear of the Escalade bowls over a row of the undead with a nauseating, muffled drumming noise, as Philip rips the shift lever back into drive, his logger boot already pushing the pedal to the floor. They all sink into the upholstery as the SUV lunges forward, Philip taking a sharp left, threading the needle between two ruined trailers.

Sparks jump in the air as the SUV swipes a side rail, and then it's through the gap and fleeing down the relatively clear and blessedly zombie-free lanes of Memorial Drive.

Hardly a minute goes by before Brian hears the scraping noise. It's a coarse, wet, keening sound coming from under the chassis. The others hear it, too. Nick looks over his shoulder. "What the hell is that noise?"

"Something's caught under the wheels," Brian says, trying to see the side of the car out his window. He can't see anything.

Philip is silent, his hands welded to the steering wheel, his jaw set and tense.

Nick is looking out at the side mirror. "One of those things is stuck under the wheel!"

"Oh *great,*" Brian says, twisting in his seat. He

notices a tiny fan of blood droplets across the back window. "What are we gonna—"

"Let it ride along," Philip says flatly, not taking his eyes off the street. "It'll be pulp in a few minutes."

They get about six blocks, bumping across a set of railroad tracks—getting deeper into the city—before encountering much more than a few isolated wrecks and roaming dead. The grid of streets threading between the buildings is choked with debris, the remnants of explosions, burned cars filled with charred skeletons, windows blown out, and piles of trash and detritus drifted up against storefronts. Somewhere along the way, the scraping noises cease, although nobody sees what has happened to the hanger-on.

Philip decides to take a north-south street into the heart of the city, but when he turns right—swerving around a mangled delivery truck on its side in the center of the intersection—he hits the brakes. The Escalade jerks to a stop.

They sit there for a moment, the engine idling. Philip doesn't move, his hands still white-knuckling the wheel, his eyes squinting as he gazes into the distant shadows of tall buildings straight ahead.

At first, Brian can't see what the problem is. He cranes his neck to glimpse the litter-strewn city street stretching many blocks before them.

Through the tinted glass, he sees high-rises on either side of the four-lane avenue. Trash swirls in the September wind.

Nick is also puzzled by the sudden stop. "What's wrong, Philip?"

Philip doesn't respond. He keeps staring straight ahead with that uneasy stillness, his teeth clenching, his jaws working.

"Philip?"

No response.

Nick turns back to the windshield and stares out at the street. His expression tightens. He sees now what Philip sees. He gets very still.

"Will somebody tell me what's going on?" Brian says, leaning forward to see better. For a moment, all he can make out is the distant canyon of high-rises, and many blocks of debris-littered pavement. But he realizes soon enough that he's seeing a still life of a desolate city beginning to rapidly change like a giant organism reacting to the intrusion of foreign bacteria. What Brian sees through that shaded window glass is so horrible that he begins moving his mouth without saying anything.

In that single instant of brain-numbing awe, Brian Blake flashes back to a ridiculous memory from his childhood, the madness of the moment gripping his mind. One time, his mom took him and Philip to the Barnum and Bailey Circus in Athens. The boys were maybe thirteen and ten respectively, and they reveled in the high-wire acts, the tigers jumping through flaming rings, the men shooting out of cannons, the acrobats, the cotton candy, the elephants, the sideshows, the sword swallower, the human dart board, the fire-eaters, the bearded ladies, and the snake charmer. But the memory that sticks with Brian the most—and what he thinks of right at this moment—is the clown car. That day in Athens, at the height of the show, a little goofy car pulled out across the center ring. It was a cartoonish sedan with painted windows, about the size of a station wagon, built low to the ground and painted in a patchwork of Day-Glo colors. Brian remembers it so vividly—how he laughed his head off at the clowns piling out of the car, one after another, and how at first it was just funny, and then it became kind of amazing, and finally it was just downright bizarre, because the clowns kept coming: six, eight, ten, twenty—big ones, little ones—they kept climbing out of that car as though it was a magic container of freeze-dried clowns. Even as a thirteen-year-old, Brian was transfixed by the gag, knowing full well there had to be a trick to it, maybe a trap-door embedded in the sawdust beneath the car, but it didn't matter because the very sight of it was mesmerizing.

That exact phenomenon—or at least a perverted facsimile of it—is now unfolding right before Brian's eyes along an urban thoroughfare in the lower bowels of midtown Atlanta. He gapes silently at it for a moment, trying to put the gruesome spectacle into words.

"Turn around, Philip." Brian's voice sounds hollow and reedy in his own ears as he stares at the countless throngs of undead awakening in every corner of the city before them. If the horde they encountered only moments ago on their way into town was a regiment of a Roman army, this—*this*—is the whole empire.

As far as the eye can see, down the narrow channel of the four-lane street, the undead emerge from buildings, from behind cars, from within wreckage, from the shadows of alleys, from busted-out display windows, from the marble porticos of government buildings, from the spindly planters of decorative trees, and from the tattered remains of sidewalk cafés. They are even visible in the far distance, where the vanishing point of the street blurs into the shadows of skyscrapers, their ragged silhouettes appearing like a myriad of slow-moving bugs roused from the darkness of an overturned rock. Their number defies logic.

"We gotta get outta here," Nick says in a rusty squeak of a voice.

Philip, still stoic and silent, works his clenched fingers on the steering wheel.

Nick nervously shoots a glance over his shoulder. "We gotta go back."

"He's right, Philip," Brian says, putting a hand gently on Penny's shoulder.

"What's the matter, what are you doing?" Nick looks at Philip. "Why aren't you turning around?"

Brian looks at the back of his brother's head. "There's too many of them, Philip. There's too many of them. There's too many."

"Oh my God, we're fucked . . . we're *fucked*," Nick says, transfixed by the ghastly miracle building across their path. The closest ones are maybe half a block away, like the leading edge of a tsunami—they look like office dwellers of both genders, still clad in corporate attire that appears shredded and chewed up and dipped in axle grease—and they stagger this way like snarling sleepwalkers.

Behind them, for blocks and blocks, countless others stumble along the sidewalks and down the center of the street. If there is a "rush hour" in hell, it most certainly can't hold a candle to *this*. Through the Escalade's air vents and windows, the tuneless symphony of a hundred thousand moans raises the hackles on the back of Brian's neck, and he reaches over and taps his brother on the shoulder. "The city's gone, Philip."

"Yeah, yeah, he's right, the place is toast, we gotta turn around," Nick babbles.

"One second." Philip's voice is ice cold. "Hold on."

"Philip, come on," Brian says. "This place belongs to them now."

"I said hold on."

Brian stares at the back of his brother's head and a cold sensation trickles down Brian's spine. He realizes that what Philip means by the phrase *hold on* is not "hold on a second while I think this over" or "hold on for a minute while I figure this thing out."

What Philip Blake means by *hold on* is—

"Y'all got your seat belts on?" he asks rhetorically, making Brian's skin turn cold.

"Philip, don't—"

Philip kicks the foot feed. The Escalade erupts into motion. He steers the vehicle straight into the teeming mob, cutting off Brian's thoughts and pressing everybody into their seats.

"PHILLY, NO!"

Nick's warning cry dissolves into a salvo of muffled thumps, like the beating of a giant tom-tom drum, as the Escalade jumps the sidewalk and mows down at least three dozen zombies.

Tissue and fluids rain across the car.

Brian is so unnerved that he ducks down against the floor and joins Penny in that place called *away*.

The smaller ones go down like ducks in a shooting gallery, bursting apart under the wheels and leaving a trail of rotting innards. The larger ones bounce off the quarter panels and hurtle through the air, smacking the sides of buildings and coming apart like overripe fruit.

The dead seem to have no capacity to learn. Even a moth will flitter away once it flies too close to a flame. But this vast society of walking corpses in Atlanta apparently have no clue as to why they can't eat the shiny black thing roaring at them—the same thundering piece of metal that just an instant ago turned their fellow zombies into blood pudding—so they just keep coming.

Hunched over the wheel, teeth gnashing, knuckles white, Philip uses the wipers, with periodic sprays of cleaning solution, to keep the windshield clean enough to see through as he chews his way north, plowing the 8,300 pounds of Detroit iron through the moving sea of zombies. Varying his speed between thirty and fifty miles an hour, he carves a path toward the center of town.

At times, he is literally cutting a swath through a crowd so dense that it's like blazing a trail through a thick forest of blood fruit, the flailing arms and curled fingers like tree limbs, clawing at the side windows as the Escalade digs through the walking excrement. At other times, the SUV crosses short sections of clear street, with only a few zombies trundling along on a sidewalk or at the edges of the pavement, and this gives Philip a chance to get his speed up, and to swerve to the right to a pick a few off, and then to the left for a few more, and then he'll hit another wall-to-wall mob, and that's probably the most fun, because that's when the shit really flies.

It's almost as though the viscera is raining down from above, from the sky, rather than from under the wheels or along the frame or over the top of the big front grill as the Escalade shears through the bodies. The wet matter streaks across the glass, again and again, with the rhythm of a giant pinwheel, a kaleidoscope of color, the palette like a rainbow of human tissue—oxblood red, pond-scum green, burnt-ocher yellow, and pine-tar black—and it's almost kind of beautiful to Philip.

He roars around a corner and plunges into another mass of zombies coming down the street.

The strangest part is the continual repetitive flashes of similar tissues and organs—some of them recognizable, some of them not so recognizable. Entrails fly in all directions, splashing the windshield and sliding across the hood. Little kernels of teeth periodically gather in the wiper blades, and something else, something pink, like little pearls of fish roe, keeps collecting in the seams of the hood.

Philip glimpses dead face after dead face, each one flashing in his window—visible one moment, gone the next—and he's in a zone now, he's somewhere else, not in the SUV, not behind the wheel, but *inside* the mob, inside the city of undead, chewing through their ranks, devouring the motherfuckers. Philip is the baddest monster of them all, and he's going to make it through this ocean of shit if he has to tear down the entire universe.

Brian realizes what is happening before he even looks. Ten excruciating minutes after they started mowing through the sea of zombies—after making it across nearly twenty-three city blocks—the Escalade goes into a spin.

The centripetal force tugs Brian against the floor, and he pops his head up—peering over the seat—as the SUV slides sideways on the grease of fifty thousand corpses. He has no time to yell or do anything about what is happening. He can only brace himself and Penny against the seat backs for the inevitable impact.

Wheels slick with gore, the SUV does a three-sixty, the rear end windmilling through the last few stray cadavers. The city blurs outside the windows, and Philip fights the wheel, tries to straighten it, but the tires are hydroplaning on a sheet of intestines and blood and spoor.

Brian lets out a strangled yelp—part warning and part inarticulate cry—as the vehicle spins toward a row of storefronts.

In the frenzied moments before the crash, Brian glimpses a row of derelict shop windows: hatless busts of bald mannequins, empty jewelry displays, frayed wires growing out of vacant floorboards, all of it blurred behind the wire-meshed display windows. But it's just a vague impression of these things, Brian's vision distorted by the violent spinning of the SUV.

And that's when the right side of the Escalade collides with the display window.

The crash has that suspension-of-time feeling for Brian, the store window turning to stardust, the noise of shattering glass like a wave slamming a breakwater as the Escalade punctures the burglar bars and plunges sideways into the dark shadows of the Goldberg Fine Jewelry Center of Atlanta.

Counters and display cases explode in all directions, a sparkling, silver sleet of debris as the gravitational forces yank all passengers to the right. The Escalade's airbags deploy in tiny explosions—great heaving balloons of white nylon filling the interior before it has a chance to collapse—and Nick is thrown sideways into the white fabric. Philip is flung sideways into Nick, and Penny is thrown across the rear floor into Brian.

The SUV skids sideways for an eternity through the empty store.

The vehicle finally comes to rest after slamming hard into a weight-bearing pillar in the center of the store, shoving everybody hard against the padded lining of the airbags, and for a moment, nobody moves.

● ● ●

White, feathery debris snows down through the dark, dusty air of the jewelry store, and the sounds of something collapsing behind them creaks in the sudden silence. Brian glances through the cracked rear window and sees the front of the store, a pile of fallen girders blocking the hole in the window, a cloud of dust obscuring the street.

Philip is twisting around in his seat, his face ashen and wild with panic. "Punkin? Punkin? You okay? Talk to me, little girl! You all right?"

Brian turns to the child, who is still on the floor, looking woozy and maybe in some kind of shock, but otherwise unharmed. "She's good, Philip, she's good," Brian says, feeling the back of the child's head for any blood, any sign of injury. She seems fine.

"Everybody else okay?" Philip looks around the dust motes of the dark interior. A thin ray of daylight filtering across the store is the only illumination. In the gloom, Brian can see the other men's faces: sweaty, stone-still with terror, eyes glinting.

Nick raises a thumb. "I'm good."

Brian says he is, too.

Philip already has his door open, and is struggling out from behind the airbag. "Get everything you can carry," he tells them, "but make sure you get the shotguns and all the shells. You hear me?"

Yes, they hear him, and now Brian and Nick are

climbing out of the SUV. Over the course of a mere minute, Brian makes a series of observations—most of them, apparently, already calculated by Philip—beginning with the front of the store.

From the chorus of moaning noises and thousands of shuffling feet, it is clear to Brian that the zombie horde is closing in on the accident scene. The Escalade is finished, its front end nearly totaled, its tires blown, its entire length shellacked with gore.

The rear of the store leads toward a hallway. Dark, narrow, lined with drywall, the corridor may or may not lead to an exit. There's no time to investigate. All they have time to do is grab their packs, their duffels, and their weapons. Dazed from the collision, dizzy with panic, bruised and battered, ears ringing, Brian and Nick each grab a goose gun, and Philip takes as many bladed tools as he can stow on his body, a bad-axe in each side of his belt, the Ruger and three extra magazines.

"Come on, kiddo, we gotta skeedaddle," Brian says to Penny, but the child looks lethargic and confused. He tries to pull her from the mangled interior, but she hangs on to the back of the seat.

"Carry her," Philip says, coming around the front of the SUV.

"Come on, sweetie, you can ride piggyback," Brian tells the girl.

Penny reluctantly climbs out, and Brian lifts her onto his back.

The four of them quickly creep through the jewelry store's back hall.

They get lucky. Just past the glass doorway of a back office, they find an unmarked metal door. Philip throws the bolt, and he cracks the door open a few inches, peering out. The smell is incredible—a black, greasy stench that reminds Brian of the time his sixth-grade class took a field trip to the Turner stockyards outside Ashburn. The smell on the abattoir floor was like this. Philip raises a hand, motioning for everybody to stop.

Over Philip's shoulder, Brian can see a long, narrow, dark alley lined with overflowing garbage Dumpsters. But it's the actual *content* of the receptacles that registers most sharply in Brian's brain: pale human arms dangling over the sides, ragged, ulcerated legs, matted hair hanging down, and pools of old blackened blood dried beneath them.

Philip motions to the others. "Y'all follow me, and do exactly what I say," he says, snapping the cocking mechanism on the Ruger—eight rounds of .22-caliber bullets ready to rock—and then he's moving.

They follow him out.

As quietly and quickly as possible, they make their way through the stench and shadows of the deserted slaughterhouse of an alley toward a side street visible at one end. Weighed down by the duffel bag over one shoulder, and the child clinging to his back, Brian limps along in between Philip and Nick—Penny's sixty-five pounds never feeling as heavy as they do now. Nick, who is bringing up the rear, walks with his Marlin 20-gauge cradled in his arms. Brian has his own shotgun wedged underneath his backpack—not that he has any idea how to use the damn thing.

They reach the end of the alley, and they are about to slip out and make their way down the deserted side street, when Philip accidentally steps on a human hand protruding from under a garbage Dumpster.

The hand—connected to a zombie with some fight still in it—instantly recoils under the container. Philip jerks backward with a start.

"DUDE!" Nick cries out, and the hand shoots back out and grabs Philip's ankle.

Philip sprawls to the ground, his Ruger spinning off across the pavement.

The dead man—an ashy-skinned, bearded homeless person in bloodstained rags—crabs toward Philip with the speed of a giant spider.

Philip claws for his gun. The others fumble for their weapons, Brian going for his shotgun while trying to balance the child on his back. Nick thumbs back the hammers on his Marlin.

The dead thing clutches Philip's leg and opens its

jaws with the rigor-mortis creak of rusty hinges as Philip fumbles for his axe.

The zombie is about to take a chunk out of Philip's lower calf when the barrel of Nick's goose gun presses down on the back of the thing's skull.

The blast rips through the zombie's brain, sending half its face through the air on a geyser of blood and matter, the booming echo of the shotgun reverberating through the canyons of steel and glass.

"Now we're screwed," Philip says, struggling to his feet, scooping up the Ruger.

"What's the matter?" Brian says, adjusting the weight of the little girl on his back.

"Listen," Philip says.

In the brittle silence, they hear the ocean-wave sound of moaning suddenly change, altering its course as though on a shifting wind, the masses of undead drawn by the boom of the shotgun.

"So, we'll go back inside," Nick says in a strident, tense voice. "Back inside the jewelry store—there's gotta be a second floor."

"Too late," Philip says, checking the Ruger, looking down into its breech. He's got four rounds of hollow tips left in the hilt, and three mags of eight each in his back pockets. "I'm bettin' they're already flooding in the front of the place."

"What do you suggest?"

Philip looks at Nick, and then at his brother. "How fast you think you can run with all that weight?"

• • •

They take off at a moderate clip, Philip in the lead, Brian hobbling along after him, Nick bringing up the rear, past caved-in storefronts and petrified, charred funeral pyres of bodies burned by enterprising survivors.

Brian can't tell for sure but it seems like Philip is madly looking for a safe exit off the streets—a clean doorway, a fire escape ladder, *something*—but he's distracted now by an increasing number of moving corpses appearing around every corner.

Philip blasts the first one at fifty paces, sending a slug through its forehead, dropping it like a bad habit. The second one surprises him at closer range, lurching out of a shadowy doorway, and Philip puts it down with his second shot. More of them are materializing from porches and gaping store windows. Nick puts the goose gun and two decades of boar hunting to good use, taking down at least a dozen of them in the space of two blocks.

The blasts echo up over the skyline like sonic booms in the stratosphere.

They turn a corner and hurry down a narrower side road of herringbone brick, perhaps a landmark antebellum street that once rang with buckboards and horses, now bordered on either side by boarded condominiums and office buildings. The good news is that they seem to be moving away from the congested area, encountering fewer and fewer walking dead with each passing block.

The bad news is that they feel trapped now. They sense the city closing in around them, swallowing them whole in its glass-and-steel gullet. By this point, the sun has begun its afternoon descent, and the shadows thrown by the massive skyline have begun to lengthen.

Philip sees something in the distance—maybe a block and a half away—and instinctively ducks under the canopy of a torn awning.

The others hunker down with him against the boarded window of a former dry cleaner, and they crouch in the shadows to catch their breaths.

Brian is panting with exertion, little Penny still clinging soporifically to his back, like some kind of sleepy, traumatized monkey. "What is it, what's the matter?" Brian asks, realizing that Philip is craning his neck to see something in the distance.

"Tell me I'm seeing things," Philip says.

"What is it?"

"Gray building up there on the right," Philip says, nodding to the north. "See it? 'Bout two blocks away? See the doorway?"

In the distance, a three-story apartment building rises out of a row of dilapidated two-story condominiums. A massive postwar pile of chalk-colored brick and jutting balconies, it's the largest building on the block, the top of it reaching out of the shadows and reflecting the cold, pale sunlight off its array of antennas and exhaust stacks.

185

"Oh my God, I see it," Brian utters, still balancing Penny on his sore back as he kneels. The child clutches at his shoulders with a desperate grip.

"That ain't no mirage, Philly," Nick comments, a trace of awe coloring his voice.

They all stare at the human figure in the distance, too far away to identify as a man or a woman, adult or child, but there it is . . . *waving at them.*

ten

Philip approaches cautiously from the opposite side of the street, the .22 at his side, cocked and ready, but not exactly raised. The others follow along behind him in a single file, all of their hackles up, their eyes wide open and prepared for anything.

The young woman across the street calls to them in a low, hissing whisper: "Hurry up already!"

She appears to be in her late twenties, maybe early thirties, with long dishwater-blond hair pulled back in a tight ponytail. She wears jeans and a loose-fitting cable-knit sweater that's severely stained, the red smudges and spatters visible even from this distance as she waves them over with a small-caliber revolver, maybe a police .38, swinging it like it's an air traffic control baton.

Philip wipes his mouth, thinking, catching his breath, trying to get a bead on the woman.

"C'mon!" she yells. "Before they smell us!" She's obviously anxious for them to follow her inside, and it's very likely she means them no harm; the way she's swinging the gun, it would not surprise Philip if it wasn't even loaded. She calls out: "And don't let any of those Biters see you come inside!"

Philip is wary, guarded, and he pauses on the curb before crossing the street. "How many of you *are* there?" he calls out to her.

Across the street, the blond woman lets out an exasperated sigh. "For God's sake, we're offering you food and shelter, come on!"

"How many?"

"Jesus, do you want help or not?"

Philip tightens his grip on the Ruger. "You're gonna answer my question first."

Another nervous sigh. "Three! Okay? There's three of us. You happy now? This is your last opportunity because if y'all don't come now, I'm going to go back inside, and then you're gonna be shit outta luck." She speaks with the faint drawl of a native Georgian, but has some big city in her voice, too. Maybe even a little bit of the North.

Philip and Nick exchange glances. The distant choir of rusty moaning drifts closer on the wind like a coming storm. Brian nervously readjusts Penny's weight on his back, and then shoots a jittery glance over his shoulder at the end of the block. He looks at Philip. "What other options do we have, Philip?"

"I agree, Philly," Nick whispers under his breath, swallowing his fear.

Philip looks at the young lady across the street. "How many men, how many women?"

She hollers back at him, "You want me to fill out a questionnaire? I'm going back inside. Good luck with everything—you're gonna need it!"

"Wait!"

Philip nods at the others, and then cautiously leads them across the street.

"You got any cigarettes?" the young woman asks, leading the group into the building's outer vestibule, securing the door behind her with a makeshift cross-brace. "We're down to our last bent butts."

She's a little beat-up, with scars on her chin, bruises on the side of her face, and one eye that's so bloodshot it looks like a mild hemorrhage. Beyond those rough edges, though, she strikes Philip as a fine-looking woman, with cornflower-blue eyes, and the kind of sun-kissed skin you might see on a farm girl—a sort of easy, low-maintenance beauty. But from the defiant tilt of her head, and the zaftig curves hidden under her bulky clothes, she gives off the air of an earth mother, and one does not fuck with earth mothers.

"Sorry, no smokers," Philip says, holding the door for Brian.

"Y'all look like you got banged up out there," the woman says, leading them across a reeking, littered chamber lined on one side with eighteen pairs of mailboxes and buzzers. Brian gently puts Penny down. The little girl staggers for a moment, getting her bearings. The air smells of must and zombie. The building does not feel safe.

The young woman kneels down by Penny. "Aren't you a sweet one."

Penny doesn't say anything, just looks down.

The woman looks up at Brian. "She yours?"

"She's mine," Philip says.

The woman brushes a strand of matted black hair from Penny's face. "My name's April, honey, what's yours?"

"Penny."

The voice that comes out of the child is so meek and nerve-racked it sounds like the mewl of a kitten. The woman named April smiles and strokes the girl's shoulder, then rises and looks at the men. "Let's get inside before we draw more of those things." She goes over to one of the intercoms and thumbs the button. "Dad, let us in."

Through a burst of static, a voice replies, *"Not so fast, little girl."*

Philip grabs her arm. "You got *power* in there? You got electricity?"

She shakes her head. "Afraid not . . . intercom's

189

on a battery." She pokes the button. "Dad, come on."

Through the crackling static: *"How do we know we can trust these yahoos?"*

Click: "You gonna let us in or what?"

Crackle: *"You tell 'em to give up their guns."*

She lets out another anguished sigh and turns to Philip, who is shaking his head, giving her a no-way-in-hell kind of look.

Click: "They got a little girl, for chrissake. I'll vouch for 'em."

Crackle: *"And Hitler painted roses . . . we don't know these folks from Adam."*

Click: "Dad, open the damn lock!"

Crackle: *"You saw what happened up to Druid Hills."*

April slams her hand down on the intercom: "This ain't Druid Hills! Now let us in, goddamnit, before we grow moss on our asses!"

A harsh, metallic buzz is followed by a loud clunk as the autolatch on the inner security door springs open. April leads them through the doorway, and then down a shopworn, sour-smelling hallway with three apartment doors on either side. At the far end of the corridor stands a metal door marked stairs, with criss-crossing boards nailed over it.

April knocks on the last door on the right—Apartment 1C—and within moments, a heavier, older, coarser version of April opens the door. "Oh my God, what an adorable little girl," the big gal says, seeing Penny, who is now holding Brian's hand. "Come on in, folks . . . can't tell ya how good it is to finally see people who can keep their drool in their mouths."

April's sister, who introduces herself as Tara, is plump and rough around the edges. She smells of smoke and cheap shampoo, and is dressed in a faded floral-print muumuu to hide her excess flesh. Her cleavage rises like bread dough out of the top of her dress, a little Woody Woodpecker tattoo on the crest of one bosom. She has the same striking blue eyes as her younger sister, but keeps them heavily lined and decorated with steel-blue eye shadow. Her long Lee press-on nails look like they could open a tin can.

Philip enters the apartment first, the Ruger still in his hand at his side.

The others follow.

At first, Philip barely notices the cluttered living room, the chairs draped with clothing, the battered luggage along one wall, and the oddly shaped musical instrument cases leaning against the boarded sliding door. He hardly notices the small kitchenette off to the left, the peach crates of provisions and the sink full of dirty dishes. The smell of cigarette smoke and stale fabric and dried sweat hanging in the air barely registers in Philip's nostrils.

Right now, all he can focus on is the barrel of

a 12-gauge shotgun pointed directly at him from a rocking chair across the room.

"That's far enough," says the old man with the shotgun. A lanky, weathered old duffer, he has the farmer-tanned face of a cigar-store Indian, with an iron-gray flattop haircut and ice-chip blue eyes. The slender tube of an oxygen rig is clipped under his buzzard's beak of a nose, the tank sitting next to him like a faithful pet. He barely fits into his stovepipe jeans and flannel shirt, his white, hairy ankles showing above the tops of his shit-kickers.

Philip instinctively raises the .22, instantly going into Mexican showdown mode. He aims it at the old man and says, "Sir, we got enough trouble out there, we don't need any in here."

The others freeze.

April pushes her way past the men. "For God's sake, Dad, put that thing down."

The old man waves the girl aside with the barrel. "You hush now, little girl."

April stands there with her hands on her hips, a disgusted look on her face.

Across the room, Tara says, "Can we all just dial it down a little bit?"

"Where'd you folks come from?" the old man asks Philip, the shotgun still raised and ready.

"Waynesboro, Georgia."

"Never heard of it."

"It's in Burke County."

"Hell, that's almost South Carolina."

"Yessir."

"You on drugs? Speed, crack . . . something like that?"

"No, sir. Why the hell would you think that?"

"Something going on behind them eyes, they look all jacked up on speed."

"I don't do drugs."

"How'd you end up on our doorstep?"

"Heard there was some kinda refugee center set up here, but it ain't lookin' too good."

"You got that right," says the old man.

April chimes in, "Sounds like we all got something in common."

Philip keeps his eyes on the old man, but says to the girl, "How's that?"

"That's the same reason *we* ended up in this godforsaken place," she says. "Looking for that damned refugee center everybody was talking about."

Philip stares at the shotgun. " 'Best laid plans,' I guess."

"Damn straight," says the old man, the faint whistle of oxygen seeping from the tank. "I don't suppose you realize what you done to us."

"I'm listening."

"You got them Biters all stirred up. By sundown, there's gonna be a goddamn convention of them things outside our door."

Philip sniffs. "I'm sorry about that but it ain't like we had a choice."

The old man sighs. "Well now . . . I suppose that's true."

"Your daughter's the one pulled us off the street . . . we had no bad intentions. Hell, we had no intentions at all . . . other than keepin' from getting bit."

"Yeah, well . . . I can see your point there."

A long beat of silence follows. Everybody waits. The two firearms begin to lower.

"What are them cases for?" Philip finally asks, nodding toward the row of tattered instrument cases across the rear of the living room. His gun is still raised but the fight-or-flight juice has drained from him. "You got tommy guns in them things?"

The old man finally lets out a flinty laugh. He lays his gun on his lap, crosswise, letting up on the hammers, all the tension draining out of his gaunt face. The oxygen tank pings. "My friend, you're lookin' at what's left of the World Famous Chalmers Family Band, stars of stage, screen, and state fairs across the South." The old man sets the gun down on the floor with a grunt. He looks up at Philip. "I apologize for the ornery reception." He struggles to his feet, rising to his full height until he looks like a withered Abe Lincoln. "Name's David Chalmers, mandolin, vocals, and father of these two ragamuffins."

Philip shoves his gun back behind his belt.

"Philip Blake. This is my brother Brian. And that wallflower over there is Nick Parsons . . . and I thank you kindly for saving our asses out there."

The two patriarchs shake hands, and the tension goes out of the room with the suddenness of an off switch being thrown.

It turns out there *was* a fourth member of the Chalmers Family Band—Mrs. Chalmers—a portly little matron from Chattanooga who sang high soprano on the group's bluegrass and old-timey numbers. According to April, it was a blessing in disguise that the matriarch of the family succumbed to pneumonia five years earlier. If she had lived to see this horrible shit inflicting the human race, she would have been crushed, would have seen it as the end-time, and probably would have walked right off the pier at Clark's Hill Lake.

So it was that the Chalmers Family Band became a trio, and went on with the act, playing the carny circuit across the tristate area, with Tara on bass, April on guitar, and Daddy on mandolin. As a single father, the sixty-six-year-old David had his hands full. Tara was a pothead, and April had her mother's temper and single-mindedness.

When the plague broke out, they were in Tennessee at a bluegrass festival, and they made their way back home in the band's camper. They got as far as the Georgia border before the camper broke down. From there, they got lucky enough to find an Amtrak train that was still running between Dalton and Atlanta. Unfortunately, the train deposited them smack-dab in the middle of the southeast side, at King Memorial Station, which was now lousy with the dead. Somehow, they managed to work their way north without getting attacked, traveling at night in stolen cars, searching for the mythical refugee center.

"And that's how we ended up here in our little low-rent paradise," April tells Philip in a soft voice late that night. She sits on the end of a tattered sofa, while Penny dozes restlessly next to her in a wad of blankets. Philip sits nearby.

Candles are lit on the coffee table. Nick and Brian are asleep on the floor across the room, while David and Tara are each snoring in a different musical key in their respective rooms.

"We're too petrified to go upstairs, though," April adds with a trace of regret in her voice. "Even though we could use whatever supplies are still up there. Batteries, canned goods, whatever. Jesus, I'd give my left tit for some toilet paper."

"Never give *that* up for a little toilet paper," Philip says with a grin, sitting barefoot in his stained T-shirt and jeans at the other end of the sofa, his belly full of rice and beans. The Chalmerses' supplies are running low, but they still had half of the ten-pound bag of rice that they pilfered from a broken shop window a week ago, and enough beans to make dinner for everyone.

April cooked. The grub wasn't bad, either. After dinner, Tara rolled cigarettes with the last of her Red Man tobacco and a few buds of skunkweed. Philip partook in a few puffs, even though he had sworn off pot years ago—it usually made him hear things in his head that he didn't want to hear. Now his brain feels woolly and thick in the strange afterglow.

April manages a sad smile. "Yeah, well . . . so close and yet so far."

"What do you mean?" Philip looks at her, and then slowly looks up at the ceiling. "Oh . . . right." He remembers hearing the noise earlier, and making note of it. They've quieted down now, but the shuffling, creaking noises from the higher floors have intermittently been crossing the ceiling all evening, moving with the insidious, invisible presence of termites. The fact that Philip almost forgot about these noises is a testament to how desensitized he's becoming to the prospects of such proximity to the dead. "What about the other ground-floor apartments?" he asks her.

"We picked them clean, got every last bit of usable stuff out of them."

"What happened in Druid Hills?" he asks after a moment of silence.

April lets out a sigh. "Folks told us there was a refugee center up there. There wasn't."

Philip looks at her. "And?"

April shrugs. "We got there and found a whole

bunch of people hiding out behind the gates of this big scrap-metal place. People just like us. Scared, confused. We tried to talk some of them into leaving with us. Strength in numbers, all that gung-ho shit."

"So, what happened?"

"I guess they were too scared to leave and too scared to stay." April looks down, her face reflecting the candlelight. "Tara and Dad and I found a car that would run, and we gathered up some supplies and took off. But we heard the motorcycles coming when we were pulling away."

"Motorcycles?"

She nods, rubs her eyes. "We got about a quarter of a mile down the road—maybe not even that far—and we round this hill and all of a sudden we hear, way in the distance behind us, these screams. And we look back across the valley, where this dusty old salvage yard is, and it's like . . . I don't know. Fucking *Road Warrior* or something."

"It's what?"

"This motorcycle gang is tearing the place apart, running people down, entire families, God knows what else. It was pretty damn ugly. And the weird thing is, it wasn't the near-miss that got to us. It wasn't the bullet we dodged. I think it was the guilt. We all wanted to go back and help, and be good upstanding citizens and all that, but we didn't." She looks at him. "Because we ain't good upstanding citizens; there ain't any of those left."

Philip looks at Penny. "I can see why your daddy wasn't crazy about the idea of taking in boarders."

"Ever since that scrap-yard fiasco, he's been real paranoid about running across any survivors— maybe more paranoid than he is about the Biters."

"*Biters* . . . I heard you say that before. Who came up with that one?"

"That's my dad's term; it kinda stuck."

"I like it." Philip smiles at her again. "And I like your daddy. He takes care of business, and I don't blame him for not trusting us. He seems like a tough old nut, and I respect that. We need more like him."

She sighs. "He's not as tough as he used to be, I'll tell you that."

"What's he got? Lung cancer?"

"Emphysema."

"That's not good," Philip says, and then he sees something that stops him cold.

April Chalmers has her hand on Penny's shoulder and is almost absently stroking the little girl as she sleeps. It's such a tender, unexpected gesture—so natural—that it reaches down into Philip and awakens something inside him that's long been dormant. He can't understand the feeling at first, and his confusion must be showing on his face because April looks up at him.

"You okay?"

"Yeah, I'm . . . I'm good." He touches the Band-

Aid on his temple where he smacked himself in the collision earlier that day. The Chalmerses dug out their first-aid kit and patched everybody up before dinner. "Tell you what," Philip says. "You go get some sleep, and in the morning, the boys and I will clear out the upstairs."

She looks at him for a moment like she's wondering whether or not to trust him.

The next morning, after breakfast, Philip shows April that his word is good. He enlists Nick, and he grabs extra magazines for the Ruger and a box of shells for one of the Marlins. He shoves the bad-axes down either side of his belt, and gives a small pickaxe to Nick for close encounters.

Pausing by the door, Philip crouches down to tighten the laces of his logger boots, which are so spattered with mud and gore that they look like they're embroidered with black and purple thread.

"Y'all be careful up there," old David Chalmers says, standing in the doorway of the kitchenette. He looks gray and washed out in the morning light, leaning on the metal caddy in which his oxygen tank is mounted. The tube under his nose softly whistles with each breath. "Y'all don't know what you're gonna find."

"Always," Philip says, tucking his denim shirt inside his jeans, checking the axes for quick and easy access. Nick stands over him, waiting with the goose gun on his shoulder. There's a taut expression on Nick's face, a combination of grim determination and excitement.

"Most of 'em will be on the second floor," the old man adds.

"We'll clear 'em on out."

"Just watch yer backs."

"Will do," Philip says, rising to his feet and checking the axes.

"I'm coming."

Philip whirls around to see Brian standing there with a clean T-shirt on—an REM logo on the front, the pride of Athens—and a dour, purposeful expression on his face. He's cradling one of the shotguns in his arms like it's a living thing.

"You sure?"

"Hell yeah."

"What about Penny?"

"The gals will watch her."

"I don't know."

"Come on," Brian says. "You need an extra pair of eyes up there. I'm up for it."

Philip thinks it over. He glances across the living room and sees his daughter sitting Indian-style on the floor between the two Chalmers women. The ladies are playing crazy eights with a tattered deck of cards, making Penny periodically smile and slap down a card. It's been a long time since the little girl has smiled. Philip turns to his brother and offers a grin. "That's the spirit."

They get up there via the stairs at the end of the first-floor corridor—the elevators at the other end as dead as the zombies—but first they have to tear the wooden bracings off the door. The noise of axe blows and nails squeaking out seems to stimulate movement above them, in the dark chambers behind apartment doors. At one point, Philip passes gas with all the exertion, a reminder of April's bean dinner from the night before.

"That fart's gonna wipe out more zombies than any twenty-gauge shell," Nick comments.

"Hardy-har-har," Philip says and tears off the last of the bracing planks

On their way up the dark stairwell, Philip says, "Remember, y'all—*be quick*. They are slippery motherfuckers but they're slow as shit, and dumber than Nick here."

"Hardy-har, back atcha," Nick says, expertly injecting a pair of .20-gauge shells into his goose gun.

They reach the top landing, and find the fire door to the second floor shut tightly. They pause. Brian is shaking.

"Calm down, sport," Philip tells his brother, noticing the barrel of the shotgun is wavering, trembling slightly. Philip gently pushes the muzzle away from the general vicinity of his ribs. "And try not to accidentally send a ball of that bird shot into one of *us*."

"I got it under control," Brian retorts in a shaky, tense voice, revealing that he obviously has *nothing* under control.

"Here we go," Philip says. "And remember, go at them hard and quick."

A single, fierce kick with the shank of his boot heel sends the door lurching open.

eleven

For a millisecond, they stand there with hearts beating like trip-hammers. Other than a few scattered candy wrappers and empty, broken pop bottles, and one hell of a lot of dust, the second-floor hall—identical to the ground-floor corridor—is empty. Dim daylight shines through the far windows and laces through streaks of dust motes, which cant down across the closed doors: 2A, 2C, and 2E along one side, 2B, 2D, and 2F along the other.

Nick whispers, "They're all locked inside their places."

Philip nods. "Gonna be like shooting fish in a damn barrel."

"Come on, let's do it," Brian says unconvincingly. "Let's get it done."

Philip glances at his brother, then glances at Nick. "John Rambo here."

They go over to the first door on the right—2F—

and raise the business ends of their guns. Philip snaps the slide on the Ruger.

Then he kicks the door in.

A giant ball of stink punches them in their faces. It is the first thing that registers: a hideous stew of human degradation, urine and feces—and zombie stench—vying for dominance over the sharper odors of rancid food and moldy bathrooms and mildewed clothes. It is so overwhelming and unbearable that it literally drives the men back a half step each.

"Jesus wept," Nick says in a choked utterance, involuntarily averting his face, as if the stench is a wind blowing at him.

"Still think my fart stinks?" Philip says as he takes a careful step into the reeking shadows of the apartment. He raises the .22.

Nick and Brian follow with shotguns at the ready, eyes wide and shiny with tension.

A moment later, they find four of them in repose, on the floor of a ransacked living room, each one slumped in a corner, slack jawed and catatonic, growling languidly at the sight of intruders, but too stupid or sick or demented to move, as though they have grown weary of their hellish fate and now have forgotten how to use furniture. It's hard to tell in the gloomy light, especially with their faces all bloated and blackened with mortified flesh, but it looks as though it's another family: mom and dad and two grown kids. The walls have weird patches of scratch marks, like a giant abstract painting, showing evidence that the things were following some flickering instinct to claw their way out.

Philip goes over to the first one, its shark eyes glimmering as the Ruger looms. The blast sends its brains across the Jackson Pollock of scratch marks behind it. The thing sinks to the floor. Meanwhile, Nick is across the room putting another one out of its misery, the boom of the Marlin like a great dry paper sack popping. Brain matter paints the walls. Philip takes the third one down as it is slowly rising, Nick moving toward the fourth—BOOM!—and the sounds of fluids spattering surfaces are buffered by the ringing in their ears.

Brian is standing ten paces behind them, his gun poised, his spirit drowning inside him on a rising tide of repulsion and nausea. "This is—this is not—" he starts to say, but a flash of movement to his left cuts off his words.

The errant zombie comes at Brian from the depths of a side hallway, plunging out of the shadows like a monstrous clown with a black fright wig and candy eyes. Before Brian even has a chance to identify it as a daughter or girlfriend, dressed in a torn robe with one shriveled breast exposed like a flap of chewed meat, the thing pounces on him with the force of a defensive back making a tackle.

Brian sprawls backward to the floor, and it all

happens so fast that Philip and Nick have no time to intercede. They are too far away.

The moving cadaver lands on top of Brian, the thing snarling with black, slimy teeth and—in that split instant before Brian realizes that he is still holding the shotgun—the zombie opens its jaws so wide it looks as though its skull is about to unhinge.

Brian gets one horrible glimpse down the recesses of the thing's throat—an endless black well straight down into hell—before he instinctively jerks the shotgun up. Almost by accident, the muzzle lodges itself in the gaping hole of the thing's mouth, and Brian screams out a garbled cry as he squeezes off a single blast.

The back of the thing's skull explodes, sending up a cloud of blood mist and tissue. The backwash hits the ceiling in deep purple arterial matter, and Brian is thunderstruck for a moment, his back pinned to the floor. The thing's head is still skewered on the shaft of the shotgun. He blinks. The silver eyes of the girlfriend or daughter, or *whoever* she was, are frozen now and fixed on Brian.

He coughs and turns away as the girl's head slowly slides down the length of the barrel, a giant shish kebob, the dead eyes still locked on Brian. He feels the moist slime of her face on his hands. He closes his eyes. He can't move. His right hand still glued to the trigger, his left still welded to the stock, he grimaces with horror.

Cold laughter brings him back around. "Look who just scored his first touchdown," Philip Blake says, standing over his brother in a cloud of cordite smoke, grinning from ear to ear with mirthless delight.

Nick is the one who finds the egress to the roof, and Philip is the one who gets the idea to deposit all the rotting carcasses up there so they don't stink up the place any further (or make the scavenger hunt through the upper floors any more unpleasant than it has to be).

It takes them a little over an hour to drag all the inhuman remains up the stairwell to the third floor, and then up through a narrow stairwell to the fire door. They have to shoot the lock off, and have to work in a sort of modified bucket brigade, dragging the smelly flesh sacks down the hallways and up two flights of stairs to the roof, leaving leech trails of gore on the cabbage-rose carpet runners.

They manage to get every last one of them—they terminated fourteen of them altogether, going through two entire clips of .22-caliber rounds, as well as half a box of shells—up the passageway and onto the roof.

"Look at this place," Nick marvels as he puts the last carcass down on the tarpaper warning track along the east side of the roof, the wind whipping his pant legs and tossing his hair. The corpses lie in a row like cordwood lined up for the winter. Brian stands at the opposite end of the file, gazing down at the dead things with a strange, implacable expression on his face.

"Pretty cool," Philip says, walking over to the edge of the roof.

At this height, he can see the distant buildings of the exclusive Buckhead area, Peachtree Plaza, and the glass cathedral of skyscrapers to the west. The frozen spires of the city rise in pristine summits, impassive, stoic in the sunlight, untouched by the apocalypse. Down below, Philip sees the scattered wandering dead moving in and out of shadows like broken toy soldiers come to life.

"Cool place to hang out," Philip says, turning and surveying the rest of the roof. Around a giant conglomeration of antennae, rent stracks, and heating and air-conditioning machinery, now cold and powerless, an apron of pea gravel offers enough space to play a touch football game. A forgotten tangle of lawn furniture leans against an air duct. "Grab a chair and take a load off."

They drag tattered chaise lounges over to the edge of the roof.

"I could get used to this place," Nick says, settling down on a lounger facing the skyline.

Philip sits down next to him. "You mean the roof or this place in general?"

"All of it."

"Copy that."

"How do you do it?" Brian says, standing behind them, fidgeting with nerves. He refuses to sit down, refuses to relax. He's still wired from his encounter with the impaled head.

"Do what?" Philip says.

"I don't know, like, the killing and stuff, and then the next minute you're—"

Brian stops himself, unable to put it into words, and Philip turns and looks at his brother. He sees the man's hands shaking. "Sit down, Bri, you did good down there."

Brian pulls a chair over, sits down, wrings his hands, ruminating. "I'm just saying—"

Again, he can't articulate what he's "just saying" and he falters.

"It ain't killing, sport," Philip says. "Soon as you get that straight, you're gonna be fine."

"What is it then?"

Philip shrugs. "Nicky, what would you call it?"

Nick is staring out at the skyline. "God's work?"

Philip has a big laugh at that one, and then says, "I got an idea."

He gets up and goes over to the closest corpse, one of the smaller ones.

"Check this out," he says, and drags the thing over to the edge of the roof.

The other two join Philip at the ledge. The rancid wind tosses their hair as they gaze over the ledge at the street thirty-five feet below them.

Philip shoves the cadaver with the toe of his boot until it slips over the side.

The thing seems to fall in slow motion, its limp appendages flopping like broken wings. It strikes the cement parkway down below, in front of the building, and comes apart with the sound, color, and texture of a very ripe watermelon erupting in a starburst of pink tissue.

In the master bedroom of the first-floor apartment, David Chalmers is sitting in his wifebeater T-shirt and boxer shorts, sucking on an inhaler, trying to get enough Atrovent into his lungs to quell the wheezing, when he hears the commotion outside the boarded sliding-glass doors of the rear portion of the apartment.

The sound instantly raises the hairs on his neck, and he quickly fumbles himself into his clothes, including the breathing tube, which he gets half-way on, one side dangling under a hairy nostril.

He storms across the room on creaking knees, yanking the oxygen tank along on its castors like a stubborn child being pulled by an impatient nanny.

Crossing the living room, he catches a glimpse out of the corner of his eye of three figures standing rapt and terrified at the threshold of the kitchen. April and Tara had been making cookies with the little girl—using up the last of their flour and sugar—and now the three females stand there, gaping in the direction of the noise.

David hobbles over to the boarded, meshed, burglar-barred sliding doors.

Through a narrow gap in the plywood planks, in between the branches of skeletal trees, he can just barely see the far end of the courtyard, and beyond that a slice of the street running parallel to the front of the apartment building.

Another body rains down as if dropped by God himself, hitting the pavement, making a wet, lurid, smacking sound not unlike a giant water balloon popping. But that's not the noise that's getting to David Chalmers right now. That's not the noise that's penetrating the apartment, coming in waves, a vast, distant, tuneless symphony.

"Sweet jumpin' Jesus," he mutters in a breathy wheeze, whirling around so fast he nearly tips over the tank in its caddy.

He drags the thing toward the door.

On the roof, Philip and Nick pause after heaving the fifth body off the ledge.

Panting from the effort and a sort of morbid giddiness, Philip comments: "They blow up good, don't they?"

Nick is trying unsuccessfully not to laugh. "This is ten kinds of wrong but I gotta admit it feels good."

"You got that right."

"What's the point, guys?" Brian wants to know, standing behind them.

"The point is, there *is* no point," Philip says without looking at his brother.

"What is that, like a Zen saying?"

"It is what it is."

"Okay, now you lost me. I mean, I don't see how throwing these things off the roof is *accomplishing* anything."

Philip turns and gives his brother a look. "Lighten up, sport. You bagged your first trophy today. It wasn't pretty but it got the job done. We're just blowing off a little steam."

Nick sees something in the distance that he hadn't noticed until now. "Hey, check out—"

"I'm just saying," Brian interrupts. "We gotta keep our wits about us and shit." He has his hands in his pockets, nervously kneading the change and the penknife that he has stashed in there. "April and her family are good people, Philip, we gotta behave ourselves."

"Yes, Mom," Philip says with a cold smile.

"Hey, you guys, check out that building down there on the corner."

Nick is pointing at a squat, ugly brick edifice on the northeast corner of the closest intersection. Blackened around the edges with the fumes of the city, the faded letters painted above the first-floor display windows say DILLARD'S HOME FURNISHINGS.

Philip sees it. "What about it?"

"Look at the front corner of the building, there's a pedestrian thing."

"A what?"

"A walkway or a breezeway or whatever you call it. See it?"

Sure enough, Philip sees a grimy glass bridge spanning the adjacent street, connecting the office building catty-corner to them to Dillard's second floor. The glass-encased footbridge is empty and sealed at either end. "What are you thinking, Nicky?"

"I don't know." Nick stares at the pedestrian bridge, pondering. "Could be—"

"Gentlemen!" The husky boom of the old man's voice interrupts.

Brian turns and sees David Chalmers trundling toward them from the open stairwell door. Urgency burns in the old man's eyes, and he drags his oxygen tank along with a practiced limp. Brian takes a step toward him. "Mr. Chalmers, did you get all the way up here by yourself?"

The old man is breathing hard as he approaches. Through his wheezing, rattling breaths, he says, "I may be old and sick, but I ain't helpless . . . and call me David. I see y'all cleaned out them floors real nice and tidy, and for that I thank you, I truly do."

Philip and Nick turn and face the man. "Is there a problem?" Philip asks.

"Hell yeah, there's a problem," the old man says, eyes flashing with anger. "What you been doin' up here, pitchin' them bodies off the roof like that? You're just cutting off your own *feet!*"

"What do you mean?"

The old man lets out a grunt. "Y'all deaf or somethin'? You can't hear that?"

"Hear what?"

The old man shuffles out to the edge of the roof. "Take a gander." He points a gnarled finger at two buildings in the distance. "You see what you done?"

Philip gazes off to the north, and all at once he realizes why he's been hearing that infernal noise of a thousand and one moans for the past fifteen minutes. Legions of zombies are migrating toward their building, most likely drawn to the noise and spectacle of bodies hitting the pavement.

Maybe ten or twelve blocks away now, they move with the undulating slither of blood clots traveling down arteries. For a moment, Philip can't tear his eyes away from the hideous migration.

They're coming from all directions. Percolating through the shadows, oozing out of alleys, choking the main drags, they meet up and multiply at intersections like a great amoeba growing in size and strength, inexorably drawn to the catalyst of humans in their midst. Philip looks away finally and pats the old man on the shoulder. "Our bad, David . . . our bad."

• • •

That night, they try to eat dinner and pretend that it's just an ordinary meal among friends, but the persistent clawing noises outside the building keep killing the conversation. The sounds are a constant reminder of their exile, of the mortal threat just outside their door, of their isolation. They tell each other their life stories, and they try to make the best of it, but the menacing noises keep everybody on edge.

Considering there are seventeen other apartments in the building, they had expected to harvest a bounty of provisions from the upper floors that day. But all they found was a few dry goods in the pantries, some cereal and hard pasta, maybe half a dozen cans of soup, a bunch of stale crackers, and a few bottles of cheap grocery store wine.

It had been weeks now since the building lay abandoned, without power, infested with the dead, and all the food had rotted. Maggots crawled in most refrigerators, and even the bedding and the clothes and the furniture had mildewed and soured with the stink of zombies. Maybe folks took their essentials with them when they fled. Maybe they took all the bottled water and batteries and flashlights and wooden matches and weapons.

They left their medicine cabinets untouched, though, and Tara manages to collect a shoe box full of pills: tranquilizers like Xanax and Valium, stimulants like Adderall and Ritalin, blood pressure meds, diet pills, beta-blockers, anti-depressants, and cholesterol medications. She also finds a couple of bottles of bronchodilators that will serve the old man well. Philip gets a kick out of Tara's flimsy pretense of being concerned for everybody's health when he knows full well she is mostly interested in anything that will provide her with a recreational buzz. And who the hell can blame her? Pharmaceutical relief in this situation is as good an escape as any.

The truth is, by that second night, despite the constant din of the undead outside their windows, the Chalmers family has begun to grow on Philip. He likes them. He likes their Bohemian-country style, he likes their pluck, and he just plain likes being with other survivors. Nick also seems reenergized by the union of the two families, and Penny is actually talking again, her eyes clear for the first time in weeks. The presence of other females, in Philip's estimation, is just what the doctor ordered for his daughter.

Even Brian, his chest cold almost completely gone now, seems stronger, more confident. He still has a long way to go, in Philip's humble opinion, but he seems galvanized by the possibility of some kind of community, no matter how small and ragged.

The next day, they begin settling into a routine. From the roof Philip and Nick keep track of the zombie quotient on the streets, while Brian checks the weak spots around the first floor—the windows, the fire escapes, the courtyard, the front foyer. Penny is getting to know the Chalmers sisters, and David mostly keeps to himself. The old man is battling his lung disease as best he can. He naps and takes his inhaler and visits with the newcomers as much as possible.

In the afternoon, Nick starts working on a makeshift catwalk, which he plans to run between the roof of the apartment building and the roof of the neighboring structure. He's got it in his head that he can make it to the pedestrian bridge at the corner without ever having to set foot on ground level. Philip thinks he's crazy but tells him to go ahead and waste his time if he wants to.

Nick believes this maneuver is actually the key to their survival, especially since they are all secretly concerned—you can see it on the face of anyone who goes into the kitchen—that they will soon run out of supplies. The water is turned off in the building, and carrying bucketfuls of human waste from the bathroom to the back window overlooking the courtyard (for dumping) is the least of their problems. They have a limited supply of water, and *that* has everybody very worried.

After dinner that night, at a little after about eight o'clock, when an awkward silence in the conversation reminds everybody of the unrelenting noises coming from the dark outside, Philip gets an idea.

"Why don't y'all play something for us," he says. "Drown those bastards out."

"Hey," Brian says, his eyes lighting up. "That's a great idea."

"We're a little rusty," the old man says from his rocker. He looks tired and drawn tonight, the sickness working on him. "If you want to know the truth, we haven't strummed a note since this all started up."

"Chicken," Tara remarks from the couch, rolling a number with the flecks of tobacco, seeds, and stems at the bottom of her little Band-Aid canister. The others sit around the living room, ears perking up at the prospect of hearing the World Famous Chalmers Family Band.

"Come on, Daddy," April chimes in. "We can play 'The Old Rugged Cross' for 'em."

"Naw, they don't want to hear no religious claptrap, occasion such as this."

Tara is already maneuvering her portly self across the room toward her gigantic bass fiddle case, her makeshift cigarette dangling from her lip. "You name it, Daddy, I'll slap a bass line to it."

"Aw, what could it hurt?" David Chalmers relents as he levers his creaking body out of the rocker.

The Chalmers dig their instruments out of their cases, and then tune up. When they're ready, they seem to position themselves in a tight formation before they begin, as synchronized as a marine drill team, with April in front, on guitar, and David and Tara on the flanks in back, on mandolin and bass respectively. Philip can just imagine them on the stage at the Grand Ole Opry, and he can see Brian soaking it all in across the room. One thing about Brian Blake, he knows his music. Philip has always marveled at his brother's depth of knowledge on the subject, and now, with this unexpected boon, Philip figures that Brian must be delighted.

They start playing.

Philip gets very still.

It feels as though his heart is suddenly being inflated with helium.

It's not just the stark and unexpected beauty of their music—that first number a lovely old Irish jig, with a sad, thumping bass line and a rolling guitar pattern that sounds like a hundred-year-old hurdy-gurdy. Nor is it the fact that sweet little Penny seems suddenly transported by the melody as she sits on the floor, her eyes going all dreamy. Nor is it the fact that a simple, delicate tune in the face of all this ugliness practically breaks Philip's heart. It's the moment when April begins to sing that floods Philip's soul with electric honey:

There's a shadow on my wall, but it don't
  scare me at all
I'm happy all night long in my dreams

As clean and crisp as a glass bell, with perfect pitch, April's spectacular, velvety alto voice rings in the room. It caresses the notes, and even has a hint of the church in it, a slight soulful sauciness that reminds Philip of a choir singer in a country chapel:

> In my dreams, in my dreams
> I'm happy all night long in my dreams
> I'm safe here in my bed, happy thoughts
>   are in my head
> And I'm happy all night long in my
>   dreams

The voice awakens an aching desire in Philip—something he hasn't felt since Sarah died. He has X-ray vision all of a sudden. He can see little things about April Chalmers as she strums her six-string and warbles joyously that he hadn't noticed before. He sees a tiny anklet chain around her ankle, and a small tattoo of a rose inside the crook of her arm, and the pale half-moons of her breasts—as white as mother-of-pearl—between the bunched buttons of her blouse.

The song comes to an end and everybody applauds—Philip's clapping the most vigorous of all.

The next day, after a meager breakfast of stale cereal and powdered milk, Philip notices April, off to herself, near the front door, putting on her hiking boots, and wrapping the sleeves of her sweatshirt with duct tape.

"Thought you might like a second cup," Philip says to her innocently, coming up to her with a cup of coffee in each hand. "It's instant but it ain't half bad." He notices her wrapping her ankles with tape. "What the hell are you doing?"

She looks at the coffee. "You use the rest of that gallon jug for that?"

"I guess so."

"We got one more gallon to last the seven of us until the twelfth of never."

"What do you got in that head of yours?"

"Don't make a big deal out of it." She zips up her sweatshirt, and tightens the rubber band on her ponytail, tucking it into the hood. "I've been planning this for a while, and I want to do it by myself."

"Planning what?"

She reaches into the front coat closet and pulls out a metal baseball bat. "We found this thing in one of the apartments, knew it'd be useful one day."

"What are you doing, April?"

"You know that fire escape ladder on the south side of the building?"

"You're not going out there by yourself."

"I can slip out 3F, climb down the ladder, and draw the Biters away from the building."

"No . . . *no*."

"Draw them away long enough to go get supplies and slip back in."

Philip sees his own filthy logger boots by the door, where he left them the night before. "Mind handing me those boots?" he says. "If your mind's made up, you sure as shit ain't doing this alone."

twelve

Once again, it's the smell that first jabs him sharply in the face as he leans out the south window of apartment 3F—a coppery gumbo of human waste slow cooked in bacon fat—an odor that is so horrendous it makes Philip flinch. His eyes start watering as he shimmies through the opening. He doesn't think he will *ever* get used to that smell.

He climbs out onto a rusty, ramshackle cast-iron landing. The platform, which is connected to a ladder that zigzags down three floors to a side street, wobbles under Philip's weight. His stomach lurches with the sudden shift in gravity, and he braces himself against the rails.

The weather has turned dreary and damp, the sky the color of asphalt, with a northeast wind curling through the distant concrete canyons. Luckily, down below, a minimum number of Biters are roaming the narrow side street running along the south side of the apartment building. Philip glances at his watch.

In roughly one minute and forty-five seconds, April is going to be risking her life in front of the building, and this urgency gets Philip going. He quickly climbs down the first flight, the rickety ladder groaning with his weight, trembling with each step.

As he descends, he senses the silver eyes of dead things noticing him, drawn by the metallic rattle of the ladder, their primitive senses tracking him, smelling him, sensing his vibrations like spiders sensing a fly in their web. Dark silhouettes, glimpsed in his peripheral vision, start lazily shuffling toward him, more and more of them coming around the front of the building to investigate.

They ain't seen nothing yet, he thinks as he drops to the ground and then runs across the street. Sixty-five seconds. The plan is to get in and get out quickly, and Philip moves along the boarded storefronts with the stealth of a Delta Force marine. He reaches the east end of the block and finds an abandoned Chevy Malibu with out-of-state plates.

Thirty-five seconds.

Philip can hear the shuffling footsteps closing in on him as he crouches behind the Malibu and quickly slips his backpack off. His hands do not shake as he digs out the sixteen-ounce bottle of

Coke filled with gasoline (April had found a spare plastic tank of gas in the apartment building's basement maintenance room).

Twenty-five seconds.

He twists the cap, stuffs in the gas-soaked rag, and shoves the pointed end in the Malibu's tailpipe, letting a twelve-inch length of rag dangle. Twenty seconds. He digs out a Bic lighter, sparks it, and sets the rag alight. Fifteen seconds. He runs away.

Ten seconds.

He makes it across the street, brushing past a cluster of Biters, and into a dark alcove, diving behind a row of garbage cans, before he hears the *WHOOMP* of that first eruption—the bottle catching in the tailpipe—followed by a much bigger explosion.

Philip ducks and covers as a sonic boom shakes the street and sends up a fireball that turns the shadows into well-lighted places.

Right on time, April thinks as she crouches down in the shadows of the foyer, the concussion blast rattling the glass door. The light popping overhead is like an unseen photographer's strobe. She peers out through the bottom half of the barred door and glimpses the sea change in the ocean of dead.

Like a moving tide of ragged, livid faces, shifting with the gravitational tug of the moon, they start following the noise and light, heading in a disorganized mass toward the south side of the building.

Tinsel shimmering in the sun couldn't attract a flock of sparrows better than this explosion works on these Biters. Within a minute or so, the street in front of the building is practically deserted.

April girds herself. She takes a deep breath. She secures the straps of her duffel bags. She closes her eyes. She says a quick, silent prayer . . . and then she springs up, yanks the cross-brace, and shoves the door open.

She creeps outside. The wind tosses her hair, and the stench strangles her. She stays low as she darts across the street.

The sensory overload threatens to distract her—the smells, the proximity of the horde half a block away, the thunderous beating of her heart—as she frantically moves from dark storefront to dark storefront. Thankfully, she is familiar enough with the neighborhood to know where the convenience store is located.

If measured by the clock, it only takes April Chalmers eleven minutes and thirty-three seconds to slip through the jagged maw of broken glass and visit the ransacked interior of the convenience store. Only eleven and half minutes to fill one and a half canvas bags with enough food and water and miscellaneous stuff to keep them going for quite a while.

But to April Chalmers, those eleven and half minutes feel suspended in time.

She grabs nearly twenty pounds of groceries from the convenience store—including a small canned ham with enough preservatives to keep until Christmas, two gallons of filtered water, three cartons of Marlboro reds, lighters, beef jerky, vitamins, cold remedies, antibacterial ointment, and six extra large rolls of blessed, blessed toilet paper—throwing it all in her duffel bag with lightning speed.

The back of her neck prickles as she works with constant awareness of the ticking clock. The street will fill up again soon and the army of Biters will block her path if she doesn't get back within minutes.

Philip goes through another half a clip of .22-caliber rounds, working his way back around the rear of the apartment building. The majority of the Biters are now clustered around the flaming debris of the Malibu, a riot of moving corpses like June bugs drawn to the light. Philip clears a path around the back of the courtyard by squeezing off two shots. One of them cracks open the cranium of a lumbering cadaver dressed in a running suit, the zombie dropping like a puppet whose strings have been cut. Another blast opens a trough in the top of a skull belonging to what looks like a former homeless woman, her geode eyes flickering out as she falls.

Before the other Biters have a chance to close in on him, he vaults over the rear fence of the courtyard and charges across the leprous brown grass.

He climbs up the back wall of the building, using an awning as a foothold. A second fire escape ladder is folded halfway up the stucco wall of the first story, and Philip gets a grip on it and starts to pull himself the rest of the way up.

But all at once, he pauses, and has second thoughts about the plan.

April reaches the critical point in her mission—twelve minutes have elapsed since she emerged—but she risks visiting one more merchant.

Half a block south, an Ace Hardware store sits empty, its display windows broken, its burglar gates loose enough for a smallish woman to negotiate. She slips through the gap and enters the dark store.

She fills the remainder of the second canvas bag with water filters (for making the standing water in toilets drinkable), a box of nails (to replenish their supply, which they used securing the barricades), markers and rolls of large-format paper (for making signs to alert any other survivors), light bulbs, batteries, a few cans of Sterno, and three small flashlights.

On her way back toward the front of the store, now lugging nearly forty pounds of merchandise in two bulging duffels, she passes a figure slumped at the end of a side aisle stacked with fiberglass insulation.

April pauses. The dead girl on the floor, slumped and leaning against the far wall, is missing one leg. From the snail-trail of gore leading across the floor, it's clear that the thing dragged itself here. The dead girl is not much older than Penny. April gapes for a moment.

She knows she has to get out of there but she can't tear her gaze from the pathetic, ragged corpse sitting in its own juices, which have obviously leaked out of the blackened stump where its right leg used to be.

"Oh God, I can't," April says under her breath, to herself, uncertain what it is she can't do: Put the thing out of its misery, or leave it to suffer for eternity in this deserted hardware store.

April pulls the metal bat from her belt and sets down her packs. She approaches cautiously. The dead thing on the floor hardly moves, just slowly gazes up with the trembling stupor of a fish dying on the deck of a boat.

"I'm sorry," April whispers, and buries the end of the bat in the girl's skull. The blow makes the wet, snapping noise of green wood breaking.

The zombie folds silently to the floor. But April stands there, closing her eyes for a moment, trying to will the image from her mind, an image that will probably haunt her for the rest of her life.

Seeing the shank of the bat cleave open a skull is bad enough, but what April just saw in the horrible brief instant before she brought the bat down, as she was drawing it back, winding up, was this: Either through some meaningless flicker of deadened nerves, or through some deeper understanding, the dead girl turned her face away in that moment before the bat arced down.

A noise near the front of the store gets her attention and she hurries back to her duffel bags, throws the straps over her shoulders, and starts toward the exit. But she doesn't get far. She slams on the brakes when she sees a *second* young girl blocking her path.

It stands fifteen feet away, just inside the mangled burglar screens, in the identical soiled dress as that of the girl April just dispatched.

At first, April thinks her eyes are playing tricks. Or maybe it's the ghost of the girl she just put down. Or maybe April is losing her mind. But as the second dead girl starts shuffling down the aisle toward April with black drool falling off its cracked lips—this one has both its legs—April realizes that it's a *twin*.

It's the other girl's identical twin.

"Here we go," April says, drawing back the bat, dropping her load, preparing to fight her way out.

She takes one step toward the pint-sized monster, raising the bat, when a dry popping blast rings out behind the twin, and April blinks.

The bullet shatters a corner of the front window and takes off the top of the twin's head. April flinches back at the kick of blood mist, as the girl collapses in a heap. April lets out a pained sigh of relief.

Philip Blake stands outside the store, out in the middle of the empty street, clicking a new magazine into his .22-caliber Ruger.

"You in there?" he calls.

"I'm here! I'm okay!"

"I know it ain't polite to rush a lady but they're comin' back!"

April grabs her treasures, and then leaps over the bloody remains blocking the aisle and slips through the burglar gate and out into the street. Instantly, she sees the problem: The throng of zombies is returning, coming around the corner with the collective fervor of a demented chorus line moving in haphazard formation.

Philip grabs one of the bags and they both make a run for the apartment building.

They cross the street in seconds flat, with at least fifty Biters on either flank.

Brian and Nick are peering out the reinforced glass of the outer vestibule door when they see the situation in the street rapidly changing.

They see wolf packs of zombies coming down the street from both directions, returning from wherever the hell they had just gone. In the midst of all this, two human beings, one male and one female, like ball carriers in some obscure, surreal, twisted sport, come charging toward the apartment building with duffel bags slung and bouncing against their backs. Nick perks up.

"There they are!"

"Thank God," Brian says, lowering the Marlin shotgun until the butt rests on the floor. He's shaking. He shoves his left hand in his pocket, and he tries to get a grip on himself. He does not want his brother to see him shaking.

"Let's get the door open," Nick says, leaning his shotgun in the corner.

He gets the door open just as Philip and April are roaring up the walk, a multitude of Biters on their heels. April roars through the doorway first, shaking and hyperventilating with adrenaline.

Philip follows her in, his dark eyes aglow with testosterone-fueled mania. "That's what I'm talkin' about!"

Nick slams the door just in time. Three Biters crash into the outer glass, rattling the steel-impregnated door, their drooling mouths leaving streaks. Several pairs of milky-white eyes gaze in through the greasy glass at the people in the foyer. Dead fingers claw at the door. Other Biters are staggering up the walk.

Brian has his shotgun raised at the figures outside the door. He backs away. "What the hell is going on, man! Where were you guys?"

Nick ushers them through the inner door and into the foyer. April drops her bulging duffel. "That was—that was—*Jesus,* that was close!"

Philip sets down his pack. "Girl, you got some *cojones*, I'll give you that."

Nick steps up. "What's the idea, Philly! You guys just disappear without telling anybody?"

"Talk to *her,*" Philip says with a grin, shoving his Ruger inside his belt.

"We were totally freaking out!" Nick rants. "We were about one second away from going outside to look for you!"

"Calm down, Nicky."

"Calm down? Calm *down!* We were turning the place upside down looking for you! Tara was about to have a shit fit!"

"It's my fault," April says, wiping the grime from her neck.

"Look at our take, man!" Philip indicates the loot stuffed into the bags.

Nick has his fists clenched. "Then we hear a fucking *explosion?* What are we supposed to think? Was that *you* guys? Did you have something to do with that?"

Philip and April exchange a glance, and Philip says, "That idea was kinda both of ours."

April cannot stifle her victorious grin as Philip takes a step toward her, raising his hand. "How about a high five, darlin'?"

They high-five each other, with Nick and Brian

staring in disbelief. Nick is about to say something else when a figure appears on the other side of the foyer, pushing through the inner door.

"Oh my God!" Tara storms into the room and goes to her sister. She pulls April into a bear hug. "Oh my God, I was so freaked! Thank God you're okay! Thank God! Thank *God!*"

April pats her sister. "I'm sorry, Tara, it was something I had to do."

Tara lets go, her face flashing with anger. "I ought to beat the *shit* outta you. Seriously! I'm telling that little girl you're just upstairs, but she's getting as freaked as I am! What am I supposed to do? That was a goddamn stupid, irresponsible thing to do! Which is so goddamn typical of you, April!"

"What the hell does that mean?" April gets into her sister's face. "Why don't you say what you mean for once?"

"You fucking *bitch*." Tara winds up like she's going to slap the younger woman when Philip suddenly steps in between them.

"Whoa there, Tonto!" Philip gives Tara a reassuring pat. "Hold on a second. Take a deep breath, sis." Philip nods toward the duffel bags. "I want to show you something. Okay? Just cool your pits for a second."

He kneels down and unzips the bags, displaying the contents.

The others stare silently at the supplies. Philip

straightens back up and looks Tara in the eyes. "That 'fucking bitch' there saved our asses today—there's food and water in there. That 'fucking bitch' risked her ass, not knowing if she'd be able to pull it off and not wanting anybody else to get hurt. You ought to be kissing that 'fucking bitch's' feet."

Tara looks away from the duffel bags and looks down at the floor. "We were worried, that's all," she says in a feeble, low voice.

Nick and Brian are now both kneeling by the duffel bags, looking through the treasures. "Philly," Nick says, "I have to admit: You guys kicked *ass*."

"You guys rock," Brian mutters almost under his breath with awe as he rifles through the toilet paper and the beef jerky and the water filters. The emotional atmosphere in the room begins to shift with the slow certainty of clouds parting. Smiles appear on all their faces.

Soon, even Tara is throwing grudging glances over their shoulders at the contents of the duffel bags. "Any cigarettes in there?"

"Here's three cartons of Reds," April says, leaning down and digging out the cigarettes. "Enjoy them, you fucking bitch."

With a good-natured smile, she hurls the cartons at her sister.

Everybody laughs.

Nobody sees the small figure standing across the

room, in the inner doorway, until Brian glances up. "Penny? You okay, kiddo?"

The little girl pushes the door open and walks into the foyer. She is still dressed in her pajamas, and her little peaches-and-cream face is chiseled with seriousness. "That man in there? Mr. Chah-merz? He just fell down."

They find David Chalmers on the floor of the master bedroom, amid a litter of tissues and medications. Granules of broken glass from a fallen aftershave bottle sparkle like a halo around his trembling head.

"Jesus!—Daddy!" Tara kneels by the fallen man, pulling his oxygen tube free. David's grizzled face is the color of nicotine as he involuntarily gasps for air, a fish out of water trying to breathe the poisonous atmosphere.

"He's choking!" April hurries around to the other side of the bed, checking the oxygen tank, which lies on the floor on its side near the window, tangled in its tubing. The old man must have pulled it off the bedside table when he fell.

"Daddy? Can you hear me?" Tara gives the man's ashen face a series of quick, light slaps.

"Check his tongue!"

"Daddy? Daddy?"

"Check his tongue, Tara!" April rushes back around the bed, the oxygen tank and a coil of tubing in her hands. While she does this, the others—Philip, Nick, Brian, and Penny—watch from the doorway. Philip feels helpless. He doesn't know whether to jump in or just watch. The girls seem to know what they're doing.

Tara gently levers open the old man's mouth, looking down his gullet. "It's clear."

"Dad?" April kneels on the other side of him, positioning the tiny breathing apparatus under his hooked nose. "Daddy, can you hear me?"

David Chalmers keeps silently gasping, the back of his throat clucking painfully like a record skipping. His eyelids—as ancient and translucent as a mayfly's wings—begin fluttering. Tara frantically feels under the back of his skull for signs of injury. "I don't see any bleeding," she says. "Daddy?"

April feels his forehead. "He's ice-cold."

"Is the oxygen running?"

"Full blast."

"Daddy?" April gently repositions the old man so he's lying supine with the oxygen tube across his upper lip. Again they give him little slaps. "Daddy? Daddy? Daddy, can you hear us? Daddy?"

The old man coughs, eyes fluttering. He blinks. He tries to get a good lungful of air, but his shallow breaths keep hitching in his throat. His eyes are rolled back in his head, and he appears to be only semiconscious.

"Daddy, look at me," April says, her hand gently turning his face toward hers. "Can you see me?"

"Let's get him on the bed," Tara suggests. "Fellas, you mind giving us a hand?"

Philip, Nick, and Brian step into the room. Philip and Nick take one side of the old man, and Tara and Brian the other, and on the count of three, they carefully lift the old man off the floor and lay him on the bed, making the springs squeak and tangling the tube on one side.

Moments later, they have the tube clear and the old man covered in blankets. Only his pale, sunken face is visible above the linens, his eyes shut, his mouth lolled open, and his breathing coming in fits and starts. He sounds like a combustion engine that refuses to turn over. Every few moments, his eyelids flutter and something flickers behind them—lips stretched into a grimace—but then his face goes slack. He is still breathing . . . barely.

Tara and April sit on either side of the bed, stroking the lanky form under the blankets. For a long while, nobody says anything. But chances are, they're all thinking the same thing.

"You think it's a stroke?" Brian asks softly, minutes later, sitting out by the sliding glass doors.

"I don't know, I don't know." April paces the living room, chewing her fingernails, while the others sit around the room, watching her. Tara is in the bedroom, at her father's bedside. "Without medical attention, what chance does he have?"

"Has anything like this ever happened before?"

"He's had trouble breathing before but nothin' like this." April stops pacing. "God, I knew this day was gonna come." She wipes her eyes, which are moist with tears. "We're on the last tank of oxygen."

Philip asks about medication.

"We got his medicine, sure, but that ain't gonna do him much good now. He needs a doctor. Stubborn old coot blew off his last appointment a month ago."

"What do we have in the way of medical supplies?" Philip asks her.

"I don't know, we got some shit from upstairs, antihistamines and shit." April paces some more. "We got first-aid kits. Big deal. This is serious. I don't know what we're gonna do."

"Let's stay calm and think this thing through." Philip wipes his mouth. "He's resting peacefully now, right? His airways are clear. You never know, something like this . . . he could bounce back."

"But what if he doesn't?" She stops moving and looks at him. "What if he doesn't bounce back?"

Philip gets up and goes over to her. "Listen. We gotta keep our heads clear." He pats her shoulder. "We'll keep a close watch on him, we'll figure something out. He's a tough old bird."

"He's a tough old bird who's dying," April says, a single tear tracking down her face.

"You don't know that," Philip says, wiping the tear from her cheek.

She looks at him. "Good try, Philip."

"Come on."

"Good try." She looks away, her crestfallen expression as desolate as a death mask. "Good try."

That night, the Chalmers girls sit watch at their father's bedside, their chairs drawn up on either side of the bed, a battery-powered lantern painting the old man's pallid face in pale light. The apartment is as cold as a meat locker. April can see Tara's breath across the room.

The old man lies there for most of the night in stony repose, his hollow cheeks contracting periodically with his labored breathing. The grizzled whiskers of his chin look like metal filings, shifting in a magnetic field, moving occasionally with the tics of his stricken nervous system. Every once in a while his dry, cracked lips will begin to work impotently, trying to form a word. But other than little dry puffs of air, nothing comes out.

At some point in the wee hours, April notices that Tara has dozed off, her head down on the edge of the bed. April grabs a spare blanket and carefully drapes it over her sister. She hears a voice.

"Lil?"

It's coming from the old man. His eyes are still closed, but his mouth is working furiously, his expression furrowed with anger. Lil is short for Lillian, David's late wife. April hasn't heard the nickname in years.

"Daddy, it's April," she whispers, touching his cheek. He recoils, his eyes still closed. His mouth is contorted, his voice slurred and drunken with nerve damage on one side of his face.

"Lil, get the dogs in! There's a storm comin'—a big one—a nor'easter!"

"Daddy, wake up," April whispers softly. Emotion wells up inside her.

"Lil, where are you?"

"Daddy?"

Silence.

"Daddy?"

At this point, Tara is sitting up, blinking, startled at the sound of her father's strangled voice. "What's going on?" she says, rubbing her eyes.

"Daddy?"

The silence continues, the old man's breaths coming hard and fast now.

"Da—"

The word sticks in April's throat as she sees something horrible crossing the old man's face. His eyelids flick open to half-mast, the whites of his eyes showing, and he begins to speak in an alarmingly clear voice: "The devil has plans for us."

In the gloomy half-light of the lantern, the two sisters exchange mortified glances.

The voice that comes out of David Chalmers is low and gravelly, an engine dieseling: "The day of reckoning is drawing near . . . the Deceiver walks among us."

He falls silent, his head lolling to one side of the pillow as if the wires to his brain have been abruptly cut.

Tara checks his pulse.

She looks at her sister.

April looks at her father's face, his expression now slackened and relaxed into a sanguine, tranquil mask of deep and endless sleep.

With the morning's light, Philip stirs in his sleeping bag on the living room floor. He sits up and rubs his sore neck, his joints stiff from the cold. For a moment, he lets his eyes adjust to the gloomy light, and he orients himself to his surroundings. He sees Penny on the sofa, cocooned in blankets, sound asleep. He sees Nick and Brian across the room, also encased in blankets, also asleep. The memory of the previous evening's deathwatch returns to Philip in stages, the agonizing, hopeless struggle to help the old man and to assuage April's fears.

He glances across the room. In the shadows of the adjacent hallway, the door to the master bedroom is visible in the gloom, still closed.

Climbing out of his sleeping bag, Philip hurriedly and silently gets dressed. He pulls on his pants and pushes on his boots. He runs fingers through his hair and goes into the kitchen to rinse his mouth out. He hears the murmur of voices behind the walls. He goes over to the bedroom door and listens. He hears Tara's voice.

She's praying.

Philip knocks softly.

A moment later, the door clicks open and April is standing there, looking as though someone threw acid in her eyes. They are so bloodshot and wet that they look scourged. " 'Morning," she says in a low whisper.

"How's he doing?"

Her lips tremble. "He ain't."

"What?"

"He's gone, Philip."

Philip stares at her. "Aw God . . ." He swallows hard. "I'm real sorry, April."

"Yeah, well."

She starts to cry. After an awkward moment—a wave of contrary emotions punching through Philip's gut—he pulls her into an embrace. He holds her, and he strokes the back of her head. She trembles in his arms like a lost child. Philip doesn't know what to say. Over April's shoulder, he can see into the room.

Tara Chalmers is kneeling by the deathbed, praying silently, her head down on the tangled linen. One of her hands is lying on the cold, gnarled hand of her late father. For some reason that Philip can't figure out, he finds it difficult to take his eyes off the sight of the girl's hand caressing the bloodless fingers of the dead.

"I can't get her to come out of there." April is sitting at the kitchen table, sipping a cup of weak, tepid tea brewed on a Sterno can. Her eyes are clear for the first time since she came out of the death room that morning. "Poor thing . . . I think she's trying to pray him back to life."

"No shame in that," Philip says. He sits across the table from her, a half-eaten bowl of rice in front of him. He has no appetite.

"Have you thought about what you want to do?" Brian asks from across the kitchen. He stands at the sink where he's pouring water, which was collected from some of the toilets upstairs, into filter canisters.

The sounds of Nick and Penny playing cards in the other room drift in.

April looks up at Brian. "Do about what?"

"Your father . . . you know . . . like, burialwise?"

April sighs. "You've been through this before, haven't you?" she says to Philip.

Philip looks at his uneaten rice. He has no idea if she's talking about Bobby Marsh or Sarah Blake, both of whose deaths Philip recounted to April the other night. "Yes, ma'am, that's true." He looks at her. "Whatever you want to do, we'll help you do it."

"Of *course* we'll bury him." Her voice breaks a little bit. She looks down. "I just never pictured myself doing it in a place like this."

"We'll do it together," Philip says. "We'll do it right and proper."

April looks down, a tear falling into her tea. "I hate this."

"We gotta stick together," Philip says without much conviction. He says it because he doesn't know what else to say.

April wipes her eyes. "There's a patch of ground out back under the—"

A sharp noise from the hallway interrupts, and all heads turn.

A muffled thump is followed by a crash, the sound of furniture overturning.

Philip is out of his chair before the others even realize that the noise is coming from behind the closed door of the master bedroom.

thirteen

Philip kicks the door open. Advent candles on the floor. The carpet burning in places. The smoky air vibrating with screams. A blur of movement smears across the darkness and it takes breathless nanoseconds for Philip to realize what he's looking at in the flickering shadows.

The overturned dresser—the source of the

crashing noise—has landed inches away from Tara, who's on the floor, crawling with animal instinct, trying desperately to pull herself free of the vise grip of dead fingers on her legs.

Dead fingers?

At first, just for an instant, Philip figures something got in through a window, but then he sees the withered form of David Chalmers—completely turned now—on the floor, on top of Tara's legs, digging yellowed fingernails into her flesh. The old man's sunken face is livid now, the color of mold, his eyes frosted with glassy-white cataracts. He snarls with a ravenous guttural groan.

Tara manages to extricate herself and struggles to her feet, and then slams sideways into the wall.

Right then, many things happen at once: Philip realizes what's going on, and that he left his gun in the kitchen, and that he has a limited amount of time to eradicate this threat.

That is the key—the fact that the kindly old mandolin player is long gone—and what *this* is, this hulking mass of dead tissue rising up and growling a garbled, drooling cry, is a *threat*. More than the flames licking across the carpet, more than the smoke—already forming a nightmarish haze in the room—this *thing* that has materialized inside their sanctuary is the biggest threat.

A threat to all of them.

At this same moment, before Philip has a chance

to even move, the others arrive, filling the open doorway. April lets out an anguished yelp—not really a scream, more like a shriek of pain, like an animal getting gut shot. She pushes her way into the room, but Brian grabs her and holds her back. April writhes in his arms.

All this happens in the space of an instant as Philip sees the bat.

In all the excitement on the previous night, April had left her Hank Aaron autographed metal baseball bat in the corner by the barred window. Now it sits gleaming in the flickering flames, maybe fifteen feet away from Philip. There is no time to consider the distance or even map out a maneuver in his mind. All he has time to do is make a lunge across the room.

By this point, Nick has whirled around and is racing across the apartment for his gun. Brian tries to pull April out of the room, but she's strong and she's frantic and she's screaming now.

It takes Philip mere seconds to cover the distance between the door and the bat. But in that brief span of time, the thing that was once David Chalmers goes for Tara. Before the large woman can get her bearings and flee the room, the dead man is upon her.

Cold, gray fingers ply themselves awkwardly toward her throat. She slams back against the wall, flailing at it, trying to push it away. Rotting jaws part, rancid breath wafting up in her face.

Blackened teeth gape open. The thing goes for the pale, fleshy curve of her jugular.

Tara shrieks, but before the teeth have a chance to make contact, the bat comes down.

Up until this moment—especially for Philip—the act of vanquishing a moving corpse had become an almost perfunctory deed, as mechanical and obligatory as stunning a pig for the slaughter. But this feels different. It takes only three sharp blows.

The first one—a hard crack to the back temporal region of David Chalmers's skull—stiffens the zombie and arrests its progress toward Tara's neck. She slips to the floor in a paroxysm of tears and snot.

The second blow strikes the side of the skull as the thing is involuntarily turning toward its attacker, the tempered steel of the bat caving in the parietal bone and part of the nasal cavity, sending threads of pink matter into the air.

The third and final whack totals the entire left hemisphere of its skull as the thing is falling—the sound like a head of cabbage smashed in a drill press. The monster that was David Chalmers lands in a wet heap on one of the spilled candles, the ribbons of drool, blood, and gluey gray tissue hitting the flames and sizzling across the floor.

Philip stands over the body, out of breath, his hands still welded to the bat. Almost as punctuation to the horror, a high-pitched beeping noise begins to shrill. Battery-operated fire alarms across the first floor are loudly chirping, and it takes Philip a second to identify the sounds in his ringing ears. He drops the bloody bat.

And *that* is when he notices the difference. *This* time, after *this* extermination, nobody moves. April stares from the doorway. Brian releases his grip on her, and he *too* gapes. Even Tara, sitting up against the wall across the room, gripped in tears of revulsion and agony, settles into an almost catatonic stare.

The strangest thing is, rather than staring at the bloody heap on the floor, they are all staring at Philip.

In due course, they put out all the fires, and they clean the place up. They wrap the body and move it out into the corridor where it will be safe until burial.

Luckily, Penny witnessed very little of the debacle in the room. She *heard* enough of it, though, to make her withdraw back into her mute, invisible shell.

In fact, for quite a long time, nobody *else* has much to say, either, and the edgy silence continues throughout the rest of that day.

The sisters seem to be in some kind of shocked stupor, just going through the motions of the cleanup, not even talking to each other. They have each cried their eyes dry. But they keep staring at

Philip; he can feel it like cold fingers on the back of his neck. What the hell did they expect? What did they want him to do? Let the monster feed on Tara? Did they want Philip to try and *negotiate* with the thing?

At noon the following day, they hold a makeshift memorial service in a section of the courtyard surrounded by a security fence. Philip insists on digging the grave himself, refusing assistance from even Nick. It takes hours. The Georgia clay is stubborn in this portion of the state. But by mid-afternoon, Philip is drenched in sweat and ready.

The sisters sing David's favorite song—"Will the Circle Be Unbroken"—at his graveside. This reduces both Nick and Brian to tears. The sound of it is heartrending, especially as it carries up into the high blue sky and mingles with the omnipresent choir of groaning noises coming from outside the fence.

Later, they all sit around the living room, sharing the liquor that they had recovered from one of the apartments (and were saving for God knows what). The Chalmers sisters tell stories of their old man, his childhood, his early days in the Barstow Bluegrass Boys Band, and his time as a deejay on WBLR out of Macon. They speak of his temper, and his generosity, and his womanizing, and his devotion to Jesus.

Philip lets them talk and just listens. It's good to

finally hear their voices again, and the tension of the past day seems to be easing a little bit. Maybe it's all part of their process of letting go, or maybe they just need to let it set in.

Later that night, Philip is in the kitchen, alone, refilling his glass with the last couple of fingers of sour mash whiskey, when April comes in.

"Look . . . I wanted to talk to you . . . about what happened and stuff."

"Forget it," Philip says, looking down into the caramel liquid in his glass.

"No, I should have . . . I should have said something sooner, I guess I was in shock."

He looks at her. "I'm sorry it went down like it did, I truly am. I'm sorry you had to see that."

"You did what you had to do."

"And I thank you for saying that." Philip pats her shoulder. "I took an instant liking to your daddy, he was a great piece of work. Lived a long good life."

She chews the inside of her cheek, and Philip can tell she's fighting the urge to cry. "I thought I was prepared for losing him."

"Nobody's ever prepared."

"Yeah, but like *this* . . . I'm still trying to wrap my brain around it."

Philip nods. "Hell of a thing."

"I mean . . . a person doesn't . . . you just don't have any reference point for this kinda shit."

"I know what you mean."

She looks at her hands, which are shaking.

Maybe the memory of Philip bashing her father's skull in is still lingering. "I guess all I wanted to say is . . . I ain't blaming you for what you done."

"Appreciate that."

She looks at his drink. "We got any more of that cheap wine left?"

He finds a little bit left in one of the bottles and pours it for her. They drink in silence for a long while. Philip finally says, "What about your sis?"

"What about her?"

"She doesn't seem to be . . ." His voice trails off, the proper words escaping him.

April nods. "In a forgiving kind of mood?"

"Something like that."

April gives him a bitter smile. "She still blames me for stealing her lunch money back at Clark's Hill Elementary."

Over the next few days, the new blended family solidifies as the Chalmers sisters go through their grieving process, sometimes arguing over nothing, sometimes giving everybody else the silent treatment, sometimes holing up in their rooms for extended periods of crying or brooding.

April seems to be handling the transition better than her sister. She clears out her father's things and moves into the master bedroom, giving Philip the room she originally occupied. Philip sets up a nice area for Penny with shelves and some coloring books he found upstairs.

The child is becoming attached to April. They spend hours together, exploring the upper floors, playing games, and experimenting with ways to stretch their meager provisions into nominal yet creative dinners cooked on Sterno flames, such as crumbled jerky stir-fry, peach and raisin casserole, and canned vegetable surprise (the surprise, sadly, turning out to be more shredded pieces of beef jerky).

Gradually, the hordes of undead drift away from the immediate area, leaving behind only a few stragglers, giving the Blakes and Nick a chance to test the limits of their reconnaissance missions to neighboring buildings. Philip notices that Brian is getting bolder, willing to venture out of the building now and again on quick trips. But it's Nick Parsons who truly seems to be taking to this place.

Nick sets up a room for himself in a studio apartment on the second floor—number 2F—at the east end of the corridor. He finds books and magazines in other apartments, and drags spare furniture into the studio. He spends time hanging out on the balcony, sketching pictures of the neighboring streets, mapping out the immediate area, reading his Bible, starting a garden for winter vegetables, and thinking a lot about what has happened to the human race.

He also completes his ramshackle catwalk between the two adjacent buildings.

The narrow walkway is hewn out of plywood and paint ladders lashed together with rope and duct tape (and more than a little praying). The footbridge extends off the back of the roof, spanning a twenty-five-foot gap over an alley, and connecting up with the top rail of a fire escape on the adjacent roof.

The completion of the catwalk marks a turning point for Nick. Getting up his courage one day, he shimmies across the rickety structure and—just as he had predicted—he makes it all the way to the southeast corner of the block without walking outside. From there, he figures out how to get into the pedestrian bridge to the department store. When he comes back that night with armfuls of goodies from Dillard's, he is greeted like a returning war hero.

He brings them fancy gourmet candy and nuts; warm clothing; new shoes and embossed stationery; expensive pens; a collapsible camp stove; satin sheets and luxurious three-hundred-thread-count linens; and even stuffed animals for Penny. Even Tara lightens up at the sight of the European cigarettes with the pastel wrappers. And Nick is doing something else on these solo runs, something that he keeps to himself at first.

On the one-week anniversary of David Chalmers's death, Nick talks Philip into tagging along on a little reconnaissance mission so Nick can reveal what he's been doing. Philip is not crazy about crossing the ladder-bridge—he claims he's worried about it breaking under his weight, but the thing that truly bothers Philip is his secret fear of heights. Nick persuades him by piquing his curiosity. "You gotta see this, Philly," Nick enthuses on the roof. "This whole area is a goldmine, man. I'm tellin' you it's perfect."

With great reluctance, Philip goes ahead and drags himself across the catwalk, on his hands and knees behind Nick, grumbling all the way (and secretly petrified). Philip doesn't dare look down.

They reach the other side, hop down, descend a fire escape ladder, and then slip into the adjacent building through an open window.

Nick leads Philip through the deserted hallways of an accounting firm, the floors littered with forgotten forms and documents like so many fallen leaves. "Not much farther now," Nick says, ushering Philip down a staircase and across a desolate lobby strewn with overturned furniture.

Philip is hyperaware of their echoing footsteps, crunching over cinders of debris. He feels the blind spots and empty spaces in his solar plexus, he hears every snap and every tick as though something might lumber out at them at any moment. He keeps his hand on the stock of the .22 thrust into his jeans. "Over here, right off the parking garage," Nick says, pointing to an alcove at the end of the lobby.

Around a corner. Past an overturned vending machine. Up a short flight of steps. Through an unmarked metal door, and suddenly, almost without warning, the entire world opens up for Philip.

"Holy mother-of-pearl," Philip marvels as he follows Nick across the pedestrian bridge. The enclosed walkway is filthy, scattered with trash and reeking of urine, the thick, reinforced Plexiglas walls so filmed with grime they distort the surrounding cityscape. But the view is spectacular. The passageway is flooded with light, and it feels like you can see for miles.

Nick pauses. "Pretty cool, huh?"

"Pretty fucking outstanding." Thirty feet above the street, the wind buffeting the structure, Philip can look down and see scattered zombies wandering underneath them like exotic fish drifting below a glass-bottom boat. "If it wasn't for those ugly motherfuckers, I'd show this to Penny."

"That's what I wanted to show *you*." Nick walks over to the south side of the walkway. "You see that bus? About half a block down there?"

Philip sees it—a hulking silver MARTA bus sitting at the curb.

Nick says, "Look above the bus's front door, by the mirror, on the right side, you see the mark?"

Sure enough, Philip sees a hand-drawn symbol above the passenger entrance—a hastily scrawled five-point star—done in red spray paint. "What am I looking at?"

"It's a safe zone."

"A what?"

"Been working my way down that street and up this one back here," Nick tells him with the innocent pride of a kid showing a soapbox derby model to his dad. "There's a barber shop over there, clean as a whistle, secure as a bank, the door unlocked." He points farther up the street. "There's an empty semitrailer up there a ways, in good shape, just sitting there, with a good, strong— whattya call 'em—*accordion door?* On the back end."

"What's the point here, Nicky?"

"Safe zones. Places you can duck into. If you're on a supply run and you get in trouble or whatever. I'm finding them farther and farther down the street. Putting marks on 'em so we don't miss 'em. There's all sorts of cubbyholes out there, you wouldn't believe it."

Philip looks at him. "You've been going all the way down to the end of that street by yourself?"

"Yeah, you know—"

"God*damn*it, Nick. You shouldn't be goin' all the way out there without any backup."

"Philly—"

"No, no . . . don't just 'Philly' me on this, man. I'm serious. I want you to be more careful. You understand? I'm serious about this."

"Okay, okay. You're right." Nick gives Philip a good-natured punch in the arm. "I hear you."

"Good."

"You gotta admit, though, this place rocks. Considering the situation we're in?"

Philip shrugs, looking down through the grimy glass at the cannibal fish circling. "Yeah, I guess."

"It could be a lot worse, Philly. We're not in the tall buildings, it's flat enough around here for you to see your way around. We got plenty of room to spread out at the apartment building, we got stores with supplies within walking distance. I'm even thinking we could find a generator somewhere, maybe hot-wire a car to get it back. I could see us staying here, Philly . . . I don't know . . . for a long time." He thinks about it some more. "Indefinitely . . . you know?"

Philip gazes through the filthy glass at the necropolis of empty buildings, and the ragged monsters meandering in and out of view. "*Everything*'s indefinite nowadays, Nicky."

That night, Brian's cough returns. The weather is getting colder and damper by the day, and it is taking a toll on Brian's immune system. After dark, the apartment is freezing. By morning, it's an icebox, the floor like a skating rink on the soles of Brian's stocking feet. He's taken to wearing three layers of sweaters and a knit scarf that Nick procured from Dillard's. With his fingerless gloves and his thatch of unruly black hair and his hollow Edgar Allan Poe eyes, Brian is starting to look like a waif from a Charles Dickens novel.

"I think this place is really good for Penny," Brian says to Philip that night on a second-floor balcony. The Blake brothers are having an after-dinner drink—more of the cheap wine—and gazing out at the desolate skyline. The cool evening air rustles their hair, and the zombie stink wafts just under the smell of rain.

Brian stares out at the distant silhouettes of dark buildings as if in a trance. For a person in twenty-first-century America, it is almost incomprehensible to see a great metropolis completely dark. But that's exactly what the Blakes are looking at: a skyline so dead and black it looks like a mountain range on a moonless night. Every few moments, Brian thinks he sees the faint glint of a fire or a light twinkling in the black void. But it could very easily be his imagination.

"I think that gal *April* is the thing that's doin' the most good for Penny," Philip says.

"Yeah, she's really good with her." Brian is also growing fond of April, and he's been noticing that Philip may very well have a bit of a crush on her as well. Nothing would make Brian happier than to have Philip find a little peace right now, a little stability with a girlfriend.

"That other one's a slice, though, ain't she?" Philip says.

"Tara? Yeah. Not a happy camper."

For the past few days, Brian has been generally avoiding Tara Chalmers—she is a walking ulcer, always irritable, paranoid, still in the throes of grief over her dad. But Brian figures she'll eventually work her way through it. She seems like a decent person.

"The girl does not realize I saved her fucking life," Philip says.

Brian lets out a series of dry coughs. Then he says, "I've been meaning to talk to you about that."

Philip looks at him. "What."

"The old man turning like that?" Brian measures his words. He knows he's not the only one worrying about this. Ever since David Chalmers came back from the dead and tried to devour his oldest daughter, Brian has been ruminating about the phenomenon, and the implications of what happened, and the rules of this savage new world, and maybe even the prognosis for the entire human race. "Think about it, Philip. He didn't get bit. Right?"

"No, he didn't."

"So, why did he turn?"

For a moment, Philip just stares at Brian, and the darkness seems to expand around them. The city seems to stretch into infinity like the landscape of a dream. Brian feels gooseflesh on his arms as though the very act of putting it into words— saying it out loud—has unleashed a malevolent genie from a bottle. And they will never, ever be able to put that genie back.

Philip sips his wine. In the darkness, his face is grim and set. "Hell of lot we don't know. Maybe he got infected with something earlier, maybe came into contact with just enough of it to start working on his system. The old man was on his way out anyway."

"If that's true, then we all—"

"Hey, professor. Give it a rest. We're all healthy and we're gonna stay that way."

"I know. I'm just saying . . . maybe we ought to think about taking more precautions."

"What precautions? I got your precautions right here." He touches the stock of his .22-caliber Ruger stuffed behind his belt.

"I'm talking about washing up better, sterilizing stuff."

"With what?"

Brian lets out a sigh and looks up at the overcast night sky, a low canopy of haze as dark as black wool. Autumn rains are brewing. "We got the water upstairs in the toilets," he says. "We got the filters and the propane, and we got access to cleaning products down the street, soaps and cleansers and shit."

"We're already filtering the water, sport."

"Yeah, but—"

"And we're washing up with that contraption Nicky found." The so-called contraption is an outdoor camp shower that Nick found in Dillard's sporting goods department. About the size of a small cooler, it has a collapsible five-gallon tank and a shower hose that operates off a battery-powered pump. For five days now, they've each been enjoying the periodic luxury of a brief shower, recycling the water as much as possible.

"I know, I know . . . I'm just saying, maybe it's like, better to go overboard right now with the cleanliness. That's all. Until we know more."

Philip gives him a hard look. "And what if there ain't nothing more to learn?"

Brian has no answer for that one.

The only response comes from the city, humming darkly back at them, with a blast of foul-smelling wind and a big, silent fuck you.

Maybe it's the alarming conglomeration of unappetizing ingredients concocted that night by April and Penny for dinner—a mixture of canned asparagus, Spam, and crumbled potato chips cooked over a propane flame—sitting like a dropped anchor in the pit of Philip's stomach. Or perhaps it's the cumulative effect of all the stress and rage and sleeplessness that does it. Or maybe it's the conversation he had on the balcony with his brother. But regardless of the cause, after he turns in for the night, and drifts off into an uneasy sleep, Philip Blake experiences an elaborate and lurid dream.

He has the dream in his newly established private quarters (April's former bedroom was apparently once somebody's home office—while clearing out the owner's things, Philip and April found stacks of Mary Kay Cosmetics order forms and makeup samples). But now, lying on the queen-sized bed shoved against the wall, Philip writhes in semiconsciousness, drifting in and out of a feverish horror show. It's the kind of dream that has no shape. It has no beginning, middle, or end. It just keeps spinning in its rut of circular terror.

He finds himself back in his childhood home in Waynesboro—the shabby little bungalow on Farrel Street—in the back bedroom he used to share with Brian. Philip is not a child in the dream, he is an adult, and somehow the plague has time-traveled back to the 1970s. The dream is almost three-dimensionally vivid. There's the lily of the valley wallpaper, and the Iron Maiden posters, and the scarred school desk, and Brian is somewhere in the house, unseen, screaming, and Penny is also there, in some adjacent room, crying for her daddy. Philip runs through the hallways, which form an endless labyrinth. Plaster is cracking. The zombie horde is outside, clamoring to get in. The boarded windows are trembling. Philip has a hammer and tries to secure the windows with nails, but the head of the hammer falls off. Crashing noises. Philip sees a door cracking open and he rushes over to it, and the doorknob comes off in his hand. He searches drawers and cabinets for weapons, and the facings fall off the cabinets, and plaster sifts down from the ceiling, and his boot breaks through a hole in the floor. The walls are collapsing, and the linoleum is buckling, and the windows are falling from their frames, and Philip keeps hearing Penny's desperate, shrieking voice calling for him: "DADDY!"

Skeletal arms thrust through crumbling window casements, blackened, curled fingers groping.

"DADDY?"

Bone-white skulls burst up through the floor like gruesome periscopes.

"DADDY!"

Philip lets out a silent scream as the dream shatters apart like spun glass.

fourteen

Philip gasps awake with a start. He jerks forward on the bed, blinking and squinting at the pale morning light. Someone stands at the foot of his bed. No. Two people. He sees them now—one tall and one short.

"Good morning, sunshine," April says with her hand around Penny's shoulder.

"Jesus." Philip sits up against the headboard in his wifebeater and sweatpants. "What the hell time is it?"

"It's like almost noon."

"Holy Christ," Philip utters, getting his bearings. His entire sinewy form is filmed with cold sweat. His neck aches and his mouth tastes like a litter box. "I can't believe it."

"We gotta show you something, Daddy," the little girl tells him, her big eyes ablaze with excitement. The sight of his daughter looking so happy sends a soothing wave of relief through Philip, driving the last remnants of the dream from his feverish brain.

He gets up and gets dressed, telling the two ladies to calm down. "Gimme a second to put my face on," he says in a hoarse, whiskey-cured grunt, running fingers through his greasy hair.

They take him up to the roof. When they emerge from the fire door and plunge into the cool air and light, Philip balks at the glare. Despite the fact that the day is overcast and dark, Philip is hungover and the light makes his eyeballs throb. He squints up at the sky and sees the foreboding storm clouds churning and roiling into the area from the north. "Looks like rain," he says.

"That's good," April says, giving Penny a wink. "Show him why, honey."

The little girl grasps her father's hand and drags him across the roof. "Look, Daddy, me and April made a garden to grow stuff in."

She shows him a small makeshift planter in the

center of the roof. It takes a moment for Philip to realize that the garden is constructed out of four wheelbarrows, their wheels removed, their housings taped together. A six-inch layer of soil fills each of the four cavities, a few unidentified shoots of green already transplanted into each barrow. "This is pretty damn fine," he says, giving the child a squeeze. He looks at April. "Pretty damn fine."

"It was Penny's idea," April says with a little gleam of pride in her eyes. She points at a row of buckets. "We're gonna collect the rain, too."

Philip drinks in April Chalmers's beautiful, slightly bruised face, her sea-foam blue eyes, her ashy blond hair undone and hanging over the collar of her scroungy cable-knit sweater. He can't take his eyes off her. And even as Penny starts jabbering happily about all the things she wants to grow—cotton candy plants, bubblegum bushes— Philip cannot help but extrapolate: The way April kneels down next to the child, listening intently with her hand on Penny's back, the look of affection on the woman's face, the easy rapport between the two, the sense of connection—all of it suggests something deeper than mere survival.

Philip can barely allow himself to think the word, and yet it comes to him right then, on that windy precipice, in a rush: *family.*

"Excuse me!"

The gruff voice comes from the fire door behind

them, on the other side of the roof. Philip whirls. He sees Tara in one of her stained muumuus and one of her patented moods in the open doorway. She holds a bucket. Her heavily jowled face and Maybelline eyes look even more lined and surly than usual. "Would it be too much to ask for a little help?"

April rises and turns. "I told you I'd help you in a minute."

Philip can see that Tara has been collecting water from toilet basins. He considers getting in the middle of this but decides against it.

"That was half an hour ago," Tara says. "Meantime, I been lugging water while you've been lollygaggin' up here in Mr. Rogers's neighborhood."

"Tara, just . . . calm down." April sighs. "Gimme a second, I'll be right there."

"Fine—whatever!" Tara turns in a huff and swishes angrily back down the inner stairs, leaving the sour vibration of contempt in her slipstream.

April looks down. "I'm sorry about that, she's still dealing with . . . you know . . . *stuff*."

By the downtrodden expression on April's face, it's clear that it would take too much energy for her to run down the litany of what's needling at her sister. Philip's no dummy. He knows it's complicated and it has something to do with jealousy and sibling rivalry, and maybe even the fact that April seems to be going through her grieving period with someone other than Tara.

"No need to apologize," Philip tells her. "There *is* somethin' I want you to know, though."

"What's that?"

"Just want you to know how grateful I am, the way you been treatin' my daughter."

April smiles. "She's a great kid."

"Yes, ma'am . . . she is . . . and you ain't so bad yourself."

"Why, thank you." She leans over and gives Philip a peck on the cheek. Nothing fancy, just a quick little kiss. But it makes an impression. "Now I gotta get back before my sister shoots me."

April walks off, leaving Philip thunderstruck and reeling in the wind.

As kisses go, it wasn't anything special. Philip's late wife, Sarah, had been a blue ribbon kisser. Hell, Philip had encountered prostitutes over the years since Sarah's death who had given up more in the kissing department. Even hookers have feelings, and Philip would usually ask at the beginning of a session if they would mind terribly if he slipped in a few kisses, just for good measure, just to pretend there was love involved. But this little smooch of April's is more like hors d'oeuvres, a hint of things to come. Philip wouldn't call it a tease. Nor would he call it the platonic kind of kiss a sister might give a brother. It exists in that irresistible limbo between two

267

extremes. It is—from Philip's perspective—a knock on the door, an attempt to see if anyone's home.

That afternoon, Philip expects the rain to come but it doesn't. It's already mid-October—he has no idea what day it is—and everybody keeps expecting the gulley-washers that traditionally sweep through central Georgia this time of year to roll in, but something keeps them at bay. The temperature is dropping, and the air buzzes with latent moisture, but still the rain doesn't come. Maybe the drought has something to do with the plague. But for whatever reason, the unsettled sky, with its dark underbelly of storm clouds, seems to reflect the strange, inexplicable tension building in Philip.

Late in the day, he asks April to go with him on a quick trip down the street.

It takes some convincing—despite the fact that the zombie quotient has thinned dramatically since the last time they went out. Philip tells April he needs help scouting the vicinity for a Home Depot or a Lowe's that might have generators lying around. It's getting colder and colder, especially at night, and they're going to need power soon in order to survive. He says he needs somebody who knows the area.

He also tells her that he wants to show her the safe routes Nick has been carving out. Nick offers to go along but Philip says it would be better if he stuck around and kept watch on the place with Brian.

April is up to the task, and is willing to go, but she's a little dubious about the rickety, homemade catwalk. What if it starts raining when they're on the ladders? Philip assures her it's a piece of cake, especially for a little drink of water her size.

They get their coats on and get their weapons ready—April brings along one of the Marlins this time—and they prepare to embark. Tara is seething with anger at them, disgusted by what she calls "a stupid, dangerous, immature, retarded waste of time." Philip and April politely ignore her.

"Don't look down!"

Philip is halfway across the makeshift ladder-bridge over the back alley. April is ten feet behind him, holding on for dear life. Gazing over his shoulder at her, he smiles to himself. Major *cojones* on this girl.

"I'm cool," she says, crabbing along with white knuckles and clenched jaw. The wind tousles her hair. Thirty feet beneath her, a pair of moving cadavers dumbly gaze around the air for the source of the voices.

"Almost home free," Philip urges as he reaches the other side.

She crabs the remaining twenty feet. He helps

her down onto the fire-escape landing. The cast-iron grating squeaks under their weight.

They find the open window and slip inside the former home of Stevenson and Sons Accounting and Estate Planning. The office corridors are darker and colder than they were the last time Philip traversed their length. The storm front has brought dusk to the area earlier than usual tonight.

They cross the empty hallways. "Don't worry," Philip assures her as they crunch across debris and crumpled tax returns, "This place is as safe as you can get, this day and age."

"That's not very reassuring," she says, cradling the shotgun, thumbing the hammer nervously.

Dressed in tattered fleece and jeans, April has her arms and lower legs wrapped with gaffer's tape. Nobody else does this. Philip asked her about it once and she told him she saw an animal trainer do it on TV—a last-resort defense against a bite breaking the skin.

They cross the lobby and find the access stairs just past the ruined vending machines.

"Get a load of this," Philip says as he leads her up the single flight to the unmarked door. He pauses before opening the door. "You remember Captain Nemo?"

"Who?"

"That old flick *Twenty Thousand Leagues Under the Sea*? That old loony captain, playing his organ in that submarine, while the giant squids swim across them big picture windows?"

"Never saw it."

Philip smiles at her. "Well, you're about to."

The last thing April Chalmers expects is for something other than horrific violence to take her breath away, but that's pretty much what happens when she follows Philip through the unmarked door and onto the pedestrian bridge. She pauses on the threshold and just stares.

She's been in these urban breezeways before—maybe even this very bridge—but somehow, tonight, the gauzy light and space of the thing, as it stretches across the intersection, thirty feet above the streets, connecting up with the second floor of Dillard's, seems almost miraculous. Through the glass roof, veins of lightning flicker and thread across the storm clouds. Through the transparent walls, the darkening shadows of the city teem with wandering zombies. Atlanta looks like a vast game board in chaotic disarray.

"I see what you mean," she says. Her voice comes out in a murmur, as she takes it all in, feeling a weird mixture of emotions—giddiness, fear, excitement.

Philip strolls down the center of the bridge, pausing by one wall and shrugging off the straps of his duffel bag. He nods to the south. "Want you to see something," he says. "C'mere."

She joins him, putting down her shotgun and backpack against the glass wall.

Philip points out the marks on the abandoned vehicles and doorways left by Nick Parsons. Philip explains the theory of "safe zones" and he talks about how cunning Nick has become. "I think he's got something really good going here," Philip concludes.

April agrees. "We could use those hiding places when we find that generator everybody's talking about."

"You got that right, sister."

"Nick's a good guy."

"That he is."

The encroaching darkness is drawing down over the city, and in the bluish shadows of the bridgeway, Philip's rugged face looks even craggier to April than usual. With his inky black Fu Manchu whiskers and dark eyes nested in laugh lines, he reminds April of a cross between a young Clint Eastwood and . . . who? Her dad as a young man? Is that why she's feeling these twinges of attraction toward the big, lanky redneck? Is April so retarded that she's attracted to a man just because he's the doppelgänger of her father? Or does this pathetic puppy love have something to do with the stress of fighting to survive in a world suddenly doomed with extinction? This is the guy who cracked open her daddy's skull, for God's sake. But maybe that's unfair. That was *not* David

Chalmers back there. Her daddy's spirit, as the song goes, had flown away. His soul had departed long before he climbed out of his bed and tried to make a meal out of his eldest daughter.

"I gotta tell you," Philip is saying, gazing out at the ragged figures, like stray dogs, roaming the streets for scraps. "We get a few things in place, and we could stay for a long time in that apartment building."

"I think you're right. All we gotta do is figure out a way to slip some Valium into Tara's oatmeal."

Philip laughs—a good, clean laugh—which shows a side of him that April has not yet seen. He looks at her. "We got an opportunity here, we can make this work. We can do more than just survive. And I'm not just talking about getting a generator."

April looks up into his eyes. "Whaddaya mean?"

He turns toward her. "Met a lotta girls in my day, ain't never run across one quite like you. Tough as nails . . . but the tenderness you show toward my kid? Never seen Penny take to somebody like she's taken to you. Hell, you saved our asses, pulling us off the streets. You're a very special lady, you know that?"

All at once April feels her skin flush hot with chills, and her midsection weaken, and she realizes Philip is looking at her in a new way. His eyes shimmer with emotion. She knows now that he's been thinking the same thing that she has. She looks down, embarrassed. "Your standards must be low," she mutters.

He reaches out and gently puts one of his big, callused workman's hands on the curve of her jaw. "I got the highest standards of anybody I know."

A clap of thunder booms outside the glass, rattling the bridge and making April jump.

Philip kisses her on the lips.

She pulls back. "I don't know, Philip . . . I mean . . . I don't know if this is . . . you know."

Second thoughts and third thoughts and fourth thoughts flow through April in the space of an instant. If she takes this to the next level, what will happen with Tara? How will it fuck up the dynamics at the apartment? How will it complicate things? How will it affect their safety, their chances of survival, their future (if they even have one)?

Philip's expression brings her back—the way he's looking at her, his gaze almost glassy with emotion, his mouth slack with desire.

He leans in and kisses her again, and this time she finds herself putting her arms around him and returning the kiss, and she doesn't even notice the droplets of rain beginning to ping off the glass over her head.

She feels her body go limp in Philip's forceful embrace. Their lips part, and electricity flows through April as they explore each other with their tongues, the taste of coffee and spearmint gum and

Philip's musky odor filling her senses. Her nipples harden under her sweater.

A flash of blue lightning turns the dusk to brilliant silver daylight.

April loses track of herself. She loses track of *everything*. Her head is spinning. She doesn't notice the rain slapping against the glass roof. She doesn't even notice the fact that Philip is gently lowering both of them to the floor of the walkway. Their lips locked and working sensually, Philip's big hands caressing April's breasts, he carefully lays her back against the glass wall, and before April knows what is happening, he is on top of her.

The storm unleashes its fury. The rain comes down now in sheets against the roof. Thunder rolls and lightning crackles and sparks like static electricity in the anxious air as Philip fumbles April's sweater up across her bare midriff, exposing her bra in the blue light.

Gnarled fingers wrestle open belt buckles. Thunder booms. April feels the urgent nudge of Philip's loins burrowing between her legs. Lightning flickers. Her jeans are halfway down her legs, her breasts free now.

The edge of a fingernail brushes her belly, and all at once, like a switch flipping inside her—accompanied by a single volley of thunder—she thinks, *WAIT*.

BOOOOOOOM!

WAIT!

• • •

A tidal wave of desire carries Philip Blake off on its roaring currents.

He can barely hear April's voice coming from somewhere far away, telling him to *Stop, wait, hold on, listen, listen, this is too much, I'm not ready for this, please, please, stop right now, stop.* None of it registers in Philip's brain as it swims with lust and passion and pain and loneliness and a desperate need to *feel something,* because now his entire being is wired to his groin, all his pent-up emotion coursing through him.

"God, I'm begging you to stop!" the faraway voice pleads, April's body stiffening.

Philip rides the writhing woman beneath him as if surfing a pipeline of white noise, knowing that she secretly wants him, *loves him,* despite what she's saying. So, he keeps shoving himself into her, again and again, in great magnesium-bright flashes of lightning and raw energy, filling her, taking her, nourishing her, transforming her, until she goes limp beneath him, limp and silent now.

The soft white explosion of pleasure erupts like a skyrocket launching inside Philip.

He slides off her, landing on the floor next to her, staring straight up at the rain—momentarily oblivious to the shadowy, desecrated souls thirty feet below them, captured in the flicker-show of lightning like monstrous figures in a silent movie.

● ● ●

Philip takes April's silence as a sign that maybe, just maybe, everything's going to be okay. As the storm settles into a steady deluge, its muffled jet-engine roar filling the walkway, the two of them pull their clothes back on and lie there side by side for a long time, not saying a word, staring up at the strafing sheets of rain crashing off the glass roof.

Philip is in a state of shock, his heart racing, his skin clammy and cold. He feels like a broken mirror, as if a shard of his own soul has fractured off and reflected back the face of a monster. What did he just do? He knows he did something wrong. But it almost feels like somebody else did it.

"Got a little carried away there," he says at last, after many minutes of terrible silence.

She doesn't say a word. He glances over at her, and sees her face in the darkness, reflecting the liquid shadows of rain streaming down the sides of the glass walkway. She looks semiconscious. Like she's having a waking dream.

"Sorry about that," he says, the words sounding tinny and hollow in his own ears. He shoots another glance at her, trying to gauge her mood. "You okay?"

"Yes."

"You sure?"

"Yes."

Her voice has a mechanical quality to it, completely colorless, barely audible above the noise of

277

the rain. Philip is about to say something else when a volley of thunder interrupts his thought. The rumbling reverberates through the iron framework of the walkway, a teeth-rattling vibration that makes Philip cringe.

"April?"

"Yes."

"We ought to get back."

The return trip is shrouded in silence. Philip walks a few paces behind April through the deserted lobby, up a staircase, and down the empty, litter-strewn corridors. Every now and then, Philip considers saying something, but he doesn't. He figures it's probably best to let it ride right now. Let her work through it. Anything Philip says might make it worse. April walks ahead of him with the shotgun on her shoulder, looking like a tired soldier returning from a rough patrol. They reach the top floor of the accounting firm and find the gaping window, the rain blowing in past jagged, broken glass. Only a few words are spoken—"You go first" and "Watch your step"—as Philip helps her climb out and cross the rain-swept fire escape. The pounding wind and rain that lashes down on them as they shimmy across the treacherous makeshift catwalk almost feels good to Philip. It braces him and wakes him up and gives him hope that maybe he can repair whatever damage has been done here tonight with this woman.

By the time they get back to the apartment—both of them soaked to the bone, exhausted, and dazed—Philip is confident he can fix this.

Brian is in the office bedroom with Penny, putting her to sleep on her cot. Nick is in the living room, working on his map of safe zones. "Hey, how'd it go?" he asks, looking up from his papers. "You guys look like drowned rats; you find any Home Depots out there?"

"Not this time," Philip replies, heading for the bedroom, not even pausing to take off his shoes.

April says nothing, doesn't even meet Nick's gaze as she heads toward the hallway.

"Look at you two," Tara says, coming out of the kitchen with a surly expression and a lit cigarette dangling out of the corner of her mouth. "Just like I thought—a wild fucking goose chase!"

She stands there with her hands on her hips as her sister vanishes without a word into her room at the end of the hall. Tara gives Philip a look, and then storms away, following her sister.

"I'm going to bed," Philip says flatly to Nick and then adjourns to his room.

The next morning, Philip stirs awake just before dawn. The rain still pounds the streets outside. He can hear it drumming off the window. The room is dark and cold and dank, and smells of mold. He sits on the edge of the bed for the longest time, looking at Penny, who slumbers across the room on her cot, her tiny body all balled up in a fetal position. The half-formed memories of a dream cling to Philip's woozy brain, as well as the sickening sensation that he doesn't know where the nightmares end and the episode with April the previous evening begins.

If only he had *dreamed* those events in the pedestrian walkway instead of actually acting them out. But the hard, sharp edge of reality comes back to him in that dark room in a series of flash frames in his mind, as though he's watching someone else perpetrate the crime. Philip hangs his head, trying to push the feelings of dread and guilt from his mind.

Running fingers through his hair, he talks himself into being hopeful. He can work through this with April, figure out a way to move forward, put it behind them, apologize to her, make it up to her.

He watches Penny sleep.

In the two and a half weeks since Philip's little cadre joined up with the Chalmers, Philip has noticed his daughter coming out of her shell. At first, he detected little things: the way Penny had begun to look forward to concocting their god-awful dinners, and the way she lit up every time April walked into a room. With each passing day, though, the child has become more and more talkative, remembering things from before the "turn," commenting on the strange weather patterns, asking questions about the "sickness." Can animals get the disease? Does it wear off? Is God mad at them?

Philip's chest hitches with emotion as he gazes at the slumbering child. There has to be a way to make a life for his daughter, make a family, make a home—even in the midst of this waking nightmare—there has to be a way.

For a brief instant, Philip imagines a desert island and a little cottage nestled in a grove of coconut trees. The plague is a million light-years away. He imagines April and Penny on a swing set, playing together out by a vegetable garden. He imagines himself sitting on a back porch, healthy, brown from the sun, happily watching the two ladies in his life sharing contented moments. He imagines all this while he watches his daughter sleep.

He gets up and pads over to her, kneeling and lightly putting a hand on the downy softness of her hair. She needs to bathe. Her hair is matted and greasy, and she has a faint body odor. That smell somehow reaches out to Philip and pinches his gut. His eyes well up. He has never loved anyone other than this child. Even Sarah—whom he adored—came in second. His love for Sarah was—like that of all married people—complicated, conditional, and fluid. But when he first laid eyes on his baby girl as a blotchy little newborn, seven and half years ago, he learned what it means to love.

It means to be afraid, to be vulnerable for the rest of your life.

Something catches Philip's attention across the room. The door is half ajar. He remembers shutting it before turning in. He remembers that very clearly. Now it's cracked open about six inches.

At first, this doesn't really make much of an impression or worry him all that much. Maybe he accidentally neglected to latch the door, and the thing drifted open on its own. Or maybe he got up to piss in the middle of the night and forgot to close it. Or maybe *Penny* had to pee and left it open. Hell, maybe he's a sleepwalker and doesn't even know it. But then, just as he's turning back to continue gazing down at his daughter, he notices something else.

Things are missing from the room.

Philip's heart starts thumping. He left his back-pack—the one he was wearing when he arrived here over two weeks ago—leaning against the wall in the corner, but now it's gone. His gun is missing as well. He left the .22 pistol on top of the dresser with the last magazine of bullets beside it. The ammo is gone, too.

Philip springs to his feet.

He looks around. The gloomy dawn is just beginning to lighten the room, the window shade projecting tears of rain, the ghostly reflections of water sluicing down the glass outside it. His boots are not where he left them. He left them on the floor by the window, but now they're gone. Who the hell would take his boots? He tells himself to calm down. There has to be a simple explanation. No reason to get all jacked up. But the absence of the gun is what troubles him the most. He decides to take this one step at a time.

Silently, careful not to awaken Penny, he crosses the room and slips out the open door.

The apartment is silent and still. Brian dozes in the living room on the pull-out bed. Philip pads into the kitchen, lights up the propane stove, and makes himself a cup of instant coffee with some rainwater left in a bucket. He splashes some of the cold water on his face. He tells himself to stay calm, take some deep breaths.

When the coffee is hot, he takes the cup and walks down the hallway to April's room.

Her door is also ajar.

He looks in and sees that the room is empty. His pulse quickens.

A voice says, "She ain't here."

He whirls and comes face-to-face with Tara Chalmers, who holds the Ruger pistol, the muzzle raised and aimed directly at Philip.

fifteen

"All right . . . go easy, sis." Philip makes no move. He just stands there, frozen in the hallway, with his free hand raised, and the coffee in his other hand, jutting out to the side like he's interested in offering it to her. "Whatever it is, we can work it out."

"Really . . . ?" Tara Chalmers glowers at him with her painted eyes flaring. "Ya think?"

"Look . . . I don't know what's going on—"

"What's going on," she says without a trace of nerves or fear, "is that we're changing the lineup around here."

"Tara, whatever you're thinking—"

"Let's get something straight." Her voice is steady and flatlined of emotion. "I need you to shut the fuck up and do what I say, or I will blow you the fuck away and don't think I won't."

"This ain't—"

"Put the cup down."

Philip obliges, slowly setting the cup on the floor. "Okay, sis. Whatever you say."

"Stop calling me that."

"Yes, ma'am."

"Now we're gonna go get your brother, your friend, and your kid."

Philip buzzes with adrenaline. He doesn't think

Tara has the balls to do any real harm, and he considers making a move for the weapon—a distance of six to eight feet lies between him and the barrel of the Ruger—but he resists the temptation. Better to comply at this point and try and get her talking.

"May I say somethin'?"

"MOVE!"

Her sudden cry shatters the stillness, loud enough to not only awaken Penny and Brian, but probably be heard up on the second floor where Nick—an early riser—is likely already up and about. Philip takes a step toward her. "If you'd just give me a chance to—"

The Ruger barks.

The blast goes wide—maybe on purpose, maybe not—chewing a divot in the wall eighteen inches from Philip's left shoulder. The roar of the gun is enormous in the enclosed space of the hallway, and Philip's ears are ringing as he realizes a particle of the plaster wall has stuck to his cheek.

He can barely see Tara through the blue smoke of cordite. She is either grinning or grimacing, it's hard to tell at this point.

"The next one goes in your face," she tells him. "Now, you gonna be a good boy or what?"

Nick Parsons hears the gunfire just after opening his Concordance Bible for his morning read. Sitting in bed, with his back against the headboard, he jumps at the noise, the Bible flying out of his hands. It was open to the Revelation to John, Chapter 1 Verse 9, the part where John says to the church, "I am John your brother who shares with you in Jesus the tribulation and the kingdom and patient endurance."

Leaping out of bed, he goes to the closet where his Marlin shotgun is supposed to be resting against the wall in the corner, except it's not there. Panic vibrates down through Nick's spine, and he spins, and he looks around his room at all the missing gear. His knapsack—gone. His boxes of shotgun shells—gone. His tools, his pickaxe, his boots, his maps—all gone.

At least his jeans are still there, neatly folded over the back of a chair. He yanks them on and charges out of the room. Through the studio apartment. Out the door. Down the corridor. Down a flight of steps and out onto the first floor. He thinks he hears the sound of a voice raised in anger but he's not sure. He rushes toward the Chalmers's apartment. The door is unlocked and he pushes his way inside.

"What's going on? What's going on?" Nick keeps repeating as he slams to a stop in the living room. He sees something that doesn't make any sense. He sees Tara Chalmers with the Ruger pointed at Philip, and Philip with this weird look on his face, and Brian standing a few feet away with Penny drawn close to him, his arms around the little girl in a protective posture. And weirder still: Nick sees their belongings piled on the floor in front of the sofa.

"Move over there," Tara says, brandishing the gun, and directing Nick toward Philip, Brian, and Penny.

"What's wrong?"

"Never mind, just do what I say."

Nick slowly complies but his mind is swimming with confusion. What in God's name happened here? Almost involuntarily, Nick looks at Philip, looks into the big man's eyes for answers, but for the first time since Nick has known Philip Blake, the big guy looks almost sheepish, almost blank with indecision and frustration. Nick looks at Tara. "Where's April? What happened?"

"Never mind."

"What are you doing? What's the idea putting of all our stuff in a—"

"Nicky," Philip chimes in. "Let it go. Tara's gonna tell us what she wants us to do. And we're gonna do it, and everything's gonna be okay."

Philip says this to Nick but as he's saying it, he's looking at Tara.

"Listen to your pal here, Nick," Tara says, and she too says this to Nick but doesn't take her gaze off Philip. Her eyes practically glow with contempt and anger and vengeance and something else—something incomprehensible to Nick, something that feels disturbingly intimate.

Now it's Brian's turn to pipe in: "What is it you want us to do exactly?"

Tara still doesn't take her eyes off Philip as she says, "Get out."

At first, this simple imperative sentence sounds to Nick Parsons like a rhetorical statement. To his stunned ears, it sounds as though she's not exactly telling them to do something as much as she's making some kind of a point. But this initial reaction—and maybe hopeful thinking—is immediately short-circuited by the look on Tara Chalmers's face.

"Hit the road."

Philip keeps staring at her. "Where I come from, that's called murder."

"Call it whatever you want. Just take your shit and go."

"You're gonna send us out there without weapons."

"I'm gonna do more than that," she says. "I'm gonna climb up on that roof with one of them high-powered pigeon guns and I'm gonna make *sure* you leave."

After a long, horrible moment of silence, Nick looks at Philip.

And finally, Philip tears his gaze away from the stout, buxom girl with the pistol. "Get your stuff," he says to Nick, and then to Brian he says, "There's a rain poncho in my pack, put it on Penny."

• • •

The amount of time it takes them to get dressed and ready to leave is nominal—mere minutes, with Tara Chalmers standing guard like a stone sentry—but it gives Brian Blake plenty of time to wildly ruminate to himself about what could have happened. Tying his boots, and putting the slicker on Penny, he realizes that all indications point to some kind of sick triangle going on. April's absence speaks volumes. As does Tara's unmitigated, righteous anger. But what *caused* it? It couldn't be something Philip said or did. What could offend the girls this deeply?

For a crazy instant, Brian's mind casts back to his insane ex-wife. Compulsive, volatile, flaky Jocelyn had done stuff like this. She would vanish without a trace for weeks. One time, while Brian was at night school, she actually put all his shit out on the stairs of their tenement building, as though she were removing a stain from her life. But *this*. This is different. The Chalmers girls have shown no previous signs of being irrational or nuts.

The thing that bothers Brian the most is the way his brother is behaving. Beneath the surface of his simmering anger and frustration, Philip Blake almost seems *resolved,* maybe even hopeless. This is a clue. This is important. But the problem is, there's no time to figure it out.

"Come on, let's roll," Philip says, his backpack slung over his shoulder. He has his denim jacket on now—the black, oily grime and gore from their earlier journey still visible all over it—and he's heading toward the door.

"Wait!" Brian says. He turns to Tara. "At least let us take some food. For Penny's sake."

She just levels her gaze at him and says, "I'm letting you walk outta here alive."

"Come on, Brian." Philip pauses in the doorway. "It's over."

Brian looks at his brother. Something about that deeply lined, weathered face is galvanizing to Brian. Philip is family, he's blood. And they've come a long way. They've survived too many jams to die now like homeless pets abandoned on the side of the road. Brian feels a strange sensation building in the base of his spine, filling him with an unexpected strength. "Fine," he says. "If this is the way it has to be . . ."

He doesn't finish the sentence—there is nothing more to say—he simply puts an arm around Penny and ushers her out behind her father.

The rain is both a blessing and a curse. It bullwhips across their faces as they emerge from the building's front entrance, but as they crouch under spindly trees along the parkway to get their bearings, they see that the storm has apparently driven the Biters off the streets. The sewers are flooding, the roads streaming with overflow, and the gray sky hangs low.

Nick squints into the distance to the south, the streets relatively clear. "That way's best! Most of the safe zones are down there!"

"Okay, we'll head south," Philip says and turns to Brian. "Can you piggyback her again? I'm countin' on you, sport. Watch her back."

Brian wipes moisture from his face and gives his brother a thumbs-up.

Turning to the child, Brian starts to go about the business of gently lifting her onto his back, but he abruptly stops. For the briefest instant, he just stares in amazement at the little girl. She is also giving a thumbs-up sign. Brian glances at his brother, and the two men acknowledge something beyond words.

Penny Blake just stands there, waiting, chin jutting defiantly. Her soft little eyes are blinking away the rain, and the look on her face is reminiscent of the expression her late mother would often display when impatient with male nonsense. Finally, the child says, "I'm not a baby . . . can we go now?"

They make their way to the corner, staying low, slipping on the slimy walk, the rain a constant drag on their progress. It gets in their faces and in their clothes and into their joints almost immediately. It's an icy, needling autumn rain with no signs of slowing down.

Up ahead, a few shabby, cadaverous zombies

cluster near an abandoned bus stop, their greasy heads of hair like moss matted across their dead faces. They look like they're waiting for a bus that will never come.

Philip leads his group across the corner and under an awning. Nick points the way to the first safe zone—the city bus sitting in mothballs half a block south of the pedestrian bridge. A quick hand gesture from Philip, and now they hurry along the storefronts toward the bus.

"I say we go back," Nick Parsons is grumbling as he crouches down on the floor of the bus and fishes through his backpack. The rain makes a muffled tommy-gun noise on the bus's roof. Nick finds a T-shirt, pulls it out, and wipes the moisture from his face. "We're talking about a single girl here—we can take the place back from her—I say we go back and kick her the hell out."

"Think we can take it from her, huh?" Philip is up in the pilot area, searching the compartments for things left behind by the driver. "You got a bulletproof vest in that backpack of yours?"

The bus—a thirty-foot fuselage of molded seats facing inward along either side—reeks with the ghostly secretions of former passengers, a sort of wet dog-fur smell. In the rear of the bus, resting on the second-to-last seat, with Penny in the seat next to him, Brian shivers in his wet sweatshirt and jeans. He has a bad feeling, and it's not only because of their exposure to the stormy, urban wilderness of Atlanta.

Brian's sense of doom has more to do with the mystery of what happened back at the apartment building last night. He can't stop wondering just exactly what transpired between the hours of 5 P.M. (when Philip and April embarked on their mission) and 5 A.M. the following morning (when everything suddenly blew up in their faces). From the gravelly tension in his brother's voice and the cold determination on his face, it's becoming clear to Brian that it may already be a moot point. Their immediate priority is now survival. But Brian can't stop thinking about it. The mystery speaks to something deeper, something gnawing at Brian to which he can't quite put words.

Lightning flashes outside the bus, as brilliant as a photographer's strobe.

"We had a good thing going at that place," Nick goes on, his voice whiny and unsteady. He stands up, grabbing a hand strap for purchase. "Those are our guns, man. All the work we did? That's our stuff as much as theirs!"

"Stay down, Nick," Philip says flatly. "I don't want any of them pus bags seeing us in here."

Nick ducks down.

Philip sits down in the driver's seat, the springs squeaking. He checks a map case on the dash and finds nothing useful. The keys are in the ignition. Philip turns it over and gets nothing but a clicking noise. "I'm not going to say it again. That place is *over* for us."

"Why, though? Why can't we take it back, Philly? We can take that fat bitch. The three of us?"

"Let it go, Nick," Philip says, and even Brian, all the way in the back of the bus, hears the icy warning tone in Philip's voice.

"I just don't get it," Nick complains under his breath. "How something like this could happen—"

"Bingo!" At last, Philip has found something useful. The four-foot-long steel rod—about the width and heft of a short length of iron rebar—is attached to clips under the driver's side window. Hooked on one end, the tool is likely used to reach across the cab to the accordion door (in order to manually pull it shut). Now, as Philip wields the thing in the gloomy light, it looks like an excellent makeshift weapon. "This'll do," he murmurs.

"How did this happen, Philly?" Nick persists, crouching down in the flickering stutter of lightning.

"GODDAMNIT!"

Philip suddenly slams the iron rod against the dash, sending shards of plastic flying and making everybody jump. He smacks it again, cracking the two-way radio. He strikes it again and again with all his might, caving in the controls and shattering the fare box, sending coins flying. He keeps striking the console until the dashboard is totaled.

Finally, with the veins in his neck bulging, his face livid with rage, he turns and burns his gaze into Nick Parsons. "Would you please shut the fuck up!"

Nick stares.

In the rear of the bus, sitting next to Brian, Penny Blake turns away and gazes out the window, the dirty rain tracking down in rivulets. Her expression hardens as though she's working out a complicated mathematical problem that's far too complex for her grade level.

Meanwhile, up front, Nick is frozen with shock. "Take it easy, Philly . . . I'm just . . . babbling. You know? Didn't mean anything. The place just kinda grew on me."

Philip licks his lips. The fire in his eyes dwindles. He takes a deep breath and lets out a pained exhalation. He puts the rod down on the driver's seat. "Look . . . I'm sorry . . . I understand how you feel. But it's better this way. Without electricity, that place is going to be a walk-in freezer by mid-November."

Nick keeps looking down. "Yeah . . . I guess I see your point."

"It's better this way, Nicky."

"Sure."

At this point, Brian tells Penny he'll be right back, and he pushes himself off his seat.

He moves up the aisle, staying low, moving just beneath the level of the sliding windows, until he joins Nick and his brother. "What's the plan, Philip?"

"We'll find someplace we can build fires. Can't build fires in an apartment building."

"Nick, how many more of these 'safe zones' have you got mapped out?"

"Enough to get outta this part of town, if we catch a break or two."

"Sooner or later, we're gonna have to find a car, though," Brian says.

Philip grunts. "No shit."

"You think there's gas in this bus?"

"Deisel, probably."

"Guess it doesn't matter *what* it is. We got no way to siphon it."

"And no way to store it," Philip reminds him.

"And no way to move it," Nick adds.

"That metal thing over there?" Brian points at the metal reacher on the driver's seat. "You think that thing's sharp enough to puncture the gas tank?"

"On the bus?" Philip glances at the steel rod. "I suppose. What good's that gonna do?"

Brian swallows hard. He has an idea.

One by one, they each quickly slip through the accordion door and into the rain, which has now settled into a low, cold drizzle. The daylight is muddy. Philip carries the steel rod, Nick the three brown Miller Light bottles that Brian found wedged under the rear seats. Brian keeps Penny close—there are dark figures visible in all directions, the closest ones maybe a block away—and the clock is ticking.

Every few moments, the lightning turns the city magnesium bright—illuminating the dead coming from either end of the street. Some of the Biters have noticed humans scurrying around the back of the bus, and those zombies approach now with a more defined purpose in their lumbering gait.

Philip knows the location of the gas tank from his days as a truck driver.

He crouches down near the massive front tire, and he quickly feels under the chassis for the bottom edge of the tank as the rain drips off his chin. This bus has two separate reservoirs, each one containing a hundred gallons of fuel.

"Hurry, man, they're coming!" Nick kneels behind Philip with the bottles.

Philip slams the pointed end of the steel rod into the bottom of the forward tank, but it only dents the iron enclosure. He cries out a garbled howl of white-hot anger and drives the point again into the reservoir.

This time, the point punctures the skin of the tank and a thin stream of yellow, oily liquid suddenly shoots out all over Philip's arms and hands. Nick leans in and quickly fills the first twelve-ounce bottle.

Thunder pounds the sky, followed by another salvo of lightning. Brian glances over his shoulder and sees an entire regiment of walking corpses—closer now in the flash of heavenly daylight, only twenty-five yards away—many of their faces clearly discernible in the photostrobe radiance.

One of them is missing a jaw, another one walking along with a streamer of intestines lolling out of a gaping hole in its stomach.

"Hurry, Nick! Hurry!" Brian has pieces of a torn shirt ready to go in one hand, the lighter in the other. He fidgets restlessly next to Penny, who is trying her best to be brave, clenching her little fists, chewing her lip as she keeps tabs on the advancing army of upright cadavers.

"There's one—go, GO!" Nick hands the first bottle of fuel to Brian.

Brian stuffs the rag into it, then quickly turns the bottle upside down until the cloth is soaked. This procedure only encompasses a few seconds, but Brian can feel the time running out, the presence of hundreds of Biters closing in. A flick of the lighter produces a flame that is instantly extinguished by the wind.

"C'mon, sport . . . c'mon, *c'mon!*" Philip is turning to the oncoming horde, raising his steel implement. Behind him, Brian cups his hands around the wick and finally gets it lit. The rag flares, the flames curling down the side of the bottle, feeding off the fumes and spill.

Brian hurls the Molotov cocktail at the leading edge of the crowd.

The bottle shatters five feet away from the closest zombies and blooms in a yellow sunburst of fire, making a crackling sound in the mist. Several corpses stagger backward at the unexpected light and heat, some of them bumping into their counterparts, knocking them over like dominoes. The sight of these monsters tumbling would ordinarily be almost funny, but not now.

Now Philip grabs the second full bottle, and stuffs the rag in. "Gimme the lighter!" Brian hands over the Bic. "Now get moving!" Philip commands, lighting the rag and hurling the flaming bottle at the army of monsters coming from the opposite direction.

This time, the bottle lands in their midst, erupting in their ranks, setting ablaze at least a dozen Biters with the ferocity of napalm.

Brian doesn't look back as he scoops Penny off the ground and follows Nick in a desperate run for the barbershop.

Brian, Penny, and Nick get halfway to the next safe zone when they realize that Philip is lagging behind them.

"What the hell's he doing!" Nick's voice is shrill and frantic as he ducks into the doorway of another boarded storefront.

"Hell if I know!" Brian says, ducking into the doorway with Penny, gazing back at his brother.

A hundred yards away, Philip is yelling something obscene and inarticulate at the monsters, swinging his iron weapon at an attacker. The flaming zombie comes at him in a wreath of smoke and sparks.

"Oh my God!" Brian shields Penny's face. "Get down—GET DOWN!"

In the distance, Philip Blake is backing away from the mob with the lighter raised in one hand and the bloody iron raised in the other, some kind of Viking brazenness taking over now, all his pent-up rage coming out in a series of big, portentous gestures.

He pauses and lights a spreading pool of fuel seeping out from underneath the bus, and then turns and flees the scene with the full-tilt abandon of a ball carrier charging toward open field.

Behind him, the puddle of fuel catches and spreads, the blue flames billowing toward the massive steel girth of the bus. Philip traverses about fifty yards of wet pavement, cracking the skulls of half a dozen Biters along the way, while the fire crawls up the side of the bus.

A low, subsonic thump rises above the rain and moaning noises. Philip can't see Brian and the others in the mist ahead of him.

"PHILIP! IN HERE!"

Brian's howl is a beacon, and Philip dives

toward the sound of it as the explosion rocks the ground and turns a dark, gray afternoon into the surface of the sun.

None of them gets a good look at it. They are all slammed against a door inside the boarded alcove, shielding their faces from the flaming shrapnel—pieces of the bus, jagged shards of metal bulwark, and fountains of glass—flying past the doorway. Brian manages to glimpse a reflection off the glass of a store window across the street: The explosion, half a block away, has launched twenty tons of bus straight up, a mushroom cloud of dazzling, horrifying fire, the force of the blast bursting open the cabin, the molten hot shock wave punching through multitudes of dead with the violent brilliance of a supernova—countless bodies swept away on the wave, incinerated in the furnace, some of them torn to pieces by the flying debris, the mortified body parts flying up into the storm-lashed sky like a flock of birds attempting to escape.

A flaming piece of fender lands fifteen feet from the doorway.

Everybody jumps at the clanging noise, their eyes wide with shock. "Fuck! FUCK!" Nick exclaims, hands shielding his face. Brian holds Penny in a locked embrace, speechless, momentarily paralyzed.

Philip wipes his face with the back of his hand

and gazes around the doorway with the stupor of a sleepwalker just coming awake. "Awright then." He glances over his shoulder, and then back at Nick. "Where's this barber shop?"

sixteen

Half a block south—in the darkness of a festering, airless tile room, among scattered remnants of *True Detective* magazines, plastic combs, dust bunnies of human hair, and tubes of Brylcreem— they dry their faces with towels and barber smocks, and then find more ingredients for homemade Molotov cocktails.

Bottles of hair tonic get emptied, and then filled with alcohol and plugged with wads of cotton. They also find an old, scarred Louisville Slugger hidden under the cash register. The baseball bat probably once warded off unruly customers or neighborhood punks looking to boost the day's receipts. Now Philip gives the nascent weapon to Nick and tells him to use it wisely.

They scavenge for any other supplies they might be able to use. An old vending machine in back yields a handful of candy bars, a couple of Twinkies, and an ancient sausage stick. As they stuff their knapsacks, Philip tells them not to get too comfortable. He can hear noises outside— more dead encroaching on the area, drawn to the explosion. The rain is slowing down. Noises are carrying. They have to keep moving if they're going to get out of the city before dark. "C'mon, c'mon," Philip says. "Let's get our asses in gear and get to that next zone—Nicky, you take the lead."

Reluctantly, Nick leads them out of the barbershop, into the drizzle, and down another row of storefronts. Philip brings up the rear with the iron bar ready to rock, keeping a watchful eye on Penny, who clings with simian instinct to Brian's back.

Halfway to the next safe zone, a stray corpse lurches out from behind a wreck, shuffling menacingly toward Brian and Penny. Philip lashes out at the back of its head with the hooked end of the iron prod—hitting it just above the six cervical vertebrae—so hard that the cranium detaches and hangs down across its chest as it collapses to the wet paving stones. Penny averts her gaze.

More cadavers are materializing in the mouths of alleys and the shadows of doorways.

Nick finds the next painted symbol, near the corner of two cross streets.

The star is scrawled above the glass door of a small shop of some sort. The store's façade is draped in iron burglar screens, and other than a few frayed wires, broken neon tubes, and wads of gaffer's tape, the display windows are empty. The door is shut but unlocked (just as Nick had left it three days earlier).

Yanking the door open, Nick waves everybody inside, and they enter in a hurry.

In fact, they slip inside so quickly that nobody notices the shop's sign over the door's lintel, the letters formed by dark, cold neon script: TOM THUMB'S TINY TOY SHOPPE.

The front of the store, barely five hundred square feet, is littered with brightly colored debris. Overturned shelves have spilled their inventory of dolls and race cars and trains across the soiled tiles. A tornado of destruction has swirled through the shop. Wires dangle where mobiles once hung, the shattered plastic remains of LEGO sets and planes piled here and there. The feathery stuffing of ripped plush toys stirs like dead leaves in the slipstream of the visitors slamming the door behind them.

For a moment, they stand in the vestibule, dripping, catching their collective breaths, gaping at the startling ruins strewn before them. Nobody moves for the longest time. Something about the wreckage mesmerizes them, and keeps them glued to the threshold.

"Everybody stay put," Philip finally says, pulling a handkerchief and wiping moisture from his neck. He sidesteps a mangled stuffed bear, and then he cautiously moves deeper into the shop. He sees an unmarked rear exit, maybe a stockroom, maybe a way out. Brian gently puts Penny down, and checks her for any signs of injury.

Penny stares at the sad rubble of decapitated Barbies and disemboweled stuffed animals.

"When I ran across this place," Nick is saying from across the room, looking for something, "I was thinking they might have stuff we could use, gadgets, walkie-talkies, flashlights . . . *something*." He moves around the end of the cashier's counter, up a few steps, and over to a perch behind the register. "Place like this, in this part of town . . . hell, they might even have a gun."

"What's back there, Nicky?" Philip shoots a thumb at a curtained doorway in the rear of the store. The black privacy drape hangs down to the floor. "You get a chance to check it out?"

"Stockroom is my guess. Be careful, Philly. It's dark back there."

Philip pauses by the curtain, shrugs off his backpack and fishes in it for the small penlight he keeps in the side pocket. He flips it on, and he pushes his way through the drape . . . vanishing into the gloom.

Across the store, Penny is transfixed by the broken dolls and eviscerated teddy bears. Brian watches her closely. He aches to help her, aches to get everybody back on track, but all he can do right now is kneel next to the child and try to keep her distracted. "You want one of those candy bars?"

"Nope." It comes out of her like the crackle of a pull-string doll, her eyes fixed on all the busted toys.

"You sure?"

"Yep."

"We got Twinkies," Brian tells her, trying to fill the silence, trying to keep her talking, trying to keep her occupied. But right now, all Brian can think about is the look on Philip's face, and the violence in his eyes, and the whole world—*their world*—falling apart.

"No, I'm okay," Penny says. She sees a little Hello Kitty backpack lying in a pile of trash, and she goes over to it. She picks it up, inspects it. "You think anybody would get mad if I took some of these things?"

"What things, kiddo?" Brian looks at her. "You mean the toys?"

She nods.

A stab of sorrow and shame cleaves Brian's midsection. "Go for it," he says.

She starts gathering up pieces of trampled dolls and tattered stuffed animals. It looks almost like a ritual to Brian, like a rite of passage for the little girl, as she selects Barbies with missing limbs and teddy bears with torn seams. She slips the injured toys into the knapsack with the care of someone performing triage at a clinic. Brian lets out a sigh.

Right then, Philip's voice calls out from somewhere deep in the guts of the back hallway, cutting off Brian's thoughts—he was about to fecklessly offer Penny the sausage stick—and now Brian springs to his feet. "What did he say?"

Across the shop, behind the cash register, Nick perks up. "I don't know—I didn't hear."

"Philip!" Brian starts toward the back curtain, his flesh crawling with nervous tension. "You okay?"

Hasty footsteps shuffle inside the draped doorway, and all at once, the curtain flaps open and Philip is peering out at them with a wild expression contorting his face, somewhere between excitement and mania. "Grab your shit, we just won the Irish fucking sweepstakes!"

Philip takes them down a narrow, dark corridor, past shelves of unopened toys and games, around a corner, and through a security door apparently left unlocked amid the previous occupants' hurried exodus. Down another narrow hallway, guided by the thin beam of Philip's penlight, and they come to a fire escape. The metal door is slightly ajar, the shadows of a passageway visible on the other side.

"Get a load of what's on the other side of our little toy store." Philip pushes the fire door open with his boot. "Our ticket out of this hellhole."

The metal door swings wide, and Brian finds himself staring across another narrow hallway at the mirror image of the first fire door.

The metal door across the hall is also ajar, and

through the gap Brian sees, cloaked in shadows, rows of gleaming spoked wheels. "Oh my God," he utters. "Is that what I think it is?"

The space is huge—encompassing the entire corner of the adjacent building's first floor—lined with reinforced window glass on three sides. Visible through the windows is the street corner outside, where shadowy forms wander aimlessly, drifting through the rain like doomed souls, but *inside*—in the shiny, happy world of Champion Cycle Center, Atlanta's premier motorcycle dealership—all is warm and tidy and polished to a high sheen.

The showroom appears to be untouched by the plague. In the wan, overcast light filtering in through the massive display windows, motor-cycles of all makes and models are lined up in four neat rows extending from one end of the dealership to the other. The air smells of new rubber and oiled leather and finely honed steel. The edges of the showroom are carpeted with logo-embroidered pile as lush and new as a fancy hotel lobby. Powerless neon signs hang down at junctures with product legends: Kawasaki, Ducati, Yamaha, Honda, Triumph, Harley-Davidson, and Suzuki.

"You think any of them have gas in them?" Brian turns in a slow three-sixty, taking in the whole of the showroom.

"We got our pick of the litter, sport." Philip nods

toward the rear of the room, past the sales counter and desks and shelves brimming with parts. "They got a workspace back there with a garage out back . . . we can siphon fuel into any one of them things easy enough."

Penny stares emotionlessly at the banquet of chrome and rubber. She has the Hello Kitty pack strapped securely to her tiny shoulders.

Brian's head is swimming. Contrary emotions crash up against each other like whitecaps— excitement, anxiety, hope, fear. "Only one problem," he utters under his breath, the weight of his anguish and uncertainty pressing down on his shoulders.

Philip looks at his brother. "What the hell's the problem now?"

Brian wipes his mouth. "I have no idea how to work one of those things."

They all have a much-needed laugh—nervous, brittle laughter, perhaps, but laughter nonetheless— at the expense of Brian. Philip assures his brother that it doesn't make one lick of difference that Brian has never ridden a motorcycle—a "retard" could learn it in two minutes. More importantly, both Philip and Nick have owned hogs over the years, and the last time Philip checked, there was only four of them, so the two nonoperators can ride along on the saddles.

"Faster we get outta A-T-L, the better chances we

got with no guns," Philip says minutes later, rifling through a rack of leathers in the rear corner of the store—jackets, trousers, vests, and accessories. He chooses a bomber-brown Harley jacket and a pair of heavy-duty black boots. "I want everybody changed outta their wet clothes and ready to go in five minutes—Brian, you help Penny."

They get changed as the rain eases up outside the big windows. The street corner crawls with shambling figures now—scores of frayed, tattered souls, some of them scorched from the explosion, others in advanced stages of decomposition. Faces are starting to cave in, some of them dripping with parasites and blackening into moldy masks of putrefied flesh. None of them, however, notices the movement inside the dark showroom.

"You see them Biters gathering out there?" Nick says to Philip under his breath. Nick already has dry clothes on, and is zipping up a black leather jacket. He gives a little nod toward the gray light of the storefront. "Some of them things are pretty ripe."

"So?"

"Some of them got—what?—three, four weeks on 'em?"

"At least." Philip thinks about it for a moment, changing out of his wet denims. His underwear is stuck to him and he has to practically peel it off. He turns away so that Penny doesn't see his package. "Whole thing broke out over a month ago . . . so what?"

"They're rotting."

"Huh?"

Nick lowers his voice so that he doesn't catch Penny's ear; the little girl is busying herself across the showroom with a size small winter coat, which Brian is trying to figure out how to snap. "Think about it, Philly. The normal course of affairs, a dead body is dust in a year or so." He lowers his voice further. "Especially one that's exposed to the elements."

"What are you saying, Nick? All we gotta do is wait out the clock? Let the maggots do the work?"

Nick shrugs. "Well, yeah, I guess I just thought—"

"Listen to me." Philip jabs a finger in Nick's face. "Keep your theories to yourself."

"I didn't mean to—"

"They ain't going away, Nicky. Get that through your thick fucking skull. I don't want my daughter hearing any of this shit. They eat the living, and they reproduce, and when they rot away, there's gonna be more of them to take their place, and judging from the fact that old man Chalmers turned without even getting bit, the whole goddamn world's days are numbered, so drink up, bubba, it's later than y'all think."

Nick looks down. "All right, man, I get it . . . cool down, Philly."

At this point, Brian has Penny bundled up, and the two of them come over. "We're as ready as we'll ever be."

"What time you got?" Philip asks Brian, who looks semiridiculous in a Harley leather jacket that's a size and half too big for him.

He looks at his watch. "Almost noon."

"Good . . . gives us a good six, seven hours of daylight to get the hell outta Dodge."

"You guys pick out your bikes?" Brian asks.

Philip gives him a cold smile.

They choose two of the biggest metal masterpieces in the place—a couple of Harley-Davidson Electra Glides, one in pearl blue and the other in midnight black. They choose them for the size of the engines, the roominess of the seats, the cubic inches of storage space, and also because—hey—they're fucking Harleys. Philip decides that Penny will ride with him, and Brian will ride with Nick. The gas tanks are empty but several bikes in the repair garage in the rear have fuel in them so they siphon as much as they can into the Harleys.

Over the course of the fifteen minutes it takes them to get the bikes ready and find helmets that fit and transfer all their belongings into the luggage carriers, the street outside the front of the place grows hectic with dead. Hundreds of Biters crowd the intersection now, wandering aimlessly in the gray drizzle, brushing against the glass, groaning their rusty groans, drooling their black bile, fixing their pewter-colored eyes on the moving shadows inside the windows of Champion Cycle Center.

"It's busy out there," Nick mumbles to no one in particular as he rolls the massive two-wheeler toward the side exit, where a small vertical garage door faces the parking lot along the side of the dealership. He straps on his helmet.

"Element of surprise," Philip says, pushing his black Harley over to the door. His stomach growls with hunger and nerves as he puts on his helmet. He hasn't eaten in nearly twenty-four hours. None of them has. He shoves the iron rod from the bus into a seam between the handlebars and windscreen (for quick and easy access). "C'mon, punkin, hop on," he says to Penny, who stands sheepishly nearby with a kiddie helmet on. "Gonna take a little spin, get outta this place."

Brian helps the child climb up onto the rear seat, a padded perch above the black lacquer luggage compartment. There's a safety belt in one of the side compartments, and Brian snaps it around the little girl's waist. "Don't worry, kiddo," he says softly to her.

"Gonna head south and then west, y'all," Philip says as he mounts the iron beast. "Nicky, you follow me."

"Copy that."

"Everybody ready?"

313

Brian goes over to the door and gives a nervous nod. "Ready."

Philip kicks the Harley to life, the engine howling and filling the dark showroom with noise and fumes. Nick kicks his bike on. The second engine sings a noisy aria in dissonant unison with the first. Philip revs the throttle and gives Brian the high sign.

Brian jacks the manual lock on the door and then throws it open, letting in the wet wind. Philip kicks the gear and takes off.

Brian leaps onto the back of Nick's bike and they blast off after Philip.

"OH SHIT! OH GOD! PHILIP! PHILIP! LOOK DOWN! LOOK DOWN, MAN! PHILIP, LOOK DOWN!"

Brian's frantic wail is muffled by his helmet and drowned by the noise of the cycles.

It happens mere moments after they slam through a mass of Biters choking the intersection, the ragged bodies bouncing off their fenders. After making a hard left turn and zooming south on Water Street, leaving the throngs in their dust and fumes, Brian sees the mangled corpse dragging along the pavement behind Philip's bike.

The bottom half of the thing is torn away, its intestines like electrical wiring flagging in the wind, but the torso still has fight left in it, its moldering head still intact. With its two dead arms, it clings to the rear fenders, and it starts pulling itself up the side of the Harley.

The worst part is, neither Philip nor Penny seem to be aware of it.

"PULL ALONGSIDE HIM! NICK, PULL UP!" Brian screams, his arms clutched around Nick's midsection.

"I'M TRYING!"

At this point, roaring down the deserted, wet side street, the bike hydroplaning on slick pavement, Penny notices the creature stuck to the bike, clawing its way toward her, and she starts screaming. From Brian's vantage point, thirty feet behind her, the child's scream is inaudible—like an exaggerated gesture of a silent-movie actress.

Nick opens up the throttle. His Harley closes the distance.

"GRAB THE BAT!" he screams over the din, and Brian tries to root the baseball bat out from beneath the luggage carrier behind him.

Up ahead, almost without warning, Philip Blake notices the thing attached to the back of his bike. Philip's helmet cocks around quickly as he gropes for his weapon.

By this point, Nick is within five or six feet of the black Harley's taillights, but before Brian can intercede with the bat, he sees Philip drawing the iron rod from its makeshift scabbard on the front of his bike.

With a quick and violent motion, which causes

the black Harley to veer slightly off course, Philip twists around in his seat—one-handing the handlebars—and thrusts the hooked end of the metal rod into the zombie's mouth.

The skewered head of the monster gets stuck inches below Penny, the rod wedged between the gleaming exhaust pipes. Philip draws his right leg up and—with the force of a battering ram—he kicks the corpse (rod and all) off the bike. The thing tumbles and rolls, and Nick has to swerve suddenly to avoid it.

Philip increases his speed, staying on course, heading south, not even bothering to look back.

They continue on, zigzagging through the south side of town, avoiding the congested areas. A mile down the road, Philip manages to find another main artery that's relatively clear of wreckage and roaming dead, and he leads them down it. They are now three miles from the Atlanta city limits.

The horizon line is clear, the sky lightening slightly to the west.

They have enough gas to get four hundred miles without refueling.

Whatever awaits them out there in the gray rural countryside has to be better than what they suffered through in Atlanta.

It *has* to be.

PART 3

Chaos Theory

No man chooses evil because it is evil;
he only mistakes it for happiness,
the good he seeks.
—Mary Wollstonecraft

seventeen

Around Hartsfield airport, the rain lets up, leaving behind a scoured, metallic sky of low clouds and dismal cold. It feels terrific, however, to get this far in less than an hour. Highway 85 has far less wreckage blocking its lanes than Interstate 20, and the population of dead has thinned considerably. Most roadside buildings are still intact, their windows and doors battened and secured. The stray dead walking about here and there almost seem like part of the landscape now—blending into the skeletal trees like a ghastly fungus infecting the woods. The land itself seems to have turned. The towns *themselves* are dead. Riding through this area leaves one with more of an impression of *desolation* than the end of the world.

The only immediate problem is the fact that every abandoned filling station or truck stop is infested with Biters, and Brian is getting very concerned about Penny. At every pit stop—either to take a leak or to forage for food or water—her face seems more drawn, her tiny little tulip lips more cracked. Brian is worried she's getting dehydrated. Hell, he's worried they're *all* getting dehydrated.

Empty stomachs are one thing (they can go without food for extended lengths of time), but the lack of water is becoming a serious issue.

Ten miles southwest of Hartsfield, as the landscape begins to transition into patchworks of pine forests and soy bean farms, Brian is wondering if they could drink the water from the motorcycles' radiators, when he sees a green directional sign looming up ahead with a blessed message: REST AREA—1 MI. Philip gives them a signal to pull off, and they take the next exit ramp.

As they roar uphill and into the lot, which is bordered by a small wood-framed tourist center, the relief spreads through Brian like a salve: The place is mercifully deserted, free of any signs of the living *or* the dead.

"What really happened back there, Philip?" Brian sits on a picnic table situated on a small promontory of grass behind the rest area shack. Philip paces, sucking down a bottle of Evian that he wrested from a broken vending machine. Nick and Penny are fifty yards away, still within view. Nick is gently spinning Penny on a ramshackle old merry-go-round under a diseased live oak. The girl just sits on the thing, joylessly, like a gargoyle, staring straight out as she turns and turns and turns.

"I told you once already to give that a rest," Philip grumbles.

"I think you like owe me an answer."

"I don't owe you shit."

"Something happened that night," Brian persists.

He isn't afraid of his brother anymore. He knows Philip could beat the shit out of him at any moment—the potential for violence between the Blakes seems more imminent now than ever—but Brian doesn't care anymore. Something deep within Brian Blake has shifted like a seismic plate changing with the landscape. If Philip wants to wring Brian's throat, so be it. "Something between you and April?"

Philip gets very still and looks down. "What the fuck difference does it make?"

"It makes a big difference—it does to *me*. Our lives are on the line here. We had a pretty fair chance of surviving back there at that place, and then, just like that . . . poof?"

Philip looks up. His eyes fix themselves on his brother, and something very dark passes between the two men. "Drop it, Brian."

"Just tell me one thing. You seemed so hell-bent to get outta there—do you have a plan?"

"Whaddaya mean?"

"Do you have, like, a strategy? Any idea where the hell we're headed?"

"What are you, a fuckin' tour guide?"

"What if the Biters get thick again? We basically got a piece of wood to fight 'em with."

"We'll find something else."

"Where are we going, Philip?"

Philip turns away and lifts the collar of his leather bomber, staring out at the ribbon of pavement snaking off into the western horizon. "Another month or so, winter's gonna set in. I'm thinking we stay moving, heading southwest . . . toward the Mississippi."

"Where's that gonna get us?"

"It's the easiest way to go south."

"And?"

Philip turns and looks at Brian, a mixture of purpose and anguish crossing Philip's deeply lined face, as though he doesn't really believe what he's saying. "We'll find a place to live—long-term—in the sun. Someplace like Mobile or Biloxi. New Orleans, maybe . . . I don't know. Someplace warm. And we'll live there."

Brian lets out an exhausted sigh. "Sounds so easy. Just head south."

"You got a better plan, I'm all ears."

"Long-term plans are like a luxury I haven't even thought about."

"We'll make it."

"We gotta find some food, Philip. I'm really worried about Penny getting some nourishment."

"You let me do the worrying about my daughter."

"She won't even eat a Twinkie. You believe that? A kid who doesn't want a Twinkie."

"Cockroach food." Philip grunts. "Can't say I blame her. We'll find something. She's gonna be okay. She's a tough little thing . . . like her mother."

Brian can't argue with that. Lately, the little girl has shown miraculous spirit. In fact, Brian has started wondering whether Penny might actually be the glue that's holding them all together, keeping them from self-destructing.

He glances across the rest area and sees Penny Blake dreamily spinning on that rusty merry-go-round in the little scabrous playground area. Nick has lost his enthusiasm for turning it and now just gives it little incremental nudges with his boot.

Beyond the playground, the land rises up to an overgrown wooded knoll, where a small wind-swept cemetery sits in the pale sun.

Brian notices that Penny is talking to Nick, grilling him about something. Brian wonders what the two of them are talking about that has the girl looking so worried.

"Uncle Nick?" Penny's little face is tight with concern as she slowly turns on the merry-go-round. She has called Nick "Uncle" for years, even though she knows very well he is not her real uncle. The affectation has always given Nick a secret twinge of longing—the desire to be somebody's *real* uncle.

"Yes, honey?" A leaden feeling of doom presses down on Nick Parsons as he absently pushes Penny on the merry-go-round. He can see the Blake brothers in his peripheral vision, arguing about something.

"Is my dad mad at me?" the little girl asks.

Nick does a double take. Penny looks down as she slowly spins. Nick measures his words. "Of course not. He's not mad at you. Whaddaya mean? Why would you even think that?"

"He don't talk to me as much as he used to."

Nick gently pulls the merry-go-round to a stop. The little girl jerks slightly back against the bar. Nick tenderly pats her on the shoulder. "Listen. I promise you. Your daddy loves you more than anything else in the world."

"I know."

"He's under a lot of pressure. That's all."

"You don't think he's mad at me?"

"No way. He loves you something fierce, Penny. Believe me. He's just . . . under a lot of pressure."

"Yeah . . . I guess so."

"We all are."

"Yeah."

"I'm sure *none* of us have been talking all that much lately."

"Uncle Nick?"

"Yes, sweetie?"

"Do you think Uncle Brian's mad at me?"

"God, no. Why would Uncle Brian be mad at you?"

"Maybe 'cause he's gotta carry me all the time?"

Nick smiles sadly. He studies the look on the girl's face, her little brow all furrowed with seriousness. He strokes her cheek. "Listen to me. You are the bravest little girl I ever met. I mean that. You are a Blake girl . . . and that's something to be proud of."

She thinks about this and smiles. "You know what I'm gonna do?"

"No, honey. Tell me."

"I'm gonna fix all them broken dolls. You'll see. I'm gonna fix 'em."

Nick grins at her. "That sounds like a plan."

The little girl's smile is something that Nick Parson's wondered if he would ever see again.

A moment later, on the other side of the rest area, among the picnic tables, Brian Blake sees something out of the corner of his eye. A hundred yards away, beyond the playground, amid the crumbling headstones, long-faded markers, and tattered plastic flowers, something moves.

Brian locks his gaze on three distant figures emerging from the shadows of the trees. Shuffling along in haphazard formation, they approach like lazy bloodhounds smelling the kill. It's hard to tell at this distance but they look as though their clothes have been fed through a reaper, their mouths hanging open in perpetual torment.

"Time to get our asses in gear," Philip says with very little urgency, and he starts toward the playground with a kind of heavy, mechanical stride.

As he hurries after him, it occurs to Brian, just for an instant, that the way his brother is walking, his muscular arms limp at his sides, the weight of the world on his shoulders, he could very easily—from a distance—be mistaken for a zombie himself.

They put more miles behind them. They skirt small towns as empty and still as dioramas in a vast museum. The blue light of dusk starts pulling its shade down on the overcast sky, the wind turning bitter against their visors as they weave around wrecks and deserted trailers, working their way west on 85. Brian starts thinking that they need to find a place to spend the night.

Perched on the saddle behind Nick, his eyes watering, his ears deafened by the wind and the roar of the Harley's twin-cam engine, Brian has plenty of time to imagine the perfect place for the weary traveler in the land of the dead. He imagines an enormous, sprawling fortress with gardens and walks and impenetrable moats and security fences and guard towers. He would give his left nut for a steak and French fries. Or a bottle of Coke. Or even some of the Chalmerses' mystery meat—

A reflection off the inside of his helmet visor interrupts the flow of his thoughts.

He glances over his shoulder.

Strange. For the briefest instant there, at the precise same moment he saw a dark blot blur across the inside of his visor, he thought he felt something on the back of his neck, a faint sensation, like the kiss of cold lips. It might just be his imagination, but he also thought he saw something flicker across the side mirror. Just for an instant. Right before they began banking to the south.

He gazes over his shoulder and sees nothing behind them but empty lanes tumbling away, receding into the distance and then vanishing around the curve. He shrugs and turns back to his rambling, chaotic thoughts.

They venture deeper into the rural hinterlands, until they see nothing but miles and miles of broken-down farms and unincorporated boonies. The rolling hills of bean fields plunge down steep moraines on either side of the highway. This is old land—prehistoric, tired, worked to death by generations. Carcasses of old machinery lie dormant everywhere, buried in kudzu and mud.

Dusk starts settling into night, the sky fading from pale gray to a deep indigo. It's after seven o'clock now and Brian has completely forgotten about the peculiar flash of movement reflecting off the inside of his visor. They need to find cover. Philip's headlamp comes on, flinging a shaft of silver light into the gathering shadows.

Brian is about to shout something about finding a hideout when he sees Philip signaling up ahead—a stiff wave, and then a gloved finger jabbing to the right. Brian glances off to the north and sees what his brother is pointing at.

327

Way off in the distant rolling farmland, rising above a prominence of trees, the silhouette of a house is visible—so far away, it looks like a delicate cutout of black construction paper. If Philip had not pointed it out, Brian never would have noticed it. But now he sees why it has sunk a hook into Philip: It looks like a grand old relic of the nineteenth century, maybe even the eighteenth century, probably once a plantation house.

Brian sees another flicker of dark movement out of the corner of his eye, flashing across the side mirror, something behind them, passing just for a fraction of a second through the outer edges of his vision.

Then it's gone, vanishing as Brian twists around in his seat to gaze over his shoulder.

They take the next exit and boom down a dusty dirt road. As they close in on the house—which sits all by its lonesome at the crest of a vast foothill at least half a mile off the highway—Brian shivers in the cold. He has a terrible feeling all of sudden, despite the fact that the closer they get to the farmhouse, the more inviting it looks. This area of Georgia is known for its orchards—peaches, figs, and plums—and as they roar up a winding drive that leads to the house, they see that it's an aging beauty.

Surrounded by peach trees, which spread off into the distance like the spokes of a wheel, the central building is a massive two-story brick pile with ornate garrets and dormers rising off the roof. It has the flavor of an old, decrepit Italian villa. The porch is a fifty-foot-long portico with columns, balustrades, and mullioned windows choked with vines of brown ivy and bougainvillea. In the fading light, it looks almost like a ghost ship from some pre–Civil War armada.

The noise and fumes of the Harleys swirl in the dusty air as Philip leads them across the front lot, which is bordered by a massive, decorative fountain made of marble and masonry. Apparently fallen into disrepair, the fountain has a film of scum across its basin. Several outbuildings— stables, perhaps—lie off to the right. A tractor lies half-buried in crabgrass. To the left of the front façade sits a massive carriage house, big enough for six cars.

None of this antique opulence registers with Brian as they cautiously pull up to a side door between the garage and the main house.

Philip brings his Harley to a stop in a thunder-head of dust, revving the motor for a moment. He kills the engine and sits there, staring up at the salmon-colored brick monstrosity. Nick pulls next to him and snaps down his kickstand. They don't say a word for the longest time. Finally, Philip lowers his stand, dismounts, and says to Penny, "Stay here for a second, punkin."

Nick and Brian dismount.

"You got that baseball bat handy?" Philip says without even looking at them.

"You think there's anybody in there?" Nick asks.

"Only one way to find out."

Philip waits for Nick to go around the back of his Electra Glide and fetch the bat, which is sheathed down one side of his luggage carrier. He brings it back and hands it over.

"You two stay with Penny," Philip says, and starts toward the portico.

Brian stops him, grabbing his arm.

"Philip—" Brian is about to say something about dark shapes flashing across his side mirror back on the highway, but he stops himself. He's not sure he wants Penny to hear this.

"The hell's the matter with you?" Philip says.

Brian swallows air. "I think there's somebody following us."

The former occupants of the villa are long gone. In fact, the inside of the place looks as though it's been sitting empty since long before the plague broke out. Yellowed sheets cover the antique furniture. The many rooms are empty, dusty chambers frozen in time. A grandfather clock still ticks stubbornly in a parlor. Niceties of a bygone era festoon the house: ornate moldings and French doors and circular staircases and two separate and massive fireplaces with hearths the size of walk-in closets. Under one sheet sits a grand piano, under another a Victrola, under another a wood-burning stove.

Philip and Nick sweep the upper floors for Biters and find nothing other than more dusty relics of the Old South: a library, a corridor of oil paintings of Confederate generals in gilded frames, a nursery with a dusty old cradle dating back to Colonial times. The kitchen is surprisingly small—another holdover from the nineteenth century when only servants dirtied their hands with cooking—but the enormous pantry has shelves brimming with dusty canned goods. The dry grains and cereals are all mealy and crawling with worms, but the array of fruits and vegetables is staggering.

"You're seeing things, sport," Philip says under his breath that night in front of a crackling fire in the front parlor. They found piles of cordwood in the backyard by the barn and now they've managed to warm their bones for the first time since leaving Atlanta. The warmth and shelter of the villa—as well as the nourishment of canned peaches and okra—caused Penny to instantly doze off. She now slumbers on a luxurious down comforter in the nursery on the second floor. Nick sleeps in the room next to her. But the two brothers have insomnia. "Who the hell would bother following *us* anyway?" Philip adds, taking another sip of the expensive cooking sherry he found in the pantry.

"I'm telling you, I saw what I saw," Brian says, nervously rocking on a bentwood chair on the other side of the fire. He's got a dry shirt on and a pair of sweatpants, and he feels almost human again. He looks over at his brother, and sees that Philip is staring intensely at the fire as though it holds a secret coded message.

For some reason, the sight of Philip's gaunt, troubled face, reflecting the flicker of firelight, breaks Brian's heart. He flashes back to epic childhood journeys into the woods, overnight stays in pup tents and cabins. He remembers having his first beer with his brother, back when Philip was only ten and Brian was thirteen, and he remembers Philip being able to drink him under the table even then.

"It might have been a car," Brian goes on. "Or maybe a van, I'm not sure. But I swear to God, I saw it back there just for a second . . . and it sure as hell seemed like it was tailing us."

"So what if there *is* somebody following us, who gives a rat's ass?"

Brian thinks about it for a second. "The only thing is . . . if they were friendly . . . wouldn't they, like, catch up with us? Signal to us?"

"Who knows . . ." Philip stares at the fire, his thoughts elsewhere. "Whoever they are . . . if they're out there, chances are, they're as fucked up as us."

"That's true, I guess." Brian thinks about it some

more. "Maybe they're just . . . scared. Maybe they're like . . . checking us out."

"Ain't nobody gonna be able to sneak up on us up here, I'll tell you that."

"Yeah . . . I guess."

Brian knows exactly what his brother is talking about. The location and position of the villa is ideal. Situated on a rise that overlooks miles of thinning trees, the house has sight lines that would give them plenty of warning. Even on a moonless night, the orchards are so still and quiet that nobody would be able to creep up on them without being heard or seen. And Philip is already talking about setting booby-trap wires around the periphery to alert them to intruders.

On top of that, the place offers them all sorts of benefits that could sustain them for quite a while, maybe even into the winter. There is a well out back, gas in the tractor, a place to hide the Harleys, miles of fruit trees still bearing edible albeit frost-shriveled fruit, and enough wood to keep the stoves and fireplaces going for months. The only problem is their lack of weapons. They scoured the villa and only found a few implements in the barn —a rusty old scythe, a pitchfork—but no firearms.

"You okay?" Brian says after a long stretch of silence.

"Fit as a fucking fiddle."

"You sure?"

"Yes, Grandma." Philip stares into the fire.

"We're all gonna be fit as fucking fiddles after a few days in this place."

"Philip?"

"What is it now?"

"Can I say something?"

"Here it comes." Philip doesn't take his eyes off the fire. He wears his wifebeater and a dry pair of jeans. His socks have holes in them, his big toe showing through one of them. The sight of this in the firelight—Philip's gnarled toenail sticking out—is heartrending for Brian. It makes his brother seem, maybe for the first time ever, almost vulnerable. It is highly unlikely that any of them would be alive right now if it weren't for Philip. Brian swallows back his emotion.

"I'm your brother, Philip."

"I'm aware of that, Brian."

"No, what I'm saying is . . . I don't judge you, I never will."

"What's your point?"

"My point is . . . I appreciate what you've been doing . . . risking your ass protecting us. I want you to know this. I appreciate it."

Philip doesn't say anything, but the way he's staring at that fire begins to change a little bit. He starts gazing *beyond* it, the flames making his eyes glimmer with emotion.

"I know you're a good person," Brian goes on. "I *know* this." A brief pause here. "I can tell something is eating at you."

"Brian—"

"Wait a minute, just hear me out." The conversation has crossed a Rubicon, now beyond the point of no return. "If you don't want to tell me what happened back there with you and April, that's fine. I'll never ask you again." There's a long pause. "But you can tell me, Philip. You can tell me because I'm your brother."

Philip turns and looks at Brian. A single tear tracks down Philip's chiseled, leathery face. It makes Brian's stomach clench. He can't remember ever having seen his brother cry, even as a child. One time, their daddy whipped a twelve-year-old Philip unmercifully with a hickory switch, raising so many welts on Philip's backside that he had to spend nights sleeping on his stomach, but he never cried. Almost out of spite, he refused to cry. But now, as he meets Brian's gaze in the flickering shadows, Philip's voice is drained as he says, "I fucked up, sport."

Brian nods, says nothing, just waits. The fire crackles and sizzles.

Philip looks down. "I think I sorta fell for her." The tear drips on him. But his voice never breaks, it just remains flat and weak: "Ain't gonna say it was love but what the fuck is love anyway? Love is a fucking disease." He cringes at some demon twisting in him. "I fucked up, Brian. Could've had something with her. Could've had something solid for Penny, something good." He grimaces as though holding off a tide of sorrow, tears welling up in his eyes until every time he blinks, they run down his face. "I couldn't stop myself. She said stop but I couldn't do it. I couldn't stop. See . . . the thing is . . . it felt so goddamn good." Tears dripping. "Even when she was pushing me away, it felt good." Silence. "What the fuck is wrong with me?" More silence. "I know there ain't no excuse for it." Pause. "I'm not stupid . . . I just didn't think I would ever . . . I didn't think I could . . . I didn't think . . ."

His voice crumbles until there's nothing but the crackle of the fire and the huge dark silence outside the villa. At length, after an interminable period of time, Philip looks up at his brother.

In the dancing light, Brian sees that the tears are spent. Nothing but barren anguish remains on Philip Blake's face. Brian doesn't say a word. He simply nods.

The next few days take them into November, and they decide to stay put and see what the weather does.

A freezing sleet sweeps across the orchards one morning. On another day, a killer frost grips the fields and takes down much of the fruit. But for all the signs of winter rolling in, they feel no compulsion to leave just yet. The villa might be their best bet to wait out the harsh days on the horizon. They've got enough canned goods and fruit—if they're careful—to keep them going for months. And enough wood to keep them warm. And the orchards seem relatively free of Biters, at least in the immediate vicinity.

In some ways, Philip seems to be doing better now that the burden of his guilt has been off-loaded. Brian keeps the secret to himself, thinking about it often, but never broaching the subject again. The two brothers are less edgy with each other, and even Penny seems to be settling in nicely to this new routine that they are carving out for themselves.

She finds an antique dollhouse in an upper parlor, and stakes out a little place for herself (and all her broken, misfit toys) at the end of the second-floor hallway. Brian comes up there one day and finds all the dolls lying in neat little rows on the floor, all the severed appendages lying next to their corresponding bodies. He stares for quite a long while at the strange miniature morgue before Penny snaps him out of his daze. "C'mon, Uncle Brian," she says. "You can be a doctor . . . help me put them back together."

"Yeah, that's a good idea," he says with a nod. "Let's put them back together."

On another occasion, early in the morning, Brian hears a sound coming from the first floor. He goes down into the kitchen and finds Penny standing on a chair, covered in flour and gunk, fiddling with pots and pans, her hair matted with makeshift pancake batter. The kitchen is a disaster area. The others arrive, and the three men just stand there, in the doorway of the kitchen, staring. "Don't be mad," Penny says, glancing over her shoulder. "I promise I'll clean up the mess."

The men look at each other. Philip, grinning now for the first time in weeks, says, "Who's mad? We ain't mad. We're just hungry. When's breakfast gonna be ready?"

As the days pass, they take precautions. They decide to burn firewood only at night, when the smoke cannot be seen from the highway. Philip and Nick construct a perimeter of baling wire stretched between small wooden stakes at each corner of the property, placing tin cans at key junctures, to alarm them of possible intruders— Biters and human alike. They even find an old antique double-barrel 12-gauge in the villa's attic.

The shotgun is filmed in dust and engraved with cherubs, and looks as if it might blow up in their faces if they tried to fire the thing. They don't even have any shells for it—the gun looks like the kind of thing somebody would hang in their study on the wall next to old photographs of Ernest Hemingway—but Philip sees some value in having it around. It looks threatening enough—on a galloping horse, as his dad used to say.

"You never know," Philip says one night, leaning

the shotgun against the hearth and settling back to numb himself with more cooking sherry.

The days continue to slip away with shapeless regularity. They catch up on their sleep, and they explore the orchards, and they harvest fruit. They set box traps for stray critters and one day they even catch a scrawny jackrabbit. Nick volunteers to clean the thing, and he ends up making a fairly decent braised rabbit on the woodstove that night.

They have only a few encounters with Biters during this time. One day, Nick is halfway up a tree, reaching for some withered plums, when he sees a walking corpse in farmer's overalls way off in the shadows of a neighboring grove. He calmly climbs down and sneaks up on the thing with his pitchfork, skewering the back of its head as though popping a balloon. On another occasion, Philip is siphoning gas from a tractor when he notices a mangled corpse in a nearby drainage ditch. Legs smashed and contorted underneath it, the woman-thing looks like it dragged itself miles to get here. Philip chops off its head with the scythe, and burns the remains with a squirt of gas and a spark of a Bic.

Piece of cake.

All the while, the villa seems to be adopting them as much as they are adopting it. With all the sheets removed from the opulent old furniture, it seems almost like a place they could call home.

They each have their own room now. And although they're each still plagued by nightmares, there's nothing more soothing than coming down to an old elegant kitchen with the November sun streaming through French windows, and the fragrance of a coffeepot that's been simmering all night.

In fact, if it weren't for the periodic feelings of being watched, things would be pretty close to perfect.

The feelings began to intensify for Brian as early as the second night they were there. Brian had just moved into his own bedroom on the second floor—an austere sewing parlor with a quaint little four-poster bed and an eighteenth-century armoire—when he sprang awake in the middle of the night.

He had been dreaming that he was a castaway, adrift on a makeshift raft on a sea of blood, when he saw a flash of light. In the dream, he thought it might be a distant lighthouse on some distant shore, summoning him, rescuing him from this endless plague of blood, but when he awakened, he realized he had just seen *actual* light in the *waking* world—just for a second—a rectangular slice of light, sliding across the ceiling.

In a blink, it was gone.

He wasn't even sure he had actually seen it, but every fiber of his being told him to get up and go to the window. He did, and gazing out at the black void of the night, he could have sworn he caught a glimpse of a car, a quarter mile away, turning around at the point where the highway met the farm road. Then the thing vanished, sliding into nothingness.

Brian found it exceedingly difficult to get any more sleep that night.

When he told Philip and Nick about it the next morning, they simply wrote it off as a dream. Who the hell would pull off the highway, and then turn around and take off?

But the suspicion grew in Brian over that next week and a half. At night, he kept catching glimpses of slowly moving lights out on the highway or on the far side of the orchard. Some nights, in the wee hours, he could swear that he was hearing the crunch of tires on gravel. The furtive, fleeting quality of these sounds was the worst part. It gave Brian the feeling that somehow the villa was being *cased*. But he got so tired of having his paranoid suspicion dismissed by the others that he simply stopped reporting it. Maybe he *was* imagining all of it.

He didn't say another word on the matter until the two-week anniversary of their stay in the villa, when, at a point just before dawn, the sound of tin cans rattling stirred him from a deep sleep.

eighteen

"What the hell?" Brian snaps awake in the darkness of his room. He fumbles for one of the kerosene lanterns on his bedside table, knocking over the hurricane glass and spilling fluid. He gets up and goes to the window, the floor icy on the soles of his bare feet.

Moonlight shines down from a crystalline cold autumn night sky, lining every shape outside with a luminous halo of silver. Brian can still hear the tin cans on the trip wires rattling out there somewhere. He can also hear the others stirring in their bedrooms behind him, down the hall. Everybody is up now, awakened by the jangling cans.

The strangest part is—and Brian wonders if he's imagining this—the rattling sounds are coming from all directions. Tin cans are clattering in the groves *behind* the villa as well as in front of it. Brian is craning his neck to see better when his bedroom door bursts open.

"Sport! You up?" Philip is shirtless, wearing jeans and logger boots that he hasn't had a chance to tie yet. He holds the old shotgun with one hand, his eyes wide open with alarm. "I'm gonna need you to go get that pitchfork in the back hallway —pronto!"

"Is it Biters?"

"Just get moving!"

Brian gives a nod and hurries out of the room, his brain swimming with panic. He wears only his sweatpants and a sleeveless T-shirt. As he pads through the darkness of the house—down the stairs, across the parlor, and into the back hall—he senses movement outside the windows, the presence of others closing in on them from outside.

Grabbing the pitchfork, which leans against the back door, Brian whirls and heads back to the front room.

By this point, Philip, Nick, and even Penny have reached the bottom of the steps. They go to the front bay window, which offers a wide-angle view of the surrounding yards, the sloping drive down to the adjacent road, and even the edge of the closest orchard. Immediately they see dark shapes—low to the ground—sliding across the property from three different directions.

"Are those cars?" Nick utters in barely a whisper.

As their eyes adjust to the moonlit night, they each realize that yes, indeed, those *are* cars moving slowly across the property toward the villa. One comes up the winding drive, another one from the north end of the orchard, a third just visible to the south, crunching slowly over the gravel path leading out of the trees.

Almost with perfect synchronous timing, each

vehicle suddenly stops at an equidistant point from the house. They sit there for a second, each one maybe fifty feet away, their windows too dark to reveal their occupants. "This ain't no welcome wagon," Philip murmurs, the understatement of the evening.

Again, almost in perfect concurrence, each pair of headlights suddenly snaps on. The effect is fairly dramatic—almost theatrical, in fact—as the beams strike the windows of the villa, filling the dark interior with cold chromium light. Philip is about to go outside and make a stand with the defunct shotgun when the sound of a crash is heard, coming from the rear of the villa.

"Punkin, you stay with Brian," Philip says to Penny. Then he shoots a glance at Nick. "Nicky, I want you to see if you can slip out a side window, take the machete, double back on 'em if you can. You follow me?"

Nick understands exactly what he's saying, and he takes off down the side hallway.

"Stay behind me, but stay close." Philip raises the shotgun, the butt against his shoulder. Carefully and focused with cobralike calm, Philip shuffles commando-style toward the sound of footsteps on broken glass now coming from the kitchen.

"Nice and easy does it, hoss," the home invader says in a cheerful Tennessee twang, raising the barrel of a nine-millimeter Glock as Philip enters the kitchen with the shotgun also raised.

Before being so rudely interrupted, the intruder had been calmly looking around the kitchen as though he had just climbed out of bed for a midnight snack. Headlamps, coming from outside, pierce the room with harsh radiance. The pane of glass above the doorknob behind the man is busted in, and the faint light of dawn is just beginning to glow.

Well over six feet tall, dressed in shopworn camo-pants, muddy jackboots, and a blood-soaked Kevlar flak vest, the home invader is completely bald, with a scarred, missile-shaped head and eyes like craters cut by tiny meteors. On closer scrutiny, he looks sick, like he's been exposed to radiation, his jaundiced skin mottled with sores.

Philip points the worthless antique shotgun at the bald man's cranium—about eight feet between the two men—and Philip concentrates on pretending—maybe even believing—that the shotgun is loaded. "I'll give y'all the benefit of the doubt," Philip says. "I'll assume you thought the place was empty."

"That's exactly right, hoss," the bald man says, his voice calm, maybe medicated, like that of a dreamy disc jockey. His teeth are capped in gold, and they shimmer dully as he smiles a reptilian smile.

"So, we'll thank y'all to just leave us be—no harm, no foul."

The man with the Glock apes a hurt frown. "Now, that ain't too neighborly of you." The man has a slight tremor, a tic, percolating with latent violence. "I see y'all got a cute little thang back there."

"Never mind that." Philip stands his ground. He can hear the front door squeak, footsteps crossing the parlor. His brain crashes with panic and warring impulses. He knows the next few seconds are critical, maybe even mortally so. But all he can think of doing is to stall. "We don't want any bloodshed, and brother, I guarantee you, no matter what happens, yours and mine's gonna be the first blood that's shed."

"Smooth talker." The bald man calls out suddenly to one of his comrades in the dark. "Shorty?"

A voice answers from outside the back door. "Got him, Tommy!"

Almost on cue, Nick appears outside the jagged window of the back door, a large Bowie knife held against his windpipe. His captor, a skinny kid with pimples and a marine jarhead haircut, pushes open the door and shoves Nick into the kitchen.

"I'm sorry, Philly," Nick says as he is shoved against the cabinets—hard enough to steal his breath. The slender young man with the crew cut holds the knife against Nick's Adam's apple, a machete thrust down the young man's belt. A jittery, bony specimen with fingerless Carnaby gloves on his hands, the skinny kid looks like an escapee from a marine brig. His fatigue jacket has the sleeves torn off, and his long bare arms are riddled with jailhouse hieroglyph.

"Hold on, now," Philip says to the bald man. "There's no reason to—"

"Sonny!" The bald man calls out to another accomplice at the precise same moment Philip hears the footsteps creaking across the hundred-year-old hardwood floor out in the front parlor. Philip keeps the shotgun raised and aimed, but shoots a quick side glance back over his shoulder. Brian and Penny huddle in the shadows directly behind Philip, maybe five feet off his heels.

Two more figures have suddenly appeared behind Brian and Penny, making the little girl jump.

"Got it covered, Tommy!" says one of the figures as the steel-plated barrel of a large-caliber revolver—maybe a .357 Magnum, maybe an Army .45—becomes visible for all to see, pressing against the back of Brian Blake's skull. Brian stiffens like a cornered animal.

"Hold on now," Philip says.

In his peripheral vision, he can see that the two figures holding guns on Brian and Penny are a man and a woman . . . although he would use the word *woman* loosely in this case. The gal clutching a piece of Penny's collar is an androgynous marionette of skin and bones, clad in leather pants and layers of mesh, with lampblack eyeliner, spikey hair, and the slightly greenish pallor of a junkie. She nervously taps the barrel of a .38 police special against the shank of her beanpole thigh.

The man next to her—the one apparently named Sonny—also looks as though he's no stranger to the needle. His sunken eyes stare out from a pockmarked mask of ignorance and meanness, his emaciated form clad in army-surplus rags.

"I want to thank you, brother," the bald man says, shoving his nine-millimeter back into its belt sheath, acting like the showdown has now officially ended. "You dug up quite a spot here. I'll give you that." He goes over to the sink and calmly helps himself to the jug of well water sitting on the counter, quaffing down an entire glassful. "This'll do nicely as a home base."

"That's all well and good," Philip says, not making any move to lower his faux weapon. "Only problem is, we can't take on any more people."

"That's okay, brother."

"Then what exactly are you planning to . . . ? What are your intentions?"

"Our *intentions?*" The bald man enunciates the word with mock profundity. "Our intentions are to take this place from y'all."

Somebody that Philip can't see snickers with great amusement.

Philip's brain is a fractured chessboard, pieces moving now in herky-jerky motion. He knows that it's likely that these hardened road rats mean to kill him and everybody else in the house. He knows they're parasites, and they've most likely been circling the place like buzzards for weeks—Brian wasn't hearing things, it turns out.

Even now, Philip can hear others outside—low voices, twigs snapping—and he does the quick mental arithmetic: There are at least six of them, maybe more, and at least four vehicles, and each one seems to be heavily armed, with plenty of ammo—Philip can see mags and speed-loaders clipped to some of the belts—but the one thing they seem to lack that maybe, just maybe, Philip can work with, is the appearance of intelligence. Even the big bald guy—who seems to be the honcho—has the look of a dull stoner in his eyes. There won't be any appeals to mercy, no appeals to the better angels here. Philip has only one chance at survival.

"You mind if I say something?" he asks. "Before y'all do anything rash."

The bald man raises his glass as though giving a toast. "You got the floor, friend."

"We got two ways this can go down, is all I'm trying to say."

This seems to pique the bald man's curiosity. He sets down his glass and turns to Philip. "Only two ways?"

"One way is, we start blazing and I can tell you how that's gonna play out."

"Do tell."

"Your folks will overpower us and that'll be that, but the only thing is, I promise you one thing and—I'll be honest with you—I've never been so sure of anything in my life."

"And what's that?"

"No matter what, I know that I'll be able to get off a single shot, and I say this with no disrespect, but I will make damn sure that the overwhelmin' majority of these steel beads go into the top half of your body. Now, sir, do you want to hear option two?"

The bald man has lost his sense of humor. "Keep talkin'."

"Option two is you let us walk outta here alive, and you take our place with our compliments, and nobody has to clean up no messes and you get to keep the top half of your body."

For quite a while, things proceed in a very orderly fashion (on the bald man's orders). The junkie couple—in his stricken brain, Philip is coming to think of them as Sonny and Cher—simply back away slowly from Brian and Penny, allowing Brian to lift the child off the floor and carry her across the front parlor to the door.

The agreement—if you can call it that—is for Philip and his group to simply walk away from the villa, leaving all their things, and that's that. Brian watches Philip backing out of the house with the shotgun still raised. *Thank God for that piece of shit antique.* Nick follows. The two of them join Brian and Penny in the doorway, and Brian nudges the door open with Penny in his arms.

They shuffle outside, the shotgun still aimed at the intruders inside.

A number of things flood Brian's senses—the cool wind, the pale light of dawn rising behind the orchards, the silhouettes of two additional gunmen on either flank of the house, the cars angled with their high beams still on like theatrical spotlights heralding the next act of a nightmarish play.

The bald man's voice calls out from inside: "Boys! Let 'em pass!"

The two accomplices outside, dressed in ragged military fatigues and wielding heavy artillery—each man cradles a sawed-off pistol-grip shotgun—watch with the baleful interest of predatory birds as Brian carefully transfers Penny onto his shoulders, piggyback style. Philip whispers low, "Stay close, and follow me. They still mean to kill us. Just do what I say."

Brian follows Philip—who is still bare-chested and still has that ridiculous gun raised commando-style—across the yard, past one of the watchful gunmen, and toward the neighboring grove of peach trees.

It takes an excruciating amount of time for Philip to get everybody across the property and into the shadows of the closest orchard—mere seconds by the clock, but an eternity for Brian Blake—because now the methodical transfer of ownership has begun to fall apart.

Brian can hear troubling things behind him as he hurriedly carries Penny toward the tree line. Brian is still barefoot, and the soles of his feet sting from the brambles and stones. Voices raised in anger drift out of the villa, footsteps, movement across the front porch.

The first shot rings out just as Philip and his group are plunging into the trees. The blast shatters the air, and chews through a branch six inches from Brian's right shoulder, spitting bark at the side of his face and making Penny yelp. Philip shoves Brian—still with Penny on his back—forward into the deeper shadows. "RUN!" he orders them. "RUN, BRIAN! NOW!"

For Brian Blake, the next five minutes pass with the chaotic blur of a dream. He hears more gunfire behind him, bullets sizzling through the foliage as he hurtles through the woods, the watery light of dawn not yet driving away the deeper shadows of the orchards. Brian's bare feet—getting more and more chewed up by the second—dig into the soft undercarpet of leaves and fruit slime, his brain sparking with roman candles of panic. Penny bounces along on his back, hyperventilating with terror. Brian has no idea how far to go, where to go, or when he can stop. He just keeps churning deeper into the shadows of the orchard.

He crosses about two hundred yards of wooded shadows before reaching a huge deadfall of rotting timber, and he ducks behind it.

Gasping to get air into his lungs, his breath visible in the chilled atmosphere, his heart thumping in his ears, he gently shrugs Penny off his back. He sits her down next to him in the weeds.

"Stay down low, kiddo," he whispers. "And be very, very, very quiet—quiet as a mouse."

The orchard vibrates with movement in all directions—the gunfire momentarily ceasing—and Brian risks peering over the top of the deadfall to get a better view. Through thick columns of peach trees, Brian can see a figure about a hundred yards away, coming toward him.

Brian's eyes have adjusted to the wan shadows well enough to see that it's one of the dudes from outside the house, the pistol-grip shotgun jutting up and ready to rock. Others are threading through the trees behind him, a shadowy figure coming toward the dude at a right angle.

Ducking back behind the rotted timbers, Brian frantically weighs his options. If he runs, they'll hear him. If he stays put, they'll stumble upon him for sure. Where the hell is Philip? Where is Nick?

Right then, Brian hears the rhythmic snapping of twigs in another part of the grove speeding up, somebody moving quickly toward the gunman.

Peering over the top of the deadfall, Brian sees the silhouette of his brother—fifty yards away—creeping low through the undergrowth, coming at a right angle toward the shooter. Brian's spine goes cold with dread, his stomach clenching.

Nick Parsons appears in the shadows on the other side of the gunman with a rock in his hand. He pauses and then hurls the stone—which is the size of a grapefruit—a hundred feet across the orchard.

It bangs off a tree, making an enormous clapping sound, which startles the gunman.

The dude whirls and squeezes off a wild shot at the noise, the sonic boom waking up the orchard and making Penny jump. Brian ducks down, but not before witnessing, almost simultaneously, a blur of movement streaking toward the gunman before the dude even has a chance to pump another shell into the breech.

Philip Blake bursts out of the foliage with the old double-barrel already in midswing. The petrified wooden stock strikes the gunman square on the back of his skull, hitting him so hard that he nearly flies out of his jackboots. The pistol-grip shotgun flies. The gunman lurches and sprawls to the mossy earth.

Brian looks away, covering Penny's eyes, as Philip quickly—savagely—finishes the job with four more tremendous blows to the fallen gunman's skull.

● ● ●

Now the balance of power subtly shifts. Philip finds a throw-down pistol—a snub-nose .38—behind the fallen gunman's belt. A pocketful of shells and a speed-loader give Philip and Nick another boost. Brian watches all this from the deadfall fifty yards away.

A surge of relief courses through Brian, a glimmer of hope. They can get away now. They can start over. They can survive another day.

But when Brian signals to his brother from behind the deadfall, and Philip and Nick come over to the hiding place, the look on Philip's face in the pale light sends a sharp dagger of panic through Brian's gut. "We're gonna take these motherfuckers out," he says. "Each and every last one of them."

"But Philip, what if we just—"

"We're gonna get this place back, it's ours, and they're going down."

"But—"

"Listen to me." Something about the way Philip locks his eyes on to Brian's makes Brian's skin crawl. "I need you to keep my daughter out of harm's way, no matter what. Do you understand what I'm saying?"

"Yeah, but—"

"That's all I need you to do."

"Okay."

"Just keep her safe. Look at me. Can you do that for me?"

Brian nods. "Yeah. Absolutely, Philip. I will. Just don't go and get yourself killed."

Philip doesn't say anything, doesn't react, just stares as he pumps a shell into the pistol-grip 20-gauge, then gives Nick a look.

In a matter of moments, the two men have sprung back into action, vanishing into the grove of trees, leaving Brian to sit in the weeds, weaponless, petrified with fear, frantic with indecision, his bare feet bleeding. Did Philip want him to stay put? Was that the plan?

A gunshot thunders. Brian jumps. Another one answers, the echo boomeranging across the cold heavens above the treetops. Brian clenches his fists hard enough to draw blood. Is he supposed to sit here?

He pulls Penny close as another gunshot rings out, closer, the muffled, strangled sound of a watery death gasp reverberating after it. Brian's thoughts begin to race again, the tremors rocking through him.

Footsteps crunch toward the hiding place. Brian ventures another quick peek over the top of the timbers, and he sees the creepy bald dude with the nine-millimeter Glock weaving quickly through the trees, coming this way, his scarred face burning with killing rage. The crumpled body of the skinny kid named Shorty lies in the mud a hundred feet to the north, half his head blown away.

Another blast makes Brian duck down, his heart in his throat. He's not sure if the bald man is down or if the blast just came from the bald man's weapon.

"Come on, kiddo," Brian says to a nearly catatonic Penny, who is curled up in the undergrowth, covering her head. "We gotta get outta here."

He pries her out of the weeds and takes her hand—it's too dangerous to carry her anymore—and he drags her away from the firefight.

They creep along behind the shadows of peach trees, staying under the cover of thickets, avoiding the footpaths radiating through the orchards. The bottoms of his feet almost numbed now by the pain and the cold, Brian can still hear voices behind him, scattered gunfire, and then nothing.

For a long time, Brian hears nothing but wind in the branches, and maybe a series of frantic footsteps now and again, he's not sure, his heart is beating too loudly in his ears. But he keeps going.

He gets another hundred yards or so before ducking down behind an old broken-down hay wagon. Catching his breath, he holds Penny close. "You okay, kiddo?"

Penny manages to give him a thumbs-up, but her expression is crumbling with terror.

He inspects her clothes, her face, her body, and she seems physically unharmed. He pats her and tries to comfort her but the adrenaline and fatigue are making Brian shake so badly, he can barely function.

He hears a sound and freezes. He hunches down and peers through the slats of the rotted wagon. About fifty yards away, a figure skulks through the shadows of a gulley. The figure is tall and rangy, and is carrying a pistol-grip shotgun, but is too far away to identify.

"*Daddy—?*"

Penny's voice startles Brian, coming out of her barely on a whisper, but loud enough to give them away. Brian grabs the child. He puts his hand over her mouth. Then Brian cranes his neck to see over the wagon. He catches a glimpse of the figure coming up the slope of the gulley.

Unfortunately, the figure coming toward them is not the little girl's daddy.

The blast practically vaporizes half the wagon, as Brian is thrown to the ground in a whirlwind of dust and debris. He eats dirt, and he claws for Penny, and he gets a hold of a piece of her shirt, and he drags her toward the deeper woods. He crawls several yards, yanking Penny along, and then he manages to finally struggle to his feet, and now he's dragging Penny toward the deeper shadows, but something's wrong.

The little girl has gone limp in his grasp, as though she has passed out.

Brian can hear the crunch of boot steps behind

him, the clang of the pump, as the gunman closes in on them for the kill shot. Frantically lifting Penny onto his shoulder, Brian hobbles as quickly as possible toward the cover of trees, but he doesn't get far before he realizes he is covered in blood. The blood is streaming down the front of his shirt, soaking him, pulsing in rivulets.

"Oh God no, God no, God no no no—" Brian lowers Penny to the soft earth, laying her on her back. Her bloodless face is the color of a bed sheet. Her eyes are glassy and fixed on the sky as she makes hiccup noises, a tiny rivulet of blood leaking from the corner of her mouth.

Brian hardly hears the gunman now, pounding toward him, the snap of the pump injecting another shell. Penny's little shirt, a cotton T-shirt, is soaked with deep scarlet, the ragged exit tear at least six inches in diameter. Grains of deer shot propelled by a 20-gauge shell are powerful enough to penetrate steel, and it looks like the child took at least half the expanding cloud of shot through her back and out the side of her tummy.

The gunman closes in.

Brian lifts the child's shirt and lets out an almost primal moan of anguish. His hand can't stanch the profuse bleeding, the gaping wound a crescent-shaped mess. Brian presses his hand down on the wound. The blood bubbles. He rips a piece of his shirttail and tries to plug the jagged hole in her midsection, but the blood is everywhere now.

Brian stammers and cries and tries to talk to her as the oily blood seeps through his fingers, and the gunman draws near: "It's okay, you're gonna be okay, we're gonna get you fixed up, it's gonna be fine, you're gonna be all better . . ."

Brian's arms and waist are baptized in the warmth of her life force draining out of her. Penny utters a single feeble whisper: *". . . away . . ."*

"No, Penny, no, no, don't do that . . . don't go away yet, not now . . . don't go away . . . !"

At this point, Brian hears the twig snap directly behind him.

A shadow falls across Penny.

"Goddamn shame," a gravelly voice murmurs behind Brian, the cold end of a shotgun muzzle pressing down on the back of Brian's neck. "Take a good look at her."

Brian twists around and glances up at the gunman, a tattooed, bearded man with a beer belly, aiming the shotgun directly at Brian's face. Almost as an afterthought, the man growls, "Look at her . . . she's the last thing you're gonna ever see."

Brian never takes his hand off Penny's wound, but he knows it's too late.

She's not going to make it.

Brian is ready now . . . ready to die.

The boom has a dreamlike quality, as though Brian has suddenly flown out of his body and is now high above the orchard, witnessing things from the perspective of a disembodied spirit. But almost instantly, Brian—who instinctively jerked forward at the boom—jerks back in shock. Blood mists across his arms and across Penny. Was the impact of the point-blank blast so catastrophic that it was painless? Is Brian already dead and not even aware of it?

The shadow of the gunman begins falling, almost in slow motion, like an old redwood giving up the ghost.

Brian whirls around in time to see that the bearded man has been shot from behind, the top of his skull a mass of red pulp, his beard matted in blood. Eyes rolling back in his head, he collapses. Brian stares. Like a curtain dropping, the falling man reveals two figures behind him, charging toward Brian and Penny.

"GODDAMNIT NO!" Philip throws the pistol-grip shotgun—still smoking hot—to the ground and races through the trees. Nick follows on his heels. Philip roars up to Brian and shoves him aside. "NO! NO!"

Philip drops to his knees by the dying child, who is now asphyxiating, drowning in her own blood. He scoops her up and tenderly touches the gaping wound as though it's just a boo-boo, just a scrape, just a little bump. He draws her into an embrace, her blood soaking him.

Brian lies on the ground a few feet away,

breathing the musty earth, a curtain of shock pulling down over his eyes. Nick stands nearby. "We can stop the bleeding, right? We can fix her up? Right?"

Philip cradles the bloody child.

Penny expires in his arms in a breathy little death rattle, which leaves her face as white and cold as porcelain. Philip shakes her. "C'mon, punkin . . . stay with us . . . stay with us now. Come on . . . stay with us . . . please stay with us . . . Punkin? Punkin? Punkin?"

The terrible silence hangs in the air.

"Sweet Jesus," Nick utters to himself, his gaze going down to the ground.

For the longest time, Philip holds the child while Nick stares into the dirt, silently praying. For most of that time, Brian lies prone on the ground, five feet away, crying into the moist earth, babbling softly, more to himself than to anyone else: "I tried . . . happened so fast . . . I couldn't . . . it was . . . I can't believe it . . . I can't . . . Penny was—"

All at once, a big, gnarled hand wrenches down on the back of Brian's shirt.

"What did I say?" Philip snarls, a guttural growl, as he yanks his brother off the ground, and then slams Brian against the trunk of a nearby tree. Brian goes limp. He sees stars.

"Philly, no!" Nick tries to step in between the two brothers, but Philip shoves Nick away hard enough to send the smaller man sprawling to the ground. Philip still has his right hand locked around his brother's throat.

"What did I say?" Philip slams Brian against the trunk. The back of Brian's skull bounces off the bark, sending veins of light and pain through his field of vision, but he makes no effort to fight back or escape. He wants to die. He wants to die at the hands of his brother.

"WHAT DID I SAY?" Philip heaves Brian away from the tree. The ground flies up at Brian like a battering ram, smashing one shoulder and the side of his face, and then a fusillade of kicks descends upon Brian as he rolls involuntarily across the ground. One kick from the steel-toed logger boot strikes him in the jaw hard enough to crack his mandible. Another one fractures three ribs, sending white-hot pain up his side. Yet another strikes the small of his back, dislocating vertebra and nearly puncturing his kidney. Shiny, bright pain splinters his tailbone. And after a while, Brian can hardly feel the pain anymore, he can only watch it all unfold from way up above his mangled body, as he surrenders to the beating as a supplicant surrenders to a high priest.

nineteen

The next day, Philip spends an hour in the toolshed out behind the villa, going through the collection of weapons taken from the intruders, as well as all the bladed tools and farm implements left by the former inhabitants. He knows what he has to do, but choosing the mode of execution is agonizing for him. At first, he decides on the nine-millimeter semiauto. It'll be the fastest and the cleanest. But then he has second thoughts about using a gun. It just seems unfair somehow. Too cold and impersonal. Nor can he bring himself to use an axe or a machete. Too messy and uncertain. What if his aim is off by half an inch and he botches the job?

At last he decides on the nine-millimeter Glock, shoving a fresh mag of rounds into the hilt and snapping back the cocking slide.

He takes a deep breath, and then goes over to the shed's door. He pauses and braces himself. Scratching noises sporadically travel across the exterior walls of the shed. The villa's property buzzes with Biter activity, scores of the things drawn to the commotion of the previous day's firefight. Philip kicks the door open.

The door bangs into a middle-aged female zombie in a stained pinafore dress who was sniffing around the shed. The force of the impact sends her skeletal form stumbling backward, arms pinwheeling, a ghastly moan rising out of her decomposed face. Philip walks past her, casually raising the Glock, hardly even breaking his stride as he quickly squeezes off a single shot into the side of her skull.

The roar of the Glock echoes as the female corpse whiplashes sideways in a cloud of scarlet mist, then folds to the ground.

Philip marches across the rear of the villa, raising the Glock and taking out another pair of errant Biters. One of them is an old man dressed only in yellowed underwear—maybe an escapee from a nursing home. Another one is most likely a former fruit grower, his bloated, blackened body still clad in its original sappy dungarees. Philip puts them down with a minimum of fuss— a single shot each—and he makes a mental note to clear the remains later that day with one of the snow-shovel attachments on the riding mower.

Almost a full day has passed since Penny died in his arms, and now the new dawn is rising clear and blue, the crisp autumn sky high and clean over the acres of peach trees. It's taken Philip nearly twenty-four hours to work up the nerve to do what he has to do. Now he grips the gun with a sweaty palm as he enters the orchard.

He has five rounds left in the magazine.

· · ·

In the shadows of the woods, a figure writhes and moans against an ancient tree trunk. Bound with rope and duct tape, the prisoner strains with futile desperation to escape. Philip approaches and raises the gun. He points the barrel between the figure's eyes, and for just an instant, Philip tells himself to get it over with quickly: *Lance the wound, remove the tumor, get it done.*

The muzzle wavers, Philip's finger freezing up on the trigger pad, and he lets out a tormented sigh. "I can't do it," he utters under his breath.

He lowers the gun and stares at his daughter. Six feet from him, tied to the tree, Penny growls with the feral hunger of a rabid dog. Her china doll face has narrowed and sunken into a rotted white gourd, her soft eyes hardened into tiny silver coins. Her once innocent tulip-shaped lips are now blackened and curled away from slimy teeth. She doesn't recognize her father.

This is the part that tears the biggest chunk out of Philip's soul. He can't stop remembering the look in Penny's eyes each time he would pick her up at the day care center or at her aunt Nina's house at the end of a long, hard work day. The spark of recognition and excitement—and hell yes, unadulterated *love*—in those big, brown doelike eyes each time Philip returned was enough to keep Philip going no matter what. Now that spark is gone forever—cemented over with the gray film of the undead.

Philip knows what he has to do.

Penny snarls.

Philip's eyes burn with agony.

"I can't do it," he murmurs again, looking down, not really addressing Penny or even himself. Seeing her like this sends a bolt of electric rage down through his system, arcing like the pilot of a welding torch, touching off a secret flame deep within him. He hears the voice: *Tear the world open, tear it apart, rip open its fucking heart . . . do it now.*

He backs away from the horror in the orchard, his brain roiling with fury.

The villa's property—now basking in a mild autumn morning—is a half-moon-shaped plot of land, the main house at its center. Several out-buildings rise along the gentle curve behind the house: the carriage house, a small storage shed for the riding mower and tractor, a second shed for tools, a coach house on elevated pilings for guests, and a large wood-sided barn with a huge weather vane and cupola on top. This last structure, the worm-eaten wood siding faded to a sun-bleached pink, is where Philip now heads.

He needs to drain off this poisonous current coursing through him; he needs to vent.

The main entrance of the barn is a double door at one end, latched with a giant timber across its center. Philip walks up and throws open the plank, the doors squeaking apart, revealing the dust motes floating in shadows inside. Philip enters, closing the double doors behind him. The air smells of horse piss and moldy hay.

Two more figures wriggle and squirm in the corner, gripped in their own brand of hellish torment, bound and gagged with duct tape: *Sonny and Cher.*

The twosome tremble against each other on the floor of the barn, their mouths taped, their backs pressed against the door of an empty horse stall, their bodies in the throes of some kind of withdrawal. Either heroin or crack or something else, it doesn't really matter to Philip. The only thing that matters now is that these two have no idea how much worse life is about to get for them.

Philip walks over to the dynamic duo. The skinny gal is trembling with spasms, her painted eyes caked with dried tears. The man is breathing hard through his nostrils.

Standing in a narrow beam of sunlight teeming with dust and hay dander, Philip stares down at them like an angry god. "You," he says to Sonny. "Gonna ask you a question . . . and I know it's hard to nod with your head taped up and shit, so just blink once for yes, twice for no."

The man looks up through raw, watery, sunken eyes. He blinks once.

Philip looks at him. "You like to watch?"

Two blinks.

Philip reaches down to his belt buckle and starts to unfasten it. "That's a shame, because I'm gonna give one hell of a show."

Two blinks.

Again . . . two blinks.

Two blinks, two blinks, two blinks.

"Easy, Brian, not so fast," Nick says to Brian the next night, up in the second-floor sewing room. In the light of kerosene lanterns, Nick is helping Brian drink water through a straw. Brian's mouth is still swollen and clumsy, and he dribbles on himself. Nick has been doing everything he can to help Brian recover, and keeping food down him is paramount. "Try some more of the vegetable soup," Nick suggests.

Brian has a few spoonfuls. "Thanks, Nick." Brian's voice is choked, thick with pain. "Thanks for everything." His words are slightly slurred, his soft palate still inflamed. He speaks tentatively, haltingly. Lying in bed, he has rags wrapped snugly around his broken ribs, Band-Aids on his face and neck, his left eye puffy with a purplish bruise. Something might be wrong with his hip; neither of them can tell for sure.

"You're gonna be fine, man," Nick says. "Your brother is another story."

"What do you mean?"

"He's lost it, man."

"He's been through a lot, Nick."

"How can you say that?" Nick sits back, lets out a pained sigh. "Look what he did to you. And don't say it's because he lost Penny—we've all lost people we love. He came very close to taking you out."

Brian looks at his own mangled feet sticking out of the bottom of the blankets. With great effort, he says, "I deserve everything I got."

"Don't say that! It wasn't your fault, what happened. Your brother's turned a corner with this thing. I'm really worried about him."

"He'll be okay." Brian looks at Nick. "What's wrong? Something else is bothering you."

Nick takes a deep breath and wonders whether he should confide in Brian. The Blake brothers have always had a complex relationship, and over the years, Nick Parsons has often felt that *he* was more of a brother to Philip Blake than his biological sibling. But there's always been an X factor with the Blakes, a bond of blood that runs deep within the two men.

Nick finally says, "I know you aren't exactly the religious type. I know you think I'm a Holy Roller."

"That's not true, Nick."

Nick waves it off. "Doesn't matter . . . my faith is strong, and I don't judge a man by his religion."

"Where you going with this?"

Nick looks at Brian. "He's keeping her alive, Brian . . . or maybe *alive* is not the right word."

"Penny?"

"He's out there with her now."

"Where?"

Nick explains what's been going on over these last two days since the firefight. While Brian has been recovering from the beating, Philip's been busy. He's keeping two of the intruders—the only ones who survived the firefight—locked up in the barn. Philip claims he's questioning them about possible human settlements. Nick is worried he's torturing them. But that's the least of their worries. The fate of Penny Blake is what's eating at Nick. "He's got her chained to a tree like a pet," Nick says.

Brian frowns. "Where?"

"Out in the orchard. He goes out there at night. Spends time with her."

"Oh God."

"Listen, I know you think this is bullshit, but the way I was brought up, there's a force in the universe called Good and a force called Evil."

"Nick, I don't think this is—"

"Wait. Let me finish. I believe that all this—the plague or whatever you want to call it—is the work of what you would call the Devil or Satan."

"Nick—"

"Just let me say my piece. I've been thinking about it a lot."

"Go ahead, I'm listening."

"What's the thing Satan hates the most? The

371

power of love? Maybe. Somebody being born again. Yeah, probably. But I kinda think it's when a person passes, and their spirit flies up to Paradise."

"I'm not following you."

Nick looks into Brian's hollow gaze. "That's what's going on here, Brian. The Devil's figured out a way to keep people's souls trapped here on earth."

A moment passes as Brian absorbs this. Nick doesn't expect Brian to believe any of this, but maybe, just maybe, Nick can get him to understand.

In that brief silence, the north wind whistles in the shutters. The weather is turning. The villa creaks and moans. Nick lifts the collar of his mothball-scented sweater—days ago, they found some warm clothes in the villa's attic—and now he shivers in the frigid air of the second floor. "What your brother's doing is wrong, it's against God," Nick says then, and the statement hangs in the gloom.

At that moment, out in the darkness of the orchard, a small campfire crackles and flickers on the ground. Philip sits on the cold earth in front of the fire, his shotgun next to him, a musty little book he found in the villa's nursery open on his lap. " 'Let me in, Let me in, Little Pig,' " Philip reads aloud in a stiff, labored singsong voice.

"'Or I'll huff and I'll puff and blow your house in!'"

Three feet away, tied to the tree trunk, Penny Blake snarls and drools at every word, her tiny jaws snapping impotently.

"'Not by the hair of my chinny chin chin,'" Philip recites, turning a delicate page of onionskin. He pauses and glances up at the thing that used to be his daughter.

In the flicker of firelight, Penny's small face contorts with unyielding hunger, as wrinkled and bloated as a jack-o'-lantern. Her midsection, wound with baling wire, strains against the tree. She reaches out with curled, clawlike fingers and clutches at the air—yearning to break free and make a meal of her father.

"'But of course,'" Philip continues, his voice breaking, "'the wolf *did* blow the house in.'" An agonizing pause before Philip says in a shattered voice, filled with equal parts sorrow and madness, "'And he ate the pig.'"

Over the remainder of that week, sleep does not come easily for Philip Blake. He tries to get a few hours each night but the nervous energy keeps him tossing and turning until he has to get up and do something. Most nights, he goes out to the barn and works off some of his rage on Sonny and Cher. They are the ostensible reasons Penny has turned, and it is up to Philip to make sure they suffer like no man or woman has ever suffered. The delicate process of keeping them just this side of death is not easy. Every once in a while, Philip has to give them water to make sure they don't die on him. He also has to be careful they don't kill themselves in order to escape their torments. Like a good jailer, Philip keeps the ropes tight, and all sharp objects out of their grasp.

On *this* night—Philip thinks it's a Friday—he waits until Nick and Brian are asleep before he slips out of his room, pulls on his denim jacket and boots, and makes his way out the back door and across the moonlit grounds to the weather-beaten barn on the northeast corner of the property. He likes to announce himself as he arrives.

"Daddy's home," he murmurs in a convivial tone, his breath showing in puffs of vapor as he pulls the padlock and pushes open the double doors.

He flips on a battery-powered lantern.

Sonny and Cher are slumped in the shadows where he left them, two ragged creatures trussed up like suckling pigs, side by side, sitting in a spreading pool of their own blood, piss, and shit. Sonny is barely awake, his head lolled to one side, his heavy-lidded junkie eyes rimmed in red. Cher is unconscious. She lies next to him, her leather pants still down around her ankles.

Each of them bear the festering marks of Philip's tools of punishment—needle-nosed pliers, barbed wire, two-by-fours with exposed rusty nails, and various blunt objects that occur to Philip in the heat of the moment.

"Wake up, sis!" Philip reaches down and flips the woman onto her back, the restraints cutting into her wrists, the rope around her neck keeping her from squirming too much. He slaps her. Her eyes flutter. Philip slaps her again. She comes awake now, the muffled cries dampened by the hank of duct tape over her mouth.

At some point in the night, she managed to pull her bloody panties back up and over her privates.

"Let me once again remind you," Philip says, yanking her panties back down to her knees. He stands over her, wrenching her legs apart with his boots as though clearing a path for himself. She writhes and wriggles below him as if she might be able to squirm out of her own skin. "Y'all are the ones took my daughter from me—so we're all gonna go to hell together."

Philip unbuckles his belt, and drops his pants, and it doesn't require much imagination for him to instantly produce an erection—his rage and hate burn so warmly in his solar plexus, it feels like a battering ram. He drops to his knees between the woman's trembling legs.

The first thrust is always the trigger—the voice in his brain abruptly chiming out, taunting him, urging him on with fragments of old biblical nonsense that his daddy used to mumble while drunk: *Vengeance is mine, vengeance is mine sayeth the Lord!*

But tonight, after the third or fourth thrust into the limp woman, Philip stops.

A combination of things steals his focus, hooks his attention. He hears footsteps outside, crunching across the rear of the property, and he even sees, through the slatted siding, the shadow of a figure blurring past the barn. But what gets Philip to draw back and stand up, and hurriedly pull his pants back on, is the fact that this figure is moving toward the orchard.

Toward the place where Penny resides.

Philip exits the barn and instantly sees a figure plunging into the shadows of the orchard. The figure is a compact, trim man in his thirties clad in a sweater and jeans, carrying a huge rusty spade over his shoulder.

"Nick!"

Philip's warning cry goes unheeded. Nick has already vanished into the trees.

Drawing the nine-millimeter from behind his belt, Philip charges toward the orchard. He snaps a round into the chamber as he plunges into the woods. Darkness gives way to the beam of a flashlight.

Fifty feet away, Nick Parsons is shining a light on the livid face of the Penny-thing.

"NICK!"

Nick whirls suddenly with the shovel raised, and the flashlight tumbles out of his hand. "It's gone too far, Philly, it's gone too far."

"Put the shovel down," Philip says as he approaches with the gun raised. The flashlight beam shines up into the leaves, casting an eerie, pale glow over everything, like a grainy black-and-white film.

"You can't do this to your daughter, you don't realize what you're doing."

"Put it down."

"You're keeping her soul from entering heaven, Philly."

"Shut up!"

Twenty feet away, the Penny-thing yanks on its bonds in the shadows. The cockeyed beam of the flashlight highlights her monstrous features from below. Her eyes reflect the dry silver light.

"Philly, listen to me." Nick lowers the shovel, his voice unsteady with emotion. "You have to let her die . . . she's one of God's children. Please . . . I'm begging you as a Christian . . . please let her go."

Philip aims the Glock directly at Nick's forehead. "If she dies . . . you die next."

For a moment, Nick Parsons looks crestfallen, absolutely beaten.

Then he drops the shovel, hangs his head, and walks back toward the villa.

Throughout all this, the Penny-thing keeps its sharklike gaze on the man it once called father.

Brian continues to heal. Six days after the beating, he feels strong enough to get out of bed and limp around the house. His hip twinges with every step, and the dizziness comes in waves whenever he goes up and down the stairs, but on the whole, he's doing pretty well. His bruises have faded and the swelling has gone down, and he feels his appetite returning. He also has a good talk with Philip.

"I miss her something fierce," Brian says to his brother late one night in the kitchen, each man suffering from severe insomnia. "I'd trade places with her in a heartbeat if it meant bringing her back."

Philip looks down. He has developed a series of very subtle tics, which emerge when he's under pressure—sniffing, pursing his lips, clearing his throat. "I know, sport. It ain't your fault . . . what happened out there. I never should have done that to you."

Brian's eyes moisten. "I probably would have done the same thing."

"Let's put it behind us."

"Sure." Brian wipes his eyes. He looks at Philip. "So, what's the deal with the people in the barn?"

Philip looks up. "What about 'em?"

"The whole thing has Nick on edge . . . and you can hear things out there . . . at night, I'm talking about. Nick thinks you're, like . . . pulling their fingernails off."

A cold smile twitches at the corner of Philip's mouth. "That's sick."

Brian isn't smiling. "Philip, whatever you're doing out there, it's not going to bring Penny back."

Philip looks down again. "I know that . . . don't you think I know that?"

"Then I'm begging you to stop. Whatever it is you're doing . . . *stop*." Brian looks at his brother. "It's not serving any purpose."

Philip looks up with embers of emotion in his eyes. "That trash out there in the barn stole everything that mattered to me . . . that bald motherfucker and his crew . . . them two junkies . . . they destroyed the life of a beautiful innocent little girl and they did it outta sheer meanness and greed. Ain't nothing I could do to them would suffice."

Brian sighs. Further protest seems futile, so he simply stares at his coffee.

"And you're wrong about it not serving any purpose," Philip concludes, after a moment of thought. "It serves the purpose of making me feel better."

The next night, after the lanterns go out, and the fires in the three separate fireplaces dwindle down to coals, and the northeasterly wind begins toying with the dormers and loose shingles, Brian is lying in bed in the sewing room, trying to lull himself into a troubled sleep, when he hears the door latch click and sees the silhouette of Nick Parsons slipping into his room. Brian sits up. "What's going on?"

"Sssshhh," Nick whispers, coming across the room and kneeling by the bed. Nick has his coat on, his gloves, and a bulge on his hip that looks like the grip of a handgun. "Keep it down."

"What is it?"

"Your brother's asleep . . . finally."

"So what?"

"So we gotta do a—whaddaya callit—an intervention."

"What are you talking about? Penny? You're talking about trying to take Penny out again?"

"No! The barn, man! The barn!"

Brian moves to the edge of the bed and rubs his eyes, stretches his sore limbs, shakes the cobwebs off. "I don't know if I'm ready for this."

They slip out the back, each one of them armed with a handgun. Nick has the bald man's .357 steel-plated revolver, Brian has a snub-nose that belonged to one of the thug gunmen. They steal across the property to the barn, and Brian shines a flashlight on the padlock. They find a piece of timber in a woodpile, and they use it to pry open the rotted doors, making as little noise as possible.

Brian's heart hammers in his chest as they slip inside the dark barn.

The stench of mold and urine fills their senses

as they work their way back through the fetid shadows to the rear of the barn, where two dark heaps lie on the floor in puddles of blood as black as oil. At first, the shapes don't even look human, but when the beam of Brian's flashlight falls on a pale face, Brian lets out a gasp.

"Holy fucking shit."

The man and woman are still alive, barely, their faces disfigured and swollen, their midsections exposed like raw meat. A thin tendril of steam rises from festering, sucking wounds. Both captives are semiconscious, their parboiled eyes fixed on the rafters. The woman is brutalized, a broken doll with legs akimbo and blood patterns covering her pasty, tattooed flesh.

Brian begins to tremble. "Holy shit . . . what have we . . . ? Holy *fucking shit . . .*"

Nick kneels by the woman. "Brian, get some water."

"What about—"

"Get it from the well! Hurry!"

Brian hands over his flashlight, spins, and hustles back the way he came.

Nick shines the light on the constellation of wounds and sores—some old and infected, some fresh—across a hundred percent of their twisted bodies. The man's chest rises and falls quickly, convulsively, with shallow breaths. The woman struggles to fix her rheumy gaze on Nick. She is blinking wildly.

Her lips move beneath the duct tape. Nick starts to carefully peel the gag away from her mouth.

"P-p-pleeee . . . kuhhh . . ." She's trying to say something urgent but Nick can't understand her.

"It's okay, we're gonna get you outta here, it's okay, you're gonna make it."

"K-khhh . . ."

"Cold?" Nick tries to pull her pants back on her. "Try to breathe, try to—"

"K-khhlll."

"What? I can't—"

The woman tries to swallow, and again she says, "K-kill uss . . . p-please . . ."

Nick stares. His guts go cold. He feels something softly nudging his hip and he looks down and sees the woman's scabby hand fumbling at the pistol grip sticking out of his belt. Nick feels all the fight go out of him. His heart sinks down through the floor.

He pulls the .357 from his belt and stands up and gazes down at the abominations on the floor of the barn for a long time.

He says a prayer: the Twenty-third Psalm.

Brian is on his way back to the barn with a plastic pail of well water when he hears the two muffled pops from inside the barn. Like firecrackers bursting inside tin cans, the blasts are short and sharp. The sound of them makes Brian freeze in his tracks, the water sloshing over the rim of the bucket. He sucks in a startled breath.

Then he sees, out of the corner of his eye, a faint light flickering on in one of the villa's second-floor windows: Philip's room. A flashlight up there plays across the window, then vanishes. This is followed by a series of muffled footsteps banging down the stairs and through the house, hard and fast, and this gets Brian moving again.

He drops the pail. He charges back across the property to the barn. He slams through the doorway, plunging into the dark. Then he hurtles through the shadows, toward the silver beam of light on the floor in the rear. He sees Nick standing over the captives.

A ribbon of cordite smoke rises from the muzzle of the .357 in Nick's right hand, now hanging at his side as he stares down at the bodies.

Brian joins Nick and starts to say something when all at once Brian looks down and sees the head wounds: blossoms of gore bloom up the stall door—shimmering in the horizontal light beam.

The man and the woman are stone-cold dead, each one of them now lying supine in their drying fluids, their faces at peace, released from their contortions of misery. Again, Brian tries to say something.

He can't get out any words.

A moment later, in the darkness across the barn, the double doors burst open and Philip storms in. Fists clenched at his sides, face chiseled with rage, eyes flashing with white-hot madness, he marches toward the light. He looks as though he's going to devour somebody. He has a pistol shoved down the side of his belt and a machete banging on one hip.

He gets about halfway across the barn before he starts to slow down.

Nick has turned away from the bodies and is now standing his ground, staring at Philip as he approaches. Brian steps back, a tidal wave of shame crashing down over him. He feels like his soul is being ripped in half. He stares at the floor as his brother approaches slowly now, warily, glancing nervously from the dead bodies to Nick, and then to Brian, and then back at the dead bodies.

For the longest time, nobody can think of anything to say. Philip keeps looking at Brian, and Brian keeps trying to conceal the paralyzing shame spreading through him, but the more he tries to conceal it, the more it drags him down.

If Brian only had the guts for it, he would put the barrel of the snub-nose in his mouth right now and put *himself* out of his misery. In some strange way, he feels responsible for this—for all of it—but he's too much of a coward to kill himself like a man.

He can only stand there and look away in abject shame and humiliation.

And like an invisible chain reaction, the pathetic, gruesome tableau of desecrated bodies—combined with the unyielding silence of his brother and his friend—begins to break Philip down.

He fights the tears pooling in his eyes and juts his quivering chin out in a mixture of defiance and self-loathing. He works his mouth like he's got something important to impart, and it takes a huge effort to speak, but he finally manages to say in a choked mutter, "Whatever."

Nick looks mortified, staring at Philip in disbelief. " 'Whatever'? "

Philip turns and walks away, pulling the Glock from his belt as he goes. He snaps the slide and fires into the wall of the barn—BOOOOMMMMMM!—the recoil kicking in his hand, the loud bark making Brian jump. BOOOOOMMMM! Another blast flashes in the darkness, taking a chunk of the door. BOOOOOMMMM! The third shot puts a chink in the rafter and rains debris down on the floor.

Philip angrily kicks the doors open and storms out of the barn.

The silence left behind seems to ripple for a moment with afterimages of Philip's fiery wrath. Brian hasn't taken his eyes off the floor throughout all this, and he continues to hang his head and stare miserably at the moldy matted hay. Nick takes one last look at the bodies, and then lets out a long, pained, unsteady breath. He looks at Brian, and he shakes his head. "There you have it," he says.

But something behind his words—the subtle tone of dread in his voice—tells Brian that things have now irrevocably changed in their little dysfunctional family.

twenty

"What the fuck is he doing?" Nick stands at the villa's front window, staring out at the overcast morning.

Across the front of the property, at the top of the driveway, Philip has Penny on a modified dog leash, assembled from spare parts found in the toolshed—a long length of copper pipe with a spiked collar threaded through one end. He drags her toward a Ford S-10 pickup parked on the grass. The truck is one of the vehicles owned by the bald man's crew, and Philip has now loaded its cargo bed with canned goods, guns, provisions, and bedding.

Penny sputters and growls as she is yanked along, grabbing at the pipe leashed to her neck, biting at the air. In the diffuse, watery light, her dead face looks like a living Halloween mask, sculpted out of wormy-gray modeling clay.

"That's what I've been trying to tell you," Brian says, standing next to Nick, gazing out at the bizarre scene unfolding in the front yard. "He got up this morning convinced we can't stay here anymore."

"And why's that?"

Brian shrugs. "I don't know . . . after all that's happened . . . I guess the place is like poison for him, full of ghosts . . . I don't know."

Brian and Nick have been up all night, guzzling coffee and discussing their situation. Nick has been dancing around the fact that he thinks Philip has gone off his spindle, succumbing to the stress of losing Penny, and to the cumulative pressure of protecting them. Although Nick has stopped short of verbalizing it, he has alluded to the possibility that the Devil has gotten his hooks into Philip. Brian is too exhausted to argue metaphysics with Nick, but there is no denying the fact that things have become dire.

"Let him go," Nick says finally, turning away from the window.

Brian looks at him. "What do you mean? You mean you're staying?"

"Yeah, I'm staying, and you should, too."

"Nick, come on."

"How can we keep following him . . . after all this shit . . . the stuff that's gone down?"

Brian wipes his mouth and thinks about it. "Look. I'll say it again. What he did to those people is, like, *beyond awful*. He lost his way. And I'm not sure I'll ever be able to look at him the same way again . . . but this is about survival now. We can't split up. Our best shot is sticking together no matter what."

Nick glances back out the window. "You really think we're gonna make it to the Gulf Coast? That's like four hundred miles and change."

"Our best shot is doing it together."

Nick fixes his gaze on Brian. "He's got his dead daughter on a fucking leash. He pretty near beat you to death. He's a loose cannon, Brian, and he's gonna blow up in our faces."

"That loose cannon got us all the way across Georgia from Waynesboro in one piece," Brian says, a flare of anger burning in his gut. "So, he's nuts, he's volatile, he's possessed by demons, he's the prince of fucking darkness . . . he's still my brother and he's our best chance of survival."

Nick looks at him. "Is that what we're calling it now? Survival?"

"You want to stay here, be my guest."

"Thanks, I'll do that."

Nick walks away, leaving Brian to turn back to the window and nervously watch his brother.

Utilizing a radiator hose as a siphon, they consolidate all the fuel on the property—from tractors, from vehicles, even from the Harleys—into the Ford S-10. All told, they're able to top off the seventeen-gallon tank and then some. Philip arranges a place for Penny in the rear cargo bay by moving the boxes of supplies around into a semicircle and laying blankets down on the deck.

He chains her to a U-bolt so she can't get herself into any mischief or fall over the side.

Nick watches all this from his second-floor window, pacing the room like a caged animal. The reality of the situation starts to set in. He'll be alone in this big old drafty villa. He'll spend nights alone. He'll spend the whole winter alone. He'll hear the north winds shrieking through the gutters and the distant moaning of Biters wandering the orchards . . . all while biding his time alone. He'll wake up alone and eat alone and forage for food alone and dream of better days alone and pray to God for deliverance . . . all by himself. As he watches Philip and Brian finish up the last of the preparations for departure, a twinge of regret tightens Nick's midsection—*seller's remorse.* He crosses the room to his closet.

It takes him a matter of seconds to stuff his essentials into a duffel bag.

He rushes out of the room and takes the stairs two at a time.

Brian is just settling into the passenger seat, and Philip is just putting the truck in gear, just beginning to pull away from the villa, when the sound of the front door ripping open reaches their ears.

Brian glances over his shoulder and sees Nick with a duffel bag slung over his shoulder, running across the front parkway, waving them back.

• • •

It's hard to believe that Philip would neglect to check under the pickup's hood. Had he taken three minutes to make sure everything was in working order, he would have found the perforated hose. But Philip Blake is not exactly a hundred percent these days. His mind is a shortwave radio tuned to different stations now.

But regardless of whether it was a deliberate cut made by the home invaders after the firefight broke out (to ensure that nobody escaped), or it was a piece of flak that had pierced the truck's grill, or it was simply a coincidental failure, the pickup begins to smoke and sputter less than five miles from the villa.

At a point approximately fifty miles southwest of Atlanta, in a place most folks around these parts call the Middle of Nowhere, the pickup hobbles off the highway and onto the gravel shoulder, where it stutters to a stop, all the warning lights across the dash flickering on. White vapor seeps out from under the hood, and the ignition won't turn over. Philip lets out an alarming barrage of profanity, nearly kicking his logger boot through the floor. The other two men look down, silently waiting for the squall to pass. Brian wonders if this is what a battered wife feels like: too afraid to escape, too afraid to stay.

At length, Philip's tantrum passes. He gets out and opens the hood.

Brian joins him. "What's the verdict?"

"Screwed and tattooed."

"No hope of fixing it?"

"You got a radiator hose on you?"

Brian glances over his shoulder. The side of the road slopes down to a ravine filled with old tires, weeds, and rubbish. Movement draws his gaze to the far end of the ravine—about a quarter of a mile away—where a cluster of Biters mill about in the garbage. They stumble around and root for flesh in the rocks like truffle-nuzzling pigs. They haven't yet noticed the disabled vehicle now smoking on the side of the road three hundred yards away.

In the rear of the pickup, Penny yanks at her chain. The chain is threaded through her dog collar and bolted to the corrugated deck. The proximity of other upright corpses seems to be tweaking her, exciting her, disturbing her.

"What do you think?" Brian finally asks his brother, who has carefully lowered the hood and clicked it shut with a minimum of noise.

Nick is climbing out of the cab. He joins them. "What's the plan?"

Brian looks at him. "The plan is . . . we're fucked."

Nick chews his fingernail, glancing back over his shoulder at the zombie conclave slowly working its way down the ravine, getting closer every minute. "Philip, we can't sit here. Maybe we can find another car."

Philip exhales a pained sigh. "All right, you fellas know the drill . . . grab your shit, I'll get Penny."

They light out with Penny on the leash, their backs laden with supplies. They hug the shoulder, following the highway. Brian limps along without complaint, despite the stabbing pain in his hip. Around Greenville, they have to take a detour due to an inexplicable pileup of wrecked vehicles, the scorched tangle of metal spanning across both northbound and southbound lanes, the area crawling with zombies. From a distance, it looks as though the earth itself has split open and vomited up hundreds of walking corpses.

They decide to take a two-lane—Rural Route 100—which wends its way southward, through Greenville, and around the congestion. And they get maybe a mile or two before Philip puts his hand up and stops.

"Hold on a second," he says, frowning. He cocks his head. "What is that?"

"What is *what?*"

"That noise."

"What noise?"

Philip listens. They all listen. Philip turns in a slow circle, trying to pinpoint the direction from which the sound is coming. "Is that an engine?"

Brian hears it now. "Sounds like a fucking tank."

"Or maybe a bulldozer," Nick ventures.

"What the fuck." Philip narrows his eyes as he listens. "That can't be too far away."

They continue on. Less than a mile down the road, they come upon a dented sign:

WOODBURY—1 MI.

They continue on down the road, all eyes on the smoke-clogged western sky.

"Whoever they are, they got fuel," Nick says.

Brian sees a cloud of dust on the horizon. "You think they're friendly?"

"I ain't taking any chances," Philip says. "C'mon . . . we'll find a back way in, take it one step at a time."

Philip leads them across the shoulder, then down a weedy slope.

They scuttle across an adjacent farm field, a vast and fallow valley of soft earth. Their boots sink into the mire as they go. The chill wind lashes at them, and it takes them an interminable amount of time to circumnavigate the outskirts before the remnants of an abandoned town begin to materialize ahead of them.

A Walmart sign rises above a stand of ancient live oaks. The golden arches of a McDonald's are visible not far beyond the Walmart. Litter tumbles down empty streets, past postwar brick buildings and cookie-cutter condos. But on the north side of the town, within a maze of cyclone fences, the sounds of engines and hammering and the occasional voice reveal the presence of humans.

"Looks like they're building a wall or somethin'," Nick says as they pause under the cover of trees. In the distance, about two hundred yards away, a handful of figures labor over a tall wooden rampart closing off the north edge of town. The barricade already stretches nearly two blocks.

"Rest of the place looks dead," Philip comments. "Can't be many survivors."

"What the hell is that?" Brian is pointing at a semicircle of high stanchions a few blocks west of the barricade. Clusters of arc lights point down at a large open space, obscured behind buildings and fences.

"Football field for the high school maybe?" Philip is reaching for his Glock. He pulls it out and checks the remaining rounds in the magazine. He's got six hollow-points left.

"What are you thinking, Philip?" Nick looks anxious, jittery.

Brian wonders if Nick is worried about walking into another trap. Or maybe he's just edgy around Philip. The truth is, Brian isn't too keen on waltzing uninvited into this little ragtag community, especially considering the fact that they have a moldering zombie in tow, and a father of said zombie so tightly wound he seems capable of almost anything at any moment. But what choice do they have? Dark clouds are gathering on the western horizon again, and the temperature is plummeting.

"What do you got there, sport?" Philip nods toward the gun bulging out the side of Brian's belt. "The .38?"

"Yeah."

"And you got the .357?" Philip says to Nick, who nods nervously. "Okay . . . here's what we're gonna do."

They enter from the northeast corner of town, from the trees along the railroad tracks. They come slowly, with their hands raised in a nonthreatening gesture. At first, they're surprised by how far they get—in plain sight of at least a dozen humans—before anyone even notices strangers strolling into town.

"Hey!" A hefty, middle-aged man in a black turtleneck sweater hops off a bulldozer, pointing at the newcomers. "Bruce! Look! We got company!"

Another worker—a tall black man in a pea-coat with a glistening shaved head—pauses his hammering. He looks up and his eyes widen. He goes for a shotgun leaning against a nearby cooler.

"Take it easy, fellas!" Philip approaches slowly across a dusty truck lot, his hands raised. His expression is an approximation of calm, as mild and friendly as he can muster. "Just passin' through . . . not lookin' for any drama."

Brian and Nick follow closely on Philip's heels, each with their hands up.

The two men come over with shotguns. "You boys packin' heat?" the black man wants to know.

"The safety's on," Philip says, pausing to carefully reach for his Glock. "I'm gonna show you the piece, nice and easy like."

He shows them the nine-millimeter.

"What about you two?" The man in the turtleneck addresses Brian and Nick.

They each show their guns.

"Is it just the three of ya?" The man wearing the turtleneck has a Northern accent. His close-cropped blond hair is peppered with gray, and he has a wrestler's neck and a stevedore's barrel chest. His big porcine belly hangs over his belt.

"Just us three," Philip says, and it's essentially the truth. He left Penny tied to a tree in the shadows of the hickory grove a hundred yards outside the barricade. Philip secured her with extra rope and put a bandana around her mouth so she wouldn't make any noise. It killed him to gag her like that, but until he knows what he's dealing with here, he figures it's best to keep her out of sight.

"What happened to you?" the turtleneck guy says to Brian, nodding at his wounds.

"He had a bad time fightin' off some Biters," Philip explains.

The man in the turtleneck lowers his shotgun. "You boys from Atlanta?"

"No, sir. Little hole-in-the-wall called Waynesboro."

"You seen any National Guard out there?"

"No, sir."

"You been traveling on your own?"

"Pretty much." Philip puts his gun back. "We just need to rest up and we'll be on our way."

"You got food?"

"Nope."

"Any cigarettes?"

"No, sir." Philip indicates his companions. "If we could just get a roof over our head for a short spell, we won't bother anybody. You fellas okay with that?"

For a moment, the two workmen give each other a glance like they're sharing a private joke. Then the black man bursts out laughing. "Boys, this is the wild fucking west . . . nobody gives two pieces of a rat's ass *what* you do."

It turns out that the black man was understating the situation in Woodbury.

Over the remaining hours of that day, Philip, Brian, and Nick get the lay of the land and it's not exactly Mayberry RFD. There are about sixty inhabitants clinging to the secure sector on the north side of town, keeping to themselves mostly, eking out an existence on scraps, most of them so paranoid and mistrustful of each other that they rarely even come out of their private hovels. They live in deserted condos and empty stores, and they have no organized leadership whatsoever. It's amazing that any of them had the initiative to begin building a wall. In Woodbury, it's every man, woman, and child for themselves.

All of which suits Philip, Brian, and Nick just fine. After scouting the edges of town, they decide to hole up in an abandoned two-unit apartment building on the southern border of the safe zone, near the uninhabited commercial district. Somebody has moved school buses and empty semi-trailers into rows around the periphery of town, forming a makeshift bastion to keep out the Biters.

For now, the place seems relatively safe.

That night, Brian can't sleep, so he decides to sneak out and explore the town. Walking isn't easy—his ribs are still bothering him, and his breathing is labored and wheezy—but it feels good to get out and clear his head.

In the diamond-chip moonlight, the sidewalks lie desolate and barren, threading through what was once a typical little blue-collar burg. Trash blows willy-nilly across deserted playgrounds and squares. Storefronts housing the requisite small-town merchants—the local dentist, DeForest's Feed and Seed, a Dairy Queen, the Piggly Wiggly—are all dark and boarded. Evidence of the "turn" lies everywhere—in the lime pits at Kirney's Salvage Yard, where bodies have been recently deposited and torched, and in the community gazebo at Robert E. Lee Square, where bloodstains from some gruesome battle still glisten like black tar in the moonlight.

Brian isn't surprised to learn that the open field in the center of town—which he first glimpsed from the neighboring farm field—is an old dirt racetrack. Apparently, the residents have enough fuel to keep generators going around the clock; and as Brian soon discovers, every so often, in the dark of night, the huge arc lights over the racetrack flare on for no good reason. On the far side of the track, Brian passes a semitrailer pulsing like a great steel heart with the muffled vibrations of combustion engines—the cables snaking out the back and tying into neighboring buildings.

By the time dawn starts to glow on the eastern horizon, Brian decides he better head back to the two-flat. He crosses a deserted parking lot, and then takes a shortcut down a litter-strewn alley. He reaches the adjacent street and passes a group of old men huddled around a flaming trash barrel, warming their hands against the chill and passing around a bottle of Thunderbird.

"Watch your back, sonny," one of the men says to Brian as he passes, and the two other men chuckle humorlessly. The three men are ancient, grizzled, spavined codgers in moth-eaten Salvation Army coats. They look like they've been hunkered around this barrel for eternity.

Brian pauses. He has the snub-nosed .38 pistol wedged behind his belt, under his jacket, but he feels no compulsion to brandish it. "Got Biters in the area?"

"Biters?" one of the other men says. This one has a long white beard and his wrinkled eyes narrow with confusion.

"He means them dead things," says the third old derelict, the fattest of the three.

"Yeah, Charlie," says the first old man. "You remember . . . them walkin' pus bags that ate Yellow Mike . . . the reason we're stuck in this shitheel town?"

"I know what he's talkin' about!" snaps the bearded codger. "Just never heard 'em called such a thing before."

"You new in town, son?" The fat one is giving Brian the once-over.

"As a matter of fact, yeah . . . I am."

The fat old man shows a grin full of rotten, green teeth. "Welcome to hell's waiting room."

"Don't listen to him, son," the first old man says, putting a bony, arthritic arm around Brian's shoulder. Then, in a low, mucousy voice, the old guy says confidentially: "It ain't the dead things you gotta be mindful of around here . . . it's the living."

The next day, Philip tells Brian and Nick to keep their mouths shut while they're in Woodbury, stay under the radar, avoid any contact with other residents, refrain from even telling people their names. Thankfully, the apartment serves them well as a temporary refuge. Built in the 1950s, with furnishings at least that old—chipped mirror tile on one wall, a moth-eaten sleeper sofa in the living room, a huge rectangular fish tank next to the TV, brimming with scum and the tiny floating corpses of neglected goldfish—the place has three bedrooms and running water. It smells like rancid cat shit and rotting fish, but as Brian's dad used to say, "Beggars can't be choosers." They find canned goods in the pantries of both apartments, and they decide to stay for a while.

Much to Brian's amazement, the townspeople leave them alone, as though they are ghosts. Brian can tell that word has spread among the inhabitants of newcomers in their midst, but still, it's as though the Blakes and Nick are apparitions haunting the broken-down apartment. Which is not too far from the truth. Nick keeps to himself and reads his Bible and doesn't say much. Philip and Brian, still edgy around each other, also go about their business with minimal conversation. It doesn't even occur to them to find a vehicle and continue on their southward journey. It feels to Brian like they've given up . . . on getting to the coast, on the future, maybe on each other.

Brian continues to heal, and Philip tends to his own obsession with Penny, stealing away to the hickory grove every chance he gets.

● ● ●

Late one night, Brian hears the apartment door clicking open and shut.

He lies there in bed, listening for nearly an hour, when finally he hears Philip returning in a flurry of shuffling steps and gurgling noises. This is the third night in a row Philip has silently slipped out of the apartment—presumably to check on Penny while the townspeople are asleep—but up until tonight, his return has been as quiet and discreet as his departure. But now Brian can hear Philip breathing heavily out in the living room, murmuring something that is drowned out by watery groaning sounds and the clank of a chain.

Brian climbs out of bed and goes into the living room. He freezes when he sees Philip dragging Penny on her leash, yanking her across the floor like a whipped dog.

For a brief instant, Brian is speechless. All he can do is stare at the little moving corpse in her pigtails and muddy clothes, her feet tracking filth across the apartment floor, and hope that she's a temporary visitor and not—God forbid—a new roommate.

twenty-one

"What the hell are you doing?" Brian asks his brother as the dead girl claws at the air with stupid hunger. She fixes her milky eyes on Brian.

"It'll be okay," Philip says, yanking his dead daughter toward the back hall.

"You're not—"

"Mind your own goddamn business."

"But what if somebody—"

"Nobody saw me," he says, kicking open the door to the laundry room.

It's a small, claustrophic chamber of linoleum tile and corkboard walls with a broken-down washer and dryer, and ancient cat litter ground into the seams of the floor. Philip drags the drooling, snarling thing into the corner and attaches her leash to the exposed water pipes. He does this with the firm yet gentle hand of an animal trainer.

Brian watches from the hall, appalled at what he's seeing. Philip has blankets spread out on the floor and duct-taped to the sharp edges of the washing machine to prevent the Penny-thing from making noise or hurting herself. It's obvious he's been preparing for this for a while now. He's been thinking about it a lot. He rigs a makeshift leather halter—fashioned from a belt and pieces of the leash—around her head, attaching it to the pipes.

Philip goes about his business with the gentle rigor of a caretaker securing a wheelchair for a handicapped child. With the steel separator, he holds the tiny monster at arm's length and carefully secures the restraints to the wall. All through this, the thing that was once a child snarls and slavers and yanks at her restraints.

Brian stares. He can't decide whether to turn away, cry, or scream. He gets the feeling that he's stumbled upon something disturbingly intimate here, and for a brief instant, his racing thoughts cast back to the time he was eighteen years old and visiting the nursing home in Waynesboro to say good-bye to his dying grandmother. He'll never forget the look on her caretaker's face. On an almost hourly basis, that male nurse had to clean the shit from the old lady's backside, and the expression on his face while he did so, with relatives in the room, was horrible: a mixture of disgust, stoic professionalism, pity, and contempt.

That same weird expression is now contorting Philip Blake's features as he buckles straps around the monster's little head, carefully avoiding the danger zone around her snapping jaws. He sings softly to her as he works on her shackles—some sort of off-key lullaby that Brian can't identify.

Eventually, Philip is satisfied with the restraints. He tenderly strokes the top of the Penny-thing's head, and then kisses her forehead. The girl's jaws snap at him, missing his jugular by centimeters.

"I'll leave the light on, punkin," Philip says to her, speaking loudly, as though addressing a foreigner, before calmly turning and walking out of the laundry room, shutting the door securely behind him.

Brian stands there in the hall, his veins running cold. "You want to talk about this?"

"It'll be okay," Philip reiterates, avoiding eye contact as he walks away, heading toward his room.

The worst part is that the laundry room is next door to Brian's bedroom, and from that moment on, he hears the Penny-thing every night, clawing, moaning, straining against her bonds. She's a constant reminder of . . . what? Armageddon? Madness? Brian doesn't even have the vocabulary for what she represents. The smell is a thousand times worse than cat urine. And Philip spends a lot of time locked inside that laundry room with the dead girl, doing God-knows-what, and it drives the wedge deeper between the three men. Still in the throes of grief and shock, Brian is torn between pity and repulsion. He still loves his brother, but this is too much. Nick has no comment on the matter, but Brian can tell that Nick's spirit is broken. The silences grow longer between the men, and Brian and Nick begin spending more time outside the apartment, wandering the safe zone, getting to know the dynamics of the inhabitants better.

Keeping a low profile, roaming the periphery of the little frontier enclave, Brian learns that the town is basically broken into two social castes. The first group—the one with the most power—includes anyone with a useful trade or vocation. Brian discovers that this first group features two bricklayers, a machinist, a doctor, a gun-store owner, a veterinarian, a plumber, a barber, an auto mechanic, a farmer, a fry cook, and an electrician. The second group—Brian thinks of them as the Dependents—features the sick, the young, and all the white-collar workers with obscure administrative backgrounds. These are the former middle managers and office drones, the paper pushers and corporate executives who once pulled down six-figure incomes running divisions of huge multinationals—now just taking up space, as obsolete as cassette tapes. With echoes of old sociology courses banging around the back of his mind, Brian wonders if this tenuous, rickety assemblage of desperate souls can ever develop into anything like a community.

The sand in the works appears to be three members of the National Guard, who wandered into Woodbury from a nearby Guard Station a couple of weeks ago and started pushing people around. This little rogue clique—which Brian thinks of as the Bullies—is led by a gung-ho former marine with a flattop haircut and icy blue eyes who goes by the name of Gavin (or "the Major," as his underlings call him). It only takes a couple of days for Brian to peg Gavin as a sociopath with designs on power and plunder. Maybe the plague made Gavin flip his wig, but over the course of that first week in Woodbury, Brian observes Gavin and his weekend warriors snatching provisions out of the hands of helpless families and taking advantage of several women at gunpoint out behind the racetrack at night.

Brian keeps his distance, and keeps his head down, and as he makes these silent observations about Woodbury's pecking order, he keeps hearing the name Stevens.

From what Brian can glean from scattered conversations with townspeople, this Stevens gentleman was once an ear, nose, and throat man with his own practice in a suburb of Atlanta. After the turn, Stevens set out for safer pastures— apparently alone, some believe due to a divorce. The good doctor quickly stumbled upon the motley group of survivors in Woodbury. Seeing the ragged inhabitants gripped by sickness, mal-nourished, and many of them nursing injuries, Stevens decided to offer his services. He's been busy ever since, operating out of the former Meriwether County Medical Center three blocks from the racetrack.

On the afternoon of his seventh day in Woodbury, still wheezing, every breath a stab of pain in his side, Brian finally gets up the nerve to visit the squat, gray-brick building on the south end of the safe zone.

"You're lucky," Stevens says, snapping an X-ray into its clip at the top of a light panel. He points at a milky image of Brian's ribs. "No serious breaks . . . just three minor fractures to the second, fourth, and fifth pectorals."

"Lucky, huh?" Brian mutters, sitting shirtless on the padded gurney. The room is a depressing tile crypt in the basement of the medical center—once the pathology lab—now serving as Stevens's examination room. The air reeks of disinfectant and mold.

"Not a word I've used that often in recent days, I will admit," Stevens says, turning toward a stainless steel cabinet next to the light panel. He's a tall, trim, smartly groomed man in his late forties with designer steel-frame eyeglasses riding low on the bridge of his nose. He wears a lab coat over his wrinkled oxford shirt and has a sort of weary, professorial intelligence in his eyes.

"And the wheezing?" Brian asks.

The doctor fishes through a shelf of plastic vials. "Early stage pleurisy due to the damage to the ribs," he mumbles as he searches the medication. "I would encourage you to cough as much as possible . . . it's going to hurt, but it'll prevent secretions from pooling in the lungs."

"And my eye?" The stabbing pain in Brian's left eye, radiating up from his bruised jaw, has worsened over the last few days. Every time he looks in the mirror, his eye seems more bloodshot.

"Looks fine to me," the doctor says, pulling a pill bottle from the shelf. "Your mandible on that side has a nasty contusion, but that should heal up in time. I'm gonna give you some naproxen for the pain."

Stevens hands the vial over and then stands there with arms crossed against his chest.

Brian almost involuntarily reaches for his wallet. "I'm not sure if I have—"

"There's no payment for services rendered here," the doctor says with a raised brow, somewhat bemused by Brian's innate gesture. "There's no staff, there's no infrastructure, there's no follow-up, and for that matter, there isn't a decent cup of espresso or a half-assed daily newspaper to read."

"Oh . . . right." Brian puts the pills in his pocket. "What about the hip?"

"Bruised but intact," he says, flipping off the light panel and closing the cabinet. "I wouldn't worry. You can put your shirt back on now."

"Good . . . thanks."

"Not a big talker, are you?" The doctor washes his hands at a wall sink, dries them on a dirty towel.

"I guess not."

"Probably better that way," the doctor says, wadding the towel and tossing it into the sink. "You probably don't even want to tell me your name."

"Well . . ."

"It's okay. Forget it. You'll be known in the records as the Bohemian Fellow with the Cracked Ribs. You want to tell me how it happened?"

Brian shrugs as he buttons his shirt. "Took a fall."

"Fighting off the specimens?"

Brian looks at him. "Specimens?"

"Sorry . . . clinical-speak. Biters, zombies, pus bags, whatever they're calling them nowadays. That how you got injured?"

"Yeah . . . something like that."

"You want a professional opinion? A prognosis?"

"Sure."

"Get the hell outta here while you still can."

"Why's that?"

"Chaos theory."

"Excuse me?"

"Entropy . . . empires fall, stars wink out . . . the ice cubes in your drink melt."

"I'm sorry, I'm not following."

The doctor pushes his glasses up his nose. "There's a crematorium in the sublevel of this building . . . we destroyed two more men today, one of them the father of two children. They were attacked on the north side yesterday morning.

They reanimated last night. More Biters are getting through . . . the barricade's a sieve. Chaos theory is the impossibility of a closed system remaining stable. This town is doomed. There's nobody at the controls . . . Gavin and his cronies are getting bolder . . . and you, my friend, are simply another piece of fodder."

For the longest time, Brian doesn't say anything, he just stares past the doctor.

At last, Brian pushes himself off the table and extends his hand. "I'll keep that in mind."

That night, woozy from the painkillers, Brian Blake hears a knock at his bedroom door. Before he even has a chance to get his bearings and turn on a light, the door clicks open and Nick sticks his head in. "Brian, you awake?"

"Always." Brian grunts as he climbs out of the blankets and sits up on the side of the bed. Only a few of the apartment's wall outlets are live with generated power. Brian's room is a dead circuit. He switches on a battery-operated lantern and sees Nick pushing into the room, fully dressed, his expression tight with alarm.

"You gotta see something," Nick says, going to the window, peering through the blinds. "I saw him last night, same deal, didn't think much of it."

Still groggy, Brian joins Nick at the window. "What are we looking at?"

Through the slat, out in the darkness of a vacant

lot, Philip's silhouette can be seen emerging from the far trees. He looks like a stick figure in the darkness. Since Penny's death, he's been losing weight, going without sleep, hardly eating a thing. He looks sick, broken, like his faded denims are the only things holding his long, lanky limbs together. He carries a bucket, and he walks with a strange, wooden kind of purpose, like a sleep-walker or an automaton.

"What's with the bucket?" Brian asks under his breath, almost rhetorically.

"Exactly." Nick nervously scratches himself. "He had it last night, too."

"Just take it easy, Nick. Stay in here." Brian turns the lantern out. "Let's just see what happens."

A few moments later, the sound of the front door clicking open reverberates through the dark apartment. Philip's shuffling footsteps can be heard crossing the living room and making their way down the hall.

The click of the laundry room door is followed by the sound of Penny becoming agitated, the chain clanking, the garbled sounds of groaning—noises to which Brian and Nick have almost grown accustomed. Then something reaches their ears that they haven't heard before: the wet slosh of something hitting the tiles . . . followed by the strange, animalistic, gooey noises of a zombie feeding.

"What the fuck is he doing?" In the half-light, Nick's face is a pale gibbous moon of terror.

"Holy Christ," Brian whispers. "He can't be—"

Brian doesn't even get a chance to finish the thought, because Nick is on his way to the door with a full head of steam, heading for the hallway.

Brian chases after him. "Nick, don't—"

"This isn't happening." Nick barrels down the hallway, moving toward the laundry room. He knocks hard on the door. "Philip, what's going on?"

"Go away!"

The sound of Philip's muffled voice is clogged with emotion.

"Nick—" Brian tries to get in between Nick and the door but it's too late.

Nick turns the knob. The door is unlocked. Nick enters the laundry room.

"Oh God."

Nick's mortified reaction reaches Brian's ears a split second before Brian can get a good look at what's going on in the laundry room.

Brian pushes his way into the narrow enclosure and sees the dead girl eating a human hand.

Brian's initial reaction is not one of repulsion or disgust or outrage (which, as it happens, is exactly the combination of emotions currently twisting Nick's features as he gapes at the feeding in progress). Instead, Brian is overcome by a wave of

413

sadness. He says nothing at first, simply looks on as his brother crouches down in front of the tiny upright corpse.

Ignoring the presence of the other men, Philip calmly pulls a severed human ear from the bucket, and waits patiently for the Penny-thing to finish consuming the hand. She gobbles the middle-aged male fingers with unbridled gusto, chewing the bloodless hairy knuckles as though they were delicacies, the stringers of pink, foamy saliva dangling from her lips.

She hardly pauses long enough to swallow before Philip places the human ear within range of her blackened teeth, offering the morsel to the child with the care and concern of a priest proffering a wafer to a communicant. The Penny-thing devours the cartilage and gristly rolls of human skin with mindless abandon.

"I'm outta here," Nick Parsons finally manages to blurt, pivoting and storming out of the room.

Brian enters and crouches down next to his brother. He doesn't raise his voice. He doesn't accuse Philip of anything. Brian is drowning in sorrow right now and all he can think of saying is, "What's going on, man?"

Philip hangs his head. "He was already dead . . . they were gonna burn him . . . found his body in a bag out behind the clinic . . . he died of something else . . . I just took a few pieces . . . nobody'll notice . . ."

The Penny-thing finishes the ear, and starts groaning for more.

Philip feeds her a dripping, severed foot, the jagged bone exposed at the ankle like a slimy tusk of ivory.

"You think this is . . . ?" Brian searches for words. "You think this is a good idea?"

Philip looks down at the floor as the sticky, wet noises of the feeding frenzy fill the laundry room. The girl-thing gnaws at the bone as Philip's voice drops an octave, beginning to crack with emotion. "Think of him as an organ donor . . ."

"Philip—"

"I can't let go of her, Brian . . . I can't . . . she's all I got."

Brian takes a deep breath and fights his own tears. "The thing of it is . . . she's not Penny anymore."

"I know that."

"Then why—"

"I see her and I try to remember . . . but I can't . . . I can't remember . . . I can't remember anything but this shit storm we're living in . . . and them road rats that shot her . . . and she's all I got . . ." The pain and grief choking his voice start to thicken, hardening into something darker. "They took her from me . . . my whole universe . . . new rules now . . . new rules . . ."

Brian can't breathe. He watches the Penny-thing gnawing on that pasty severed foot. He looks away. He can't take it anymore. His stomach is clenched with nausea, his mouth watering. He can feel the heat rising in his gorge, and he struggles to his feet. "I have to . . . I can't stay in here, Philip . . . I have to go."

Whirling around, Brian stumbles out of the laundry room and gets halfway down the hall when he drops to his knees and roars vomit.

His stomach is relatively empty. What comes out of him is mostly bile. But it comes on spasms of agony. He retches and retches, the acids spattering a six-foot length of carpet between the hallway and the living room. He upchucks his guts, which instantly makes a cold sweat break out all over his body and sends him into a paroxysm of coughing. The fit goes on for endless minutes, each cough throbbing painfully in his ribs. He coughs and coughs until he finally collapses into a heap on the floor.

Fifteen feet away, in the light of a battery-powered lantern, Nick Parsons packs his knapsack. He shoves in a change of clothes, a couple of cans of beans, blankets, a flashlight, some bottled water. He searches the cluttered coffee table for something.

Brian manages to sit up, wiping his mouth with the back of his hand. "You can't leave, man . . . not now."

"Hell I can't," Nick says, finding his Bible under a pile of candy wrappers. He puts the Bible in the backpack. The muffled feeding noises drift down the hallway, fueling Nick's anxiety.

"I'm begging you, Nick."

Nick zips the knapsack shut. He doesn't look at Brian as he says, "You don't need me . . ."

"That's not true." Brian swallows the bitter taste of bile. "I need you now more than ever . . . I need your help . . . to keep things together."

"Together?" Nick looks up. He slings the backpack over his shoulder, and then he walks over to where Brian is slumped on the floor. "Things haven't been *together* around here for a long time."

"Nick. Listen to me—"

"He's too far gone, Brian."

"Listen. I understand what you're saying. Give him one more chance. Maybe this is like a one-time thing. Maybe . . . I don't know . . . it's grief. One more chance, Nick. We got a much better shot at survival if we stay together."

For a long, agonizing moment, Nick considers all this. Then, on a weary, exasperated sigh, which seems to deflate his very spirit, he drops the knapsack.

The next day, Philip vanishes. Brian and Nick don't even bother looking for him. They stay inside for most of the day, hardly speaking to each other, feeling like zombies themselves, moving silently from bathroom to kitchen to living room, where they sit staring out the barred window at the blustery sky, trying to come up with an answer, a way out of this downward spiral.

Around five o'clock that afternoon, they hear a strange buzzing noise coming from outside—like a cross between a chain saw and a boat motor. Worried that it might have something to do with Philip, Brian goes to the back door, listens, then pushes his way outside and takes a few steps across the cracked cement of the back porch.

The noise is louder now. In the distance, on the north side of town, a thundercloud of dust rises into the steel-gray sky. The howl of engines sputters and waxes and wanes on the breeze, and with a surge of relief, Brian realizes that it's merely somebody maneuvering race cars around the dirt track arena. Every so often, the sound of cheers warbles and echoes on the wind.

For a moment, Brian panics. Don't these idiots realize all this noise is going to draw every Biter within a fifty-mile radius? At the same time, though, Brian is transfixed by that buzz-saw sound drifting on the breeze. Like a wandering radio signal, it touches something sore inside him, an ache for preplague times, a series of painful memories of lazy Sunday afternoons, a good night's sleep, walking into a goddamn grocery store and buying a fucking gallon of milk.

He goes back inside, puts his jacket on, and tells Nick he's going for a walk.

The entrance to the racetrack borders the main drag, a high cyclone fence stretched between two brick piles. As Brian approaches, he sees drifts of trash and old tires scattered across the meager box office, which is boarded by graffiti-stained planks.

The noise rises to ear-piercing levels—the winding scream of motors and caterwauling crowds—tainted by the odors of gasoline and burning rubber. The sky is choked with a haze of dust and smoke.

Brian finds a gap in the fence, and he heads for it, when he hears a voice.

"Hey!"

He pauses, turns, and sees three men in ratty camo-fatigues coming toward him. Two of the men are in their twenties, with greasy long hair and assault rifles pinned up high against their shoulders patrol-style. The oldest of the three—a crew-cut hard-ass, his olive drab jacket buttoned up with a bullet bandolier across his chest—walks out front, obviously in command.

"Admission is forty bucks or the equivalent in trade," says the commander.

"Admission?" Brian says, taken aback. He sees a name patch on the older man's breast pocket: MAJ. GAVIN. Up to this point, Brian has only stolen glimpses of the vicious National Guardsman, but now, at this proximity, Brian can see a glint of crazy in the man's frosty blue eyes. His breath smells of Jim Beam.

"Forty bucks for an adult, son—you an adult?" The other men chuckle. "Kids get in free, of course, but you look over eighteen to me. Just barely."

"You're taking *money* from people?" Brian is confused. "Times like these?"

"You're free to trade, friend. You got a chicken? Some *Penthouse* magazines you been jackin' off to?"

More snickers.

Brian's gut goes cold with anger. "I don't have forty bucks."

The smile disappears from the Major's face like a switch has been thrown. "Then have a nice day."

"Who gets the money?"

This gets the attention of the other two Guardsmen. They move in closer. Gavin comes nose to nose with Brian, and says in a soft, threatening grunt, "It's for the Commons."

"The what?"

"The Commons . . . the collective . . . community improvements and what-not."

Brian feels a surge of rage twisting inside him. "You sure it's not for the collective of *you three?*"

"I'm sorry," the Major says in a flat, icy tone, "I must have missed the memo that says you're the new city clerk. You boys get the memo stating that this peckerwood is the new Woodbury city clerk?"

"No, sir," says one of the greasy-haired minions. "Didn't get that memo."

Gavin pulls a .45 semiauto from his belt holster, thumbs off the safety, and presses the barrel against Brian's temple. "You need to study up on group dynamics, son. You flunk civics class in high school?"

Brian says nothing. He stares into the Major's eyes, and a red lens draws down over Brian's vision. Everything goes red. Brian's hands tingle, his head spins.

"Say ahh," the Major says.

"What?"

"I SAID OPEN YOUR GODDAMN MOUTH!" Gavin bellows, and the other two Guardsmen swing their assault rifles into ready positions, the muzzles trained on Brian's skull. Brian opens his mouth, and Gavin inserts the cold barrel of the .45 between Brian's teeth like a dentist checking for cavities.

Something breaks inside Brian. The steel muzzle tastes like old coins and bitter oil. The entire world turns the deepest shade of scarlet.

"Go back to where you came from," the Major says. "Before you get yourself hurt."

Brian manages a nod.

The muzzle slips out of his mouth.

Moving as if in a dream, Brian slowly backs away from the Guardsmen, turns, and walks stiffly back the way he came, now traveling through an invisible mist of crimson.

● ● ●

Around seven o'clock that evening, Brian is back at the apartment, alone, still bundled in his jacket, standing at the barred window in the rear of the living room, gazing out at the dwindling daylight, his racing thoughts like contrary waves crashing against a breakwater. He covers his ears. The muffled thumping noises of the miniature zombie in the next room fuel his stupor—a phonograph needle skipping on a record—driving Brian further and further inward.

At first, he barely registers the sound of Nick returning from who-knows-where, the shuffling footsteps, the click of the closet door. But when he hears the muted mutterings drifting down the hallway, he snaps out of his trance and goes to investigate.

Nick is digging in the closet for something. His tattered nylon coat is damp, his sneakers muddy, and he's murmuring under his breath, " 'I will lift my eyes up to the hills . . . And from whence comes my help? . . . My help comes from the Lord . . . Who made heaven and earth.' "

Brian sees Nick pull the pistol-grip shotgun from the closet.

"Nick, what are you doing?"

Nick doesn't answer. He snaps open the gun's pump mechanism, and checks the breech. It's empty. He madly searches the floor of the closet, and he finds the single box of shells, which they managed to spirit all the way from the villa to Woodbury. He keeps muttering, " 'The Lord shall preserve us from all evil . . . He shall preserve our souls . . .' "

Brian takes a step closer. "Nick, what the hell is going on?"

Still no answer. Nick tries to load the shells with shaky hands and he drops one. It rolls across the floor. Nick fumbles another one into the breech, and then pumps it home with a clang. " 'Behold he who keeps Israel shall neither slumber nor sleep . . .' "

"Nick!" Brian grabs the man's shoulder and spins him around. "What the fuck is *wrong* with you?"

For a moment, it almost looks like Nick is about to swing the shotgun up and blow Brian's head off—the look of unadulterated fury contorts Nick's face. Then he gets himself under control, and swallows, and looks at Brian and says, "This can't go on."

Then, without another word, Nick turns and marches across the room and out the front door.

Brian grabs his .38, shoves it down the back of his belt, and hurries after Nick.

twenty-two

The purple light of dusk settles over the landscape. Icy winds toss the trees along the edges of the woods bordering Woodbury. The air swirls with the odors of wood smoke and carbon monoxide, as well as the unceasing whine of dirt racers emanating from the center of town. The back streets are fairly deserted, most of the inhabitants at the track . . . but still, it's a miracle nobody sees Brian and Nick stumbling across the vacant lot bordering the safe zone.

Nick prays furiously as he heads for the woods, carrying the pistol-grip shotgun on his shoulder like some kind of holy bludgeon. Brian keeps grabbing at Nick, trying to slow him down, trying to get him to stop his goddamn praying for one second and talk like a normal person, but Nick is driven by some feverish objective.

At last, as they approach the tree line, Brian yanks at Nick's coat so hard, he nearly knocks him over. "What the fuck are you doing?"

Nick spins and gives Brian a hard look. "I saw him dragging a girl out here." Nick's voice is brittle and on the verge of tears.

"Philip?"

"It can't go on, Brian—"

"What girl?"

"Someone from town, he took her by force. Whatever he's doing, it has to stop."

Brian studies Nick's quivering chin. Nick's eyes fill up with tears. Brian takes a deep breath. "Okay, calm down for a second, just calm down."

"He's got the darkness in him, Brian. Let go of me. It's gotta stop."

"You saw him take a girl but you didn't—"

"Let go of me, Brian."

For a moment, Brian just stands there, clutching at Nick's sleeve. Gooseflesh ripples down Brian's back, his midsection going cold. He refuses to accept this. There has to be a way to get things back on track, get things under control.

Finally, after an agonizing pause, Brian looks at Nick and says, "Show me."

Nick takes Brian down a narrow, untrimmed footpath that snakes through a copse of pecan trees. Overgrown with hemlock and ironweed, the path is already lousy with shadows. Magic hour is closing in, the temperature nose-diving.

Brambles and thorns tear at their jackets as they hasten toward a break in the foliage.

To their right, through a latticework of leaves, they can see the southernmost edge of the construction site, where a new section of the wooden barricade is going up. Piles of timber lie nearby. The bulldozer sits in the gloom. Nick indicates a clearing up ahead.

"There he is," Nick whispers as they approach a deadfall on the threshold of the clearing. He drops down behind the logs, looking almost like a hysterical little boy playing army. Brian joins him, crouching down and peering over the top of the rotting timber.

About twenty yards in the distance, in a natural basin of mossy earth, shrouded by a canopy of ancient live oaks and longleaf pine, Philip Blake is visible. The ground is carpeted in matted pine needles, fungus, and weeds, and a low faint glow of methane clings to the forest floor, a ghostly magenta haze that gives the clearing an almost mystical cast. Nick raises the shotgun. "'Dear Lord,'" he mumbles under his breath, "'please cleanse us of all this unrighteousness—'"

"Nick, stop it," Brian whispers.

"'I renounce all sins,'" Nick drones on, gaping at the horror in the clearing. "'They offend thee, O Lord—'"

"Shut up, just *shut up!*" Brian is trying to make sense of it all. In the shadows, it's hard to make out exactly what they're looking at. At first glance, it looks like Philip is out there, kneeling down in the weeds, hog-tying a pig. His denim jacket soaked in sweat, covered in cockleburs, he winds rope around the wrists and ankles of a writhing figure beneath him.

A frigid blast of horror swirls through Brian when he realizes it is *indeed* a young woman on the ground, her blouse torn, her mouth gagged with nylon rope. "Jesus Christ, what the hell is he—"

Nick keeps babbling under his breath: " 'Forgive me, Lord, for what I'm about to do, and with the help of Thy grace I serve Thy will—' "

"Shut the fuck up!" Brian's brain is chugging, seizing up with panic, racing with frantic assumptions: Philip is either going to rape this poor woman or kill her and feed her to Penny. Something has to be done, and it has to be done quickly. Nick is right. He was right all along. There has to be a way to stop this before—

A blur of movement next to Brian.

Nick is vaulting over the deadfall, pushing his way through the briars and into the clearing.

"Nick, wait!" Brian gets halfway through the brambles when he sees the deadly tableau taking shape in the shadowy clearing like an arrangement of players on a surreal chessboard, coming together in dreamy slow motion.

Nick stumbles out into the open with his shotgun raised at Philip, and Philip, startled by the sudden sound of Brian's warning cry, springs to his feet. Weaponless, glancing nervously from the wriggling women to the duffel bag lying in the toadstools next to her, Philip raises his hands. "Put that goddamn thing down, Nicky."

Nick raises the bead of the muzzle until it's

trained directly on Philip. "Devil's got his hooks in you, Philip. You've sinned against God . . . desecrated His name. It's in the hands of the Lord now."

Brian is staggering into the clearing, fumbling for his .38, hyperventilating with adrenaline. "Nick, don't!—DON'T DO IT!" Brian's mind races as he comes to a halt ten feet behind Nick.

By this point, the girl on the ground has managed to roll over—still bound and gagged—and she's crying into the moist earth, as if wishing it would open up and let her climb in and die. Meanwhile, Nick and Philip are standing six feet away from each other, their gazes locked.

"What are you, the avenging angel?" Philip asks his longtime friend.

"Maybe I am."

"This doesn't concern you, Nicky."

Nick is trembling with emotion, his eyes blinking away tears. "There's a better place for you and your daughter, Philly."

Philip stands as still as a stone monument, his narrow, weathered face looking positively grotesque in the gloomy light. "And I suppose you're the one who's gonna send me and Penny to Glory?"

"Somebody's gotta stop this, Philly. Might as well be me." Nick raises the sight to his eye and mutters, " 'Lord, please forgive—' "

"Nick, wait!—Please, please! *Listen to me!*" Brian circles around with the .38 pointed up in the air like he's a referee. He comes within inches of Nick, who still has his sight fixed on Philip. Brian babbles: "All the years of bumming around Waynesboro, all the laughs you shared, all the miles we put behind us—doesn't that count for something? Philip saved our lives! Things have gotten out of hand, yeah. But things can be put back together. Put the gun down, Nick. I'm begging you."

Nick shakes. He keeps the sight fixed. Sweat beads on his forehead.

Philip takes a step closer. "Don't worry about it, Brian. Nicky's always been a talker. He ain't got the stones to shoot somebody who's still alive."

Nick trembles furiously.

Brian watches, frozen with indecision.

Philip calmly reaches down to the girl, grabs her by the scruff of her collar, and yanks her up like a stray piece of luggage. He turns and starts dragging the squirming girl toward the far side of the clearing.

Nick's voice drops into a lower register. "Have mercy on us all."

The shotgun ratchets suddenly.

And the muzzle roars.

A 12-gauge shotgun is a blunt instrument. The lethal .33-caliber pellets can spread as wide as a foot or more in a short distance, tearing through its target with enough force to penetrate a cinder block.

The buckshot that hits Philip in the back punches

through the meat of his shoulder blades and the cords of his neck, sending half his brain stem out through the front of his throat. The grains also take the side of the girl's scalp off, killing her instantly. The two bodies are launched in a cloud of pink mist.

The pair tumble forward in a tangled clench before sprawling side by side on the forest floor, their arms and legs akimbo. The girl is already stone-still dead but Philip twitches in his death throes for several agonizing seconds. His face is upturned, frozen in a mask of utter surprise. He tries to breathe but the damage to his brain is shutting everything down.

The shock of what has just happened drives Nick Parsons to his knees, his finger still frozen on the trigger pad, the shotgun sizzling hot.

His vision tunnels as he gapes at the damage inflicted on the two human bodies in the path of the blast. He drops the shotgun in the weeds and moves his mouth but makes no sound. What has he done? He feels himself contracting inward like a seed pod, cold and desolate, the clanging noise of Armageddon ringing in his ears, the scalding tears of shame coming now in rivulets down his face: What has he done? What has he done? What has he done?

Brian Blake turns to ice. His pupils dilate. The sight of his brother lying in a bloody heap on the ground next to the dead girl stamps itself forever on his brain. All other thoughts drain out of his mind.

Only the noise of Nick's keening wails penetrate Brian's stupor.

Howling with sobs now, Nick is still on his knees next to Brian. All reason and sanity have drained out of Nick Parsons's face, and he caterwauls at the sight of the carnage. Bursts of gibberish come out of him in stringers of snot—part prayer, part insane pleading—his breath showing in the chill twilight. He looks up at the heavens.

Brian raises the .38 without thinking—a jolt of psychotic rage driving him—and he squeezes off a single shot, point-blank, into the side of Nick Parsons's skull.

The battering ram drives Nick over in a jet of red fluid, the slug ripping through his brain, coming out the other side and chewing through a tree. Nick folds, eyes rolling back, brain already dead.

He lands with the profound surrender of a child going to sleep.

The passage of time loses all meaning. Brian doesn't see the dark silhouettes of figures approaching through the distant trees, drawn to the noise. Nor does he have any awareness of moving across the clearing to the mangled pair of bodies. But somehow, without even being conscious of it, Brian Blake ends up on the ground next to Philip, cradling his younger brother's bloody form in his lap.

He gazes down at Philip's grizzled face, now as pale as alabaster, stippled with blood.

A flicker of life still glints in Philip's eyes, as the two brothers meet each other's gaze. For a brief instant, Brian flinches at the glacier of sorrow cutting through him, the connection between the two siblings as thick as blood, as deep as the earth, now fracturing Brian's soul with the power of shifting tectonic plates. The weight of their common history—the endless tedium of grammar school, the blessed summer vacations, the passing of late-night whispers from one bunk bed to the other, their first beers on that ill-fated Appalachian camping trip, their secrets, their fights, their small-town dreams foiled by life's cruel equations—all of it slices through his soul.

Brian weeps.

His cries—as shrill and keen as that of an animal in a trap—rise up into the darkening sky, blending with the distant whining of race cars. He sobs so hard he doesn't even notice Philip's passing.

When Brian looks back down at his brother, Philip's face has hardened into a marble-white sculpture.

The foliage trembles twenty feet away. At least a dozen Biters of all shapes and sizes are forcing their way through the thicket.

The first one, an adult male in tattered work clothes, pops through the branches with arms reaching at the nothingness, shoe-button eyes scanning the clearing. The thing fixes its gaze on the closest meal: Philip's cooling corpse.

Brian Blake rises to his feet and turns away. He can't watch. He knows this is the best option. The *only* option. Let the zombies clean up the mess.

He shoves the .38 back behind his belt and heads for the construction site.

Brian finds a perch on top of a truck cab to wait out the feeding frenzy.

His brain is a television tuned to many stations all at once. He draws his pistol and clutches it like a security blanket.

The cacophony of voices, the fragments of half-formed images, all crackle and flicker inside Brian's skull. The twilight has passed into full-bore darkness, the closest vapor light hundreds of yards off. But Brian sees the world around him in photo-negative brilliance now, his fear as keen as a knife edge. He is alone now . . . as alone as he has ever been . . . and it eats at him deeper than any zombie.

The wet, gurgling, sucking noises coming from the clearing are barely audible above the constant buzzing of dirt track racers. Somewhere in the back of Brian's hectic thoughts, he knows that the din of the racetrack is drowning the commotion in the clearing—probably part of Philip's plan, his abduction of the girl going unheard, unseen.

Through the lacing of brambles and foliage, Brian can see the silhouettes of monsters tearing into the human remains left in the clearing. Clusters of zombies hunch over their quarry, apelike, gorging on hunks of flesh, detached bones dripping with gore, flaps of skin, torn scalps, unidentified appendages, and sopping organs still warm and steaming in the chill air. More of them crowd in, clumsily shoving each other aside, grunting for a morsel.

Brian closes his eyes.

For a moment, he wonders if he should pray. He wonders if he should offer a silent eulogy for his brother, for Nick and the woman, for Penny, for Bobby Marsh, for David Chalmers, for the dead, for the living, and for this whole fucked-up, broken, godforsaken world. But he doesn't. He simply sits there as the zombies feed.

Some time later—God only knows when—the Biters drift away from the flensed, excoriated remains now lying strewn across the clearing.

Brian slips off the roof of the truck cab and makes his way back through the darkness to the apartment.

That night, Brian sits in the empty apartment, in the living room, in front of the empty, scummy fish tank. It's the end of the programming day in

Brian's brain. The national anthem has been sung, the broadcast has signed off, and now only a blizzard of white noise blankets his thoughts.

Still clad in his filthy jacket, he sits staring through the fish tank's rectangular glass side—which is filmed in green mold, and mottled with specks of chum—as though watching some monotonous still life being broadcast from hell. He sits this way, staring trancelike into the vacuous heart of that fish tank, for endless minutes. The minutes turn into hours. His mind-screen is a blank cathode-ray tube boiling with electronic snow. The coming of daylight barely registers. He doesn't hear the commotion outside the apartment, the troubled voices, the sounds of vehicles.

The day drags on—time now meaningless—until the next evening draws its curtain of darkness down over the apartment. Brian sits in the dark, oblivious to the passage of time, continuing to stare with catatonic interest at the invisible broadcast originating from the empty shell of the fish tank. The next morning comes and goes.

At some point that next day, Brian blinks. The flicker of a message sparks and sputters across the blank screen of his mind. At first, it's faint and garbled, like a poorly transmitted signal, but with each passing second, it grows stronger, clearer, louder: GOOD-BYE.

Like a depth charge in the center of his soul, the word implodes in a convulsion of white-hot energy, jerking him forward in the shopworn armchair, sitting him bolt upright, forcing open his eyes.

—*GOOD-BYE*—

He's dehydrated and stiff, his stomach empty, his pants soaked through with his own urine. For nearly thirty-six hours, he sat in that chair, comatose, as still as a divining rod, and moving isn't easy at first, but he feels cleansed, scourged, as clearheaded as he's ever been. He limps into the kitchen and finds little in the cupboard other than a couple of cans of peaches. He tears one open and wolfs the whole thing down, the juice running across his chin. Peaches have never tasted so good. In fact, it occurs to him that perhaps he has never tasted peaches before. He goes into the bedroom and changes out of his disgusting clothes . . . puts on his only other pair of jeans and his only other shirt (an AC/DC silk-screened tee). He finds his spare Dr. Martens boots and slips them on.

Mounted on the back of the door is a cracked, floor-length mirror.

A wiry, disheveled, compact ferret of a man stares back at him. The crack in the looking glass bisects his narrow visage and his thatch of long, unruly black hair. His face is fringed with straggly whiskers, his eyes sunken and rimmed in dark circles. He hardly recognizes himself.

"Whatever," he says to the mirror, and walks out of the room.

He finds his .38 in the living room, along with one last speed-loader—the last six rounds in his possession—and he shoves the gun down the back of his belt, the speed-loader into his pocket.

Then he visits Penny.

"Hey there, kiddo," he says with great tenderness as he enters the laundry room. The narrow chamber of linoleum reeks of the dead. Brian barely notices the smell. He goes over to the little creature, who growls and sputters at his presence, straining against her chains. She's the color of cement, her eyes like smooth stones.

Brian crouches down in front of her, looks in her bucket. It's empty.

He looks up at her. "You know I love you, right?"

The Penny-thing snarls.

Brian strokes the side of her delicate little ankle. "I'm going to go get some supplies, sweetheart. I'll be back before you know it, don't worry."

The little dead thing cocks its head and lets out a groan that sounds like air running through rusty pipes. Brian pats her on the leg—out of the range of her rotting incisors—and then rises to his feet.

"See ya soon, sweetie."

The moment that Brian slips unnoticed from the side door of the apartment, and starts north, striding through the raw winds of the afternoon, his head down, his hands in the pockets of his jacket, he can tell something is going on. The racetrack is silent. A couple of townspeople run past him, their eyes aglow with alarm. The air reeks of the dead. Off to the left, behind the barricade of buses and semis, scores of walking corpses wander along the barrier, sniffing for a way in. Up ahead, black smoke pours out of the clinic's incinerator. Brian quickens his pace.

As he closes in on the town square, he can see, way in the distance, at the north end of the safe zone, where the fence is under construction, men standing on wooden parapets with rifles and binoculars. They don't look happy. Brian hurries along. All his pain—the stiffness in his joints, the throb in his ribs, all of it—vanishes amid the high-voltage current of his adrenaline.

Woodbury keeps its food rations in a brick warehouse across from the old courthouse. Brian pauses in front of the warehouse when he sees the old derelict juicers loitering across the street in front of the flagstone government building with its chipped Romanesque columns. Other folks stand on the stone steps, nervously smoking cigarettes, while others crowd the entranceway. Brian crosses the intersection and approaches the gathering.

"What's going on?" he asks the fat old man in the Salvation Army coat.

"Trouble in River City, son," the old codger says,

jerking a greasy thumb at the courthouse. "Half the town's in there havin' a powwow."

"What happened?"

"Found three more residents out in the woods yesterday, picked clean as chicken bones . . . place is crawlin' with roamers now, drawn by the racetrack most likely. Damn fools makin' all that noise."

For a moment, Brian considers his options. He could very easily avoid this mess, pack up, and move on. He could boost one of the four-wheelers and take Penny in the back and be gone in a flash.

He doesn't owe these people anything. The safest bet is to not get involved, just get the fuck out of Dodge. That's the smartest way to play it. But something deep inside Brian makes him reconsider. What would Philip do?

Brian stares at the crowd of townspeople milling about the entrance to the courthouse.

twenty-three

"Does anybody even know what their names were?" A woman in her late sixties with a halo of fright-wig gray hair stands up in the back of the community room on the first floor of the courthouse building, the veins in her neck wattle pulsing with tension.

The thirty or so beleaguered residents of

Woodbury gathered around her—town elders, heads of small families, former merchants, and passers-through who landed here almost by mistake—fidget on folding chairs in tattered coats and muddy boots, facing the front of the narrow conference room. The space has an end-of-world feel to it, with crumbling plaster, overturned coffee urns, exposed wiring, and litter strewn across the parquet floor.

"What the fuck difference does it make?" barks Major Gene Gavin from the front of the room, his minions behind him with their M4 assault rifles on their hips like faux gangbangers. It feels right and proper to the Major to be standing at the head of this little town hall meeting right now, near the flagpoles displaying the American and Georgia State flags. Like MacArthur taking over Japan, or Stonewall Jackson at Bull Run, the Major relishes the opportunity to finally make his stand as the leader pro tem of this miserable town full of chickenshits and rejects. Ramrod tough in his green fatigues and jarhead brush cut, the Major has been waiting for this moment, biding his time for weeks.

No stranger to whipping pussies into shape, Gavin knows he needs respect in order to lead, and in order to be respected, he needs to be feared. Which is exactly how he used to deal with the weekend warriors under his command at Camp Ellenwood. Gavin was a survival instructor with the 221st Military Intelligence Battalion, and he used to torment those lily-livered weaklings on overnight bivouacs up to Scull Shoals by shitting in their duffels and giving them the rubber hose treatment for the smallest infractions. But that might as well have been a million years ago. *This* situation is Code *Fucked,* and Gavin is going to take every advantage to stay on top of things.

"It was just a couple of them new guys," Gavin adds as an afterthought. "And some slut from Atlanta."

An elderly gentlemen in the front stands up, his bony knees trembling: "All due respect . . . that was Jim Bridges's daughter, and she weren't no slut. Now, I think I speak for everybody when I say we need protection, maybe a curfew . . . keep people in after dark. Maybe we could take a vote."

"Sit down, old man . . . before you hurt yourself." Gavin gives the old geezer his best menacing look. "We got bigger problems to deal with now—there's a goddamn convention of them Biters closing in on us."

The old man takes his seat, grumbling to himself. "All that noise from the damn dirt races . . . that's the reason them Biters is surroundin' us."

Gavin unsnaps the holster on his hip, exposing the grip of his .45, and takes a threatening step toward the old man. "I'm sorry, I don't recall opening the floor to comments from the nursing home." Gavin jabs a finger at the old man. "My advice is for you to shut the fuck up before you get yourself in trouble."

A younger man springs to his feet two chairs away from the old man. "Take it easy, Gavin," the younger man says. Tall, olive-skinned, his hair tucked under a bandana, he wears a sleeveless shirt that reveals heavily muscled arms. His dark eyes gleam with street-level smarts. "This ain't some John Wayne movie, take it down a notch."

Gavin turns to the man in the bandana, brandishing the .45 with menace. "Shut your mouth, Martinez, and put your spic ass back in your chair."

Behind Gavin, the two Guardsmen tense up, swinging the muzzles of their M4s up and into ready positions, their eyes scanning the room.

The man named Martinez just shakes his head, and sits back down.

Gavin lets out a frustrated sigh.

"You people don't seem to grasp the seriousness of this situation," he says, holstering the .45 as he moves back to the front of the room, speaking with the cadence of a drill instructor. "We're sittin' ducks here, we don't do somethin' about them barricades. Got a bunch of freeloaders takin' up space. Expecting everybody else to carry the weight. No discipline! I got news for ya, your little vacation is over. Gonna be some new rules, and you're all gonna pitch in, and you're gonna do what you're told, and you're gonna keep your fucking mouths shut! Am I making myself clear?"

Gavin pauses, daring somebody to object.

The townspeople sit in silence, looking like children who've been sent to the principal's office. In one corner, Stevens, the physician, sits next to a young woman in her twenties. Dressed in a stained smock, the girl has a stethoscope draped around her neck. Stevens looks like a man smelling something that's been rotting for a long time. He raises his hand.

The Major rolls his eyes and lets out an exasperated sigh. "What is it now, Stevens?"

"Correct me if I'm wrong," the doctor says, "but we're stretched thin already. We're doing our best."

"What's your point?"

The doctor gives him a shrug. "What is it you want from us?"

"I WANT YOUR GODDAMN OBEDIENCE!"

The booming response barely registers on Stevens's thin, cunning features. Gavin takes long, even breaths, getting himself back under control. Stevens pushes his eyeglasses up the bridge of his nose and looks away, shaking his head. Gavin gives his men a look.

The Guardsmen nod in unison at the Major, trigger fingers on trigger pads.

This isn't going to be as easy as Gavin thought.

● ● ●

Brian Blake stands in the back of the room, in the shadow of a dusty, bankrupt vending machine, his hands in his pockets, listening, taking it all in. His heart thumps. And he hates himself for it. He feels like a laboratory rat in a maze. The crippling fear—an old nemesis—is back with a vengeance. He can feel the speed-loader like a tumor in his pocket, the bulge cold against his thigh. His throat is tight and dry, his tongue two sizes too big for his mouth. What the fuck is wrong with him?

At the front of the room, Gavin keeps pacing in front of the gallery of town founders displayed in shopworn frames across the room's front wall. "Now, I don't care what you call this cluster fuck we find ourselves in, I call it war . . . and right now, this little shit-heel town is officially under marshal-fucking-law."

Tense murmurings spread through the group. The old man is the only one brazen enough to speak up. "What does that mean, exactly?"

Gavin walks over to the old man. "That means y'all are going to follow orders, be good little boys and girls." He pats the top of the codger's bald pate like he's petting a rabbit. "Y'all behave yourselves, do what you're told, and we just might survive this shit storm."

The old man swallows hard. Most of his fellow townspeople look down at the floor. It's clear to Brian, observing from the back of the room, that

444

the inhabitants of Woodbury are trapped in more ways than one. The hatred in the room is thick enough to paint the walls. But the fear is thicker. It exudes from the very pores of everybody present, including Brian, who is hard at work fighting it. He shoves his terror back down his throat.

Somebody murmurs something near the front of the room, over by the window. Brian is too far away to make out the words, and he gazes over the tops of heads to see who it is.

"You got something you want to say, Detroit?"

Near the window, a middle-aged black man in greasy dungarees and gray beard is sulking in his seat, looking gloomily out the window. His long, tawny fingers are caked with axle grease. The town mechanic, a transplant from up North, he mumbles something to himself, not looking at the Major.

"Speak up, homeboy." The Major approaches the black man. Towering over him, Gavin says, "What's *your* beef? You don't like the program?"

Almost inaudibly, the black man says, "I'm outta here."

He gets up to make his exit, when suddenly the Major reaches for his gun.

With almost involuntary instinct, the black man reaches a big, callused hand down to the revolver shoved into his belt. But before he can draw the weapon or even give it a second thought, Gavin draws on him. "Please go for it, Detroit," Gavin snarls, pointing the .45 at the man. "So I can blow the back of your nappy fuckin' head off."

The other soldiers move in behind the Major, raising their assault rifles, fixing their eyes on the black man.

Hand still on the hilt of his pistol, eyes locked with Gavin, the black man named Detroit murmurs, "It's bad enough we gotta fight off them dead things . . . now we gotta deal with you pushin' us around?"

"Sit. The fuck. Down. Now." Gavin puts the barrel on Detroit's forehead. "Or I will take you down. And that is a promise."

With an exasperated sigh, Detroit flops back down.

"That goes for the rest of you!" The Major turns to the others. "You think I'm doin' this for my health? You think I'm runnin' for dog catcher? This ain't no democracy. This is life and fucking death!" He begins pacing across the front of the room. "You want to keep from being dog food, you'll do what you're told. Let the professionals mind the store, and keep your fuckin' pie holes shut!"

Silence hangs in the room like a poisonous gas. In back, Brian feels the skin on the back of his neck prickle. His heart is going to break through his sternum, it's hammering so hard in his chest. He can't breathe. He wants to rip this tin soldier's head off but his body is going into some kind of fight-or-flight paralysis. His brain crackles with flickering fragments of memory, sights and sounds from a lifetime driven by fear, avoiding bullies on the playground at Burke County Elementary, skirting the parking lot of the Stop-and-Go to avoid a group of leather thugs, running away from a gang of toughs at a Kid Rock concert, wondering where Philip is . . . where the hell is Philip when you need him . . .

A noise from the front of the room shakes Brian out of his rumination.

The man named Detroit is getting up. He's had enough. His chair squeaks as he rises to his full height—well over six feet—and turns to walk away.

"Where the hell are *you* going?" Gavin watches the black man move down the aisle toward the front exit. "HEY! I ASKED YOU A QUESTION, DETROIT! WHERE THE FUCK DO YOU THINK YOU'RE GOING!"

Detroit doesn't even look back, he just waves dismissively, mumbling, "I'm outta here . . . good luck, y'all . . . you're gonna need it with these motherfuckers."

"YOU SIT YOUR BLACK ASS BACK DOWN RIGHT NOW OR I WILL BLOW YOU AWAY!"

Detroit keeps walking.

Gavin pulls his sidearm.

There is an audible intake of air among the townspeople as Gavin draws a bead on the back of Detroit's head.

The blast sucks the air out of the room—so loud, it rattles the walls, accompanied by a scream from one of the older women—as a single round goes into the back of the black man's skull. Detroit is thrown forward into the vending machine next to Brian. Brian jerks. The black man bounces off the steel panel and then folds to the floor, his blood spray-painting the Coke display, the wall above the machine, and even part of the ceiling.

Many things happen in the aftermath of that blast, even before the ringing echoes of screams have had a chance to fade away. Almost immediately, three separate townspeople—two middle-aged men, and a woman in her thirties—dart toward the exit, and Brian watches as if in a dream, his ears ringing, his eyes flash-blind. He can barely hear the strangely calm voice of Major Gavin—void of regret, void of any feeling whatsoever—ordering his two Guardsmen—Barker and Manning—to go get the fleeing townspeople, and while they're at it, round up anyone else who's "still out there hiding like goddamn cockroaches," because Gavin wants every soul who's still got a pulse to hear what he has to say. The two Guardsmen hurry out of the room, leaving behind the stunned, petrified group of twenty-five residents, the Major . . . and Brian.

The room seems to turn on its axis for Brian as Gavin holsters his gun, looking down at the body of the black man sprawled on the floor as though it was a hunting trophy. Gavin turns and saunters back toward the front. He's got everybody's attention now like never before, and he seems to be enjoying every minute of it. Brian can barely hear the Major droning on now about making an example out of any cocksucker who thinks they can endanger the lives of Woodbury's residents by being a lone wolf, by bucking the system, by being a smart-ass know-it-all who thinks they can go it alone and keep their shit to themselves. These times, according to Gavin, are special times. Foretold in the Bible. Prophesied. Matter of fact, these times are maybe, just maybe, the end-time. And from now on, every last son of a bitch in this town needs to get used to the fact that this may very well be the last battle between man and Satan, and as far as the fine folks of Woodbury, Georgia, are concerned, Gavin has been hereby appointed, by default, the goddamn Messiah.

This maniacal lecture lasts for perhaps a minute—maybe two minutes at the most—but in that brief span of time, Brian Blake goes through a metamorphosis.

Frozen against the side of the vending machine, the fallen man's blood seeping under the soles of his shoes, Brian realizes he will have no chance in this world if he lets his natural inclinations drag him down. Brian's instincts—to shrink away from violence, to skirt dangers, to avoid confrontation— fill him with shame, and he finds himself casting his racing thoughts back to the very first encounter he had with the walking dead, back in Deering, at his parents' place, a million light-years away. They came out of the toolshed in back, and Brian was trying to talk to them, reason with them, warning them to stay away, throwing stones at them, running back into the house, boarding up windows, pissing his pants, behaving like the weakling he always was and always will be. And in the space of that single terrible instant—as Gavin pontificates to the townspeople—Brian is gripped with a flickering flash-frame series of visions of his cowardice and indecision along the road to western Georgia, as if he'd learned nothing along the way: huddling in the closet at Wiltshire Estates, bagging his first zombie almost by accident in the Chalmerses' building, bellyaching to his brother about this and that, always weak and scared and useless. Brian realizes suddenly—with the convulsive pain of an embolism exploding in his heart—that there is no way he can survive on his own. No way in hell. And now, as Major Gavin starts barking orders at the traumatized residents from the front of the council room, assigning arduous duties and rules and procedures, Brian feels his consciousness disconnecting, detaching from his body like a butterfly leaving its cocoon. It starts with Brian wishing that Philip were there to protect him, as he'd done since the beginning of the ordeal. How would Philip handle Gavin? What would Philip do? Soon, this simple longing transforms into agonizing pain and loss over Philip's death—the torture like an open wound—the sharp edge of grief slicing through Brian and tearing him in two. Bracing himself against that blood-spattered vending machine, Brian feels his center of gravity rising, his spirit breaking away from his body, like a primordial chunk of the earth tearing away to form the moon. Dizziness threatens to drive him to the floor but he fights it, and before he can even register what is going on, Brian has risen out of his body. His consciousness now floats above his body, a ghostly onlooker, gazing down at himself in that airless, reeking, crowded community room in the old Woodbury courthouse.

Brian sees himself grow still.

Brian sees the target at the front of the room, twenty-five feet away.

Brian sees himself take a single step away from the vending machine, reaching behind his belt, grasping hold of the beavertail grip of the .38-caliber pistol, while Gavin continues hollering orders up front, oblivious, pacing across stoic portraits of Woodbury's forefathers.

Brian sees himself taking three more tactical steps, moving down the center aisle, while simultaneously drawing the .38 from his belt in one smooth instinctual movement. He holds the gun at his side as he completes the fourth additional stride—coming within fifteen feet of Gavin, finally getting Gavin's attention, causing the Major to pause and look up—and that's when Brian raises the muzzle and empties the entire cylinder of lethal, hollow-point Glaser Safety Slugs into the general vicinity of Gavin's face.

This time, the townspeople jerk in their seats at the noise but, oddly, nobody screams.

No one is more shocked by Brian's actions than Brian, and he stands frozen for one excruciating moment in the center aisle, the .38 still raised and empty, his arm locked in the shooting position, the spectacle of Major Gavin's remains slumped on the floor against the front wall. Gavin's upper body is riddled, his face and neck pumping deep red arterial blood in oily bubbles.

The spell is broken by the sound of squeaking chairs, the shuffle of people rising. Brian lowers the gun to his side. He looks around. Some of the townspeople are moving to the front of the room. Others are staring at Brian. One of the men kneels by Gavin's body, but he doesn't bother feeling for a pulse or looking too closely. The one named Martinez comes over to Brian.

"Don't take this personally, brother," Martinez says, his voice a low, grave murmur. "But you better get your ass outta here."

"No." Brian feels as though his center of gravity has returned, his very soul rebooting like a computer powering back up.

Martinez stares. "Gonna be hell to pay when those goons get back."

"It'll be okay," Brian says, reaching into his pocket for the speed-loader. He dumps the empty shells, then fumbles the fresh round into the pistol. He's unskilled at the maneuver but his hands are rock steady. He has stopped shaking. "We outnumber them ten to one."

Some of the townspeople are gathered by the vending machine, clustered around the body of the one named Detroit. Dr. Stevens is feeling for a pulse as the sound of someone softly crying reaches Brian's ears. He turns toward the group gathered there.

"Who's armed in here?" he asks.

A few hands go up.

"Stay close," Brian says, then weaves his way through the stunned, milling townspeople to the exit. He stands inside the door, gazing out through the panes of safety glass at the blustery, overcast autumn day.

Even through the door's window glass, the unmistakable drone of zombies can be heard way off in the distance, under the wind. They now sound different somehow to Brian's ears. Segregated behind makeshift barricades, sectioned off from the stubborn little enclave of survivors by thin membranes of wood and metal, the low, ubiquitous symphony of moaning noises—as ugly and dissonant as wind chimes fashioned from human bones—no longer whisper of doom. They now speak of opportunity. They sound to Brian like an invitation to a new way of life, a new paradigm that is just now forming within Brian like the birth of a new religion.

A voice next to Brian snaps him out of his trance. He turns and sees Martinez, giving him an inquisitive look. "I'm sorry," Brian says. "What did you say?"

"Your name . . . I didn't catch it before."

"My name?"

Martinez nods. "I'm Martinez . . . and you are . . . ?"

Brian pauses for the slimmest of moments before replying, "Philip . . . Philip Blake."

Martinez reaches out to shake Brian's hand. "Pleasure to meet you, Philip."

With a firm grip, the two men clasp hands, and in that single gesture a new order begins to take shape.

Center Point Large Print
600 Brooks Road / PO Box 1
Thorndike, ME 04986-0001 USA

(207) 568-3717

US & Canada:
1 800 929-9108
www.centerpointlargeprint.com